ROGUE HEART

ROGUE HEART

Guardians Trilogy — Book 1

Stefanie Dawn

Disclaimer: The material in this book contains sexual content and is intended for mature audiences ages 18 and older.

ISBN eBook: 978-1-7636644-3-2

ISBN Paperback: 978-1-7636644-4-9

ISBN Hardcover: 978-1-7638705-5-0

Book Design by Angels and Fire Books

Paperback Cover Design by Artscandare

Hardcover Cover Design by RJ Creatives

Published by Angels and Fire Books

Also by Stefanie Dawn

The Unearthly Sins Novels

The Demon in Me

The Angel in Her

Lure of a Demon

Dark Angel

Touch of a Demon

The Demon in Him

The Elements of Abduction Novels

Savior

Rescuer

Redeemer

Liberator

Releaser

Freer

The Guardians Trilogy

Rogue Heart

Shattered Heart

Reborn Heart

Novellas

Demonic

Daemonia

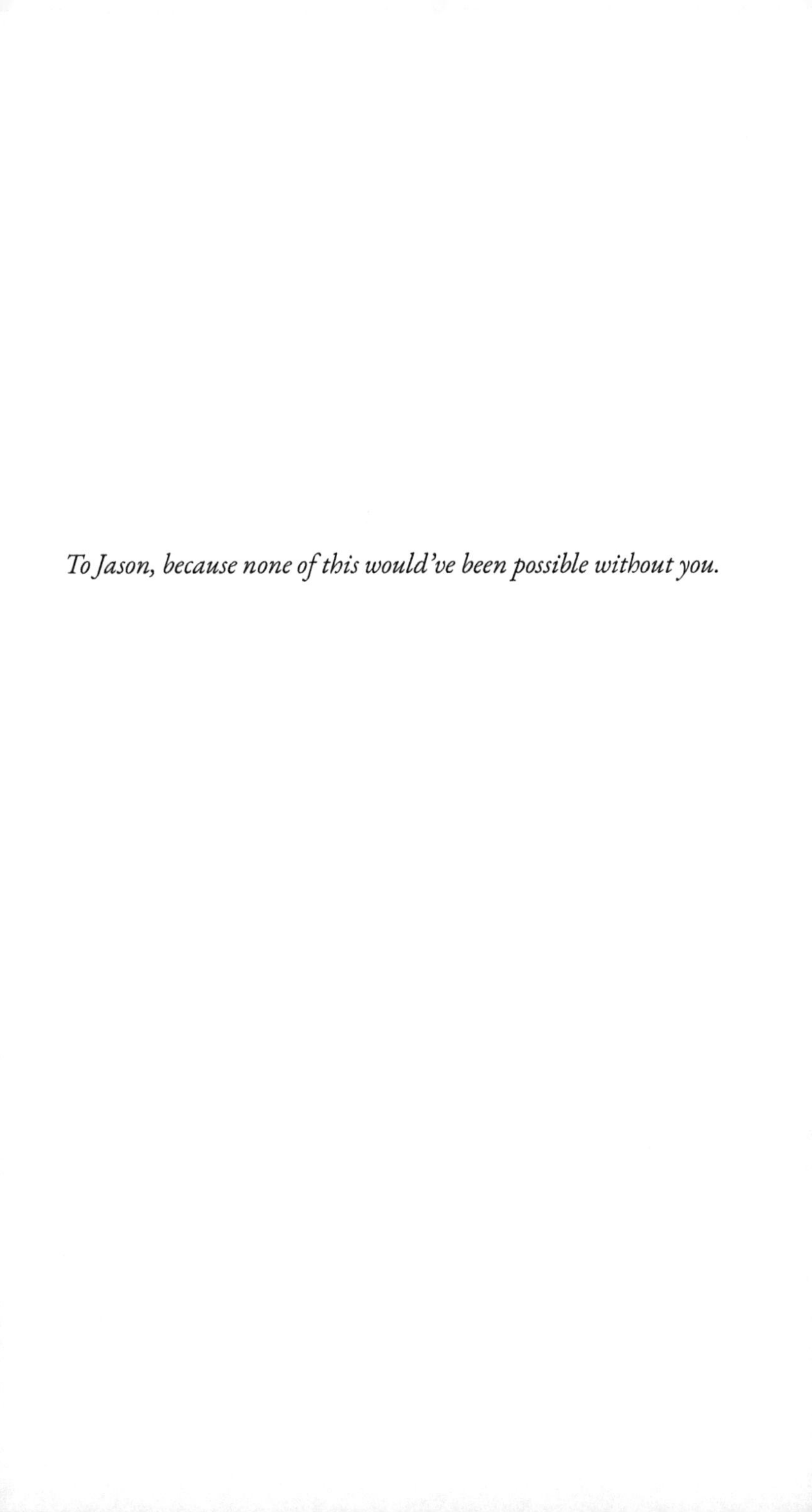

To Jason, because none of this would've been possible without you.

Would I sacrifice my duty for love?

As one of the Guardians of Earth who inhabit the two realms—Lucidis and Tenebris—my job is to maintain the Balance—a force on Earth between positive and negative energies.
These energies are constantly disrupted by human emotions.

Every laugh, smile, and act of kindness.
Every tear and heartache.
And every act of violence.

When a Tenebrian Guardian goes Rogue and disrupts the Balance, the pleasure he takes in the sadistic acts of violence makes my stomach churn. I welcome the duty I've been given—stop him, and return him to his home realm for punishment.

But everything changes when I meet her.

Anahera.

She's tangled up in the battle, and my feelings for her are clouding my judgment. I have to let her go, but each nerve in my body aches for her. She's in danger every second she's close to me.
What if he comes for her?

If I wait too long to make the choice, it will be made for me.
And I may not be able to save her.

Contents

Glossary

Guardians—Beings that inhabit the two realms, either side of Earth—Lucidis and Tenebris. The Guardians' duty is to protect and maintain the Balance, the force on which Earth exists. Their abilities include the control and manipulation of human emotions. As stoic beings, they can utilize these powers to influence humans and, if powerful enough, even one another. Depending on age and power, they can calm or anger humans on an individual or large scale. Lifespans average around one hundred and twenty to one hundred and fifty years, rarely living beyond two hundred. They do not take on life partners—instead, they engage with various partners within their communities to breed, and the community raises the children.

Lucidis—The light realm, representing all that is positive. The Guardians of Lucidis (Lucidians) balance the negative on Earth with the positive. While negative emotions—pain, fear, grief—can cause them physical pain, positive emotions entice the opposite result. Laughter and joy can re-energize Lucidians and be an energy source on Earth. Guardians still require sustenance and rest to live, but the ability to use their powers relies on the energies around and within them.

Tenebris—The dark realm is a polar opposite of Lucidis, but cannot be considered evil, as light cannot exist without dark. Both realms are equally necessary. Tenebris plays a crucial role in the Balance, as a shift too far in either direction could be disastrous. The Guardians of Tenebris (Tenebrians) balance out positive with negative, creating darkness where there is too much light. Humans' pain and fear create a pleasurable rush in Tenebrians.

The Balance—The force on which Earth exists—a balance between light and dark, good and evil, positive and negative. Every human on Earth and every emotion they feel shifts the Balance, creating a constant push-and-pull between positive and negative. Ultimately, this requires the interception of the Guardians, who use their powers of influence over human emotions to balance the energies when they are pushed too far in one direction or another. Individual humans are inconsequential to Guardians, and maintaining the Balance is the only essential priority.

The Shift—The result of the Balance being shifted too far in one direction past the point of no return. A Shift toward either negative or positive will have equally devastating effects. Devastation would occur across the planet as the walls between the realms weaken, ultimately creating one unstable realm where surviving humans and Guardians would be forced to live together. Until the Shift reaches its final stage, all light turns dark, ending life on Earth.

Gateway—The means of transport for Guardians to move between their home realms and Earth after taking on their human form. They may go to Earth for a few hours to influence where the use of Portholes isn't enough. Gateways contain a healing power and are a rip in the thin wall between the realms—a blast of powerful energy that can heal and recharge a Guardian as they pass through. Gateways opened from Earth are difficult to control, and it is almost always certain that a Guardian will need to open both a Gateway to Lucidis and Tenebris simultaneously, before closing the one they do not need. Opening a Gateway from Lucidis directly to Tenebris, or vice versa, is impossible, and the two realms can only be reached via Earth.

Porthole—A partially formed Gateway, which can be used to view humanity from Lucidis or Tenenbris or impart emotional influence without setting foot on Earth. As both Lucidis and Tenebris contain energy that re-energizes the Guardians in their home realms, it is preferable not to go to Earth unless required. As Earth exists on the point of the Balance, where negative and positive can cancel each other out, Earth does not contain the energy needed for a Guardian to draw from, which is why they draw from humans' emotions to recharge.

Rogue—A Guardian who has abandoned their duty and gone to Earth purely for pleasure. Regardless of the potential damage to the Balance, they may go out of their way to create extreme human reactions and emotions and take pleasure in the results.

Rogue Guardians will be hunted down by their kind and sent back to their respective homes. The penalty for becoming a Rogue is death.

Elders—Chosen Guardians to lead their communities. Elders are chosen when they are in or nearing their eighth decade and remain Elders until the day they die. Through the transference of emotional imprints, they gain insight from the Elders before them and use this to guide the community, becoming more effective in maintaining the Balance.

Emotional Imprints—A recognizable emotional fingerprint, individual to every human and Guardian. Guardians can recognize one another through these imprints and use them to gauge the nature of beings they have not met. Names and faces cannot be gained through these imprints, but an idea of who someone is, their values, and their power levels can be felt. Strong imprints can be detected long after a Guardian or human has physically left a location.

Fog—The result of the buildup of too many positive or negative emotions in one place. It can occur when a large group of people is gathered together, particularly in the aftermath of a disaster. All the emotions merge in the air, creating a thick, invisible fog that Guardians struggle to penetrate as their senses become lost amidst the jumble of information blocking them.

Moonstone—The only substance on Earth that can be used to return a Guardian to their home realm forcibly. Used on Earth, the most minor injury or cut will open a Gateway within the injured Guardian and transport them back to their home realm, whether they wish to or not. Moonstone, used within Lucidis or Tenenbris, will kill a Guardian more effectively than a blade of any other material. Human blood drawn by moonstone and dripped onto a Guardian's skin in human form will force them to reveal their true form.

Reflections—As the relationship between humanity's emotions and the Balance grew more complex over thousands of years, semi-transparent human forms known as Reflections began to appear in Tenebris and Lucidis. They have no identities and are not alive in the conventional sense, but they represent all humans on Earth. There is a connection between the souls of humans on Earth and the Reflections in the other realms. The Reflections absorb energy from the realms—positive from Lucidis and negative from Tenenbris—and this energy is transferred to humanity through their souls. The Guardians need not interact with the Reflections, as their presence in the realms brings them the energy they need. Tenebrian Guardians, however, take pleasure in torturing them, increasing the negative influence on humanity, and forcing Lucidians to work harder to counteract the energy and maintain the Balance. If you were to ask a Guardian to explain the connection between human souls and the Reflections, the answer would be simple—*it always was, and always shall be.* As far as they saw it, no further explanation was required.

Prologue

Ana

Present day

Some might call it selfish or weak, but I called it self-preservation.

It was the oldest story in the book, the way so many people dealt with grief and pain. Yet every time someone chose that path, there was judgment from those who didn't understand. Close yourself away from any chance of getting too close to people, because it's simpler that way. Love hurts, and losing someone you love hurts more than I could've ever prepared for.

If I didn't allow myself to love or be loved, my heart could not be ripped from my chest.

But still, a few people wormed their way into my heart even after I shut it down.

I could count them on one hand.

Hell, I could still count them on one hand, even if you took a few fingers.

But meeting him shattered that all apart. Without even trying, he opened me up to a world of emotions I had worked so hard to ignore. Once the dam cracked, the crack grew into a break, and even self-preservation couldn't stop me from falling for him.

Kyle came into my life by chance, and now I couldn't bring myself to let him go. There was a connection between us, something unspoken and invisible. A line that drew us together, wrapped around us both, and threatened to squeeze the life from us if we dared to pull away from each other. Painful if we were too far apart, but strengthened every second we were together.

I understood our connection over time, although I didn't when we first met.

I loved him.

I would die for him.

And maybe I would need to.

Chapter One

Kyle

Three weeks ago

The essence of pain crept through the Porthole. So slowly, it was barely enough to register on my senses at first as I watched over the area. Earlier, we had detected unusual activity—spikes of pain and fear that indicated something bigger was happening than was immediately apparent. Human emotions were like messages delivered directly to us through the air, and keeping them from constantly breaking into our senses took control and practice. But while on duty watching over humanity, we welcomed them inside us.

But this one hurt.

I breathed deeply, even though the pain of the humans pained me. Every beat of their heart that pushed them through their moments of struggle was a sharp ache inside of my chest, but I took it all in anyway.

Soon, the trickles of pain were replaced with the imprint of death, followed by a spike of grief, and a shudder ran down my spine as I glanced at the Guardian next to me, Sasha. Her hands trembled as she held them out toward the Porthole, ready to ease the negativity with positive energies and do what was needed to maintain the Balance.

Her gaze darted from me to the Porthole and back again as neither of us moved. The pain filtering through was stronger than we were used to. Strong enough to be felt through the fragile walls that separated our realm from Earth, even without the Porthole open.

I almost dry-retched when it doubled.

Then tripled.

The emotional blocks I attempted to create to protect myself were too little, too late. The humans' pain filtered into me through my senses, and it was like trying not to hear a jet engine. You could cover your ears, but the sound would still penetrate.

There was no escaping it.

Their screams might have well been my own.

My stomach lurched when the screams ended abruptly, and another human's emotional imprint came to a complete stop as the life was stripped from their body.

The silence after the death was filled only with grief as the ripples began, and I held up a hand as Sasha, by my side, opened her mouth to speak.

She didn't need to tell me. I already knew.

The death of a human was at the hands of a Tenebrian.

Guardians had gone Rogue before, but not like this.

Kyle.

My chosen human name rolled off my tongue nicely. It's a

simple name and straight to the point.

The name said, *I am here, and I have a job to do.*

Or at least, it sounded that way in my head.

How humans viewed me would not be my concern. I was going to Earth on a mission, and once I completed it, I would return to my home realm of Lucidis.

My home spread warmth through me, and I opened my senses to it. The realm powered me as much as Tenebris powered the Guardians who lived within it. We were polar opposites, Tenebrians and us, but we served our purpose.

Until that purpose was warped when a Guardian went Rogue.

I would need all the strength Lucidis offered me, and I absorbed as much as I could hold on to. The moment I stepped foot on Earth, my power would begin to drain. Being a neutral zone between the two Guardians' realms, Earth contained no energy I could absorb.

Humans, though, I could use them if I needed to. I could go somewhere they were happy, find the joy in the air, absorb it, and let it energize me. It wouldn't be the same as being home, but it would keep me going and allow me to concentrate my powers enough to track the Rogue Tenebrian. Negative emotions could power them as much as positive ones do for us.

But to *kill* for the sensation? That was something else.

Guardians didn't kill. It wasn't our placc.

But I would corner and send the Tenebrian back long before my energies drained.

Holding my hands before my face, I studied the skin. Being in my human form still felt strange, especially while in Lucidis. It seemed to create a partial block, and I could not connect with my home realm as I usually would, but I took what I could.

Smooth skin. Fragile. Weak.

No wonder we were to protect them.

Stronger, faster, and taller. Skin hard like diamonds.

But Guardians took a risk every time we went to Earth and opened ourselves up to injury that otherwise wouldn't have been a consideration.

I'll admit, though, the feel of a human's skin under my own was euphoric.

Being able to absorb and be strengthened by emotions made sex on Earth incredible. Human women were delicate and beautiful, so very responsive to touch, and their heart rate flared with their arousal...

No.

Concentrate.

This was not the time for games.

Once my mission was completed, perhaps if permitted, I would return to Earth to celebrate.

Find a female and spend a few hours with her.

My mentor and a community Elder, Cordus, had selected me, and me alone, to go to Earth to track down the Rogue. At first, the activity was nothing unusual—a negative influence here and there, harmless games that left humans feeling hurt, but no physical pain was delivered. Tenebrians played these games sometimes, taking their duties too far and creating negative energy where it wasn't strictly needed. They weren't doing this to keep the Balance between light and dark. They were doing it for *fun.*

We were so different.

Lucidians corrected them without complaint, knowing it

was simply more games.

Until it wasn't.

The death of a human at the hands of a Tenebrian, or any Guardian, was an unnatural and horrific act.

Cordus had grabbed my arm after the essence was picked up, his strength catching me off guard, considering his advanced age. Once the Tenebrian had killed, Cordus instructed me to prepare myself for the mission to Earth to stop him. He could not come with me, as while his strength and experience were decades beyond mine, Earth made controlling our powers difficult, and he feared that with age, he might not have the same influence on Earth as in Lucidis. His powers on Earth would be unpredictable, more so than when he first took me to Earth for training almost a decade ago.

The Guardians viewed humanity as tools for keeping the Balance in its natural state. While the Balance may move with every passing second and every human emotion is a push and pull against its invisible power, it has been successfully maintained for thousands of years.

We were the Guardians, and this was our duty.

But humans, like their emotions, were volatile. They throw them about, as they do not understand the effect they have—everything they feel and every move they make has a ripple effect on the Balance that keeps the fabric of our realms together.

Guardians *know* its effect, so one of us disregarding it was dangerous.

For the greater good, sometimes there was a need to impart negative emotions to humans to balance out the good. There should be no pleasure from this, though I suspect the

Tenebrians enjoyed their duty and the pain that resulted from it. But it seemed this particular Tenebrian did more than enjoy the pain—he *relished* it. He let it feed him and used that power to create more.

He *killed.*

No matter how often I let that fact drift through my mind, it was difficult to believe.

Why?

Even from Lucidis, I could feel the Rogue Tenebrian's strength, but as Cordus had trusted me with this task, I pushed down any doubts I had about my experience versus his.

For surely Cordus knew my power and capability better than I did.

Barely into my third decade, I was still young, and I didn't recall any other Lucidian being given a mission of this importance as their first solo. But I couldn't let my pride swell, as that was a human weakness I wouldn't succumb to.

Standing in the sun's warmth, I let the realm of Lucidis recharge me.

Somewhere in the Earth city I was about to step into, a Tenebrian was creating pain, the worst, and feeding from it, enjoying it. The results of his influence and actions were already creating a fog of negativity across the city, spreading and engulfing all those who lived within it. He was smart, concentrating his efforts within a few city blocks and letting the negativity build until it choked the happiness from the air.

I didn't know who he was, but I would find him. He couldn't hide forever.

Every move he made left a mark, an imprint, which I could use to track him.

If left too long, he could increase the fog and hide within it, using it to conceal his identity further.

If left too long, he could destroy us all.

Chapter Two

Kyle

Cornered, like the animal he was.

It had taken me three days to track the Tenebrian I was on Earth to find. Three days of waiting, scouting, and concentrating my powers on selected areas. There could be no rushing the process, and even once I had pinpointed my enemy through the thick fog of fear and pain he'd created, it was another day before I was able to cross paths with him.

Moonstone blades were handy. It was the only substance on Earth that could be used to return a Guardian to their home realm forcibly.

And if used correctly, it could kill them.

I didn't need to strike a killing wound, although after knowing this Guardian had killed humans, it was tempting. The slightest nick to the skin, the smallest cut, and a Gateway would open within the injured Guardian and drag them back to their realm, with or without their consent.

Cordus wouldn't want me to kill. He'd want me to return the guilty to Tenebris to be dealt with by their Elders.

The Tenebrian's face in human form was long and thin, with

a short crop of reddish-brown hair, spiked and unkempt. His emotional imprint was like a kick in the chest when I got too close, and the negative waves of his Tenebrian nature leaked from him even as he walked down the street. What humans were out at this late hour gave him a wide berth. They wouldn't know what exactly it was about this being that made them so afraid, but they would cross the street, sure they had seen the devil in his features.

The Tenebrian felt my presence at the same time I saw him. I'd used his creation against him and pushed down my Lucidian imprint to hide within the fog.

When I drew the blade from my pocket, he ran.

Coward.

Three days. It wasn't a record by any stretch—I had witnessed Guardians returning home after hours of searching to bring down a Rogue. But this was different. No one had killed humans before, and no Guardian had taken this level of pleasure in destruction for destruction's sake. My mission was special, one of a kind, and three days wasn't a bad record for that.

Tonight, it would end, and I would return home.

Where Cordus would warn me against pride.

But I thought I would allow myself to have this win and let the pride in, even if only for a moment.

I followed the Tenebrian down a narrow alley before it opened to a dead end, where large bins pressed against the dirty walls. When he realized he was cornered, he turned slowly to face me, raising his hands.

"I am Vena," he said, his voice as sharp as his features.

"I don't care," I replied, taking a step closer, ready to strike with the blade.

He opened his arms wide, his black jacket falling open to reveal no weapons strapped to his body. "Tell me your name, and then feel my imprint. I will not resist."

"I don't see the point in this." He arched a brow at me, and I huffed out a breath. "Cael," I offered through gritted teeth.

The darkness flashed across his eyes. "Humor me, Cael."

Sighing, I reached out with my senses. As promised, he didn't resist or block my probing and allowed me to get a read on him. My lips twisted, and I wanted to pull back. Tenebrians and Lucidians caused each other pain when too close, and intentionally sensing him from this close stung—a series of pins and needles exploded across my arms and chest as I read him.

"What did you find?" he asked when I withdrew my senses.

"You are older than I expected for someone being so reckless."

Vena's lip twitched into a snarl or a smile. I couldn't tell with his face half hidden by shadow. "That is because I am not the one you seek. I came to Earth for the same reason as you, to locate and return the Rogue to Tenebris. While we are..." There was a definite smirk this time. "*Different...* I can assure you we fight for the same cause. Despite what you may think, there are Tenebrians who still care for the Balance."

"Why should I trust you?"

Vena's anger seeped through the air, and I could feel it as clearly as though it were my own. But beyond the feeling was something else.

Contempt.

He felt I was no threat to him.

He thought he had me fooled.

"I suppose you could not trust me ordinarily, but these are no ordinary circumstances. I think you would agree."

"You don't know anything about me, *Tenebrian.*" I spat the words out. The use of his home realm name was intended as an insult, and from the rush of anger that spilled through the air toward me, it was received as such.

Vena revealed himself in that act.

If he were who he claimed to be—an older Tenebrian sent here to find the Rogue—he would have better control over his emotions.

Anger, like pride, was a human weakness.

"We must join forces," he said, quieter as though he wanted to force me to pay attention. "We both know what could happen if he is allowed to continue the damaging path he has started. The Balance could shift, and—"

"You cannot be trusted." I cut him off and ignored the rush of rage I received through the air in return. "I will do only the right thing and rid Earth of your presence."

The wave of power hit me, sent as an attack, and I stumbled back a step. Vena got a read on me. It was quick but thorough, penetrating my mind and being in one swift motion before he withdrew equally quickly—a trained attack, from years, perhaps decades more experience than I.

Yet, I smirked. I still had him cornered.

"It is not I," he yelled, and with a huff of impatience, he continued, "You are young, foolish, and full of pride that should have been beaten from you in your training."

My chuckle was empty. "You're all the same with your lies and tricks. My purpose is to protect the humans from *you.*"

I would not let Cordus down, nor the humans I was here to protect.

Vena looked as though he was about to attack or at least attempt an escape from the corner he found himself in. Before he had a chance to do either, I threw the knife, and when it pierced Vena's shoulder, he cried out in rage rather than pain.

Vena lifted his hands and watched blankly as his image began to burn away in flickers of orange and white light—a Gateway to Tenebris forming inside him, where he could not escape it. When he looked back at me, it seemed only then that he was beginning to betray his age and lose the youthful look that Guardians maintained for many decades. I suspected he would be in his seventh decade.

Why would he go Rogue now?

Vena stared at me as his body disappeared. Blackness overtook his eyes, and I was left staring into empty voids.

"Fine." Vena spat at my feet before he sneered. "You're on your own."

His hard stare penetrated me until he disappeared from Earth.

I had won.

Sighing, I pressed my forehead against the glass window of the cheap motel room, damp and cold with condensation from the night air outside. Tonight would mark the fifth day since I came to Earth to track the Rogue. Three wasted days spent locating the wrong being, and two where I had to start my search anew, and I was no closer to finding him.

I had tracked and located a Tenebrian. The *wrong* Tenebrian.

A dark scowl crossed my lips as I was again forced to replay the exchange. A reminder of the error I had made and the foolish pride that had followed. How many times must I relive it? I feared I would never escape the anger and self-loathing that bubbled in my stomach. A human weakness, first pride and then anger—was I weaker than other Guardians? Unable to fully control my emotions?

Banging my forearms against the window in frustration as the memories swam before my mind, I looked up as this elicited a shout from a neighboring room. The walls of this old building were thin.

Worse than the constant reminder of my failure, which refused to leave my mind and at times blocked me from moving forward with my duty, was knowing that after I sent Vena back to Tenebris, I felt a wave of triumphant glee.

Like a fool.

Like a human.

While I did not look down upon humanity as did many of my kind—in fact, I found them fascinating—I still knew the dangers of allowing myself the luxury of feeling emotions on that level.

Yelling an apology to the neighbor I had disturbed, I shook my hands out, forced the sneer of derision from my face, and centered my calming influences to bring myself back into line.

Earth was infecting me.

Guardians were not built to be here for days on end.

With a deep breath, I could absorb some residual positive feelings from the air left lingering from humans within the building and from the streets below, and calm my anger.

Vena had been right, and that grated against me. Tenebrians

couldn't be trusted. There had been no evidence apart from his flimsy word that he wasn't the one I was here to find. A Tenebrian's word was worth nothing, and I knew my own skills enough to know that I needed to trust my gut.

But I was wrong.

Once I had banished Vena back to Tenebris, a substantial shift in the air almost forced me to my knees as the fog increased. It was all wrong. With the negative influencer gone from Earth, the air should've begun to clear and be restored. Yet the cloud of fear and pain had grown stronger until it was practically strangling me to breathe.

There were *two* Tenebrians. It had never occurred to me that there might be two.

I had sacrificed the only help I had.

My lip lifted in irritation and regret when I remembered I had also lost the knife that had been a gift from Cordus. My first mission alone on Earth, and my first act was a major error in judgment, which ridded me of my weapon as well.

Another deep sigh, another effort to center myself, and I felt closer to whole again.

I struggled to understand the idea of a Tenebrian being helpful, but I had to push the thought from my mind.

I needed to focus.

People were in danger.

Shaking my head, I placed my fingertips against the glass and prepared my senses to take another sweep of the city. Keeping my empathetic sights within the few city blocks to which I had narrowed the target area, I brushed the shoulder-length dark blond hair out of my face and continued my search.

Human emotions left an imprint. They were all around us

all the time, so strong on Earth that it took many years to craft the skills to use them correctly. Every person feels different, and every emotion they experience is built into their imprint. Guardians were not cursed with the level of emotions humans felt and displayed, and our stoic nature allowed us to use them for our benefit.

The Rogue Tenebrian, whoever he may be, left a trail of destruction behind him.

Invisible to humans, although they would *feel* it rather than *see* it, was a cloud of negativity that would leave them sick and depressed. A build-up of anger, fear, and pain created a fog that the Tenebrian fed off and, apparently, much more disturbingly, took pleasure in.

It also allowed me to track where he had been and, hopefully, figure out where he would go next.

On the streets below, I could feel the imprints of the people who were there and had been there recently—laughing, arguing, dreaming, having sex—all regular activities for normal humans. But between all their emotional energies, I was searching for the footprint the Tenebrian left behind, the imprint of fear so strong it almost stained the air itself a sickly yellow and gray.

Once I had located the sense of the Tenebrian, I could move in on him.

But he was powerful, and with each passing hour, I needed to work harder to swallow down the reminder of just how much of a threat he was.

To Guardian, to humans.

To me.

To the fabric that held our realms together.

Surely, he knew the danger of what he was doing.

The ability to cloak one's location by internalizing one's powers was not unknown to me, but I hadn't seen it used to this extent before.

Nor for the purpose of destruction.

What was he up to?

His motivations were irrelevant, but one couldn't help but be curious.

No. I was here to protect the humans as much as I was the Balance itself.

The humans themselves posed another obstacle. Whatever terrible deeds the Tenebrian did affected the humans negatively. If he hurt them, they felt pain. If he scared them, they felt fear, perhaps anger. If he killed, those remaining felt grief. Not to mention that final, horrifying spike of terror right before they lost their life. Those who died left behind loved ones, who felt more grief, sadness, and anger, and their emotions pooled in with the others.

I rubbed my temples.

All of this clouded the area further, and by the time I felt a spike of emotional distress, the Tenebrian would have already moved on, and I would be left to deal with the fallout of his sick deeds. I'd need to drain myself to influence positive energy where he had left negative, putting out small proverbial fires everywhere I went as I stumbled down the path to finding him.

It was a vicious cycle that created a cloud of fear and pain, which in turn made the humans more afraid and only increased the fog. The fog went on and on, building and building until my senses were so clouded that even walking down the street felt like I was fighting my way through the air.

Unfortunately, I supposed, that was half the point.

I was brought crashing back to the moment when my senses tripped over an upset in the air, like a spike on a graph or the wildly swinging needle of a Richter scale. Recoiling my fingers from the glass, I cried out before I cradled my hands after a sharp pain shot through my fingertips. My eyes widened in horror as I stepped back from the window, and I almost tripped over my feet in my rush to be away from the feeling that left my stomach churning.

Whatever the Tenebrian was doing right now, it was sheer cruelty.

I could almost *taste* the pain, acidic and metallic.

Fear tasted like blood.

Grabbing my jacket, I ran.

Chapter Three

Ignis

Leaning against a tree in one of the parkland areas that dotted the city, I took a moment of solace, one foot on the bark and the other planted firmly in the grass.

The air started to smell bitter and thick, the remnants of human pain.

It was not enough, though. It was never enough. I wanted more. I wanted to see how far I could push it before things got *really* interesting.

I'd played my hand too soon and killed a handful of humans, slowly and painfully. Their fear and pain had traveled across the realms, and both a Tenebrian and a Lucidian had been sent to find me. The imprints of those who passed through into Earth were clear as I felt the Gateways open, and each came through with a sense of grim determination. One I recognized was Vena, who was being considered for an Elder.

The Lucidian, I didn't know.

But there was no doubt they were here for me.

I'd been treated to a hearty laugh two nights ago. Waves pulsed through the air as there was a clash between the two opposing Guardians, as simply being so close together sent ripples throughout the city I could pick up on. It had given me *great* pleasure to breathe deeply and absorb those sensations. Conflict, fear, and confusion from my fellow Guardians. *Bliss.*

The Lucidian must have assumed Vena was causing the damage on Earth and sent him back to our home realm without question. The Lucidian's energy pattern was weak. He was young and likely inexperienced at tracking, and therefore, not much of a threat to me.

Not that there were many Guardians I would consider a threat, perhaps only the Elders, and they wouldn't come to Earth themselves. They were too old to control their powers here anymore, and they would be more of a risk than a help. No, they would send their minions to do the job for them. The fact that a tracker had been sent from my home realm and I was not simply left to be dealt with by Lucidis spoke volumes to me. It told me my journey so far had been a success and that I was causing enough ripples to draw their attention, and therefore, I was actually *disrupting* the Balance.

Me, all on my own.

Interesting.

Let's see how far I could go.

Tenebris would not send another. If the Lucidian was foolish enough to force his only assistance back to Tenebris, they would wash their hands of me and let the Lucidian deal with me alone.

Good luck to him.

Although maybe at some point, I'd allow myself to be tracked and turn the hunter into the hunted.

But this game of cat and mouse had some potential for fun. Perhaps I could pull the Lucidian into my game and make him hurt like the humans.

Tonight, I tested my patience as I waited for a specific type of victim to wander into my spider's web. While unsure who I was waiting for, I knew I'd know them when I saw them. Someone unassuming, the sort of person who wouldn't even consider that crossing through a park after dark might be a bad idea. The city was safe enough, populated, and had plenty of good people around at this hour. But humans were too trusting, *too* good, and sometimes needed a shake-up.

I was just the one to do it.

They all had darkness within them and the ability to do cruel things. Some humans could be influenced into acting out the cruelty themselves. I enjoyed seeing how far I could turn humans against each other and draw out the darkest parts of their nature until they enacted violence upon those nearby. Those who could not be influenced to that extent, for, unfortunately, there was always an element of free will, became the victims.

My victims.

I had fun with them all the same.

Their skin was thin, their flesh weak, and their wills unable to hold up once they faced me, a being that held the negative force of my home realm. A force humans didn't and couldn't understand, but they recognized it. Good and evil have taken many forms over the centuries, but it was always the same.

Us.

"Are you the devil?" they would ask me, eyes wide and pain written on their features.

I would tell them what would hurt them most.

"Yes."

My skin exploded in goosebumps when I anticipated the pain I would cause tonight. It empowered me. The same emotions that Tenebrians found so delightful made the Lucidians ill. It was wonderful to know my Lucidian counterpart would be in such pain simply being here as he experienced the leftover aftershocks of my fun. I could create, breed, and absorb the pain, increasing my power. All the while, he would be suffering.

There was nothing to stop me now. An inexperienced Lucidis Guardian was no threat. But I'd remember he was around, for one day soon, I'd welcome him personally into my game, and he'd regret the day he stepped through the Gateway alone.

Arrogant enough to believe I was simply *another Rogue.*

I was far from it.

There had never been another like me. I was a trailblazer, and generations would remember my name and the legacy of what I had begun.

I was only getting started.

Peering around the tree trunk into the darkness, dapples of light from the street lamps, partially obscured by the overgrown treetops, crossed over the pathway. The effect created the stage as a human walked across, unaware he was being watched.

My victim.

A grin crossed over my face, darkening my already threatening features. I could be handsome if I tried, when I hid my true nature from humanity, which wasn't difficult. Humans were only animals, slaves to their own emotions and weaknesses. But once I had my victims, I allowed my negative influence to drip through and permitted my Tenebrian nature to peek out from behind the disguise that made me look like one of them.

I'd let them see the darkness in my eyes.

They would scream, and I would suck in a breath of their fear.

It took absolute control over my power to release only a hint of my being while maintaining my human form, and it had taken years of practice.

Allowing my negative energies to pump through my veins, the full potential of my influence exuded from me in a pulse. The man passing slowed in his step, overcome with a depression that he couldn't explain as he drew level with where I hid.

I pounced.

He never stood a chance.

The human woke slowly, and I doubted he remembered losing consciousness in the first place. He had put up quite a fight, but getting the upper hand against a being with strength you didn't understand was difficult with a forearm pressed against your throat.

It didn't take him long to become alert when he realized he was tied to a chair.

He looked around wildly while he yanked his arms uselessly against the binds that tied him to the office chair. That sound of plastic on plastic as the cable ties ground against the arms of the cheap chair was irritating, but I let him squirm for a while. Maybe he'll keep going until the ties cut into his skin. I kept it too dark for him to see much, but I could observe him from behind as I leaned against a desk. The illumination of the lights from a distant window cast eerie shadows across the empty office space and created squares of vague visibility through abandoned cubicles. The shadows helped me. The environment helped me. I'd use anything that played on humans' primal fears and created a spike of terror that piqued as his heart rate accelerated.

How did I get here? He'd be wondering. W*hy, I was simply walking home and was attacked. These things happen on the news, but not to people like me.*

Pathetic.

His mind was ticking over. Soon, he would notice his missing wallet, which I had taken purely to know who I was speaking to.

Alexander.

The intimacy of my knowing his name would be worse for him than a stranger he could separate himself from. He'd wonder if he knew me, too.

Then he'd wish he'd never met me.

The build-up was almost as delicious as the act itself.

After battling with whatever thoughts were going through that pathetic mind, he began fighting the binds again. It was amusing to watch, but there wasn't a hint of a weakness in those ties he could take advantage of. Everything he thought he knew about being safe and escaping a situation like this was lost and useless when faced with the real thing.

I didn't think he would be a crier, but I'd been wrong before.

I wondered what his pain tolerance was.

I'd find out.

Alexander's back stiffened, and his head turned when he finally realized he was being watched.

"Hey!" he shouted into the darkness, "Come out where I can

see you."

I approached and kept to his peripheral vision—a dark figure he couldn't even be sure was there. He'd be praying this was a nightmare.

"Usually, it is not the guy tied to the chair making the demands," I answered.

Alexander turned his head, straining his neck to see who was speaking. "What do you want? Do you want money? Who are you?"

I chuckled. "Not money. What *I* want you are not going to be happy about."

"What? What does that even mean?" He tried to keep the panic from cracking his resolve, and while I applauded his efforts, it didn't matter because I could read him. I could feel the chill that spread down his spine as though it were my own. His skin crawled with the urge to be anywhere but near me as my presence only filled him with a discomfort he couldn't explain.

Before he could blink, I was at his shoulder, my breath hot against his ear as the tip of a blade touched the edge of precious Alexander's jaw. Predictably, he tilted his head away from the blade as though his instinct, worn down by centuries of being slaves to their emotions, could save him. But he couldn't move far enough, and any movement resulted in more pressure on the blade's edge as I poised it, digging into his skin enough to draw blood but not enough to kill. A bead of sweat dripped down his neck, and I followed its trail with my gaze. I doubt he'd experienced fear like this before, fear that poisoned him through the air, seeped into his pores, and made rational thought difficult.

And made hope impossible.

But my senses danced with the pleasure of it.

He didn't even understand he was feeding the fear, making it worse by giving in to it. Fear built around humans like a bubble, and with every heavy breath, he was making it darker, breathing it in and out, and increasing its effect. Assisted by me, I focused my energies and added to it, increasing the sense of fear until I could practically hear his heart thumping against his rib cage.

Every intake of my breath absorbed his fear, and when I released it back into the air, I added to the cloud of negativity around him. Feeding it, feeding *off* him. Taking advantage of the cycle of energies that I *should* be balancing, and was instead used. Alexander squeezed his eyes shut momentarily before they snapped open again. The internal darkness was more terrifying than what he could see, and his eyes darted around rapidly as he searched for an exit, desperate for escape.

He would find none.

A shudder ran down my spine, and I felt myself grow erect.

Fear was nothing short of ecstasy.

But I wouldn't take him, not like that, not tonight.

Maybe tomorrow I will find someone, seduce them, and have them come to me of their own free will.

Then destroy them.

Humans' responses were always better when they came under my influence of their own will.

"How about I answer your last question?" I cooed.

Alexander cringed and gritted his teeth as I pushed the tip of the blade into his jaw slowly, so he could feel every bit of the metal as it passed the protective barrier of his skin and invaded his body. Blood dripped steadily down his neck and onto his shirt.

A stained shirt wouldn't be the only reminder he'd be left with tonight.

I flashed a grin. "You know how people in movies say, '*I'm your worst nightmare*?'"

Alexander's eyes started to water from the pain as I twisted the blade into his flesh. It wasn't a large knife, but it didn't have to be. I could bring any human to their knees with a nail file if I had to. Moving in front of Alexander's face, I bent to face him and placed a hand on the back of his neck in an almost intimate gesture. Too intimate for him, judging by the flare of fear in his eyes.

I watched his pupils expand and contract as though his body was trying to protect him from seeing too much.

As though not seeing me would make the pain go away.

"Well, in my case..." I bared my teeth at him, hissing slightly and causing a whimper to be drawn from his throat. Allowing my eyes to cloud black, I whispered, "... it's true."

He didn't scream, but the spike of his fear left me groaning in pleasure.

Twisting the blade again, I needed more.

More.

RELA

Chapter Four

Ana

Reaching the peak of laziness was getting irritated that the view of the television was obscured, and knowing you could easily solve the issue by moving your feet from the coffee table, but being too comfortable to do so.

I was pleased to say I had reached such a peak.

Such was my laziness at that moment that the packet of crisps I desperately wanted to finish would remain uneaten, as they were a good three inches out of my reach.

And I wasn't moving until I had to.

Which reminds me.

Slipping my cell out of my pocket, I diverted my attention from the movie to check the time. Groaning, I slid my black lace-up boots from the coffee table and dropped my feet heavily to the floor. Rustling my fingers through my hair, I groaned again, mainly for dramatic effect this time. It didn't matter that I had seen the movie countless times, more than I should admit. It still seemed a shame to miss the ending for something as mundane as work.

How could you go wrong with a seventies classic about a

killer shark?

"Spielberg, you're a fucking genius," I mumbled to myself before I heaved myself off the couch, stretched, and looked around the small apartment. It wasn't dirty by any stretch of the word, but could certainly do with some tidying up.

Seemed we were back to the lazy argument again.

Absentmindedly, I picked up several jackets I'd thrown over the backs of chairs after previous shifts. The tell-tale squeak of the taps as the shower was turned off sounded as I passed the bathroom while my roommate, Penny, got ready for her shift.

Different workplaces, *very* different people. I admired Penny's work as a nurse, but I didn't think I'd have it in me to do it. She was kindness personified, having gone through Hell and come out the other end, only to insist on giving back to the community and saving people.

Potentially much like the person who had almost torn her apart.

For me, bartending it was.

I liked the nighttime. I liked being too busy to have a meaningful conversation with any one person, and I quite enjoyed a drink.

Initially, I'd have preferred to live alone. But the reality was that even with the inheritance and the life insurance payout after my mother's death, on my salary alone, I couldn't afford the rent of a central city apartment. I had resisted looking for a roommate for as long as possible, until it became apparent that it was sheer stubbornness and I was delaying the inevitable, and wasting my savings in the process.

Although I'd been lucky to find Penny, or, more specifically, I'd been lucky Penny had found *me*.

Beyond lucky, given all the messed-up people out there.

Penny had responded to my online post seeking a roommate within a few hours of it being up. I didn't have to go through months of bad living experiences with unsuitable people before finding the right one. Penny had moved in, and we'd fallen into a routine like we'd known each other for life. She was the perfect combination of company and conversation, and she left me the hell alone when I wanted to be.

Which, honestly, was my preference most of the time.

I didn't know how she put up with me, but I'm thankful she did.

Penny had wormed her way into my heart, and I'd found myself favoring conversation with her over being alone more often than I would've thought myself capable. She was difficult not to love, and now I felt the same fierce protectiveness over her as I did over myself.

The intimate circle of people I allowed to get close to me was so small now it bordered on non-existent. Mentally, I ticked off people I counted as close.

Mom, rest her soul.

Penny, Henry.

Mr. Banks, although he was another story and...

Damn, I guess that was it.

With Penny's seemingly infinite patience and willingness to open up at my slow-ass pace—and damned if I hadn't made her work for every inch of the personality I hid so well—Penny had become my closest friend.

I was not one for second chances, and I rarely bothered with people beyond a first impression. People were mostly easy to read, and you could tell all you needed to know about someone by the initial feel of their character—how they communicated and held themselves, how they talked to you, and *about* you when you weren't there. But Penny was open and warm, despite an aura of self-preservation I could relate to. We shared a protective nature over our independence and the pain of our respective pasts.

Penny had scars that ran deep, and after we'd settled in together as roommates and ultimately friends, she was a kindred spirit to me—a rarity I knew I had to hold on to.

Because for the longest time, I'd been afraid to let myself care or be cared for.

Why let people in when they're just going to leave you, anyway?

"Penny, I'm going to work," I yelled as I walked past the bathroom.

"Okay, but there's no need to *shout,*" Penny cried, and I could hear the smirk in her voice clearly through the crack in the partially open door.

Chuckling, I pulled my t-shirt over my head as I stepped into my bedroom and discarded it onto the growing pile on the floor. A t-shirt that said *No Pants are the Best Pants* probably wasn't the best choice for working behind a bar. Slipping on a white tank top and, over that, a loose black singlet, I yanked them both down over the top of my black jeans.

Glancing in the mirror, I ruffled my blonde hair with my fingers. What used to be a pixie cut had grown past my ears. A little bit longer, and I just might be able to pull it into a ponytail.

I tried.

"Close, but no banana," I muttered.

As I released my hair from my fingers, Penny poked her head around my bedroom door, holding a towel around herself. "Did you say something?"

"I was talking to myself."

"Oh, like the crazy woman you are, of course," Penny said.

"At least it's better conversation than with you," I said and ducked as a shoe was flung into my room, missing me by inches.

I was searching for the shoe, getting ready to lob it back at her in the same manner, when Penny sheepishly shuffled her way into my room. "I actually need that for work," she said, and I laughed, playing a ridiculously short game of *keep-away* with her. A useless endeavor, considering she was almost eight inches taller.

As Penny returned to her room, I flicked my necklace out from under my tops and took a moment to debate if I should bother wearing some other jewelry.

Nope. More trouble than it was worth.

Habitually rolling the stone pendant between my finger and thumb, I shuffled through my bedside table, seeking my keys.

The necklace had once belonged to my mother, who had died in a car accident when I was a teenager. My mother told me the necklace had been a gift from my father, not that I gave a shit about that part. The man had been barely present during my childhood, and I hadn't seen him since before my mother's death.

Despite his constant disappearances, Mom would never hear a bad word against him and would tell me off whenever I called him a shit father. I never understood her unwavering loyalty to a man who didn't care to show her the same love and respect.

Shoving my cell, keys, and cards into my pockets, I moved to the front door and tossed a wave over my shoulder. My cheeks burned when the futility of the gesture hit me—Penny couldn't see through walls.

That I knew of.

"Penny, can you see through walls?"

She poked her head around the corner of her doorway. "What?"

"Can you see through walls?"

She stared at me for a beat before she barked out a laugh. "You watch too many movies, idiot."

"Aha." I held up a finger. "That's what people say when they're hiding something."

She rolled her eyes. "Be safe, Ana."

"You too."

I scoffed to myself. *As if there's such a thing as too many movies.*

Leaving, I unintentionally slammed the door behind me, hearing another laugh from Penny after I did.

Skipping down the stairs two at a time, I grabbed the handrail at the bottom of each flight and used my momentum to fling myself around in a semicircle because I was easily amused. I always took the stairs instead of the elevator. My twenty-seven years on this planet had earned me a distrust of those mechanical boxes.

There were no bad experiences to blame for the attitude, simply too many spooky stories.

For example, I'd heard if you were in an elevator that was plummeting to the ground and you jumped at the last second, you would avoid the impact breaking every bone in your body. Great in theory, but how did you know when you were at the bottom of the building? Did you jump up and down continuously and hope you nailed the timing?

It was best to avoid them altogether, rather than spend your last moments alive jumping around like a lunatic.

Reaching the ground floor, I poked my head into the open doorway of Henry's apartment. Henry was an elderly gentleman who had taken a liking to me for whatever reason. Maybe he saw some of himself in my smartassery. He could fire off one-liners with the best of them.

Surprising myself, I found I enjoyed his company.

Welcome to my circle of friends, Henry, population—two.

"All right, Henry?" I called out.

"Ana, how are you?"

"Good, good, just on my way to work."

"You be careful. I don't like you working at night."

The corner of my lip lifted. "I'm always careful. Grocery shopping next week as usual, right?"

Henry smiled, the skin around his eyes wrinkling behind his round glasses. "Ana, you don't have to help me carry my groceries. I'm stronger than I look, you know?"

"Don't let him fool you. He loves playing the old-man card."

Chuckling, I stood to the side to let Nathaniel pass as he made this quip. He worked for the aged care services, occasionally popping around to see Henry and helping with small chores around the place.

"How are you doing, Nathaniel?" I asked, more out of social obligation than anything else.

He half-smiled and lifted a shoulder into a slight shrug as though he couldn't be bothered giving even the gesture his full attention. He was tall and slender, had full-bodied dark hair, and surprisingly good dress sense for his age.

Well, what I assumed was his age anyway. I'd never asked and probably never would.

I was fairly sure he was younger than I, even if only by a few years.

"I gotta run. See you soon."

"Bye, Ana!"

Waving, I jogged out of the apartment and through the foyer.

"Right on time, never early, never late," Ed chimed as I stepped behind the bar and tied one of the off-white aprons around my waist. It was only Ed and I scheduled, and I never understood why they didn't assign more than two bartenders to a Saturday night shift. Trying to save money, I guessed. But the revelation didn't make it any less irritating.

Rush hour with only two bartenders? Why the fuck not, right?

Yet—I glanced at Ed down the bar and tutted quietly to myself—it seemed no matter how busy we got, my sleazy workmate would still find some time to charm every good-looking girl he served. The man had no shame and even fewer standards.

"Hey, I don't work for free," I quipped as I straightened the apron. "Busy?"

"Nah, not yet." Ed leaned against the bar, a casual gesture in line with his ever-casual tone. "But it's early and not a decent piece of ass in the place." He eyed me even as I narrowed my gaze at him. "Until now, anyway." Ed finished with a wink, as though a cheeky wink made his constant skeezy comments justifiable.

"You're such a sleazebag." I rolled my eyes.

"Yes, but I'm *your* sleazebag," Ed said and made a kissy face.

"Ed, you'll never be *my* anything." I turned away, feeling his eyes on me and sure he was checking out my ass as I stocked the bar fridges under the counter. I tolerated working with Ed, and part of me liked to think that, deep down, he wasn't such a bad guy.

Deep, *deep* down.

Very fucking deep.

But his attitude and sordid comments sent a shiver down my spine every damn time. I could joke with most people, but him? It was like every word from his mouth dripped with non-consensual promises. He was the sort of guy who made you feel dirty simply by being near him... and not in a good way. Ed laughed at my dismissal of him and ran his fingers through his short brown hair.

He was good-looking, and half the problem was that he *knew it*.

Something about how he looked at me had evolved over the weeks since he'd started working here. As though I had moved up from the challenge all women posed to him, to a game, then eventually a prize he must claim because I wouldn't sleep with him.

I liked to trust my gut, and with him? My initial reaction was that something about him felt uncomfortable. But that wasn't a strong enough word.

Icky was a good word.

My grasp of language was mature like that.

Chapter Five

Kyle

Standing amongst the empty shells of cubicles made my skin crawl. Even if I had walked in with my eyes closed and hadn't seen the chair dragged into the middle of the floor with severed cable ties strewn around it. Even if I hadn't viewed the splatters of blood on the worn carpet, I would've felt it. I could've walked blindfolded to the exact spot where the torture occurred because the fog of fear and pain was so thick I could almost touch it.

The entire office looked like it had been unoccupied for some time. It was the perfect setting for the Tenebrian to torture his latest victim. Whether the Tenebrian Guardian had chosen this place by design or for sheer convenience, I didn't know, and it hardly made a difference. My stomach churned with the residual fear that was heavy in the air.

It mingled with something even more disturbing.

Ecstasy.

The joy my enemy took in inflicting the pain and absorbing it, in using it to grow stronger and go on to hurt again, made me cringe. We were two sides of the same coin. The same emotions that made me sick brought Tenebrians joy, and vice versa. If I worked at it and absorbed enough happiness and joy, I could use it against him like a shield.

Or a weapon.

He could do the same to me, and was with all the fear he was spreading. It was both a shield and a weapon to him. He hid in the fog he created and weaponized it until I could barely breathe in the space. He no doubt knew it would be painful for me to walk through the energies he left around the city.

And I bet that made him even happier.

My lips pressed together in a thin line. I'd never understand Tenebrians, especially Rogues. But then again, I didn't have to *understand* them. I only needed to keep them at bay and get them to stick to their duties to preserve the Balance, and preferably away from the Earth realm.

Silently, I moved to the chair, sat, and forced myself to ignore the way the residual pain tingled through my body unpleasantly. I tried to trace the feeling of where he might have gone from here. The victim had not died in this chair or this room. I could tell that much immediately. The sense of death always lingered and stuck to the roof of my mouth, and it wasn't here.

Something else was in the air beyond the pain and ecstasy.

He was toying with me.

Feeding me a line or a clue, only to have it ripped away when I got too close.

Frowning, I honed my concentration inwards within this room, this chair, and the feel of the unfortunate human that sat in it.

My eyes snapped open, and I moved to the nearest window.

The echoes of their presence and emotional imprint shifted

around, barely beyond my senses. Looking out across the area, I tried hard to ignore the expanse of the city beyond the horizon, and I searched.

There were a lot of places he could be, but my eyes fell almost immediately on a nearby hospital.

Cordus had told me to follow my instincts.

Pinpointing my senses toward the hospital, I stumbled back at the wave of negative energy thrown back at me due to my mental probing. The ripples of it lasted long after I had withdrawn my senses and reverberated around the empty office floor.

That was it.

Wait, did he take his victim to the *hospital?*

It would make sense, I guessed, on a twisted level. Let the doctors and the nurses see the result of his torture and have them go home and wonder what kind of sick being was capable of such things, and if their families were safe. They'd move about the city, fearing what they had seen, spreading the fear without saying a word, and wondering if it could happen to them or their loved ones.

Leaving the office building, I quickened my pace as I headed toward the hospital.

More than another clue, it was a strong possibility for a hiding place, and it renewed my sense of purpose.

A hospital, of course, would be a perfect hiding spot for a Rogue to set up base. Somewhere where additional fear would initially go unnoticed by a Guardian as the waves of it would be clouded by the pain already living within the buildings.

Staring at the hospital from across the street, I kept a relatively safe distance to avoid my senses becoming too clouded and did a quick visual scan. It comprised one main building and several smaller ones covering a large area. A cancer ward with on-site housing and a nursing home was located on the same block, the signage lit with dim, flickering bulbs.

I watched people as they came and went for a while, and took readings of them as they passed.

I would know if they had been close enough to the Tenebrian, provided their imprint wasn't too clouded by the murky air of fear around this place.

Damn, it was a good choice of hiding places.

A *really* good choice.

Had he done this before?

But I couldn't go into the hospital and search, not now. I was already drained from searching for the office building, and my sense of weakness only increased as I stood there. I would be useless once I entered, and no better at tracking the other Guardian than the humans inside. Every person who passed me held within them an energy pattern almost identical to the one I was trying to trace, fueled by guilt and terror. Every ounce of negativity penetrated my being, and it felt as though gravity was dragging me down and beckoned me to lie on the ground and not move until my energy was restored.

But it wouldn't be, not here. It would drain until I had nothing left.

People generally didn't come here if they were happy.

Although there were spots of joy in the building, as new life was brought into the world.

Families. It's a nice concept, but it's foreign to me.

Vowing to return tomorrow to resume my search and focus in on this area, I turned on the spot and began walking back to my temporary home. I needed my powers to be sharp and clear to penetrate the cloud of fear.

Shoulders slumping slightly, I tried to shake off my doubts. It was becoming difficult to maintain my confidence when I was so often reminded of how limited my powers were. I was young by Guardian standards, and the air was thick overhead with the aftereffect of the Tenebrian's presence. I'd need my full concentration to penetrate the fog and pinpoint the imprint I sought.

So, I had no choice but to leave the hospital site.

I had work tonight, a small job I had picked up in the human world, and being around the humans would help me. They'd be happy where I worked, and I could use that.

Vowing to return tomorrow, I almost smiled, daring to feel hopeful that my search was nearing an end.

At a previous gig, a girl had approached me, giggling and twirling her hair around her finger, and told me I had a *Kurt Cobain* look. I wasn't sure what she meant, so I looked it up. While it turned out she was right, it was a complete accident. I made a selection from the comfortable clothes in Lucidis—a red plaid shirt worn over a grey T-shirt and black jeans. She'd reached up and twisted a lock of my mid-length blond hair around her finger and nodded to the guitar I had slung over my back.

"Perhaps you could give me a lesson?"

My mind was too clouded, so I'd shaken my head. "Maybe

another time."

I'd been distracted that night, and the sex wouldn't have been good for her. She would have picked up on my mood through my influence, which I'm certain I wouldn't have been able to control, and would've left with a dark cloud of negativity around her.

I didn't want that for her or any human.

Making my way into the bar, I sat on a stool near the rear corner and adjusted the microphone height. It wasn't much, but the money I made doing these low-key acoustic shows was enough to keep me going without borrowing too much, so I could continue my search.

An added bonus was that *most* city bars and clubs attracted people who wanted to relax and feel good. I could use that energy to recharge myself, and in turn, I fed my influence into the space around me. They'd feed off me, and I'd feed off them. Social energy, in particular, was helpful. The laughter and the joy were like a light being ignited within my being, bringing me back to normal.

Not one for introductions, I opted to simply start playing. I had nearly missed my scheduled start time, not that it would have mattered had I succeeded in bringing down the Tenebrian.

I managed to contain a grimace as I was reminded I had been too late to stop him.

Again.

But this time, at least, I had made progress and had found a likely base the Tenebrian may be using, and that was enough to keep me going.

So, for now, I had to continue as if I belonged in this realm and went to work like a regular person who didn't have to worry about supernatural beings infecting the Earth.

As the night wore on, the vibe increased and fluctuated slightly before settling into one of carefree happiness. It fueled me and built up my energy to a point where I had to actively work to control my image and maintain my human form. Humans had no idea how much power they held. They responded to Guardians because we were beacons for their emotions, without feeling them ourselves. I'd discovered firsthand the power of the bond between humans and Guardians during my first trip to Earth with my mentor.

After a day of work, I'd picked up a woman in a bar and seduced her, and she had responded so strongly to my touch and underlying power, which I was still learning to control, I almost couldn't get her to leave the motel the following morning. She pined and grabbed at my clothes, desperate for more contact and the sensation beyond the physical touch only a Guardian could provide. Cordus had reprimanded me, telling me I should never bring a human back to my place of rest, and if I *must* partake in Earthly pleasures, I should find somewhere else to do it.

Where *I* could leave *them.*

But the feel of her skin...

Grinning, I let my fingers run playfully across the guitar strings. I mostly played instrumental pieces during my gigs, and what singing I participated in carried across the room on an additional plane humans couldn't understand but could feel. Had they focused on my voice, they would've been completely absorbed in the music, unable to tear their attention away. I could influence them with my voice if I wanted, and use it as a tool to carry my powers by focusing my energy into words. I could plant ideas in their heads, and they would feel like they had changed their minds.

Although the power was limited, free will was important and strong. I couldn't *make* someone do something unless the desire existed within them.

Or unless I was particularly strong, like the Rogue appeared to be.

Shaking the thought from my head, I continued playing.

For now, I only mildly affected the room's mood, without particularly trying, and fed off the returning vibes I got from the crowd. It created a cycle of positive energy I could use, and in turn, made the bar-goers feel good too. Sometimes, I'd tune into a particular person and play music based on the reading I got from them. I translated the emotions of those around me and let them flow through the music. Occasionally, a bar-goer would stop their conversation and listen, and I'm sure they'd feel the music was from a long-ago memory, but not quite able to place it.

I felt something nearing the end of my set—a disturbance in the room's energy.

But not a negative one. This was no Tenebrian.

It was a soft feeling, almost hidden amongst the chaos of the bar as it drifted through the air and settled around me. As I played, I focused on it, drew it into me, and used it. Tilting my head, I leaned into the sensation. *Soft* was the wrong word to describe it, it was more... melancholic, and it was being carried toward me through a gentle humming. I couldn't hear the humming itself, but I didn't need to. I could feel the emotions it supplied floating through the room toward me like a river, and it built around me until my fingers couldn't help but translate it into the music.

Looking up, my eyes fell almost immediately on the blonde bartender who had smiled at me when I'd entered. I watched her while I played and drew the tune directly from her.

At that moment, she was my muse.

She remembered something. I couldn't tell much about the memory itself, but she was thinking of something or someone from the past.

I refocused.

Someone, not something. She was thinking about *someone.*

Someone whom she had loved and lost, and still loved. The trickle of her remaining love was in the air, and now it was in my music, and it was beautiful.

When she saw me watching her, I was rewarded with another genuine smile. She was quite beautiful, but her imperfections made her *extraordinary*. Her nose—a little too round and turned up at the end to be considered classic beauty—suited her, made her unique. Her brown eyes, almost too large for her face but framed by dark lashes and brows, made it feel like she was looking through me. An innocence to her, but a defiance. She was hiding, and although even from here, I could feel the purity of her essence, she was guarded. There were thick walls within her that stood to attention constantly. I imagine a slight prod from the wrong person, and those walls would slam down with reinforcements, and all inner parts of her being would be lost to them forever.

Maybe she'd open up to me.

Perhaps her company might help strengthen me further.

After finishing my set, I made my way over to her and could not stop the smile that crept over my face as she looked up and watched me approach patiently.

As though she had been waiting only for me.

I grinned. Maybe I was looking into it too much.

As I sat on a barstool near the end of the bar, she walked over and stopped as I rested my forearms on the wooden surface.

"There's thirty years of beer stickiness on that bar," she said.

"I know that now. I can't move my arms."

She laughed. What a gorgeous sound. "What can I get you?"

I smiled, and hers faltered. It almost looked like she blushed slightly, but she didn't seem the type to blush. She was responding to my energy. I could feel it.

"Just a beer, please." When I grinned at her, she raised her eyebrows, and a shadow of a smirk crossed her face before she turned and poured the beer, then placed it in front of me. She threw my cash in the register without counting it and turned back to me as she poured herself a shot.

"I liked your music," she said.

"Thank you."

"Maybe you could play privately for me sometime?"

I raised my eyebrows. "That was smooth."

She laughed again. "I know, I thought so too."

As I reached across the bar, I introduced myself, "Kyle." Holding my hand out to her had been an automatic action, having watched humans do it many times. I wasn't sure of the origin of the tradition of shaking hands, but I liked it. It allowed me to get a deep, albeit brief, reading on someone. A reading that could only be achieved through physical contact.

"Ana," she replied, shaking my hand, and electricity coursed through my veins at her touch. The skin-on-skin contact confirmed what I had already felt—she was kind.

But deep down, hiding pain.

"Short for something?" I asked.

"Anahera." She withdrew her hand.

"I haven't heard that name before."

"It's a Māori name."

"It's beautiful."

She smiled. "I'd say thank you, but I can't take any credit for it."

It was my turn to laugh. She was a strange combination of open and honest, but heavily guarded. The open part of her felt only skin deep. My lips curved as I wondered what she hid beneath the surface. My eyes moved down her neck to the hint of cleavage above her tank top.

I wondered what she looked like beneath her clothes.

When I met her eyes—my blue against her brown—she arched her back ever so slightly to give me a better view, and I gripped the beer glass as my cock twitched in my pants.

A man approached the bar, interrupting my sordid thoughts, his shirt half untucked and his suit jacket disheveled. "Another beer, please, love."

Ana assessed him. "All right. But it's gonna be your last one for tonight."

He leaned heavily against the bar and swayed slightly. "You're pretty. Wanna get together later?"

Ana handed him his beer, and I noticed she had poured light when he hadn't asked for it.

"No, thank you," she answered, swiping his credit card.

"Come on, I see you here all the time. I could show you a good time." He wiggled his eyebrows at her, and I suppressed a laugh, as that had to be the most unalluring flirtation I'd ever seen. There was a shot of pride that moved through me at the stark difference between her reaction to me and her reaction to this stranger.

She wanted me.

She felt the connection, too.

Ana's expression didn't shift. "I assure you, Sir, I'm here because it's my job, not because I'm waiting for you to sweep me off my feet."

"Come on..." The man grabbed for her hand when she handed him his credit card. Anger flashed across her face, but I stood before she could respond.

Stretching out my arm, I blocked the man from leaning across the bar. The muscles in my arm flexed and tightened as the drunken man leaned forward and put his weight against me. Ana's gaze was on me—she was checking me out as much as I had her. I was overcome with the overwhelming urge to touch her.

Or flex.

No, that was pride again.

I needed to get this guy out of here.

"Why don't you just leave her alone? She said no."

"Hey, buddy—"

Drawing myself to my full height—a bit over six foot six—I faced the man, invading his space. "I said, *leave her alone*."

There was a pause as the man responded to the energy I'd directed at him through my words, and then, without a word, he turned and walked stiff-limbed back to his table of friends. While I couldn't affect free will, simple things like getting someone to leave were easy.

Ana looked at me, and her eyes widened slightly before

returning to her bemused expression. "Oh, my knight in shining armor." She said it with a smile and only a hint of sarcasm.

"You're welcome." I sat back down and brought my energy under control.

I wasn't here to influence Ana. I liked her company.

"Seriously, thank you," she said as she wiped down the bar where the man had spilled his beer. "I wasn't in the mood to be dealing with that bullshit tonight."

"No problem. So, what time do you finish?"

Ana glanced at the clock by the bar. "In about... thirty-two seconds."

"I think I can manage the wait."

Ana grinned. "Well, aren't I the lucky one?"

OUTLET

Chapter Six

Kyle

Ana and I sat at a tram stop and sipped lukewarm convenience store coffees. I tried to focus on the conversation, but my senses piqued the closer I got to her. Humans blocks away came into clarity, and their emotional imprints opened to me like a book. The closer I shuffled next to Ana on the cold bench, the clearer my senses became. Small groups of people—lovers' arguments and friends' laughter—all echoed within my mind with almost pinpoint accuracy. I was certain that if I were to go for a walk with Ana, I could get within a few yards of any chosen human on sense alone.

It was intriguing.

Ana sharpened me and cleared away all negativity so I could think again.

So I could feel like myself again.

Ana calmed me like the best kind of drug.

As she cradled her coffee between her hands, I asked, "Shall we find a bar or something?"

Ana swung her legs back and forth from her seat on the bench. "If you don't mind, I'm quite happy here. I like the night. The tasteless coffee I can give or take, though." She raised the polystyrene cup and swirled it slightly. "How did you make that guy at the bar leave me alone?"

"*Make* him?" I glanced at her before shrugging. "I didn't make him do anything. I simply suggested he leave you alone. I guess he didn't want any trouble."

"I know that man, I mean... I see him around the bar a lot." She eyed me like she didn't believe I wasn't hiding some secret superpowers from her. "He *always* wants trouble. I've never seen him stop or leave because someone *asked him nicely*. If I knew your secret, I could deal with him next time."

I smiled, huffing a breath through my nose. "Afraid I can't help you there."

"Fine, keep your secrets." Ana hummed her acknowledgment. "Well, I appreciated it, nonetheless. Gallantry isn't dead after all."

I chuckled. "Not for me." After a pause, I said, "I like your necklace."

Ana glanced down and began twirling the stone pendant with her fingers. The motion was so natural, almost subconscious, as if she'd done it a thousand times before. "Thank you, it was my mother's."

"Birthday present?"

"Nah, I got it when she died."

"Oh, I'm sorry. I didn't know."

That explained the sense of loss and melancholy I'd picked up on while I played guitar, and that same sense came to the surface now and swirled around her.

Ana lifted an eyebrow at me, and I cursed myself. "How could you have?"

Of course. *How could I have known?* I could feel the grief on her, and I could've made a deductive leap. But she seemed so young to be without her parents.

She sighed before continuing, "It's okay. It was almost ten years ago now." Ana paused and squeezed her eyes shut for a second. "Well, it's not *okay*, but you know what I mean. It's okay to talk about. I'm better at talking about Mom now since I'm almost always thinking about her. It's not until I stop to think about her like this..." she gestured between us, indicating our conversation, "that I realize how long it has been. All that time, all the life experiences I've had without her..."

She let her words drift off with her thoughts. I liked listening to her talk. "I know what you mean." I said, "What was she like?"

Ana blew out a long breath. "Oh boy, not an easy question to answer quickly." She laughed with a quiet huff of her breath. "She was insanely stubborn. My God, we used to clash over some things. She was an incredibly strong woman, and I keep hoping I have some of her strength locked away, ready to be unleashed somewhere inside me. But she was also artistic and kind. She'd help a stranger in need without a second thought. Mom gave people second and third chances, always seeing the best in everyone and letting people into her life without judgment. The opposite of me in that respect." Ana sighed as thoughts of her mother consumed her.

"What about your father?"

Ana snapped her head up. "Sorry?"

"Your father?" I repeated. I also liked how she got lost in her thoughts and fell silent as she disappeared inside her mind. I wished I could jump in there with her, peel back the layers, and find out exactly who lay underneath.

Ana threw up her hands dramatically into the air. "Fuck knows! He left years ago. He could be dead, and I'd never know. He wasn't around much even before he left, so I can't say much about him. But I've gone this long without him, so I don't need him now."

My lips pressed together, and I'm sure the sympathy was written on my face. I tried hard not to feel, but being around humans made it difficult. They amplified a part of me I preferred to keep stoic. Especially Ana. Being with her was like shining a spotlight on feelings I didn't know myself capable of.

Ana waved her finger before me when she saw my expression change. "Now, wait a minute, don't you go pitying me. I know what you're thinking... *ooh... aah... a girl with daddy issues hangs around with random strangers at night and tries to jump into bed with them. What a cliché!*"

I chuckled despite myself. "Jumping into bed? I like to be wined and dined first."

Ana laughed, a single loud *hah* sound, but it wasn't insincere.

When Ana laughed, she laughed loudly and seemingly without a care. Either she was the rare human who didn't concern herself with what others thought, as so many claimed. Or more likely, she *did* care, but forgot to care as much when relaxed. Something stirred in me, feeling too much like the pride I kept trying to keep down.

I was glad that she could enjoy herself and relax *with me.*

The breeze ruffled her short hair around her face, enunciated by another chuckle from her. My entire being calmed in her presence, and once again, my senses piqued, and the streets around us opened up as I could read every human within my mind's reach.

The clarity would be helpful when I searched for the Tenebrian again tomorrow.

I contemplated telling Ana this for a moment, but it would have led to follow-up questions, which would have been awkward.

Hey, want to come hang out with me at a hospital? I shook my head at the thought.

I was content to be in her company for however long I had with her.

"You are beautiful," I said.

"Is that all you've got? I'm pouring my sad story out to you, and you tell me I'm beautiful?"

"It's true."

She smiled, and I returned the smile. It was difficult not to when hers was so genuine, it lit me up.

"Tell me," she said, knocking me on the elbow as her posture shifted. "*Do you read*?" The question was asked through gritted teeth while she put on a gruff voice, leaned forward, and pulled her brows together.

My jaw dropped as I tried to decipher her tone and physical stance. I couldn't think what human emotion was connected to such a move. Was she angry at me? Had I said something wrong? I was momentarily speechless before I realized I was sitting there with my mouth agape. "I'm... I'm sorry, what?" I stuttered.

She laughed, this time several loud *hahs* with a slight pause between each, the last two a higher pitch. I'd never heard anyone laugh like that. I wanted to listen to it more. "Sorry," she said, "I can't ask that question normally without thinking of the movie *Batman vs Superman*." At my blank look, she added, "You know, the movie quote? '*Tell me, do you bleed...*" she laughed again. "Never mind."

My expression remained passive as I grappled with the situation.

She was quoting a movie line at me.

Is that normal?

Ana smirked. "Whatever, just answer the question. Do you like to read?"

Regaining my composure, I answered, "I guess. I do like to learn." I caught myself before I had added *about humans*. No idea how I'd explain that slip-up. "I don't often get the time to do it, though."

"See, I always figure if something is really important, you'll make time to do it."

"You're probably right."

"Probably?" Her dark eyebrows shot up. "Oh, see, we've just met, and you don't know me yet, so I'll let you off the hook. But I will tell you now, I'm *always* right."

"Is that so?"

She grinned and nodded before looking at her feet and swinging her legs again. It was almost as if sometimes she let herself slip outside of her shell, then actively made a point to return inside, afraid to show too much of who she was. I wondered why. She was wonderful. The whole world should see how wonderful she was.

"So, what do these super senses of yours tell you about me?" I turned toward her, holding my palms out and tilting my chin in invitation, waiting to be assessed.

"First of all..." Ana held up a hand, her face lit with a grin, "... who told you about my super senses? Secondly..." she paused and looked me up and down, and I smirked as she flushed when her eyes lingered on my arms, my chest, and then my crotch. Ana cleared her throat. "You're about a million times more complicated than you let on, but... I think you're trustworthy."

"That sounds good. Anything else?"

"Yes, I suspect that you're excellent in bed."

It was my turn to raise my eyebrows. "Well, at least that's something we can put to the test."

Ana grinned and leaned in to kiss me. I wasn't ready for her to make the move, but I was saved from a potentially awkward pause when she kept it chaste and gently pressed her lips against mine. She tasted like coffee, and I felt the heat pass between us. My skin tingled at the touch of her lips.

"My place or yours?" she whispered, her lips still close to mine, seemingly hesitant to put space between us.

"Yours, but..." I grabbed her wrist as she went to slip her hand under my open shirt to caress my chest. She was one layer of thin fabric away from touching my skin, and I held back a shudder. I wanted to watch her come undone. "...no promises, Ana. I'm not someone who can be more to you than what we are tonight."

Her eyebrows involuntarily shot up, but she recovered quickly and nodded, leaning in to kiss me again. She waited a beat before making contact, and when I raised a palm to touch her cheek, she closed the small gap between us and pushed her tongue into my mouth as I parted my lips for her. As my thumb caressed her cheek, she leaned into my touch. Her skin was smooth, not rough like cut diamonds, and I was reminded that beyond her tough façade, she was only human. As she pressed into the touch of my hand, gentle but demanding, my eyes widened at the intimacy of the act.

Before I had time to think, she had pulled away.

"Come on." She stood and reached out her hand. "My place is just around the corner. My roommate should still be at work for a bit."

Taking her hand, I followed as she crossed the street.

Chapter Seven

Ana

The front door to my apartment crashed against the wall as we shoved our way through it before I kicked it closed behind us. I didn't want to break apart from Kyle for a moment. But eventually, we had to shatter the kiss to take a grateful breath of air before he returned his attention to my already swollen lips. Kyle would look at me in those brief moments between kisses, tilt his head down, and smile. Not the smirk of a man who'd won a contest or claimed another woman to add to the notches on his belt, but a smile of genuine affection. There were passing moments, so short I almost missed them, when his focus waned, and he looked to be elsewhere, and I wondered what he was thinking.

Where did you go?

I tried not to look into it too much.

Kyle's eyes were a striking blue, an impossible shade that created a mystery out of him. If touching him didn't feel so damn good, I'd want to stare into those eyes for hours.

As sappy as it sounded.

But as I continued to kiss him frantically as he shoved my

body back against the front door, I was driven entirely by need. A desire that fueled my body and made my hands move in uncoordinated motions over his chest and back, desperate to have all of him at once. I was lost in him, and it felt like something in the air around us pulled us closer together.

He was taller than I, which was not unusual, as most people were, and I instinctively stood on my toes to kiss him again. My fingers sprawled over his hard chest, and I ached to touch him more. But he was so close and pushed closer against me until I couldn't get my hands between our bodies and had to settle for clutching at his back, bunching his plaid shirt between my eager fingers. The grunge look wasn't one I usually went for, but when Kyle had entered the bar, he'd drawn my gaze as though there was an invisible rope tying us together. The definition of his muscles was clear through the t-shirt, but his face held my attention, soft features in contrast to the beginnings of a five o'clock shadow and soulful eyes that melted me.

Part of me hated the instant reaction I'd had to him. It was unlike me. I certainly didn't throw myself at men, and those whom I did intend to have a one-night stand with, it would be physical and nothing more.

But *this*...

I had no idea what *this* even was.

His words echoed in my mind. *I'm not someone who can be more to you than what we are tonight.*

Then I'd take tonight.

Kyle leaned into me and breathed in deeply, sparking embers of arousal within me that filled my senses, and a rumble of a growl moved up in his chest. I wouldn't have heard it if we hadn't been so close with his chest pressed against mine, and the vibrations made me shudder. He kissed his way down my neck and dragged his lips along my collarbone as I gasped at the sensation, so gentle compared to the desperation of our kisses. Pulling my tops down slightly, Kyle kissed the curve of my breasts, and I moaned. He growled in response, and the sound carried across to me like a punch in the gut.

I wanted more.

Kyle stood and pushed me back firmly when I went to straighten, and the door rattled slightly against its hinges as a huff of air escaped my lungs.

"How much time have we got alone?" he asked.

"I'm not sure, an hour? Maybe a bit more," I said.

He sighed. "It'll do."

I practically swooned.

What exactly does he have planned for me?

"Now..." he muttered, pulling my singlet top over my head and throwing it to the side. He then reached down and grabbed the tank I was wearing to pull it up over my head, too. As I lifted my arms, expecting him to remove the top, he instead tangled it around my wrists and loosely bound them together. "Stay like this." He held my hands above my head and pressed my wrists against the door with a growl. "It's loose. You can get out anytime, so don't feel trapped or afraid."

A smirk played across my lips. It was nice he was so sweet and considerate, but I couldn't help but think I'd never been *less* afraid and *more* turned on in my life. He'd snuck up on me with this darker side of him that wanted to hold me captive while he showered me with pleasure. All I could think of was him, in my mind and soul... in my body, *penetrating me*. I whimpered slightly, desperate to touch him and ground my hips against his.

Kyle chuckled at my eagerness, and as I breathed out heavily, he breathed in deeply and shared my breath. Something sparked in him, and his pupils dilated before a dark possession came over his features.

I responded to him on a level I didn't even know existed.

"However..." his words were a breathy whisper as he slowly kneeled before me, where I stood on trembling legs, "... I'd suggest you just go with it."

He unbuckled my belt and undid my jeans, taking his time with every clasp and button with steady fingers before he slid them down as I lifted my hips slightly from the door toward him. I was one breath away from begging him to touch me, and I didn't *beg. It* simply wasn't me.

But I would, for *him.*

Kyle guided me to step out of my boots and jeans, rubbing his hands down my calves and over my bare feet. Pushing the discarded clothes to one side, he then shrugged out of his shirt, adding it to the pile.

Watching his arms move beneath the gray fabric of the fitted t-shirt, I knocked my knuckles once, *hard,* against the door in frustration of wanting to touch him. Part of me wanted to bring my hands down, to disobey the light order he'd given and see what he'd do. But when he glanced up at the sound, he was grinning like a Cheshire cat, and he held my eye contact while he grazed his teeth down my stomach and tugged at my panties. I couldn't move, let alone *think.* His breath was hot against my skin, and the thin fabric did nothing to protect me from the sensations.

Staring intently at the ceiling momentarily, I silently admonished myself for not doing the laundry more often. But if

Kyle noticed the thin, ratty nature of my faded pink underwear, he didn't say anything as he yanked them down to my ankles. He began kissing my thighs, tasting my skin, and humming with appreciation. Whenever he found a spot that made me jump, he'd go back to give it extra attention, running his tongue in tiny circles close to where I needed him to be but teasing me until I was going crazy.

By the time he kissed my mound, my will had broken, and I was begging him to touch me, whimpering and gyrating against the door. Kyle gently swatted my ankles to get me to open my legs, and I obliged willingly. When he muttered, "Good girl," I moaned.

Usually, the sort of thing that would irk me sounded delectable coming from him.

His voice betrayed his lust and built my own. This was teasing him as well, the way he was drawing this out, but apparently, he had enough patience to push me to my limit before he even scratched the surface of his pleasure.

Kyle placed his hands on my waist before he teased around my hip bones with his fingertips. Again, he pressed me against the door with barely controlled strength and almost knocked the breath out of me. *Finally*, he gave me what I'd been begging for and began licking and sucking at my swollen clit. He was growling against me as he tasted my arousal, and the sounds he made were intoxicating in the best way.

Wanting more, I tried desperately to lift my hips toward him, but he held me still with a strength he hadn't previously displayed. He was giving me *just* enough, *exactly* enough to have me teetering on the edge. His responses to my body magnified every sensation I felt, and his tongue and fingers found all the right spots and exploited them.

"Oh God, Kyle, how are you doing that?" I gasped out.

He answered only by doubling his attention on me, and I couldn't take anymore and brought my hands down and clutched at his hair and pulled him against me as, with a final swirl of his tongue, he brought me to a screaming climax.

Slumping against him, I panted and tried to find some words, but none came.

My. God.

After breathing in my scent, Kyle leaned his cheek against my hip and hummed in contentment before abruptly standing and pressing his body against mine again. Bringing his hand to my chin, he tilted my head to his and kissed me hard as I tasted myself on his tongue.

I squealed with laughter as he lifted me easily over his shoulder with a needy grunt that I doubted had anything to do with the physical exertion and carried me through the living room.

"Which one?" he grunted.

"On the right." I pointed with my foot as I was facing the wrong way. Kyle entered my bedroom, dropped me lightly onto the bed, and watched me bounce slightly on the firm mattress. Moving away to close the door, he pulled off his t-shirt. As he turned around to face me, he unbuttoned his jeans before approaching the bed. I could feel the flush rising in my cheeks, and I was breathing heavily like I was in heat by the time he crawled over me, finally completely naked. Kyle unbound my wrists and jumped slightly when I immediately placed my palms on his chest and traced the lines of his muscles with my fingers.

"Your hands are cold," he muttered.

"Sorry." But I didn't stop touching him as I danced my fingers down his abdomen and felt his muscles tense before I wrapped my fingers around his waiting cock, already hard for me. Kyle groaned loudly as I worked him with my hand. I tried to keep the rhythm as I opened the bedside table drawer with my other hand and filtered through the contents.

Losing concentration, I stopped touching him. "Shit," I mumbled, opening the second drawer and hastily searching through the junk. "Shit, shit, *shit*. Let me check Penny's room."

Sliding off the bed, I jogged out of the room, returning moments later and waving the foil square above my head. "Success!" I cried, doing what could only be described as a victory jig.

Kyle leaned against the headboard and rubbed himself. But after my stupid dance, which left me standing in the middle of the floor as I stared at him, he paused briefly before he burst out laughing. "Wow," he chuckled. "Now *that* was sexy."

I grinned, and he smiled back. I felt free with him, relaxed, like I had lost all inhibitions. He made me feel *sexy* and *wanted*, and it practically glowed from him when he looked at me.

Unclasping my bra and letting it drop to the floor, I jumped back onto the bed. "Oh yeah? How about this then, smart ass?"

Ripping the condom packet open, I rolled it over his cock and followed quickly with my mouth.

Kyle sat bolt upright and gripped the bed sheets. *"Fuck,"* he moaned as my head bobbed up and down in his lap. Grabbing my head lightly, he thrust upward into my mouth, and I gagged slightly. He muttered an apology, but his hips were still slightly thrusting, as though he was losing control of himself. He used his grip on my hair for leverage and pulled me back from him.

"Bend over," he commanded.

"Yes, sir."

My comment earned me a slap on the ass as he kneeled behind me. Kyle wasted no time, and we moaned in unison as he penetrated me from behind. I was so ready for him, wet and waiting, but he still filled me with a delicious stretch. Kyle pressed forward slowly until he was fully sheathed within me. Dropping to my elbows, I arched my back as Kyle gripped my hips and thrust into me. He started hard and only increased his speed as he worked his way toward his release, and I squealed in pleasure, helpless at each thrust. Apparently, his teasing had pushed his patience to the limit, and now that thread of control was broken, and he fucked me hard enough to make up for the teasing earlier.

The room was filled with the scent and feel of our mingled lust.

It was something beyond the sex, and it felt like nothing short of magic.

When I heard the front door open and close, I jumped as Kyle's thrusting slowed. "*She's home,*" I whispered urgently.

Kyle leaned over, forcing me to fall forward onto the bed, and pinned my arms beneath my body. "I'm not done with you yet," he growled against my cheek. Pressing his palm over my mouth, he continued thrusting into me, harder than before, pushing me into the mattress as it groaned in protest. Shifting my arms out from underneath me, I reached forward and gripped the mattress, feeling as though he was going to fuck me off the edge of the bed if I didn't brace myself. I moaned against his palm, unable to contain the sounds, and with three final deep thrusts, Kyle came and groaned loudly as he filled the condom.

The sound of his climax had *definitely* carried through the walls, judging by the abrupt silence outside my bedroom door. The silence was followed shortly by an uncertain voice, "...Ana?"

Clearing my throat, I tried to clear the fog from my head simultaneously, before I called out, "Ah... I'm fine. All good!"

Kyle kissed my cheek and neck, and I moaned quietly before I turned my face to meet his lips in a passionate exchange. His tongue dragged over mine, the lingering taste of my arousal still on him. Slowly, he lifted himself off me and sat up on the edge of the bed before he ran his fingers through his hair and exhaled sharply. His back glistened with sweat and came up in goosebumps in the cooling air.

Rolling onto my back, I sighed. *"Whoa."*

Kyle smiled softly as he threw the condom in a scrunched-up tissue into the bin. Retrieving his pants, he paused before pulling them on, and his hands clenched into fists as his breathing slowed. Raising an eyebrow, I said nothing. It seemed as though he were meditating or something.

After a minute of silence, I started giggling to myself. I couldn't help it, and Kyle watched me as I lay sprawled on the bed.

He chuckled. "You don't seem like the giggling type. What are you laughing at?"

"I don't know," I said mid-laugh. "I think my brain has just gone on vacation." My limbs felt heavy as I lay there, and I sank into the mattress as I bathed in the cool air.

He smiled and paused by the side of the bed to arch an eyebrow at me as I watched him. I tilted my head over the back of the mattress so he looked like he was standing on the ceiling.

He had magic hands. He might as well have magic feet, too.

Kyle didn't seem to be at all abashed at his nudity, and I admired that.

Not that he had anything to be humbled about. *Damn.*

"Doesn't it bother you?" I asked.

"What?"

"Being naked."

He looked down and shrugged. "I guess I've never really thought about it. Nudity isn't an issue at home."

"Don't you get embarrassed?"

Kyle looked thoughtful, as if he were genuinely considering the question. "No."

"Ever?" I eyed him with interest, and Kyle only shrugged again.

Rolling over, I sat up and brought the sheet with me to cover my breasts. A move I only thought about after I had made it, and I realized I did even when I was alone. A thought occurred to me, and a cheeky grin spread across my face. "Are you a nudist?" I asked, leaning on one elbow.

"Maybe I am." He laughed.

He slipped his jeans on and grabbed his t-shirt off the floor. "I should, ah..." He looked toward the door and gestured vaguely with his thumb.

"Yeah, no..." I sat upright. "Of course." I rolled off the bed and pulled on a t-shirt and pajama shorts while I watched Kyle put on his shoes.

As we left the bedroom, Penny stood in the kitchen making coffee. "Well, hello, you two."

Looking at the floor, I smiled and combed my fingers through my hair as I tried to hide my smirk—unsuccessfully, judging by

Penny's look.

Kyle introduced himself, smiled dashingly, and nodded at Penny. Her eyebrow arched as he collected his plaid shirt from the living room floor and patted his pockets. "I'll, um..." Kyle's arms twitched as if he were going to embrace me, but he stopped himself. "I'll catch you around."

"Yep." Standing on my toes, I kissed Kyle on the cheek before I opened the door for him. He looked at me for a moment, and something passed across his face that almost resembled regret. But it was gone almost as quickly as I'd imagined it. He smiled sadly and left.

Closing the door behind Kyle, I watched him walk away through the shrinking gap. As I leaned against the door, it clicked closed. Penny dropped her bag on the couch and faced me with her hands on her hips. "Sooo..." she started.

Biting my bottom lip, I mouthed, *Oh my God*.

"That bad, huh?"

I opened the door a fraction to check that Kyle wasn't within earshot, and the hallway was empty. I snapped it shut again and turned the lock.

"No, I mean, *oh my God,* as in *amazing,"* I said, taking another deep breath. "As in, *whoa."* I enunciated the word, *Bill and Ted* style.

Penny raised her eyebrows. "Oh, really?"

"It was like he was in my head. He found all the right places and knew just what to do with them to push me to my limit and... well, just *wow."* I squirmed where I leaned against the door, the sensations of his touch still alive on my skin.

"Sounds like quite the stud." Penny sat on the couch and slid her laptop from her bag. "So, I guess I don't need to ask how your night was."

Sighing, I stomped across the room—Penny glanced up but said nothing. She'd already told me a thousand times I walked too heavily—and I slumped beside her. Turning to her, I frowned. Penny had dark circles under her eyes. She wasn't usually up as often as I was at night, and she definitely didn't have the luxury of sleeping in as I did most mornings. "How was your shift?" I asked.

"My placement is still in the Emergency Department, so it was hectic as usual."

I nodded, but I couldn't really understand. While I limited my contact with people, rarely engaging in anything beyond casual interactions, Penny went out of her way to help and become involved. I don't know how she did it. But if I were sick, there was no one I'd rather have looking out for me than her.

I admired her beyond words.

Penny leaned back and closed her eyes as her head tilted toward the ceiling, and she rubbed a knot out of her neck. "I don't know what's going on, but it seems to be so much busier these past few weeks. We've had people come in with injuries and no explanation of how they got them. Also, there are more extreme cases of street fights than I've ever seen, like ultra-violence. It's so bizarre."

"Must be something in the air." I mused.

"Something like that."

"Do you want to talk about it?" I asked. Something Penny had taught me. *Always ask.*

"No," she said, but then she immediately followed with, "There was a woman there tonight. Someone had..." she swallowed heavily, "I shouldn't be telling you this."

"Tell me." I sat up, tucked one leg under the other, and touched Penny's arm gently. "If you need to talk, then talk."

She smiled weakly. "Learning to socialize, I see."

I made a face. "Only with you."

"And hot-Kyle."

Smirking, I agreed, "And hot-Kyle. Now talk to me."

Penny sighed, and her fingers hovered over the keyboard of her laptop as though she were about to start her studies but couldn't bring herself to. "There was a woman..."

"A woman, right," I prompted when she stopped talking.

"She'd been grocery shopping, and she had been kidnapped or attacked somehow. Hours missing from her memory. She had this huge scar going down her face and crossing over her eye." Penny threw a significant look at me. "It won't ever heal, that eye..." She closed her eyes momentarily, and I wondered again how she stood it. It was obvious she took on board every patient's story and pain as though it were her own. "She's not the only one. We've had so many people in lately, victims of violent attacks from strangers, or sometimes even someone they know. Several have no memory of it. The other week, a guy came in, barely holding on to his sanity. It looked like he'd been buried alive and had dug his way out."

"Oh my God..."

Penny pressed her lips together. "I guess it's just... these people who've become victims, especially the ones who don't remember it, it just reminds me too much of... You know."

I placed a hand on her arm and rubbed gently with my thumb. She didn't need to tell me. "I know. I'm so sorry."

Penny hummed and said nothing further. Penny had opened up to me about her past once we'd gotten comfortable with each other. Years ago she'd been abducted, kept captive overnight, tortured, and raped, and then to the bewilderment of the police and her, she had simply been dropped off where her abductor had found her. She'd seen his face and was convinced she would die because of it. Still, despite giving an accurate description to the police and the police artist's sketch being plastered over the media, the man was never found. Penny's case moved to the bottom of the pile with thousands of others that would never be solved.

She hadn't wanted to tell me initially. She worried I would judge her or be scared of her or something else equally ridiculous. Now and then, she was still plagued by night terrors and woke up screaming and terrified. They were getting less frequent—it had been over a year since her last—but what he had done to her would haunt her forever.

When Penny had gone to the hospital following her trauma, the nurses had been her saviors. The doctors, too, of course, but the nurses looked after her, mothered her, and so she had moved to the city to pursue the career herself. They'd made her undertake a psych evaluation before she began studying as a nurse and told her she had post-traumatic stress disorder. However bad her night terrors got, she couldn't seem to accept herself under the banner of PTSD, as though she didn't deserve it because someone somewhere may have gone through something worse.

Penny took a few moments to bring herself together again, then returned to her assignment, and we sat in silence for a while as I watched her type.

"Can I help at all?" I ventured, indicating her laptop.

Penny smiled softly and shook her head, not taking her eyes

from the screen. "No, but thank you." She paused then and raised her eyes to mine. "And *thank you* for being here for me."

"Always."

The silence was filled with the sounds of typing, and shortly afterward, my thoughts returned to Kyle.

"You're grinning again," Penny said.

I started. "I am?"

Penny nodded, her face illuminated by the laptop screen, with a slight smirk on her lips. "And you smell like sex."

I laughed. "Thanks."

Penny shoved me playfully on the shoulder, the small gesture warming me. "Go have a shower, you whore. I have an assignment to bluff my way through."

Returning her playful shove, I stood and went to the bathroom. Stripping off, I dropped my clothes on the floor and turned on the squeaky taps to start the shower. Staring at myself in the mirror, already beginning to fog, I covered my hair with a shower cap before stepping into the blast of hot water.

Kyle had said no promises.

But then he had touched me like *that.*

Not to mention the date, if that's what it even was.

It certainly felt like there was something more.

Shaking my head, I closed my eyes and lifted my face under the steady stream. As the water ran down my body, it washed away the smell of him, and my skin tingled with the memory of his fingertips before that, too, almost seemed to evaporate in the steam.

But what I couldn't wash away was how he had made me feel.

Chapter Eight

Kyle

Stepping out of Ana's apartment building and into the brisk night air, I checked the time on my cell. I missed the last tram, but I could catch the after-hours bus. While I didn't have far to go, I wasn't in the mood for a walk this evening. The streets that would usually be a sanctuary, almost void of human life at this time of night, would allow me to cleanse some of the negativity building up in this city, and somehow felt like they were taunting me.

The memory of Ana's emotional imprint was all over me, along with the lingering sensation of her hands and mouth on my body.

I didn't have to wait at the stop for long and sighed as I stepped onto the bus. I paused at the top of the steps to let another passenger disembark, and they waved, smiling at the driver. I recognized the driver immediately, even though I didn't often take public transport. "Night shift again?" I asked and flashed her a smile.

"What can I say? I'm a night owl." Her skin crinkled around her eyes as she grinned in return. She wore her hair in a sensible low ponytail, gray hairs peppered throughout the brown, and a face covered in freckles betrayed a youth spent in the sun. I didn't know much about her, but I didn't need to in order to get a read on her. The happiness she portrayed wasn't purely an external front some humans put on because they felt some social obligation. Her happiness stemmed from a deep need to make others feel as happy as her.

It was refreshing, but as with most humans, something was beneath the surface.

As I sat, I dove deeper into the bus driver's imprint. It felt like she was trying to make up for something... something she blamed herself for. Underneath all the happiness and smiles was *guilt.*

If I had the time or the energy, I would ask her about it. Every human had a story that wove together like a tapestry, making them who they were. But I didn't have it in me to ask, and my chest sank when I realized I didn't *care* enough to ask. I watched as streetlights blurred into each other and flowed past the window, one light merging with the next as the bus picked up speed. I could still feel Ana around me. Something beyond the smell of her perfume and skin had permeated and followed me. It was in the air around me, the feeling that had pulled us together on a plane beyond the physical when we were in her bedroom. Something that made the smooth slide of her skin as I pushed into her so intense, my senses swelled and peaked as I did.

All humans were slightly different, but touching Ana was like setting my skin on fire. Every brush of my fingertips against her responsive body sent a shot of energy through me like an arrow through my heart.

She drew from me, and her arousal swam around the room as I absorbed it and turned it into energy that encased us both in the moment.

I'd had sex before on Earth, but fucking Ana was nothing short of incredible.

When I had taken her, my arousal mingled with hers in the air. Now, her essence was on my skin and in my blood, and it was almost too much to take. Her pleasure had only driven mine on further, and I had to force control of myself and hold onto my human form.

If I hadn't penetrated her when I did, I may have lost control of the fine thread I held on to in this realm. Guardians were tough, and the last thing I wanted to do was hurt her with unbridled strength.

Then, when we were talking and laughing, and she had gazed at me with such affection, I felt the exact moment my genuine smile became a mask as I shut down the connection between us. I put an abrupt halt to the flow of her energy into mine to protect myself from whatever was stirring inside me and to protect *her* from *me*. I couldn't afford to open up to her further. I had already opened up too much with how long we had talked, allowing us to connect in a way that I shouldn't.

She was so easy to talk to. I had talked too much.

I *felt* something, and feeling anything was already too far.

The exchange had to end at the physical.

But damn, she sparked excitement in me.

I didn't even realize I was smiling until I reached my stop, and the driver threw me a knowing grin as I stepped off the bus.

But walking the short distance to my motel—a particularly seedy apartment complex, where the rates were cheap, and they didn't ask too many questions—my smile dropped as I stared at the shabby building.

Shaking my head, I tried to shift Ana from my mind.

But I couldn't.

It was a bad idea—beyond a bad idea—to get involved with her or any other human. My prolonged exposure to this realm was affecting me, and she had triggered something in me I shouldn't even have the capacity to feel. Humanity was weakening me. I didn't know what would happen if it were the other way around—if a human spent too much time with a Guardian. There may be no ill results, but I didn't want to risk finding out. Any distractions were just that—distractions—and whatever it was Ana made me feel, whatever these feelings were, I wasn't here for them.

Stepping into the dark foyer, a single remaining fluorescent light flickered near the stairs, and I reminded myself I had to focus.

Before someone else got hurt.

Chapter Nine

Ignis

He had gotten close. Too close.

The shift in the air was palpable as the Lucidian had acted out his pathetic small deeds to counteract the things I had done. I felt him as he had stood on the threshold of the territory I had marked as my own and probed the area, searching for me.

Shaking my head, I laughed, a low rumble in my throat.

The Lucidian had no idea who he was dealing with.

If he thought I would play by the rules, he had another thing coming.

Previously, Guardians who had come from Tenebris to Earth to cause trouble had played minor games with people's emotions and fears, maybe causing them to hurt each other or themselves in small ways. But I was the first of many to come to break the mold. Humans were tools for maintaining the Balance, but they were also playthings, disposable and expendable beings I could use until they became hollow shells. Then I'd move on and find a new toy.

What *would* happen if the Balance were to Shift, really? Maybe it'd be better for Guardians, and the humans could live beneath our feet where they belonged.

Guardians held the potential for so much more than guarding and protecting the Balance, so why shouldn't we take advantage of our strength and potential? Be damned with the consequences and live.

Or perhaps, *use* the consequences to our advantage.

Did we *need* the Balance? I wasn't so sure anymore.

I had honed my powers of influence and energies to a fine point that could be directed at any one—or many—humans. I had used other Tenebris Guardians in my practice, and some of them even gained pleasure from my teachings, but not many of them had taken me too seriously.

Until now.

They would see what I was capable of. What we were all capable of.

If I could influence a Guardian, imagine what I could do to the pathetic human beings.

Locating a spot near the center of the region I had been focusing on, I closed my eyes and began drawing my energies together. If I kept to a space of a few city blocks, rather than trying to involve the entire city, the fear would build up and create an impenetrable cloud that I couldn't be tracked through. A fog that built as the negative emotions of the humans tumbled upon each other. *Why are we afraid all the time?* They would wonder. *What is it that we can't sense?* The uncertainty and the resulting depression would only make them *more* frightened, and then *all* of it would cloud up the air and delightfully fill my senses.

But building fear into a block like that took time, and as much fun as I was having to make that happen, I needed to speed things up to protect my human identity and stop the Lucidian from getting too close again. I didn't want his senses to be simply *hazy* when he tried to pinpoint me. I didn't want him to be able to find me at all.

Not until I *wanted* him to find me.

Then I would come at him and take him down with as many humans as possible.

Looking up at the sky, I threw my arms above my head and spread out my fingers to touch as much energy in the air as possible. To any passers-by, I'm sure I looked crazy. But the humans couldn't see the ripples of the air and the barely visible black ink that permeated through my fingertips and dissipated into the night.

Energy, pure dark energy.

Channeled through decades of experience and practice, drawn from the realm of Tenebris itself and pushed firmly into the air on Earth. Humans may not be able to see it, but they would certainly *feel* it. Everyone within this area would become anxious, depressed, lost, or angry, and without any discernible reason they could find within their lives.

Why is this happening to me?

Pathetic.

It made me smile.

These poor, weak creatures—there was so much fun to be had with them and at their expense. They were purely vessels for their emotions. Vessels that could scream and cry and beg.

And bleed.

The fear fog built, so strong that the low-hanging clouds cleared from the night sky as the air was forced to shift around the energy before being compelled to incorporate it. Lowering my arms, my breath came in heavy gasps. Centering and releasing that power had come at a cost and drained almost everything I had worked to build up since I arrived here.

But it was worth it.

Not only would it offer me protection from the Lucidian, as his senses would be distorted and warped, but the continuing after-effects from the fog of fear would increase the negative human emotions within it, growing and growing until they were almost self-sustaining and couldn't be stopped.

And when it can't be stopped, what will the Lucidians do then, I wonder?

How will he save the Balance?

But I was weakened and needed to recharge. Since I couldn't return home and draw from the power of Tenebris, there was only one way to do it.

I needed fear and pain.

Lots of it.

Chapter Ten

Ana

When I woke abruptly, drenched in a cold sweat, and yanked back into reality, it took a moment for me to settle. I remembered my dream so clearly. I didn't often remember my dreams or nightmares as they may be, but Mom's face had come to me so clearly. She didn't say anything, and I guessed that was because she was simply a conjuring of my subconscious and memories. But seeing her was enough to have me trembling.

My entire life changed when she died. I'd lost all my friends—if that's what they could be called with the way they walked away. Everyone I thought I could rely on disappeared one after the other until I was left alone in this world. Alone to fight through the shitstorm of life on my own.

Which is exactly how I preferred it now, to protect what was left of my heart.

Losing Mom and the grief that followed the funeral were physically painful. Once I had snapped out of the shock in the time between being told about the car accident and watching her being lowered into the ground, grief hit me as though the car had slammed into *my* chest. It felt as though I were being ripped apart from the inside, as though gremlins were living in my body, and they were shredding me, bit by bit, starting with my heart and working outwards.

It *hurt.*

A pain I'd never experienced before and didn't ever want to again.

Hence, not letting people get too close. If I did, they'd only leave me again.

Barely able to move for the first few days after the funeral, I was stuck on the couch, eating only when my stomach threatened to consume itself with a violent rumble that left me gagging. My friends tried to console me, friends I had known for years. But when I was still grieving months later, it seemed they simply lost interest. They'd told me I'd had plenty of time to grieve and needed to get over it and move on.

God, I'd wanted to shout at them. I wanted to *hurt* them and to make them feel the pain I was feeling. To tear them up from the inside, like I was experiencing. I had sarcastically apologized for my grief not being *convenient* for them, and they had replied that I'd become *toxic.* Apparently, even being near me was depressing and bringing them all down.

One by one, they had given up on me and left, and consequently, I didn't open up to people anymore. The pain of being abandoned was too much, and people didn't like being around me when I was in pain. They didn't want me hurting. They wanted me happy. It was a vicious cycle, so it was easier to keep people at an arm's length so that I couldn't be hurt like that again.

Nothing to lose. No connections.

Until Penny came and wormed her way into my heart. Henry

too.

Two people, more than I'd allowed anywhere near my heart in years.

Maybe it was my fault. Perhaps I didn't try hard enough to *move on.* But being given a deadline for the grief of losing Mom had me reeling. Maybe I had shut them out before they even left.

It hardly mattered now.

Sitting upright, I fanned my loose t-shirt to cool myself. I didn't remember any elements of the dream being a nightmare, so I wasn't sure why I was sweating so much. Perhaps the extra duvet I had draped over the bed last night after Kyle had left had been too much. But the bed had an unusual chill after he'd left, and it felt empty and cold. Shaking my head, I ran my fingers through my hair. The chill must have been an illusion, given my physical state this morning, screaming at me that I'd been too hot all night.

Looking out the window, the thin line of the sunrise was visible through the gap in the blinds. Strangely, I didn't feel tired, although I couldn't have gotten more than a few hours of sleep. Grabbing my cell off the nightstand, I checked the time.

Six AM.

What. The. Fuck.

No one gets up this early.

Surely waking up after only a few hours of sleep would catch up with me later, but since I was already sweating, I figured I might as well exercise before showering. Glancing at the cell again, I did a quick calculation. If I left now, I could be back in time before Penny started her shift today, and maybe we could have breakfast together.

Stripping off my nightshirt and throwing it on the ever-growing pile to wash, I made a mental note to get us something to eat on my way back around the block. Pulling on a pair of tights and a singlet over a sports bra, I stretched my arms above my head and then back down to touch my toes a few times before quietly leaving the apartment and heading downstairs for a run.

The streets were empty, and despite my usual preference for nighttime, there was a burst of freshness to the air at this time of day, which forced me to appreciate it. Before people started flocking to the city and before the gridlock of traffic built up and polluted the air, taking away the crispness from the night before. As I ran, the cars slowly began to build up, and all it did was remind me why I liked to live in the city. No commuting, no driving at all. I didn't even own a car. Everything was within walking distance if I was feeling motivated, or a short bus or tram ride otherwise. The nightlife was close. It was perfection.

Rounding the block, I slowed to check the usual hiding spot for a stray cat I had named Seamus, for no other reason than it seemed like an inappropriate name for a cat. If I ever spoke about him, people would ask, *Why Seamus?*

Why not?

He came trotting up to me from the alleyway where he resided, and I patted his head before he rubbed between my legs. I cooed at him, talking in a baby voice I wouldn't use if anyone else were around to hear it.

"I'll bring you some tuna tonight, okay, gorgeous boy?" The ginger cat looked up at me, his eyes round and green and full of innocence and trust. Trust I had built over some time because he had no reason to trust anyone. But I melted whenever I looked at him. If I stared at him long enough, I swear my voice would reach pitches only dogs could hear as I proclaimed his cuteness. I'd always had an affinity with animals, and they seemed to love me back equally as much. I had already discussed with Penny about moving to an apartment building that allowed pets so I could finally bring Seamus home, and Penny's only rule had been we cap the number of cats at four.

I smiled. Penny knew me so well.

Lightly booping Seamus's nose with my index finger, I continued my run.

After forty minutes, I returned to my street, hair stuck to my forehead with sweat, and looking like I had run through a waterfall. The weather had warmed up faster than anticipated, and I wished I'd worn baggy shorts instead.

Check the weather forecast, Penny always said, like the nagging mother figure she was.

Turning into a bakery close to my apartment building, I ordered two lattes while investigating the contents of the glass display cabinet for something suitable for breakfast. Standing back from the counter, convinced I smelled of body odor, I pointed and leaned to press my finger against the glass.

I left a sweat smudge, which I hastily tried to wipe away.

I only made it worse.

When I said, "And that one, too, thanks." I added a sheepish smile at the lady behind the counter.

Sorry, I'm a sweatball.

She didn't look amused.

Carrying my finds back to the apartment, I climbed the stairs much slower than I had descended, taking extra care not to spill the generously filled coffee cups. After unlocking the door, I picked up the coffees from the floor and used my hip to nudge my way inside.

Penny was leaning against the doorway to her bedroom, rubbing her eyes.

"I brought breakfast," I announced.

Penny stared blearily at me. "You're up early."

"Yeah, couldn't sleep. It's cool, I'll take a nap later." I set the coffees down on the counter.

Penny smiled and rolled her eyes. "You're such a nana sometimes."

"A nana with a soft spot for whiskey. Do you want some breakfast?"

Penny approached as I opened the white cardboard box so she could inspect the contents. She looked at me with an eyebrow cocked. "Are you serious?"

"What?"

"Cake for breakfast? A *whole* cake?"

"I'm an adult—"

"Debatable," Penny muttered.

I ignored her. "And I can have cake for breakfast if I want."

"Eat some fruit, for God's sake."

"Don't nurse me." I waved a finger at her. "Besides... *loophole!*" I cried gleefully. "It's carrot cake."

Penny laughed. "You're unbelievable."

Setting the cake box down on the kitchen counter, I put a hand on my hip. "Look, do you want some or not?"

"Of course, I want some. Gimme some fucking breakfast cake."

Serving up generous slices, I then handed Penny her coffee. Penny thanked me, and we chatted between mouthfuls of cake.

"This is the best part of being an adult," I mumbled.

"Agreed." Penny nodded. Thank you, Ana. This was really sweet of you."

Pressing my lips together, I nodded curtly, and Penny smiled knowingly.

It was hard sometimes to keep myself open for too long. My dream last night was simply a reminder of what happened when people got too close—they *left,* and it *hurt.* Sometimes, old Ana would slip through, an Ana that had existed before I'd lost Mom, a brighter Ana who smiled more, and I'd completely let my guard down and just be myself. Then Penny would say something like that, and while I *really* appreciated her words, it was almost like a slap in the face, reminding me to hide again. Sometimes I had the strength to fight against that voice and that instinct.

Mostly not.

Penny understood—of course she did—as she was also almost unmeasurably patient. She saw something in me I didn't, and she must have seen it from the start because she stuck around despite my cold shoulder for the first few months we lived together.

Last night, Kyle looked at me with affection, like Penny does sometimes.

Apparently, other people could see something I couldn't.

Chapter Eleven

Kyle

Returning to the hospital the following morning, I was ready to investigate further. Ana had re-energized me more than any other human I'd spent time with. Something about her had been overwhelming, like a spark of purity inside her, more powerful than the usual recharging abilities of humanity. While I had planned on getting some decent sleep, I found being with Ana was more soothing to the soul than sleep ever could be. So, I was up early.

Usually, spending too much time in a single human's company was draining, almost as if we developed an immunity to a human's emotional energy pattern, and they could only recharge us to a certain point. That is why I liked playing in the bar. The crowd came and went, and while the general energy in the room was positive, it was as ever-changing as the patrons who moved about, keeping the energy levels high and my ability to absorb them strong.

But this *immunity* hadn't happened with Ana. If anything, the more time I spent with her, the *more* she recharged me. But I couldn't dwell on it because we had our night, and that was done. Right now, all I was focused on was the hospital in front of me and the beings within it.

I could feel all the bodies moving around inside, and those who were lying in beds, some awaiting death's grasp. Most of the beings inside were pure souls, as pure as they could hope to be given what they were subjected to each day. But I could feel some others—a few areas that radiated increased pain and fear, like a spike in a graph. If the hospital were a thermograph, the negative energy would show up as reds and blacks, harsh colors that hurt the vision. These were the places I must focus on, though it wouldn't be easy to pinpoint a single being.

While I'd like to think I'd know him on sight, this was the perfect hiding place for the Tenebrian Guardian. I'd need to be almost toe-to-toe with him to feel his essence beyond the exterior. Too much negative energy, and it blended. If the other Guardian was hiding his identity and containing his essence within himself, this, coupled with the fog, meant I wouldn't be able to confirm who he was until I was clear of other beings. It's likely I'd even need physical contact to be one hundred percent sure.

I didn't know what his human form looked like. He could be anyone within these walls.

All I could tell about him was what I could feel, his distinct energy imprint based on his prolonged presence in this realm. I knew he was male, and I knew he was older than I and more experienced. I knew what his imprint felt like because it was the center of all the pain I'd encountered around here.

I knew he was dangerous.

The hospital was a difficult hunting ground, mainly because of the fear the buildings already contained—the fear of the unknown or of what would come. Not to mention the pain—so much pain from the patients and those who loved them, it was overwhelming. It was painful for me to even be near it because I had to open up my senses to be able to read and track, which meant I opened myself up to being flooded with negative energy.

This was why I needed Ana last night.

My head felt foggy.

There was something else. Something wrong.

Frowning, I focused and cast my senses upward and over the hospital.

Because surely—*surely*—the other Guardian couldn't have done this much damage so soon? No matter the power, hurting and scaring people, he couldn't have left this thick fog in a matter of days.

No, something else was going on.

Some blanket of protection was around here, like he had somehow focused his energies and thrown them into the air. Swallowing, it was difficult not to be intimidated by the blatant display of power.

I can do this.

I'd never understand the need to cause humans such pain. Tenebrians were simply beings as we were, beings with a purpose and a duty.

But this was intentional damage.

Some Guardians looked down on humans as lesser creatures with diminished worth, unaware and unable to understand the essence of life. But I found them fascinating. I loved watching them grow, find love, see their lives unfold, and how they dealt with loss and luck. They felt so deeply, their emotions spilling out in a rush at the slightest coercion. Humans were so much more complicated than most Guardians knew and appreciated. Being close to Ana had shown me another side to them, layers and levels I hadn't experienced before, and a spark of a feeling in my gut at her touch, which confused and thrilled me.

Still standing across the street, I stared at the hospital buildings, knowing I needed to move soon before I was drained too much. I let my concentration drop when there was a nudge on my elbow. Glancing down at the hunched-over elderly woman next to me as she grasped weakly onto my inner elbow, she blinked at me with a smile. "Would you be so kind as to help me across the street?"

The corner of my lip lifted. It may have been the oldest cliché in the book, but every little act of kindness helped. Even the smallest act could affect the Balance. In this case, any pushback against the negative blanket thrown over these city blocks would be helpful. Looking at the human next to me, I returned her smile. Humans were so fragile, so vulnerable, even when they were younger than this one.

"Of course," I replied.

Touching my hand lightly on top of hers, I felt her paper-thin skin and all the memories she held. I took the moment to take a reading on her. Inside, she felt like a young woman, full of hopes, dreams, and love spread across a vast family whom she never stopped thinking about.

How does so much love fit into such a small body?

Sometimes I envied them and their ability to love.

Holding her hand as I watched the traffic, I was flushed with pride in my role to protect humans and in my duty in this world. Looking at the people around me, I knew they needed protection.

My protection.

When an opportune moment arose, I guided her safely across the street, ensuring she stepped onto the curb without tripping. "Visiting someone?" I asked.

She nodded. "My husband. We've been married for fifty-three years."

"That's wonderful. Give him my best."

She patted my arm, a feather-light touch. "You're a good boy," she stated, then shuffled toward the hospital.

As I watched her go, there was a shift in the air. I looked up as I felt it and resisted the urge to smirk. It was all the confirmation I needed to know I was in the right place. My good deed, however small, had been a positive shift against a negative influence present here. Positive essences were consistently more powerful than negative ones and required smaller acts to outweigh the other.

With renewed purpose, I started toward the hospital, ready to search inside for the Tenebrian. Gently, I tapped my pocket and felt the outline of the new blade through the fabric. Its weight was comforting. It was crudely crafted, but it would do.

I began wandering the halls and at least tried to look like I had somewhere to be. Unfortunately, there was no better way to get a start than to pick a place at random and go from there. I followed a systematic search and planned to check each corner of the hospital grounds. Occasionally, I'd feel a shift in energies. Still, after I followed it, I was often led to a patient in particular pain or an office where someone was undoubtedly receiving bad news.

At one point, I purposefully strolled into a staff room, and the doctor inside looked up as I entered.

"Excuse me, this is for staff only."

Holding up a hand, I apologized. "I'm sorry, I must have taken a wrong turn."

But I didn't move and instead stared at the young doctor, attempting to get a read on him.

The doctor narrowed his eyes. "You need to leave."

I nodded, noting the doctor's name tag—Ken Rodriquez. I was getting a strange read from the man. Something dark lurked beneath the surface. Reluctantly, I left the room when Ken had moved toward the security alert, not having gotten my answer. Internally, I cursed the other Guardian. If this was the place he had chosen to hide his location, it was perfect. There were so many feelings clouding the area that I could be in the same room as him, and I'd still need to touch him to be sure.

I could be standing right next to him and not even know it.

Would he know me? Were my powers enough to hide my identity from him?

I wasn't sure I could simultaneously reach out my senses and search and hide my essence.

I made sure to imprint Ken in my mind, and I'd pay him closer attention while I was here.

My frustration had begun to boil over into anger. I couldn't continue to wander around in circles for hours and hoped I had close enough contact with the other Guardian to be sure of his identity. I also couldn't go around touching people at random without eventually getting myself kicked out of the hospital. Already, I had noted several members of security watching me. Perhaps my face had already been put on their alert list by some of the employees I had encountered. After all, I had been here all day without stopping or visiting anyone. The humans were bound to be suspicious of my continued presence, seemingly without purpose. It was a difficult line to walk. I was protecting them, but I couldn't explain why I was there. I had been so focused on the hospital's main building—there was still so much ground to cover and emotional fog to break through—that I hadn't even made it *near* the smaller outer buildings in the complex.

I was wasting time.

This method may have worked to help me track the first Guardian, who turned out to be Vena, here for the same reason I was, but this was different. Vena hadn't been hiding from me. He hadn't been *actively* creating a fog. The Rogue wasn't simply another Tenebrian here to make some excess chaos or have some fun. This was a being intentionally setting out to do as much damage as possible and masked his every move. It was someone who thrived not only on the pain that humans caused each other but also conducting the harm himself, injuring them, killing them, or keeping them captive for periods to feed off their fear. This Guardian was much better at internalizing his energies and controlling his influences than I had ever encountered. How long had he been honing his abilities? Decades? How many others like him were out there?

There was another path I could take.

Something I could do to *force* him out of hiding and compel him to take his proper form. I'd still have to be close, but not as close if I were to rely on my senses alone. Once I found him, or someone I suspected to be him, I could force him to show his true identity, drop his human form, and show his Guardian skin. Then I would know for sure.

There was a certain level of inner conflict I needed to deal with, though. I was resisting taking this path because of the torment it would cause me. It was a last resort. But now wasn't the time to second-guess. Now was the time for action. No matter how much I hated it, I had to take the step.

Because doubts crept into my mind and forced me to grapple with the revelation that perhaps I wasn't experienced enough to do this with my powers alone. Before coming to Earth, I thought my senses were relatively well-developed. My ability to influence was as strong as any Guardian I knew of my age, perhaps stronger. Cordus chose me. He chose *me* for this mission because he knew I was strong enough to do it.

I could do this.

All the opinions I had of my worth were being put to the test with every passing hour.

Was I falling victim to the same negative influences affecting the humans here?

My time in the hospital had resulted in two strong suspects—the doctor named Ken and a man I had encountered wearing scrubs but with no name tag or identification. The man avoided close contact and conversation with most staff members but kept ducking into patients' rooms and talking to them. He held a cloud of pain about him he couldn't possibly hide, so strong it was like a dark cloud following him around, and I'd never encountered any human with *that* level of internal darkness, with an imprint that was tainted by such overt pain.

If I were going to take this step and engage in the old methods of revealing Guardians, I first needed to recharge again and be surrounded by some good. Because this method involved going against everything I believed in, I had to harm a human.

I needed blood.

Do the ends justify the means?

Would I ever forget the feeling of drawing a human's blood? Or what it felt like to absorb a human's pain, knowing it was my hand that caused it? I shuddered at the thought, but I had no choice.

While I was aware my powers would be affected by my prolonged stay on Earth, I wasn't quite prepared for how quickly it would happen and the extent of the effect. Sometimes, it felt like I was losing control, and the influences were going to explode out of me and infect every human within a mile radius. Other times, I felt weak and useless, as though my senses were draining from me, seeping through my pores, and leaving me empty.

But it didn't matter. I had loyalties not only to my home of Lucidis but to Earth and all its occupants who relied on me to protect them, even if they didn't know it. I was here to protect them all from harm, not to mention the Balance as well.

I knew what I had to do.

As dusk fell, I straightened my shoulders and made my way toward the hospital's exit in an attempt to trick myself into thinking I was more mentally prepared than I was. Before I made the preparations and took the step to engage the old methods, I needed happiness, and light—positive energy to recharge everything I had lost today.

And for that, all I thought of was Ana.

RELA

Chapter Twelve

Kyle

Taking a chance Ana would be working, I was pleased to see her behind the bar when I entered. A small band played in the corner, covering eighties rock songs and looking as much the part as they sounded. Glancing down at my clothes, my lip twitched.

They stole my style.

My chest swelled at Ana's smile when I sat, as though she had hoped I would come back to see her. The warmth radiating from her when she approached already revitalized me. It pulsed from her and almost made her glow. I'm certain I was grinning like an idiot, unable to contain the rush of joy at being close to her. It reminded me of home, of the light and warmth that existed in Lucidis, and I sucked in a deep breath, drawing the essence toward me faster.

I needed more of her.

With Ana close by, I pushed all thoughts of the task ahead and my difficulties from my mind. However, a shadow of a thought kept resurfacing and reminded me of what lay ahead.

But I stamped it down. I didn't want to think about

something I was putting off.

I am not putting it off. I am taking some time to recharge. Preparing.

I sighed. I almost convinced myself of my bullshit.

Cordus would tell me it was for the greater good, and I wished he were here with me. His guidance and power could have kept me on task, and we probably would have found the Tenebrian and been home by now. But I understood why he couldn't be here. The Elder Guardian was losing his ability to control his powers when on Earth, but he had faith in my abilities. When I came to Earth, I was filled with that same confidence.

But now I wasn't so sure.

All I wanted now was one more night without thinking about it all.

One more night with Ana.

Those intrusive thoughts told me I was being foolish—I had important work to do. So why was I fraternizing with a human? Internally, I was trying to justify putting off my task so I could spend time with Ana, when really, the company of *any* group of humans would do to recharge my powers. I could absorb *any* happiness and laughter—it didn't have to be hers.

But I was drawn to her in a way I couldn't explain, feelings stirring deep inside me that were so much stronger when being felt firsthand. I usually only felt such things empathically through humans—feeling *them* experiencing the emotions—but the ache that resisted deep in my chest and the butterflies in my stomach were something else altogether.

I was fighting a losing battle.

I didn't know what to do with these feelings.

Tonight, I would see Ana again and tell myself *just one more time.*

Just one more night.

I could try to convince myself I wasn't taking a night off for selfish reasons. I could tell myself all sorts of things, but they would all be lies, and lying was something Guardians did rarely, if ever. Keeping information to ourselves that humans didn't need to know, of course, but lying was against our nature. We didn't see the point in it. To conserve feelings we didn't have? Pointless.

Shaking my head again, I steamrolled over the thoughts of doubt and reminded myself I'd been entrusted with this task, which meant they'd trusted me to do it *my* way.

Ill-advised additional time with a human and all.

Ana slid a beer across the counter at me as I sat, refused my money, and winked.

I pursed my lips. "I don't want to get you into trouble by not paying."

Ana shrugged. "Ed does it all the time with random women he's trying to pick up, so I'm sure I can get away with it once."

Suppressing the urge to tell her it wasn't right to steal, I accepted the drink with thanks and reminded myself to leave some money over the bar later.

Ana watched me, then said, "Wow, it's really bothering you, isn't it?"

My eyebrows shot up. "How can you tell?"

"It's written all over your face. Here..." She opened the register and dropped a handful of cash into the drawer. "Better?"

I grinned again. "Yes, but now I owe you a drink."

She beamed and leaned on the bar with her elbows, resting her chin in her palms. "You can repay the favor later."

She was close enough that I could see the flecks of different shades of brown in her eyes. I tore my gaze away from her eyes and glanced at the ornate clock behind the bar. "What time do you finish?"

"About an hour... when the band finishes and the DJ starts."

"Well, then, I shall wait for my dance."

She tilted her head and smiled in a response that, to me, was adorable. "You're an old soul, like old-fashioned."

"Guess I'm just out of my time."

"No, I like it." She squeezed my hand momentarily, sending sparks firing through my veins at the contact, before she moved away to serve other bar patrons.

She was so *pure.*

I sat and drank for the next hour and watched her. She'd come and chat with me whenever she had a free moment, which wasn't often as the bar seemed understaffed, but I was no expert. Shortly before her knock-off time, two other bartenders arrived and worked together for a while before the change of shifts.

Undoing her apron, which I tried not to focus on too much as I remembered how the curve of her waist had felt under my fingers, she threw it under the bar, ducked out from under the hatch, and approached me. Having her close again, without the barrier of the bar between us, pushed all the air from the room and replaced it with only her emotional imprint.

My jaw tensed as I gritted my teeth. I needed to think of her as nothing beyond how she could recharge my energies with her company. I had ordered a drink and handed it to her as she sat beside me, so close that her arm brushed mine.

"You're a man of your word, I see." She accepted the drink. "Ah, it's nice to be on this side of the bar. Now I can give Ralph a hard time." She raised her voice on her last few words, and the tall African man behind the bar grinned at her before returning to work.

"Been busy?" I asked, adding, "Outside of work, I mean."

Ana shrugged. "Not really."

"Not hanging out with friends today?"

"I don't really have many friends, just Penny."

"What does she do?"

"Works at the hospital. She's a student nurse."

My eyebrows arched involuntarily, and I tried not to let my interest show too much. "Oh? That must be stressful."

Ana nodded. "Yeah, I guess it is. She said they get all sorts of weird injuries in there, lately more and more. It's like the whole area has gone crazy."

"That's so strange..." My voice trailed off as I considered probing Ana for more information, but it didn't feel right. I found the hospital through my search methods and had strong leads. Ana's company was to make me feel better, not to interrogate her for information. Having a night off from the job wasn't common practice, and even less so was having *two* nights off. But then, as if responding to an internal argument, a justifying thought surfaced.

It's also not common practice for a Guardian to be on Earth for this long.

Since I was in new territory, I might as well play by my own rules.

Every time I looked at Ana, it was easy to justify almost anything to be with her.

Just one more night.

"I don't know how she does it, to be honest," Ana continued. "I think it takes a special person to be a nurse."

I nodded, humming in agreement before taking a sip of my drink.

After a pause, Ana said, "Look, I'm not very good at small talk."

"Me, either." My shoulders stiffened for a moment, and something like daggers stabbed against my back—a negative emotional imprint explicitly aimed at me.

I was being watched.

Turning, I saw the male bartender Ana had worked with staring at me. Once we made eye contact, his eyes narrowed, and he stalked toward the exit. My brows knitted together as I watched him leave, before I slowly turned back to face Ana. "Who was that guy?"

"Who?"

As I indicated the man's retreating form, Ana scoffed. "That's Ed, just ignore him. He's been trying to get in my pants since he started working here."

"I don't like him," I grunted out. He had an odd reading, again something I hadn't encountered before. Beyond the arrogance and the swagger, something darker flashed through his eyes when he stared back at me, and he did not even bother hiding his bitterness toward me. When I turned back to Ana, the remnants of the dark feeling I picked up from Ed still swirled around inside me, along with a possessiveness over Ana I couldn't explain the origin of. I had no claim over her.

Jealousy was a human response.

"I don't like him either," she said, and I resisted the urge to smile.

My frown ebbed. I didn't like the vibe I got from that guy. He was dark beyond the daggers he had drilled into my back. It was possibly only a reaction because I sat next to Ana, but maybe something else.

Add him to the list.

My thoughts were interrupted by the brightness of Ana's smile when she looked up at me as the DJ's set shifted and a nineties hit song fit for a middle-school prom started.

"I think you owe me a dance."

Smirking, I held out my hand, and the familiar electricity passed through my skin when Ana took it. "I must warn you, though, I can't dance."

Ana laughed. "Why would you tell me you wanted to, then?"

Spinning her around awkwardly before I pulled her close to me, I slid a hand around her waist and used the other to take her right hand. My fingers enclosed around hers, as I'd seen it done many times, and her body moved flush against mine. But watching the act of dancing had not prepared me for the sensation of having her so close to me, nor for the feel of her heartbeat, faster than usual, as she felt the same sparks I did. "Because I wanted to dance with you," I said, leaning close. A shiver ran up Ana's spine as our bodies pressed closer together.

Soon, I became overwhelmed with the feel of her, as her essence pushed all others from my senses, and when I breathed in the scent of her subtle perfume and, beyond that, the smell of her skin, there was no room left in me to sense anything else. It was an unnerving sensation. Next to Ana, my senses were enhanced, and I could pinpoint people and their emotions so accurately that it filled my head with dizzying power. But like this, with the music thumping through the room and the bass making it feel as though our hearts were beating as one, I was consumed by her.

But with my senses blocked, I was weakened. Overcome with a sudden need to get some space from her to rid myself of the sensation, Ana laughed freely and openly as I turned her in a clumsy spin and caught her with my forearm across her back when she tripped over her own feet, or perhaps over mine. Leading her with my hand, fingers spread across the small of her back, we danced in circles, and I couldn't help but laugh at the joy that radiated from her as her imprint enveloped me again.

This time I didn't fight it.

This was *exactly* what I needed.

There was light within her, and despite all the pain she hid, I could feel who she was *inside*, beyond all the walls. She was completely guarded—the side everyone saw socially was a front. But when she was this close, the heat from her skin was on mine, our hands joined, and she was relaxed, I could feel everything that made her herself. Ana's smile completely lit me up, and internally, I pushed down the ever-present reminder that this couldn't last, that I could not risk putting her in danger.

But that was tomorrow's problem.

Right now, it was about this, her smile, and us together.

After another spin, she collided lightly against my chest, and I stiffened against the impact to steady her. Still holding her hand, I looked down at her and drank in the depths of her eyes.

The music changed, and Ana glanced at the DJ, who winked exaggeratedly as he played a slow song. I knew this song, and I'm sure that I'd borrowed elements of the guitar from it once or twice while gigging, and I chuckled.

"What's so funny?" Ana asked

"This song is named after you."

She pulled a face. "It's called *'Annie,'* and John Denver isn't really my thing."

"It could be our thing."

She laughed as I gritted my teeth at the corniness of the line I'd somehow not had the willpower to stop myself from saying out loud. Internally, I cursed myself. There was no time in this mission for us to have *our thing.*

There was no time during this mission for *us.*

Ana looked up at me and bit her bottom lip. "If this were a movie, we'd kiss now."

"I get the impression you watch too many movies," I said.

Ana's face fell, and I smirked at her adorable pout before I leaned in to kiss her. Her lips were soft when I pressed mine against hers, and a whisper of the taste of cider was still on her. As she parted her lips, she snaked her hand around the back of my neck, her other hand still clasped in mine. She was so warm as her essence entangled with mine.

When we broke apart, she sighed and leaned her head against my chest as we danced slowly in circles on the spot.

I rested my chin on her head, closed my eyes, and breathed deeply.

This was all I needed right now.

Everything else could wait.

As the dance floor became more crowded, we broke apart,

moved back toward the bar, and slid into the first available seats. Shaking my head as Ana offered me a drink, she ordered another cider. Her cheeks were flushed, either from the alcohol, the dancing, or both, and I could feel the waves of relaxed energy pulsating from her and let myself get lost within them.

I was getting drunk off Ana.

Corny. I'm glad I didn't say it out loud.

We chatted for a while, and the words came easily. I asked her many questions and managed to keep my answers vague enough. When she asked where I was from and where I grew up, I told her somewhere far from here.

She looked expectantly at me later after asking again about my childhood, and I sighed. I couldn't avoid talking about myself all night without it appearing odd, and I didn't want her to lose interest and leave. "I didn't have much of a family," I said, picturing Lucidis. "Family values, as you know them, weren't all that important. The community raised me."

"Like a cult?"

I laughed. "No, just..." There was no easy way to explain it. "Not a cult."

"That's a bit sad, not having a close-knit family."

I shrugged. "Not really, it's just how it is." The children were raised by the community and not strictly by their parents. Matings were for pleasure or propagation, nothing more. Children slept and spent their days with carers until they were old enough to begin training to hone their natural senses and start their work in maintaining the Balance.

"What brought you to the city?" Ana asked.

"Work, mostly."

"Playing in bars?"

My lip twitched, hesitating for only a moment. If Ana noticed, she didn't say anything. "There aren't any bars at home."

She laughed. "Ah, a very small country town then."

I chuckled. "Yeah." After a beat, when she kept looking at me with those beautiful brown eyes, I continued, "I like being around the people here, they're so vibrant, and there's always so much going on." I let my gaze sweep the bar. "Look at these people. Each of them has a story. Where they come from, where they're going, and why they are here. They all have fears and happiness and memories."

Ana smiled warmly. "I often wonder about people's stories. I'll see someone on the bus and wonder about their life. Sometimes, I'll make up a back story for them."

My eyebrow arched. "Oh, you can't imagine what people hide behind their masks."

She looked at me curiously. "Like you? What's behind your mask?"

"Someone very much like me, but with more secrets."

"Maybe one day you can tell them to me."

I smiled sadly. "Maybe I will."

Steering the conversation back toward Ana, I enjoyed what she talked about when she felt free and relaxed. She spoke of wanting a horse when she was younger—apparently, that was something many young humans wanted. I understood. They were beautiful animals with so much soul, and I liked cows for the same reason. Ana told me about the stray cat she feeds—Seamus—and how she hoped to bring him home one day when she and Penny get a new apartment. There was no way to stop the smile that spread across my face. Ana revealed a previously unseen nurturing side when she talked about that cat, and it made me think about those family values I grew up without. There were so many elements to Ana that she hid behind walls. She had so many barriers that I doubted even she knew how to break through them if she wanted to. I understood she had lost people in the past, but humans usually displayed their emotions for everyone to see, yet she hid hers so carefully.

Ana glanced at the large clock over the bar. "Shall we go back to mine?" She stood before I could answer.

I smiled again, although truth be told, I hadn't stopped smiling since I first laid eyes on her hours ago. I ached to touch her, to be close to her in the way we were last night, to be inside her again. To be one with her.

While I didn't want to ruin this night by turning her down, I also couldn't risk her seeking more with me. I had already let myself get too close and couldn't risk anything further.

But looking into her eyes and seeing how she looked back at me, I feared it might already be too late.

"I can't tonight, I'm sorry."

Ana didn't appear fazed. "That's okay, another time?"

I nodded but didn't verbally respond. I didn't trust myself to, for while I mostly kept my control, there were words I longed to say to her, things that could never be. So I kept them to myself as I followed her out of the bar.

Once outside, I pulled her against me and spread my fingers across her back to absorb all the warmth from her I could.

I was going to need it.

I struggled to find a way to end this evening on a good note without offering her hope for a future that could never happen.

"Do you want me to walk you home?" I asked.

I knew what was out there.

"It's not far, I'll be okay."

Staring over her head into the darkness, I tensed. "It's late. Make sure you go straight home and text me when you arrive."

"All right, all right." She nodded against me and plugged my number into her cell with one hand, and her other arm was still wrapped around my torso.

Casually. Comfortably.

So close it hurt.

Closing my eyes, I held her, and she pulled away just enough to kiss me lightly on the lips, lingering for a whisper of a moment. She sucked in a small breath, and I relished in the feel of her essence, pushing my energy into her and, in turn, receiving more from her. Letting it surround us both, I memorized the feel of it for what I knew would be the last time.

"Good night, Kyle."

"Good night, Ana."

Watching her walk away, I thanked her internally for giving me the strength to do what I needed to do next.

Goodbye Ana.

OUTLET

Chapter Thirteen

Ana

Picking up my cell for the sixth time that hour, I glanced at the screen and checked for messages or missed calls, trying and failing to be surreptitious about it, judging by the look I got from Ed. Sighing when there were none, I placed it back under the bar. Kyle had been upfront and honest with me. He'd said no promises from the start and not led me on under false pretenses.

But we had connected.

At least, that's what *I* had felt. But at the same time, I was plagued with inner conflict. I didn't want to be chasing after someone who didn't want me back. In fact, I'd never really chased after *anyone* before. My relationships—if that was even a suitable word—usually ended with a mutual parting of ways after a few months at most, and neither of us ever looked back.

How could I know if I was looking into this too much?

I already knew the answer—I had to put myself out there.

Risk getting hurt.

Not my favorite thing.

After a moment of internal debate, I decided I'd never know

for sure if I didn't try. I'd forever ask myself, *what if*?

It sounded lame even in my head.

What really pushed me over the edge when it came to making the decision was something in my gut that told me Kyle was worth the risk.

"I'm taking my break," I shouted over her shoulder at Ed. Rather than nodding his acknowledgment, he sauntered up to me. I paused and resisted the urge to roll my eyes as I rested my hand on the hatch, ready to duck underneath and out from behind the bar.

"Who's got your attention so wrapped up?" Ed asked.

"No one you need to know about."

"It's that scrappy-looking guy from last night, right?"

"He's not *scrappy.*" I defended Kyle, even as my lip twitched and I held back a smile. I guessed he was kind of scrappy, as though his clothes were randomly selected without much thought, but it was endearing.

Ed nodded. "So, are you and Scrappy Boy dating now?"

"Kyle, his name is Kyle."

Ed shrugged as though it made no difference to him, and I doubted it did. Ed didn't care for anything that wasn't revolving around Ed. He sidled closer to me, and I moved away. The man had a way of making me feel sick simply by being too close. "What does he have that I don't?"

"A heart?"

He scoffed. "Is he good in bed?"

Tired of his intrusive questions, I switched subjects. "Earlier, a guy was here, and you slipped him something."

Ed's eyebrow arched, but he gave no other indication he was concerned by my question. "Maybe."

"What was it? You shouldn't be doing that here."

"So innocent, my little Ana." I lifted my lip into a snarl. I wasn't *his* anything. Ed chuckled and continued, "It was something for his friend. She's a bit uptight and needed some loosening up."

His words struck me like a punch in the gut. "Are you telling me you're selling date rape drugs?" I hissed through my teeth, and as my fingers gripped the bar hatch, the sound of my nails scraping on the wood drew his attention.

Ed laughed. It was a cold sound. "Seriously, Ana? Do you think I would do something like that?"

I wouldn't put it past you.

As a customer approached, Ed turned to move away from me. "Lighten up. Sometimes people just need a little something to help them relax."

I had no idea what to make of that, and my hands shook as I ducked under the bar hatch and moved outside onto the footpath. I'd be keeping an eye on Ed. If I witnessed even a *hint* of him doing that, I'd have the cops running all over that bar faster than he could blink.

The sky had a pinkish glow in the distance, and the sun lingered around for longer during the warmer months, as though it didn't want to let go of the day. I was ready to let go of the daylight and wait for night, when the world would be quieter and clearer.

Selecting Kyle's number, I dialed, pressed the cell to my ear with more force than was probably necessary, and waited. I'd only seen him last night, and the unwritten rules of courting said we should wait three days before contacting a suitor.

But to hell with social construct.

It was never my thing, anyway.

"Ana," Kyle answered after a few rings.

"Hey, Kyle, it's Ana."

I cringed as he chuckled. "I know," he said. I could hear the amusement in his tone, and I relaxed.

A little bit.

Laughing uncomfortably, it helped to picture his smile. "So, how are you?"

"I'm alright."

There was a pause, filled with all the things left unsaid. "I was wondering if you wanted to get together again sometime?" I asked.

Another pause.

"Ana..."

"Ah." Dread threatened to choke me. "That's a no."

"Look... I'm sorry."

"No, no, it's okay." Although I knew my tone betrayed my true feelings. I was excellent at being sarcastic, but not so good at hiding hurt. Clearing my throat, I said, "No harm in asking, right?"

"Ana, I'm no good for you. I am no good for anyone. You are an amazing person, but having me around can only mess you up."

Starting to pace in small circles on the pavement, I could feel myself getting worked up. I was hurt and angry. I knew my anger wasn't justified. Kyle had made his position clear from the start, and it was my fault for looking into it too much. But the *one* time I put myself out there, the first time in as long as I could remember, and I was shot down. What the *fuck?* How many times did I have to be taught the same lesson?

Opening up only led to pain and rejection.

"I thought that would've been my call to make," I said defensively.

"I'm trying to protect you."

"I can protect myself."

"Ana, I'm sorry. I like you—"

"Not enough, though."

"Ana..."

I stopped pacing. "No, Kyle, it's okay, honestly. I won't force myself on you, but I thought I'd reach out because I felt we had something more. The way we connected..." I shook my head. "I had to at least try for myself, you know? But it's okay, really. Have a good night."

Hanging up before he could respond, my shoulders dropped, and I resisted the urge to hurl my cell at the pavement. I looked up at the sky as it darkened to suit my mood. Sighing, I angrily swiped away a stray tear from my cheek and went back inside.

For the first time, I left my shift late that night. It felt better to keep working, to keep busy and distracted. I was mad at myself for allowing Kyle to get under my skin, and I hated that I cared so much about some random guy I'd had a one-night stand with.

Huffing angrily as I walked, I sidestepped a lamp post I hadn't noticed until the last second.

I needed to pay closer attention.

Whatever I had *thought* I felt, he wasn't worth it.

No one was.

But God, the sex was *so good*. I'd heard the word *transcendent* used before, which always sounded pretentious. But it was the only word that came to mind when I thought of how it felt when Kyle and I were together, physically and beyond.

Transcendent—above-normal human experience.

Sighing hard, I shoved my hands in my pockets and headed toward the bus stop, purposefully scuffing my boots on the pavement. Voices distracted me, and I was only feet from my bus stop when I heard them—angry and shouting—around a nearby corner. Backing up to the wall, I peeked around the corner. A handful of teenagers picked on younger kids and pushed them around. As the bullying escalated from light pushing into hard shoving, I frowned and sucked in a breath when one kid was knocked to the ground.

When I heard the flick of a knife, a neon sign reflected on the switchblade, my back straightened against the wall.

I took a deep breath before coming around the corner with a shout. "Hey!"

Their attention was turned to me, and I was outnumbered.

Shit.

I was well out of my depth, but it was too late. If I ran, they would only chase me down. There were three of them and one of me, and I was in boots, not running shoes.

Another reason heels were a terrible idea.

Think fast, Ana.

Grabbing my cell out of my pocket, I held it before me, covering it in my closed fist. "I have mace. Get the fuck out of here unless you want a face full of pepper spray."

The teens smirked, and one clapped the other on the

shoulder as they took a menacing step closer to me before they stopped. The moment lingered between us, and his eyes never wavered from my face as he said, "Come on, man, let's leave the hussy to it."

The tenseness of my muscles remained until they had crossed the street and disappeared into the night. Only then did I release the breath I'd been holding. As I lowered my hand, I helped the smaller kid up from the ground before wiping my forehead with the back of my wrist.

"Thanks, lady," one kid said.

"How old are you?"

"Sixteen."

Yeah right. I raised my eyebrows. "The truth, please. I just saved your asses."

They looked to their feet, ashamed. *So they should.* "Thirteen."

"Go home. Please, just... go home."

They nodded and turned to leave.

"Hey!"

I looked up from my trembling hands at their call. "Yeah?"

"Do you really have mace?"

When I opened my hand, I needed to flex my fingers to release the tension so I could reveal my cell phone to them.

"You've got some balls, lady. That could've ended real bad."

"I know," I said. My lip twitched, but I couldn't find it in me to smile. Aside from the situation, it felt like a cloud of fear surrounded me, pressing on my shoulders and back. "Think about that next time before you come out so late. Now, please, go home. I'm sure your families are worried."

They nodded, and I watched them as they ran across the

street, hoping they made no detours and went straight home as I'd suggested. They were kids, but they shouldn't be stupid enough to stay out after that little adventure. Surely, they could also feel the ominous threat that seemed to loom in the night around us. As I turned back toward my bus stop, I almost walked straight into a man who I hadn't heard approach, and I came to an abrupt halt.

"*Shit.* I'm sorry," I said.

Stepping to the side to walk around him, he grabbed me roughly by the shoulders, and his fingers dug painfully into my skin as he shook me slightly. "What did you do?" he shouted.

He was wearing a hoodie, and I couldn't see his face, but his voice alone was enough to prick up the hairs on the back of my neck. He oozed darkness, like the bad guy from all the movies.

He *was* the darkness.

It seemed a ridiculous thought to have, but I couldn't think of another way to explain how he made me feel. My skin crawled where he held me.

I tried to push against him. "What? Let go of me!"

"You should have just let it happen. You ruined it." He snarled, and I trembled at the sound.

On instinct, I lifted a knee and made harsh contact with his groin. He released me and stepped back, but he didn't appear overly winded, almost as if he'd let me go from the shock of my attack rather than any pain.

When he stepped toward me, I backed up in equal measure. "Maybe you and I can have some fun." His voice dripped with menace, and I trembled at the pain promised with his words.

Run.

I backed away a few steps before taking off, passed on his left, and ran as fast as possible.

"Next time, let people be the animals they are meant to be," He yelled after me as I ran down the street. My ankle twisted as I slipped, but I kept going and jumped on the first bus that passed.

Turning and watching the bus doors close, I bent and squinted into the night, trying to find the shape of the man as the bus pulled away, but it was too dark.

Grabbing my chest, I forced myself to slow my breathing. "Christ, what the fuck was that about?" I muttered and rubbed my arms where he had grabbed me before I rolled my foot gently. It didn't feel like I'd injured myself too badly—nothing some ice and rest wouldn't cure.

"You okay?"

Turning, I nodded at the bus driver. "I'm okay. Thanks." Trying to make my tone clear to express that further questions were not welcome. There was no way I could explain the feeling I'd gotten from the man beyond the verbal threat, and I didn't want to think about it.

Taking a seat for the short trip, my heartbeat still pounded hard behind my ribcage. Glancing out the window again as we drove, I saw nobody. Hopefully, those kids were okay and almost home, if not home safe already.

Standing before my stop, I tried to avoid too much weight on my foot and absentmindedly waved goodnight to the bus driver before I stepped off and half-jogged, half-limped to my apartment building.

I glanced around every corner and was mindful of every shadow.

Chapter Fourteen

Kyle

Sitting on the edge of my bed, I stared at my cell after Ana had hung up. The small piece of insignificant technology held more weight than it had moments before, as though having it in my hand was my one remaining link to Ana. A heavy and stifling ache filled my chest, accompanied by a fluttering in my stomach that I couldn't explain. For a moment, I thought I was going to be sick, but it passed, and I was left with the residual sensation.

Guilt.

Too clouded now to continue working, I reluctantly tilted my hand slowly until the cell phone slid from my palm and clattered onto the floor. Slumping down the side of the bed, as I slid off the mattress, the sheets bundled up with me and ended up in a pile behind my back.

It was uncomfortable, but I didn't care.

Picking up my guitar, I glanced at the small pile of tools I had been working with—refining a better replacement for my lost stone knife. It was still nowhere near the quality of the one I had lost, but it didn't need to be.

It only needed to be sharp.

When I came to doing what I had to, I didn't want to increase the human's pain by cutting into them with a blunt blade. It took time, as the moonstone resisted being sharpened without the proper tools, but I needed to ensure it was right. The marbled white blade, discarded on the floor when my cell had rung, reflected the light from outside.

Sighing, I started playing a few chords and worked them into a melody with no name—a sad, sweet tune that filled the room and left no space for the lies I had been trying to tell myself. Closing my eyes, I let the music surround me.

But it stuttered, and my fingers skipped notes.

The music infiltrated me, and I screwed my eyes shut against the emotion that rose in my chest. The notes were filled with the sense of *her*. I was surrounded by Ana's lingering emotional imprint that I had drawn forth from memory, and I'd created an invisible and painful prison.

Taking a deep breath, I sighed again, and the forceful breath fluttered the hair around my face. We *did* have something more—she was right to pick up on that. There was something about her that soothed me, something that made the rest of the world fade away. And she was *beautiful*. Beyond her looks, I found her stunning in every way.

But I had a job to do.

I couldn't endanger her or anyone else. What if the other Guardian saw us together and found her? He could use her as leverage and torture her to get to me. I couldn't be responsible for that. She was better off without me. The humans around me were in enough danger without my active involvement in their lives.

I couldn't risk it.

Dropping my head, I fought uselessly against the building sensation before I could fight no more, and a few tears escaped and landed on the guitar's smooth finish.

I brushed a finger through the tears that sprinkled my guitar.

A physical manifestation of the emotions I could no longer contain. Emotions I shouldn't be capable of. Earth was changing me. *She* had changed me.

There are worlds of physical pain I would take over the ache that filled my chest.

I didn't fully understand these feelings, and being on Earth had apparently influenced me as much as I could influence the humans in this realm.

All the more reason I couldn't risk Ana.

I was compromised, and she could *not* be put in harm's way.

Regardless of the pain it caused me.

Chapter Fifteen

Ana

Carrying the shopping basket, Henry and I strolled casually through the aisles and collected the items he had meticulously written on his list.

How does he get his handwriting so perfect?

Mine always looked like someone kicked me in the back of the knee halfway through each word.

"Do you always write such a comprehensive list?" I mused.

Henry laughed. "I only want to buy what I need."

"Where's the fun in that? Don't you ever open your cupboard and wonder what you'll cook from the random assortment of things in your pantry and fridge?"

"Ana, I'm seventy-eight. I don't like surprises."

"Henry..." Stopping in the aisle, I placed my free hand on my hip and arched a brow at him, "... all the more reason to live without boundaries."

"We all have our boundaries."

Pausing, I looked at the floor before sneering slightly—more to myself than to him. Henry often did that and caught me off guard by making me assess what he had said in case something more was written between the lines. He slipped in hidden meaning between his words because I wouldn't often let the conversation shift into something deeper and more meaningful. So, he would pepper our everyday interactions with nuggets of wisdom.

I supposed Henry had advice about many things, so I *tried* to take what he said on board.

Sometimes, I didn't want to think about things, and I was angrier about the Kyle situation than I wanted to admit.

Boundaries indeed.

"Yes, but now you also have chocolate biscuits." I snatched a packet off the shelf and added it to the basket.

"Diabetes, Ana," he reminded me gently.

Smirking, I lifted the packet from his basket to show him. "I know that. Check the label."

He leaned forward to read the label, checking their suitability, then glancing at me under his brows, he chuckled before we continued wandering slowly up and down the aisles. I kept pace with Henry and enjoyed his shopping routine's relaxed amble and strategic pattern.

He was patient and planned. I was chaotic and unorganized.

So, I appreciated these days with Henry. I liked his stories and how the memories that stuck with him about his family and friends were the simple ones. The small moments that passed each day, almost unnoticed at the time, were the ones he treasured the most. He'd speak of his children and grandchildren and the gifts they used to make for him in school crafts using toilet paper rolls. He'd told me more than once of the time he came home with his wife after a weekend away to find his teenage children passed out after a party on the front lawn, and even one person on the roof. He had been livid at the time, but now it was merely another wonderful memory that made him chuckle in that soft way he does with that toothy grin I loved so much.

His children lived in rural or interstate areas now, but Henry didn't want to go despite having offered him a home with them. He liked it in the city—it had always been and always would be his home. Henry had seen so much without ever leaving the country and regretted none of it. I admired his openness and ease at interacting with people, even down to the woman at the cash register. Her very standard questions would've brought out from me the only response I knew how to deal with—sarcasm. But Henry had an easy charm that hadn't faded with age.

I wished I had it in me.

But it was easier to keep to myself, often shrinking into the background if Henry encountered someone he knew and was conversing politely.

Sometimes my heart started breaking when we were together. Henry could be forgetful and tell me the same stories or ask the same questions more than once. I didn't mind. I had untold patience and love for Henry, and I'd thought to myself more than once that, in some way, perhaps he filled the void left by my father. Sometimes Henry had the clarity of a much younger man, but earlier today, he had asked me again how old I was.

"I'm twenty-seven, Henry."

He looked shocked for a moment. "I'm sorry, I keep forgetting... You look like a teenager."

"That would explain why I still get asked for ID to buy alcohol."

Henry smiled. "Take it as a compliment, Ana, most people would love it."

Now he asked, "Are you seeing anyone lately?"

"I like you, Henry, but I don't *like-like* you," I replied in a sing-song voice.

Default—sarcasm.

He chuckled. "I'm serious, you're a young lady who's alone a lot. You need to let someone into your life."

"I have Penny, and I have you."

"That's a good start."

Sighing, I looked at the floor again. "Well, actually, just recently, I did try to let someone in. But I made a poor judgment, and it turns out I was more invested than he was. It was silly, really, we barely knew each other, but I just thought—"

"You had a moment?"

My eyes shot to his face for a beat before I returned my gaze to the shopping list. The shopping list didn't ask questions that made the pain in my chest rise again. I wasn't even really seeing what was written on the paper before me, and I blinked my way back to clarity. "Something like that."

"I understand that. We open ourselves up to the chance of getting hurt every time. But sometimes it's worth the chance." Henry continued when I didn't reply, "What about Nathaniel?"

"What about him?" I asked.

"He's a nice young man. Good job. He's respectful." He was smiling before he even finished the sentence. "You should go on a date with him."

"I don't like being set up, Henry."

"I'll give him your number."

"I'd rather you didn't."

Henry smiled. "Do a favor for an old man."

Throwing my head back, I couldn't help but laugh. "Don't play the old-man card with me."

"Just think about it."

"Fine," I conceded. "I'll think about it."

Slowing my steps, I kept a steady pace with Henry as we returned to the apartment building. My legs may be short, but I usually moved like a madman through the city streets, ducking and weaving through the crowds as only someone shorter than average could. Slowing down like this was a nice change, but I didn't think I'd do it for anyone other than Henry. I carried his shopping bags, despite his insistence that he could do it himself. Dusk was approaching, and the late afternoon sun cast an orange hue across the city skyline and stretched out the shadows of the skyscrapers and apartment buildings into infinity. I'm sure Henry would have done his shopping at seven or eight in the morning if he were doing it alone, but he accepted I wasn't an early morning person.

Or a mid-morning person.

Sometimes not even a barely-afternoon person.

Even if I didn't have to work until the early morning hours after most night shifts, I still didn't think I'd be fond of the mornings. The night was different. It wasn't so overwhelming. The night understood me. There wasn't as much noise, as if the crowds of people buzzing about their day created a hum in my head I couldn't drown out. The night was still, the nightlife was purposeful, and they were only there for a good time. The morning was for people who worked nine to five.

As we rounded the corner, Nathaniel was waiting outside the building and glanced at the time on his cell. He looked up as we approached, and wearily, I slowed my pace.

Something was up.

"You called?" Nathaniel asked as we came level with him.

I looked at Henry as he cocked his head. "Did I?"

Realization hit, and I rolled my eyes. "Oh my God, Henry, you're the *worst* liar," I muttered.

Nathanial frowned. "Yeah, about half an hour ago?"

"Oh, I'm sorry, Nathaniel, I must've gotten confused. I am an old man, you know." He shuffled away after I handed him one of the bags, and his eyes twinkled at the unamused look I gave him. I could have sworn he chuckled as he moved away, the cheeky bastard. Nathanial turned toward me expectantly, as if I held the answers or was somehow responsible for Henry's shenanigans. His frown was still in place, marring an otherwise handsome face, and he glanced over his shoulder as though he had left something important to come here.

I shrugged. "He's been planning our wedding."

Nathaniel's attention was back on me. "I'm sorry?"

"He's setting us up."

Confusion crossed his face for a moment, and he eyed me suspiciously before he smiled. It was almost amusing to witness the cascading emotions as he tried to figure out what he was doing here. But when he smiled, it changed his entire face. It occurred to me that I hadn't seen Nathaniel smile properly before. Most of our interactions consisted of small talk with single-sentence replies for Henry's benefit. I'd never figured out if he had a dry sense of humor or no sense of humor at all.

Twisting my lips, I worked the thoughts around as though they were in my mouth as words unsaid. I supposed Henry would have spoken to Nathaniel more often than I had while he'd been helping around the apartment. *Surely* Henry wouldn't try to set me up with a stranger.

Plus, if I were honest with myself, I was still seething about the Kyle situation.

So, I took Henry's advice and took a chance.

"He's very subtle," Nathaniel said, glancing into the building and back at me. His lips were still turned into a welcoming grin that somehow morphed him from attractive to dashing.

"About as subtle as a sledgehammer," I commented.

"So... lunch then?"

I whipped around to look at him. "Huh?"

"Do you want to go to lunch with me tomorrow?"

I almost pulled a muscle in my neck, resisting the urge to do a double-take. Nathaniel had *immediately* asked me out. He didn't even *know* me.

If I were him, I would have turned and run in the opposite direction.

But then again, if everyone responded to social situations like I did, people wouldn't talk to each other at all.

Dammit, what the hell, right?

"Yeah, okay, but can we make it a late lunch? Around about the too-late-for-lunch, too-early-for-dinner window is when I eat."

"Whatever, I'm not fussy."

"Okay, it's a date, then."

We swapped numbers and stood in silence for a moment. I stepped forward, and we exchanged an awkward embrace somewhere between a half hug and a handshake, which left me tempted to make it weirder for the sake of it by adding a small jig before Nathaniel left with another grin.

Watching him go, I almost cringed. Only a fist-bump high-five combo could have been more awkward than that.

Give it a chance, Henry had said.

I'd give it a chance, and maybe I'd even try to let my guard down. The very least I could do for Henry was *try*.

Since today was the day for honesty, maybe I owed it to myself to try more often.

"You've got a date with who?" Penny asked.

"Nathaniel." At Penny's blank look, I continued, "The guy from the at-home carer's place who does maintenance at Henry's place."

Penny hummed. "Don't think I've ever met him." She watched me sort through my clothes momentarily before asking, "How did it even happen?"

Straightening from sorting through the pile of laundry on my bed, I threw my hands up. "How do you think? Henry set us up."

Penny laughed. "Oh, I do like that man's style."

"Well, maybe you and Henry can come along, and we'll make it a double date."

"As much as I'd love to be a fly on the wall, I'm going to leave you to it." Penny watched as I tossed clothes around the room for a moment. "What exactly are you looking for?"

Without pausing my search, I said, "My criteria are clean, not smelly, and comfortable."

"At least try to wear something pretty."

When I looked up, holding an option, Penny's expression added, *'Are you serious?'* without her needing to verbalize it. I looked at the black overall shorts and held them before me. "I mean, I could add a pretty t-shirt under it?" When she continued to stare at me, I threw the overalls over my shoulder and huffed out, "Fine! How about this?" I selected a black summery T-shirt dress with a floral pattern.

Penny failed to suppress her shock. "Actually, surprisingly good."

"Sweet." Throwing it on, I then shimmed out of my jeans and bent to put on my shoes.

"Sneakers, Ana?"

"Hey, I'm wearing a dress," I scoffed. "Credit where credit is due."

Penny smirked. "I don't know anyone else who could pull off that look..." She crossed her arms, "... I'm a bit jealous."

"Jealous? Of what?" I looked up from tying my laces before I stood, and she took in my complete outfit.

"*You!* You could wear heels, and you don't, while I can't wear them."

"Why?"

Penny moved her hands up and down and indicated her body. "Because, in case you hadn't noticed, I'm tall as hell."

"So?"

"So, women who are too tall are intimidating, and people don't like it."

"Penny, screw what they think! If you want to wear heels,

wear heels."

"Maybe."

Grinning, I ran my hands over the dress, feeling slightly exposed but comfortable in the sneakers' familiarity. Hesitating, I bit my bottom lip and watched Penny. Sometimes, it was like I saw her in a new light, as though every time she accidentally reminded me of her vulnerability or self-consciousness, I saw her for the first time as my friend all over again.

Sometimes I got so caught up in my shit I forgot to appreciate those around me.

Stepping forward, I placed a hand on Penny's arm. "You know I care about you, don't you?"

"Yeah, of course." Penny tilted her head and covered my hand with her own. "You okay?"

"Yeah, just something Henry said yesterday about letting people in."

"I care for you, too."

Lifting the corner of my lip into an almost smile, I squeezed Penny's arm before I grabbed my handbag.

No pockets. Stupid dress.

"I'll see you later."

Heading down the stairs, I was immediately glad of my choice of footwear. Boots, yes, but heels? I never understood them. Touching my cheek, I wondered if I should've worn makeup. *Na.* I never usually did, and doing so would be out of character now. I was already wearing a dress. That should be enough to show I was making some effort. I wasn't even sure why I cared so much, but something about Nathaniel's demeanor made me want to impress him.

Judgmental was the wrong word. It was more like he was

surveying the world, hiding behind a front until he found someone worth opening up to.

I knew that feeling.

Technically, this was the first official date I'd had in years. Usually, I'd meet someone while out for the night, and we'd hang out for a few months until its ultimate demise. Henry, of course, had my best interests at heart, and if the date was an abysmal failure, then at least I had tried.

Then I'd have a solid excuse for denying any further set-ups.

Nathaniel and I met at a small eatery a few blocks from my apartment. The best part of living in the city center was that I never had to stray far from home, so I liked to keep it local, and he didn't seem to care where we went. I'd been to the venue a handful of times, but not in a year or so. While it was usually busy, it wasn't too crowded today. Busy enough so you didn't feel like you stood out, but quiet enough to hear each other speak.

Nathaniel ordered black coffee, which somehow didn't surprise me. It seemed to suit him. As he sat there sipping it, I noticed his hands were perfect and well-manicured, and I could imagine them as they swept delicately over the pages of a book.

Or over a naked body.

Flushing slightly when he caught me watching him, I pushed the intrusive thought from my mind, unsure where it had come from.

Sipping my still-too-hot mocha and regretting it immediately, I tried to cover my discomfort and continued the conversation. "So, what do you do outside of work?"

"Not as much as I'd like, mostly get myself into trouble." He flashed that smile like a secret weapon he held close.

He seemed a different person when he smiled, as though there was something much more intriguing behind the suave, calm exterior. But I couldn't get a read on him beyond a vague sense that there was more to him. Nathaniel was a completely closed book.

Closed, sealed, and chained up.

Did that mean there was more to him or nothing at all?

"I'm often on call, so I need to keep days open as much as possible," he continued.

"Have you lived here long?"

"Honestly, too long, but work is work. I've left a few times but always seem to come back."

I was about to ask him if he liked to read, my default question for new people, when his cell phone went off. He looked at me apologetically and answered the call. The boredom was clear on his face, as if dealing with whoever was on the line was a chore and an inconvenience to his time. He kept looking at me as though he were trying to gauge my reaction to him while he half-listened to the conversation on the other end of the line.

We were two people with our guards up high, trying to get a read on each other, and it would go nowhere if I didn't give this a chance.

He sighed. "All right, gimme ten."

Looking up from my mocha and my thoughts, I asked, "Everything okay?"

"As if part of some cosmic joke, at the exact moment we were talking about it, I've been called in to help with a job downtown."

"Oh, that's okay." The disappointment stirred in me was stronger than I'd expected. The date had barely begun, but I was intrigued by him.

Maybe because I hadn't thought about Kyle while I'd been with Nathaniel.

Damn, broke the streak.

Nathaniel stood. "Can I take you out again?"

I smiled. "Yeah, that'd be good."

Standing to see him off, he kissed me lightly, his lips delicate and soft. When I brushed his hand with mine, a spark passed between us, a flame of something that could be more. But as I raised my eyes to his, the sensation disappeared. He was a closed book again.

"I'll text you," he said.

Leaving some money on the table, he turned and was gone. Sitting to finish my drink, I played a game on my cell before heading home.

Note to self—*don't tell Henry that maybe he was right.*

I'd never hear the end of it.

Penny looked up as I re-entered the apartment, a furrow immediately etched into her brow. "That was quick."

"Yeah." Closing the door, I chucked my bag onto the coffee table before sitting next to Penny. "Nothing untoward, though. He got an emergency call from work and had to go, so we'll reschedule."

"But in the half an hour or so you spent with him?"

"Actually, not bad. He's not much of a talker but seems... steady."

"Steady?"

"Predictable, reliable, but also intelligent, and he has a cute smile."

"Cute. I like that descriptive word better than predictable

and reliable. It means you might like him a little bit."

"A little bit." Half-shrugging, I smiled at Penny. "But we shall see how it goes next time. Takeout?"

Penny grinned. "Sure, I start early tomorrow morning, so we can eat before I turn in for the night."

"It's a date. But first, I'm getting out of this dress and into some sweats."

With one arm halfway through a t-shirt, I began tapping out a takeaway order into an app on my cell, already knowing what Penny's favorite dishes were. When I strolled past the doorway, Penny was watching me. I knew that look, that knowing smile. It told me she was proud I was putting myself out there. But as I paused in the doorway and she continued to watch me, biting her lower lip, I knew something was up.

"Penny?" I asked and held her gaze. "What's up?"

"Um, Lynn is coming over tomorrow night."

"Oh. Okay. Cool."

There was silence between us.

"Ana..." Penny started. While she was a patient woman, her tone had an edge.

I held up a hand. "It's not that I don't like her, it's... she doesn't like me, you know that, right?" Penny nodded, and I dropped my hand. "She's always welcome here, Penny. If she makes you happy, that's more than good enough for me."

Penny smirked, and I held up my hand and balled it into a fist. "But if she ever hurts you..." I mimed boxing, throwing a few poor punches, and added the appropriate movie sound effects. Penny laughed, and I grinned and returned to my cell to finish the dinner order.

Penny and Lynn had been on and off for a few years now,

and I could always tell Lynn was uncomfortable around me, although she denied it. It wasn't her fault. I'd hardly been the easiest person to get to know. The problem was that the awkwardness had been going on for so long that I didn't know how to break it. Whenever I made a sarcastic comment in an attempt at humor to cut the tension, Lynn would simply look at me like she didn't get it.

Didn't get *me.*

Penny had expressed a similar pride after my date with Nathaniel as when I'd grown fond of Henry. I had to let my guard down to let him into my life, and I'm thankful I did. She told me she had wished I were more outgoing when we had first met. But that passed when we got close, and some selfish part of her was glad I was so closed off. She liked me exactly as I was and wanted to keep my friendship to herself.

I didn't feel worthy of such a compliment, but I'd take it.

NO PARKING
DO NOT
BLOCK

Chapter Sixteen

Ana

She screamed.

A high-pitched scream of terror reached the walls around me and beyond. It felt loud enough to shake the very bricks of the apartment building as though her terror would claw its way into the cracks and bring the building down around us.

My mind was still fuzzy from my dream as I sat up in bed.

The screaming continued.

The realization that it wasn't part of my dream was like a slap to the face, and bounding off my bed, I raced to Penny's room. Penny screamed and scrambled madly to free herself from the tangle of sheets. Lynn was on her knees on the bed and hovered her hands over Penny's writhing form, looking halfway between shock and tears.

It occurred to me that this may be the first time Lynn had seen one of Penny's night terror episodes.

When Penny freed herself from the sheets, Lynn leaned forward and grabbed her arms, and Penny's screaming reached a new intensity.

"Let her go!" I cried out.

Lynn immediately lifted her hands as Penny struck out wildly, still screaming.

"Penny! Penny, it's not real," Lynn cried and ran her fingers through her impossibly bright red hair, the contrast making her face paler than usual. It wasn't often I saw her without makeup, and the effect in the dim lighting from the streetlights outside was ghostly.

I flicked on the light as Penny rolled out of the bed and clambered across the floor until she was in the corner of the room. She stopped screaming, hugged her knees close to her chest, and made herself as small as she could. My heart split in my chest at seeing her like this, but through experience and hesitant conversations, at least I knew what to do.

Turning to Lynn, I said, "Turn on every light in the apartment." When she sat staring at Penny, I shouted, "*Now!*" And she leaped off the bed to follow my instructions.

Dropping onto my hands and knees, I approached Penny slowly, like a wild animal.

"Penny, it was a nightmare," I whispered, not yet reaching out to her, simply inching closer. "You're safe. He's not here."

The sobs broke through and became heavy. Penny's chest heaved, and her shoulders shook. She didn't react when I reached out and tentatively touched her leg, which I took as a good sign, and crawled up next to her before I pulled her against my chest. Penny clutched me as if her life depended on it. As Lynn entered the room, I continued to rock Penny for a few minutes until her cries subsided and her breathing steadied. Then, I rocked a bit longer and whispered soothing nothings. It didn't matter what I was saying—a calm voice and a warm embrace were all she needed to cling to so she could return to reality and leave her past firmly where it belonged.

"Tell me," I said, and almost failed to keep the crack from my voice.

God, I hate this part.

Penny choked back a sob, and I squeezed her against me. "No," I said. My voice shook. "Don't clam up, you need to talk. Where were you?"

Nothing.

"Where *were you,* Penny?"

She sniffed and closed her eyes. "In a warehouse, at the edge of the city."

"What kind of warehouse?"

"An abandoned abattoir."

"And where are you now?"

Penny opened her eyes and blinked against the light. She released the word on a breath, "*Home.*"

"Who was with you?"

Penny took a shuddering breath. "*He* was. I don't know his name."

"What was he doing?"

"He tortured me for hours. With knives and tools. He ra..."

She couldn't get the word out. I squeezed her again. She didn't need to.

Lynn cut in, and her voice sounded on the edge of breaking. "Is this really necessary? To get her to say these things?"

I held her with a hard stare. "This isn't easy for me either, Lynn." Rocking Penny again, I calmed my voice and asked her, "And who's with you now?"

"You are. Ana." She looked at Lynn, whose eyes were wide and full of pain at watching Penny go through this. "And my

Lynn."

There was a heavy pause, and I could've sworn Penny was about to say that she loved Lynn but couldn't quite get the words out. Of course, they loved each other, and I would sit through a thousand awkward meals with them if it meant they would spend more time together. Penny had been so focused on her career that she hadn't yet committed to Lynn in a way I knew they both craved. I only wanted them to be happy.

"And what are we doing?" I asked.

Penny sniffed. "Keeping me safe."

"Where are you?" I asked again.

"Home."

"And?"

"Safe."

"Repeat it."

"I'm home and safe."

As Penny nuzzled into me and I pulled her close, I released a sigh as tears burned behind my eyes. It wasn't easy to force her to relive it, to bring the nightmares into the waking world. But this is how Penny needed to cope after a night terror episode, and if this is what she had asked me to do and what she needed, then I would deal with any level of discomfort to help her.

Penny touched a hand to her chest. I imagined every muscle in her core ached from the violence of the sobs that had wracked through her body. Lynn released a slow breath, and I tilted my head toward the glass of water on the bedside table. Lynn handed it to Penny, who took a few tentative sips.

She'd gone almost a year without one of her episodes, and while they were getting further apart, I doubted they would ever fully disappear. You didn't go through something like that and simply forget it one day.

Although sometimes I wished she could, seeing her in such pain cut me to my core.

Lynn helped Penny back into bed, and she leaned back, the blankets pulled up around her chest, and her head tilted against the wall.

Penny took Lynn's hand. "I'm sorry I scared you."

Lynn huffed out a humorless laugh. "Please don't apologize. I'm sorry you were so scared." She turned to me briefly. "And I'm sorry, I didn't know what to do."

Penny slowly shook her head and sank against the pillows. The exhaustion would take over soon, and she would sleep again. Hopefully, a dreamless sleep, where terrors, real or fictional, didn't plague her. Lynn stroked Penny's hair until she fell asleep. I thought she had forgotten I was in the room until she whispered something and then my name.

I straightened. "Pardon?"

Lynn turned to me as tears slid down her cheeks. "Thank you."

I nodded stiffly and left Penny's room. Once in the lounge, I closed my eyes and tilted my head back, my fists clenched at my sides as I tried to steady myself with a few deep breaths. Turning, when I felt a presence behind me, I found Lynn had followed me.

"Do I…" Her hand hovered over the light switch in the bedroom. "Do I turn off the light?"

I nodded. She looked so lost and probably blamed herself for not knowing how to deal with a situation she couldn't have possibly known how to handle. "Leave the living room light on, though, and the door open," I whispered, barely having the energy for anything else.

When I dropped myself on the couch, to my surprise, Lynn came and sat beside me, gracefully folding one leg over the other.

"I assume she told you about the kidnapping?" I asked.

Lynn nodded. "Not all the details, but enough for me to realize..." She glanced toward the bedroom. "I can't imagine what she went through."

It had been almost a decade, and still, the memories of that night were so vivid for Penny that she relived them in the nightmares that came back to haunt her. The afternoon following her ordeal, Penny had been found in the gutter with a broken rib, two broken toes, nineteen slash marks on her legs, and an additional eight on her feet. She was missing a tooth from being slapped across the face, had been hit in the stomach hard enough to cause internal bruising, and was strangled, as well as violated sexually. To the absolute bewilderment of law enforcement and herself, her kidnapper had dumped her back where he had found her after he'd grabbed her the night before when she was out clubbing and taken her out of the city.

But she'd survived.

Her parents had moved her to a different city, and while it had helped, it could never fully erase the memories of what she had endured.

Glancing at Lynn, she watched me, so much concern written on her face. I sighed, reached out, took her hand, and squeezed it briefly before pulling away again.

"Ana..." she started.

"It's okay. I know I'm not the easiest person to get to know. This isn't news to me. I only hope you don't dislike me so much that it affects your relationship with Penny."

Lynn tucked her hair behind her ear with perfectly manicured nails. When we first met, I'm sure her hair was a different color, but she'd had the bright red for so long now it was hard to imagine her without it, and it suited her. I could understand why Penny loved her. Not only was she beautiful, but she had a spunky attitude that conflicted with her well-kept image. I knew I'd only seen snippets of her because she wasn't her true self around me, and I only had myself to blame for that.

"I don't *dislike* you." She said, her voice small, as though this conversation made her as uncomfortable as it made me.

I released a small laugh. "It's okay, really."

"It's just..." Lynn searched for the words before she fixed me with a hard stare. "You say such weird things."

I laughed genuinely. "It's the movie quotes, right?"

Lynn's brow furrowed. "Yeah, and the odd comments... and you don't smile often."

My lip twitched. It was *almost* a smile. "It took Penny many months to get to know me. I'll try not to make it so difficult for you."

"Penny can be very persistent."

I smirked. "That she can." My smile dropped as I glanced into the bedroom. "Go back to bed and hold her tight. She shouldn't be alone right now."

Lynn nodded, and we stood and moved off to separate bedrooms.

"Ana?"

I turned. "Yeah?"

"I don't hate you, you know?"

"You love her, right?"

Lynn looked startled by my question, and her expression softened when she glanced in Penny's direction. "Yes, I do."

"Then that's all that matters to me. Goodnight, Lynn."

"Goodnight, Ana."

Leaning against the doorframe as Lynn retreated into Penny's room, I waited for a beat. I was about to move to my bed when I heard Lynn whisper, "Are you okay?"

Penny's voice was quiet, "I am now you're here."

My heart cracked again, but this time with happiness that they had found each other.

Chapter Seventeen

Ana

Returning to my usual attire of jeans and a t-shirt for the second attempt date with Nathaniel, I once again awarded myself points for *trying* when I added a summer jacket. Nathaniel watched me with interest and something else that twinkled in his eye as I pushed open the main doors to the apartment building. He'd offered to meet me out front, despite my offer to meet somewhere closer to wherever he lived. But he insisted it was no big issue, and his arm twitched before we started walking as though he was going to attempt another awkward half-hug, half-handshake, but thought the better of it.

"Where are we going?" I asked as we turned another corner.

"I thought we'd do an actual proper normal-people dinner date."

"Oh, I do like pretending to be a normal person."

He smiled. "Me too."

Nathaniel draped his arm loosely around my waist, and I waited for that spark again when his fingers grazed the skin on my arm. But it didn't happen. He was pleasantly warm, though, as if his entire body radiated heat even in the warm evening air.

I tried not to think about it too much—the last thing I wanted was another one-night stand straight away.

I allowed him to guide me around the streets, and Nathaniel tightened his fingers on my waist when he wanted me to turn a corner. We walked in relative silence, but it wasn't uncomfortable. We enjoyed the breath of spring air as the evening settled, and the concrete of the buildings and footpaths radiated back all the heat they had absorbed through the day, as though their job was to protect the city's inhabitants from the chill of the night for a little bit longer.

"So, what's this normal-people place we're going?"

Nathaniel gave me the name of the restaurant, and I frowned. Twisting slightly in his hold, I scanned the streets behind us before I looked back at him. "It would've been quicker to turn right two streets back."

"I know." His expression turned stony. "I'm sorry, but I'm trying to avoid walking past where my ex works."

A flutter of understanding moved through me. I could get that. Nodding, I said, "I understand. I don't mind the walk."

He squeezed me slightly against his side and let a grin slip past before he looked ahead, and we fell again into comfortable silence. There were questions I wanted to ask him, but they could wait until we got to the restaurant. It wasn't that I got the sense he didn't want to talk, but simply that he was enjoying this walk with me, and the silence between us, as though we were both taking the chance to feel each other out without words. Something about it felt so pure—two almost strangers enjoying each other's company on a level other than verbal. This sort of connection broke when you talked too much, and maybe the illusion of who we thought each other were would be broken, too. But right now, that didn't matter.

The night air took on an unseasonable chill, almost like when we had turned the last corner, we'd been doused in ice. I wrapped my arms around myself and pulled my light jacket closer to my body for whatever good it did.

Was it a trick of my eyes, or was it darker here?

Blinking a few times, I tried to clear my vision, but it didn't work.

What the hell is going on?

Glancing up and down the footpath, the streetlights were on, but they felt less effective, as though the light they emitted was being dulled or numbed somehow. The light around the lamps seemed to stop a foot from them, a glowing ball around the globe that did almost nothing to illuminate the area around it.

I must be going crazy.

Squinting into the night, my skin started to tingle. A thousand tiny pinpricks moved across my body in waves. The tips of my fingers were alight with sensations, and the same feeling lingered on the back of my neck and down my spine, making my skin crawl with discomfort. I glanced at Nathaniel, and a shudder ran down his spine as he, too, looked around the street.

Then I saw it.

Frowning, I focused ahead as an old warehouse fully entered my sight. We were in an industrial area near the city's outskirts, on the back way to the restaurant district. The warehouse was six stories high, and over half the windows were smashed. It was a dark space, empty and eerie, and it promised horror stories to those who looked too closely.

But in front of the warehouse...

I'd never seen anything like it before.

A forty-foot wall. It appeared as though it was constructed from glass, but...

The wall seemed to create light, a glow that penetrated the unnatural darkness in a way the streetlamps couldn't. I couldn't draw my eyes away from it and slowed in my steps. It shimmered and shifted, a hypnotizing back-and-forth movement as though it was affected by a thousand individual breezes. As we approached, Nathaniel gripped my waist, and we stopped across the street and stared at the apparition. Looking at Nathaniel's face, I'm unsure why, but I hoped he would hold some answers, but he stared as if it entranced him as much as it did me.

"What is it?" I whispered.

He shook his head in response. "I don't know."

Cautiously, I slipped out of Nathaniel's hold and crossed the street toward the wall. His arm lingered around me, hesitant to let go, before he dropped his hand and followed a few paces behind me. As I drew closer, the gap between us became greater until Nathaniel stopped clear of the anomaly while I continued to move ahead. He may have hissed out my name, but I couldn't be sure.

I was drawn to this wall. Something about it beckoned me.

Reaching it, I inspected it and let my gaze trail up and down over the thing. Standing within a foot of the base, I almost couldn't see the top as it towered above my head. There was nothing to keep it suspended, no supports, simply the sheer force of the wall itself. Upon closer inspection, I could see it *wasn't* glass, but what it was made of, I couldn't say.

It looked like it was made of light itself.

Almost completely transparent, it was covered in large cracks and fissures like a broken mirror, and the cracks glowed a soft orange. Squinting, I studied between the cracks—a thin, inky substance leaked through, an impenetrable black, darker than the night sky above me. The fine ink streams turned into vapor and vanished into the air around the wall, but still more came.

Subconsciously, I breathed in deeply, and abruptly, it felt like I couldn't get enough air. Some of the vapor rushed toward my parted lips as if driven by an invisible sentience, and I batted it away and waved my hand in front of my face too late. When the substance hit my lungs, I wanted to cough and drew in a sharp breath to expel it from my body.

Something in my mind was telling me I *needed* to cough.

Get it out.

But I didn't.

The fire started in my lungs, not unpleasant, but a raw power created within me, pushing its way out to my limbs. An energy built and moved to the pit of my stomach, to my heart, and spread out over my entire body. The tingling on my skin resumed, stronger this time, as though my skin rolled across my body in tiny, invisible waves.

Incredible.

"Ana, what's happening?" Nathaniel yelled, not coming any closer himself.

But I couldn't move. My eyes were wide as I looked up, completely enthralled at the sheer scale of the wall. It looked so thin, so fragile, and I could see the building behind it through the glassy areas between the bright cracks. I was light and free, yet completely unable to move away from it, my body frozen.

I don't want to move away.

I took another deep breath because I had to. I *had* to breathe it in deeply again. I *needed* it.

I closed my eyes, and the world around me seemed to disappear. The intake of my breath magnified to be the only sound I could hear—an ever-increasing echo that I'm certain the entire city could hear.

The wall was so thin—almost as if I could reach and put my hand right through it.

I raised my hand toward it.

"Ana! *No.*"

I spun around to the shadow that raced toward me through the darkness. His face wasn't visible until he came within the light the wall gave off.

"Kyle? What are you doing here?" I asked and lowered my hand, but I didn't move away from the shimmering wall. I put myself between Kyle and it, trying to protect him from it.

Or *it* from *him*.

Kyle seemed unable to tear his eyes from the wall, wide and fearful, and stared at it as though he expected it to come to life and swallow me whole.

"Ana..." Kye held his hand out toward me while keeping his distance. "Please step away from there."

"Why? What is it?" I asked, and I found it hard to reflect his concern in my voice. Nor the willpower to care *why* he was so concerned.

"Ana, I need you to listen to me—"

The fire in my chest spiked. "Why *exactly* would I listen to you, Kyle?" My tone was laced with sarcasm and zero guilt.

I was righteous in my anger toward him.

"Ana, please," he pleaded, his voice heavy with desperation.

He kept saying my name, and every time he did it, my lip would twitch. "We need to leave."

"*We?*" Laughing, I strode toward Nathaniel and stopped at his side only when our arms brushed against each other. Kyle's relief at my stepping away from the wall seemed short-lived when I determinedly planted myself next to Nathaniel before adding, "I'm with Nathaniel now."

Something sparked in me, and I turned and threw myself at Nathaniel.

Nathaniel's back straightened as I wrapped my arms around his neck and kissed him with a passion that built from within me. We'd barely touched before this, but when my tongue found his, his shock wore off, and he wrapped his arms around me, held me, and lifted my feet from the ground.

Pulling away, I sucked in a deep breath and held his eye contact, smiling with wicked intent. He returned the look as he lowered me to the ground. After a beat, I looked back at Kyle. He was watching me, but his eyes weren't angry or jealous.

They held fear.

Kyle stepped toward me and glanced uncertainly at Nathaniel, who responded only with an arched eyebrow.

"Are you okay?" Kyle asked.

"Never felt better."

He leaned forward with a deep furrow etched into his brow and studied my face.

With a stumble, he recoiled from me, his eyes wide with fear. I cocked my head at his reaction, and I noticed he continuously glanced at the wall as if he were afraid to get near it. I couldn't help the smirk that flitted across my face as I approached Kyle and walked with an unnatural swagger that I found both empowering and amusing. Stopping barely an inch from him, I pushed myself to my toes, tilted my head, and seductively pursed my lips before I blew cool air in his face.

Kyle held his breath and frowned when I laughed.

"What's the matter, Kyle?" I spoke slowly.

What's happened to my voice? It barely sounds like my own.

Kyle's fingers twitched by his sides as though he was actively trying not to shove me away from him. He had wanted to take my hand and run away with me only minutes ago, but now he looked horrified at my proximity. Laughing again, I sauntered back to Nathaniel. "Come on, Nathaniel," I said and took his hand in mine. "Let's go find something fun to do."

Nathaniel cast a glance at the wall and then back at me. I shrugged and led him away without a backward glance at Kyle.

"Ready for dinner?" Nathaniel asked as we walked. Although I practically dragged him down the street, his arm stretched out in front of him as I walked briskly ahead, clutching his hand, and tugged at him whenever I was forced to slow my gait. It was almost cute. He was so much taller than I, and I suspected stronger, and yet he complied everywhere I dragged him.

Spinning around, I fell against him, and his hands immediately found my waist. "I'm not hungry. We could find someplace fun."

"Fun?" He arched a brow at me.

With a shove, I backed him against the wall of a nearby shopfront and pressed my body against his. As I stood on my toes, he glanced down at where my breasts brushed his chest, his lips curving into the first genuine smile I had seen from him all evening.

It was clear where his thoughts were.

But I had other things in mind.

His hands caressed my waist again as I walked my fingers up his chest and leaned into him, my face close to his cheek.

I huffed out a quiet chuckle, then simply whispered, "Fun."

The corner of his mouth twitched. "Are you feeling okay?"

"I'm great. Brand new!"

Holding my shoulders, he looked into my eyes and studied my face intently.

I'm not sure what he expected to find.

He had lovely eyes, so blue.

"Do you know what that thing was?" he asked as he watched me carefully.

I waved my hand dismissively. "I don't know, and I don't care. All I know is that I feel like a new person and want to have some fun." I pressed my palms against his chest and pushed him against the window again. "Is that okay with you?" I crooned and practically batted my eyelashes at him. I had no interest in talking anymore.

Finally, he dropped his hands from my waist and smiled slowly at the way I rocked my hips against him. "I think I like this new Ana."

I smiled wickedly and snatched his hand before we headed down a side street.

Nathaniel followed me down a flight of dodgy-looking stairs and glanced uninterested at the large bouncer as he attempted to be intimidating. The bouncer asked for my identification, and I groaned loudly. From the look on Nathaniel's face, I think he thought I was about to make a scene. It was tempting, but I needed to dance. After flashing my identification, I leaned into the heavy door and shoved it open. The air inside the club was thick with sweat and smoke, and the music was loud and predominantly bass, one song indistinguishable from the next.

Sashaying toward the bar, Nathaniel followed close behind, so close I could feel him brush against me with every other step. I still had a vice-like grip on his hand, but he seemed happy to follow my lead and let the night unfold. Ordering two rounds of successive shots, I slammed some money on the bar before I threw back the vodka shots, one after the other.

Nathaniel barely managed to down his shots before I dragged him onto the dance floor, and he obliged, as if he had a choice. Immediately I turned my back to him and began grinding my ass against his groin. One of my hands twisted through his hair before I closed my eyes and reached into the air with my other hand. My head tilted back against Nathaniel's chest, and my entire body moved with the bass.

Moving with me, Nathaniel placed his hands on my waist, ran his fingers down and around my stomach, lifted my top, and brushed my skin. I pressed back into him as sparks of energy passed between us. His skin was hot as he tucked his fingers just under the waistband of my jeans and caressed my hips. Dropping a hand behind his head, I grabbed a fistful of his thick hair and yanked his face against my neck. He kissed me gently before his teeth grazed like he would rather bite.

I was moving in such a way that drew people's attention, and they were starting to stare.

"People are watching," he whispered in my ear.

"I don't care."

I kept moving as though my life depended on the dance and the music that thumped its way through my body and this dank club. All I wanted was this feeling. I needed the movement and music that pulsed through my veins to last forever. My gaze swept the club, and when my eyes came to rest on a man standing near the corner, I stared at him. There was something about him, something coming off him in waves that I couldn't see so much as feel. While he leaned against the wall as though he didn't have a care in the world, he feared judgment, the judgment of his friends and the other dancers in the club. I could *feel* his fear. He met my gaze and stared at me with disinterest until his eyes raked my body, and something about my movement, coupled with the way I stared into his soul, made his eyes widen, and the fear that ebbed from him pulsated the air between us.

His fear *moved* the air.

I saw it.

I can see it.

"What are you looking at?" Nathaniel muttered.

"That man, I can feel him," I said, aware my voice was breathy and heavy as I practically panted.

"Feel him?"

"I can *feel him.*" I drew the sentence out around my tongue and finished with a tug on my lower lip with my teeth.

Whipping around, I turned to face Nathaniel. "I think we need more shots."

He nodded, not taking his eyes from my face, halfway between a frown and a smile. "Stay here, I'll get them."

Nathaniel moved away and slid through the crowd toward

the bar. The second he was no longer touching me, the space around me cleared, and the cloud of fear I could sense from that man expanded. Closing my eyes, I forced the music from my mind and focused on the feeling I picked up from the air.

I could expand my senses.

Beyond the man in the corner, the dancefloor, and the club entirely.

If I could get outside, maybe I could feel the whole city.

Nathaniel forgotten, I shoved my way through the crowd to the door, burst into the fresh night air, and sucked in a deep intake of breath.

That sense was stronger out here, and it consumed me, surrounded my mind and body, and permeated my blood.

I wanted *more.*

Chapter Eighteen

Kyle

She had been infected.

When Ana approached me, walking as though she owned the world and leaning in close, the darkness crossed over her eyes, and I couldn't stop myself as I recoiled on instinct.

I felt the Gateway to Tenebris the moment it opened. There was no doubt that the Rogue Tenebrian had done it intentionally, but it was risky to create something so large and uncontrollable, even given what else he had done. What was its purpose? Was he playing games with me? He would have known I'd have sensed the Gateway's presence the moment it forced its way through the thin wall that separated the realms.

The Gateway would have only served to increase the negative influence in this area, leaking out onto Earth and infecting anyone who came into contact with it. More than a Tenebrian could do through influence alone. A Gateway left open like that, to that scale...

The problem was that I'd never encountered something like this before, nor had I ever heard of a Gateway being used that way.

What sort of influence could push into humans when it seeped through from Tenebris directly?

Ana had been infected with it.

The essence of Tenebris penetrated her very being and became absorbed into her, molding with her. This was beyond influence. This was what energized Guardians. At the least, she would be unpredictable and volatile for who knows how long. At the worst...

No. It wouldn't kill her.

It was the hardest decision I had to make to let her walk away with Nathaniel. Closing the Gateway was a higher priority, and it pulled at my chest to let her go and choose to follow my duty over my heart. I stared at the Gateway with hopelessness in my chest for a moment before I steeled myself and raised my hands to begin closing the Gateway.

It took several long minutes, considering a Gateway could usually be closed in seconds.

My hands dropped to my sides, and I sighed heavily. I was feeling... *things,* and I pushed them deep down so I could focus. The fog in the area had only increased since the Gateway had been opened, and tracking Ana's emotional imprint would be impossible.

I had no choice but to wait for the air to clear.

On my way back to my apartment, I broke up three fights and talked someone out of robbing a liquor store.

Humans were falling victim to the influence of the essence of Tenebris, and putting out small proverbial fires wasn't giving me the satisfaction I thought it would. I was helping, but it didn't feel like enough.

I couldn't find Ana.

Back in my apartment, my crossbow sat at my feet—a recent acquisition when I'd realized I needed to step up my game. If I couldn't get close enough to the Tenebrian, I could take him out from a distance. My hands were busied with carving tools as I adjusted the arrowheads to my needs.

But I couldn't stop my hands from shaking.

Ana had terrified me tonight.

I *had* searched for her after she disappeared. But the city was big, and I had no chance—not with my senses clouded and the air so polluted. I couldn't separate any emotional imprints at all. As I worked, I stopped every few minutes to send my senses outward and try to penetrate the fog caused by the Gateway.

Still too much interference.

Ana didn't want to come with me, I understood that. I had hurt her.

At least she hadn't tried to touch the Gateway.

But something was still wrong. Her behavior was erratic, exaggerated, and dark, and when she stared at me and I saw the shadow of the vapor cross over her eyes, turning them an inky black for a fraction of a second, my stomach dropped.

When she came too close, it was like a thousand insects crawling across my skin, and I ached to be away from her. At that moment, she felt like a Tenebrian, the mere proximity causing my body to react, two opposites too close together. The urge to shove her away from me brought a pang to my chest. But she *felt* like illness, like darkness and hate. She was sexual energy, anger, and violence. She was everything Tenebris embodied, forced into her pure being, and taken over.

How long would it take to leave her body?

Humans weren't meant to be that close to Gateways, and

Gateways were never intended to be that large or left open and unattended.

It was risky and uncontrollable, but if he hoped it would infect a human or several humans, a place too public, and it would act too quickly and draw attention. The effects were magnified, and people would begin to influence people, passing it between them in an energy chain. But hidden in the industrial area, stray groups of humans may come across it. The spread would be slow and intentional.

But why did it have to be her?

The Gateway would have quickly become unstable, and after closing it, the exertion brought me to my knees.

Another reminder I didn't need. *He was stronger than I.*

But I can do this.

The Tenebrian was sending me a message. He was playing games with me to taunt me, show off his strength and power, and increase the fog that hung over this part of the city so he could continue his sick games unabated.

It frightened me that I didn't know how long the infection would stay in Ana's system. Hopefully, it will not be long because during that time, she'd be a loose cannon controlled by the worst aspects of humanity as they leaked into her system and guided her. Part of me wanted to go to her apartment and wait for her, but when I passed the building, I felt her roommate's presence there. Her imprint was tense, and I didn't want to scare her by hanging around outside.

Sighing in frustration, my hands paused. I was constantly trying to balance what *needed* to be done, and not causing undue harm or upset to any humans, and it was becoming increasingly difficult.

I still had my plan to force the Tenebrian to reveal himself to me, but I also needed moonlight, so without a clear night, that plan was also on hold.

I felt weak, useless, and ultimately responsible.

And unable to get Ana from my mind.

Staring intently at my work, I forced my concentration back into line and continued carving, creating crossed divots deep in the arrowhead. Applying a small amount of superglue, I fused carved pieces of moonstone collected from a local street jeweler into each of the cuts and finished off by sanding them down. Holding the arrowhead up to the light, I admired the smooth finish.

Not bad. It would penetrate the skin, even Guardian skin. Nodding to myself, I moved on to the next one. I needed to be additionally prepared with another way to force my enemy back to where he came from.

Once I found him.

Or he found me.

Chapter Nineteen

Ana

While in the small, dark club, I felt my pupils dilate as they absorbed what little light there was, and magnified it until I could see the people. More clearly than I'd ever seen them before. There was a color about them, a light, bright color for positive emotions, darker shades for negative. Most people were dark colors, and they weaved and ebbed around them, pulsated, and sent vibes through the air to be absorbed by my skin. I felt the fear of the other dancers on the dancefloor. They feared the judgment of their peers and the strangers that surrounded them. Some people felt unsafe in the club and put on a front to hide it. But the fear seeped through their skin all the same.

When I focused on the feeling of discomfort from the man in the corner, I almost peaked with pleasure at the sensation. The alcohol passed through my veins and blended with the senses I seemed to absorb.

I felt his fear.

I *loved* the feeling.

I needed *more.*

As I stepped out onto the street, a rush filled my head, and

I closed my eyes for a moment and stopped moving. Every sound and physical sensation was drowned out by the feelings absorbed into my body. It was as though the air was swimming with emotions from people around me and people who *had* been here. I could pick up on them all, and they were drawn to me.

How was this happening?

I didn't care to question it much. It felt too good.

Tilting my head, I leaned forward as if picking up a scent.

A sharp inhale brought the tang into my nose.

It was a strong essence of *fear*.

Somewhere close, someone was in trouble.

I stumbled slightly at the top of the stairs in my rush to seek this new feeling. It was sharper than the others, and once I was free from the shackles of the nightclub, it practically stabbed into my heart insistently and demanded I find it. I followed the invisible trail, a game of hot and cold. I turned corners randomly and turned back on myself when the sense weakened. Stopping at a corner when it was so strong it threatened to engulf me, I breathed in deeply and let the sense flutter and settle in my lungs. It felt like a drug.

More.

Peeking around the corner, two men were in a tussle, which ended abruptly when one pulled a knife on the other and held it against his abdomen.

"I told you, man, just give me the money and I won't hurt you."

The second man was bleeding from his mouth and had a black eye. He coughed and sprayed his chin and shirt with speckles of blood. Reaching into his pocket, he scrambled for his wallet before he held it up to his attacker with a shaking hand.

"See? That wasn't so hard, was it?" the mugger mocked. He pocketed the wallet and held the knife to the man's throat.

The victim's fear spiked.

"Yes," I hissed through my teeth as I came around the corner.

Both men turned. "Who the fuck are you?" the mugger asked. "Get out of here, girly."

Now I was close to the source of the fear, it prickled pleasantly beneath my skin, and I approached the men with a skip in my step. I didn't stop until I was right next to them and breathed in the victim's fear, my face close to his neck and my body pressed against his arm.

I licked my lips. "Keep going."

"What?"

Biting my bottom lip, my head rolled lazily as I turned to the mugger. Cheek-to-cheek with the victim, my eyes flitted to the knife the mugger held against his throat. Reaching toward the blade, I withdrew my finger a whisper before I touched the sharp edge.

"I said..." I breathed out harshly, "... keep going."

A jump of anger in the air from the mugger added to the fear from the man against the wall. Turning toward him, I smiled wickedly. All his negative energy was being dragged into my body. I was taking almost no active role in this, allowing my body to be a beacon to sensations I'd never felt before. I drew the worst of this world into me.

I knew it was the worst of humanity when it left them, but it felt *so good* when it hit my body.

As I licked his cheek, he screwed up his face in disgust. "I can taste your fear." I pressed right up against him, and my breasts rubbed against his arm as I moved, desperate for more of the feeling. "I can make it stronger."

"Get the fuck out of here, you crazy bitch!"

Snatching the mugger's wrist when he yelled at me, the other man didn't hesitate to take the opportunity to flee and ran down the street and out of sight. I hissed at the mugger when I noticed the victim was gone, and his cloud of fear faded from the area as he disappeared into the night, and the mugger and I struggled. My newfound strength wavered quickly, and he pulled his wrist out of my grip. When he looked at me, I felt something move across my eyes and features, and he recoiled.

"What the fuck?" In his panic, he slashed at me with the knife, cutting a thin, straight line just above my left collarbone. I jerked backward with the sharp pain, and a sound that could only be described as a purr rumbled through my chest and throat. The mugger looked at me with a mixture of horror and anger before he, too, fled the scene and didn't look back.

Sighing in frustration as the air cleared of both fear and anger, I walked into the night in search of my next high.

Just under two hours passed before I found what I truly craved. I had kept walking and needed the next rush to be bigger than the last. Minor squabbles and disagreements wouldn't do, and I walked on by as I encountered small pockets of fear in the air, because I desired deep, penetrating fear. The kind that people felt to their core.

Maybe the kind they felt when they thought they were about to die.

Then I found it.

My feet registered no aches from the prolonged walk in my boots, and the cut on my collarbone had stopped bleeding, but only after my top and jacket had become stained a dark red around the wound. I'd made no attempt to clean the cut or cover it.

It was of no concern to me.

All I was focused on was the fear radiating from someone close, someone I'd find very soon.

My breathing became ragged as I stopped outside the small townhouse, and the air around the front door practically throbbed with fear. Leaning toward the house, the top of the short picket fence pressed hard into my thighs, and the sensation only amplified the intensity of the senses.

Muffled by the thick brick walls were screams and crying.

Pushing open the gate, I walked up the cobblestone pathway toward the front door and stopped only to pick up a loose rock and hold it in my closed fist. The street was quiet, and the nearest streetlamp was too far to illuminate my face as I knocked on the door and slid my fist behind my back. I'd learned from my previous engagement that I was too weak to take someone by sheer force, so I had to rely on surprise. The sounds inside halted at my knock, and after a moment, the front door rattled as though someone had been shoved into it and slammed their palms against the wood to stop their head from colliding with it.

The door opened barely a crack, and a woman's face appeared, half-hidden by the door. She made eye contact with me, and her eyes pleaded while her expression spoke of resignation. “Can I help you?” she asked timidly, barely louder than a whisper.

“Be a good wife and tell me who it is,” a man bellowed somewhere behind her.

The woman was afraid. I could feel it as I took a long, steady breath and let the fear rush toward me and invigorate me. Stepping right up to the crack in the door, I held out my hand. “Come,” I whispered so quietly that the sound barely traveled beyond my lips.

My words were for the woman and her alone.

She could fuel me.

She looked from my hand to my face, her eyes still wide with fear. Without breaking eye contact, she stared as though transfixed by something she could see in my expression, and slowly, she lifted her hand and took mine.

Clasping my fingers around her hand, I pulled the woman toward me, but the door swung open before she had taken a step. The man paused, taking in me and my bloody shoulder, and then his eyes trailed down to my hand, holding his wife’s tight.

“Who the fuck are you?” he yelled. He was only average height, but solid. The arms that stuck out of his tank were thick like tree trunks, and his pale skin was dotted with a thousand freckles. I felt a sudden hatred for him, fueled by more than the unfamiliar darkness and powers inside me.

Letting go of the woman’s hand, I screamed like a wild animal before I leaped at him. The woman shrieked as I hit her husband over the head with the rock in my hand, and he stumbled before he fell heavily to the floor. I fell with him and landed on him with my legs straddling his large body. Turning to look at the woman, I bared my teeth with a hiss I couldn't contain. The man beneath me breathed steadily, and there was very little blood.

He would be fine, but be out long enough for me to take his wife.

Standing, I grabbed the woman's hand again and strode toward the front door.

But this time, I was met with resistance.

"*No.* Leave me alone." She pulled hard against my grip, and I slid slightly across the wooden floor before grounding myself, bending my knees, and yanking the woman back toward me.

She was afraid of me because of my frenzied attack on her husband.

Grabbing the woman by her shoulders, I backed her against the wall. Leaning in close and breathing in her fear, my nose and lips were only inches from the sweat on the woman's neck as she arched and tried to get away.

"Please leave," the woman said shakily.

"Why? He was only hurting you, anyway," I whispered, and the resulting tremble from the woman sent a shiver down my spine.

Ecstasy.

"I don't know you, please... just leave." She whimpered and glanced down at her unconscious husband. I felt the hope for his recovery radiate from the woman, and rage overtook me.

This woman was weak. She was pathetic.

A darkness filled my vision until I could only see the fear she radiated.

"You're a beacon of fear," I hissed. "You could leave him, but you don't."

"It's not that simple." The woman was getting angry, and I was glad to see some fight in her. "You know nothing about me. Get out of my house!"

Gritting my teeth, I increased my grip on her shoulders. "All I need to know is the fear you can give me."

The woman stared in horror as I clenched my fist and raised it to my shoulder. She screwed her eyes shut as I brought my hand down and landed a blow against her stomach. She didn't fall, but her fear spiked, as did my pleasure. The woman squeezed her eyes shut and prepared for the next blow.

At that moment, I didn't see her face. I only saw a blur of all the anger I had kept inside.

"Why do you stay with him?" I asked, "He's never around. He obviously doesn't care for us."

"Wha—"

"You tell me off for speaking badly of him, but you wait and wait for him to return whenever he disappears. I don't understand, Mom!"

"I'm not—"

"And then *you* left me, too! Everyone I love leaves me."

The woman grunted as she was hit again. *Was it by me?* I couldn't even tell. I was a vessel for my anger and everything negative that swirled in my veins. I was a body only, simply there to transport all my unanswered questions and pain.

But every spike in her pain eased mine.

More.

CHAPTER TWENTY

ANA

OH GOD. MY FUCKING head.

Everything else was secondary to the pounding in my skull.

Slowly, I woke, uncertain for several minutes, or maybe it was hours, whether I was truly awake or not. Drifting off for a moment only to wake again, over and over, until eventually I could flutter my eyes open.

It was dark here, wherever *here* was.

Taking a long, shuddering breath, I pressed my nose against the cotton bedsheets.

It smelled like my shampoo.

I must be home.

How had I gotten home?

No idea.

Clutching my head, I squeezed my eyes shut. When I tried to focus, I couldn't remember much from the night before. Long before the *how did I get home* conundrum was the *what the fuck did I do last night* question.

How much did I drink?

Groggily, I reached for my cell and paused to stare at my

hands. My fingernails were caked in dirt, and… I started, and my eyes widened—*is that blood*?

Was it *mine?*

I'd come back to that later. Squeezing my eyes shut for a moment, I refocused on my cell. There were several missed calls and text messages, and the little yellow light on my phone flashed as the battery clung to life. Groaning again, I plugged it into the charger before I flicked my thumb over the screen and dialed Nathaniel's number.

He answered on the third ring. "Ana?"

"Nathaniel, hi. Umm… sorry I missed your… calls."

There was silence on the other end of the line.

I continued, "I, ah… don't remember much. Sorry. I don't usually drink that much. Can you tell me what happened?"

"Not really, you disappeared. I have no idea where you've been."

"But our date?"

"Started good, then weird… then we went clubbing, and you disappeared."

"Did we kiss?" I thought I remembered a kiss.

"Yeah." His voice flickered with pride before it edged back into anger as he grunted.

I cringed. "Are you mad?" I asked.

"Yes, Ana, I am." I bit my bottom lip against the rise of excuses I could throw out and remained quiet as he continued, "You said you wanted to have fun, then you just *left.* I thought you wanted to have fun *with me*, but I couldn't find you. I *searched* for you. I called. Where the hell were you?"

I thought I couldn't cringe any harder and closed my eyes again as I searched for the right thing to say. Was there even a right thing to say?

My thoughts were broken as Nathaniel sighed heavily. "Look, if you want, we can go out again."

"Umm..." I said, and swore I could hear as he grew angry again on the other end of the line. "I'm really not well. Just let me rest up, and then we'll sort something out. Okay?"

"Okay." He didn't sound convinced, and his voice had taken on a rough edge. "Do you remember seeing anything strange last night?"

"Strange like what?"

"Just strange... different. Something really weird..."

"No." I paused. *What was he getting at?* "Why? What happened?"

"Nothing, never mind. Glad you're alive." The phrase took on additional scorn with the harshness of his tone. Granted, I hadn't known the guy for long, but I'd never heard him talk like that.

I ignored the tone, saying, "Thanks, and sorry again." Before I hung up, dropped my cell, and rolled over as it landed with an audible clatter on the wooden floor and slid under the bed as far as the charging cord would allow. I wasn't in the mood for any games of his right now. As I rubbed my face, there was a knock on the door.

"Ana?" Penny's voice was quiet and tentative.

"Come in."

She cautiously peeked her face around the half-open door. "How are you feeling?"

"What time is it?"

"Six."

"In the morning?"

"No, you slept all day. It's six in the evening."

"Oh *shit!*" Sitting bolt upright, I immediately regretted it when a particularly vicious throb worked its way through my skull. "I'm supposed to be at work."

Penny held up her hands but didn't come any closer. "I checked your roster and called in sick for you."

"Didn't you have plans tonight?"

"I canceled them." Penny watched me with concern from the other side of the room as I rubbed my eyes again. She opened and closed her mouth a few times before finally asking, "Do you remember coming home?"

"No."

"Do you remember what happened?"

Wearily, I raised my gaze to Penny. "No."

"You were acting so weird, Ana. I mean, I was afraid of you, *for you*. What did you take?" Penny wrung her hands together as though she were conversing with a troubled teenager. "If you took something, you can tell me. I won't judge, and I might be able to help." When I didn't respond, she continued, "You came home bleeding and dirty and mumbling to yourself. You crashed on your bed, and I didn't want to disturb you. To be honest, I was a bit scared to go near you because when you walked in, it was like you didn't even see me. You stared straight through me with this haunted look..."

I was about to tell Penny I didn't take any drugs when the cramps hit—sudden and heavy like I had ingested poison, and it was eating my stomach from the inside. Dry-heaving, I clutched my stomach and curled over onto my side. My body was desperate to get rid of something. I just didn't know what it was. *Did I take something?* It seemed unlikely. I'd never taken drugs before, nor had any inclination to. Penny acted immediately, grabbed the small bin from next to my bedside table, and emptied the contents onto the floor before she held it under my face as I continued to retch.

By the time the pain subsided, I was panting and clammy, but mercifully, I hadn't been sick. Still, I was thankful for Penny's quick thinking, as I wasn't in the mood to clean vomit from the floor.

I was thankful, in general, to have her nearby.

As I calmed and my body gave me every sign it wouldn't be sick, Penny gently put the bin on the floor and retreated again. Clearing my throat, I grabbed a half-empty bottle of tepid water from the bedside table and took a few tentative sips.

"I'm sorry, Penny," I croaked out, and cleared my throat again.

Penny shook her head. "You don't have to apologize."

"I do. I'm sorry for scaring you last night. I don't remember much at all. Nathaniel is pissed at me. He said I disappeared."

Rubbing my neck, I hissed through my teeth when a sharp pain shot across my collarbone. Sitting up, my hand came away covered in flecks of dry blood. Standing, I paused to rub my temples and turn on the light before I looked in the mirror and examined the wound on my collarbone. I tried to keep my expression impassive as I poked around the cut.

What the fuck happened?

Penny peered at my reflection over my shoulder. "That's a knife wound."

Touching the cut, I jerked my hand away when it stung. "I'm struggling to remember what the hell happened."

Penny stared at me. She looked afraid at my inability to

remember, as though she, too, was wondering what secrets were held in the blank spaces in my memory. “Maybe it’s best if you don’t try too hard. Just rest up, and see what comes back to you.”

“I remember kissing Nathaniel and… something else… some weird feeling.” I rubbed my upper arms and shook my head. The broken memories didn’t make any sense. “I think I saw Kyle, too.”

“Kyle?”

“Yeah, I think I ran into him at some point. I’m not sure. He was mad at me, though.”

“Why would he be mad at you?”

Shrugging, I glanced down at my clothes, also covered in dirt and blood around the wound. “I’m going to have a shower.”

“Good idea.” Penny straightened. “I’ll make you something to eat. Maybe some plain toast is best.”

“Thanks, Penny, you’re amazing.”

Penny retreated from my bedroom, leaving me to my thoughts. But there wasn’t much going on in my mind, and I was too exhausted to think too hard about anything. Alcohol wasn’t unfamiliar to me. I probably drank more than I should, but I had a high tolerance, and it would take a lot to create vast gaps in my memory.

Had someone drugged me?

Surely Nathaniel wouldn’t do such a thing.

No. Something else had happened.

The problem was that I wasn’t entirely convinced I wanted to remember what.

RELA

Chapter Twenty-One

Kyle

Standing outside the large window of the bar, the ornate gold text on the glass partially obscured my view. I watched Ana work. Straining my senses, I could not pick up on anything unusual in or around her. She felt like Ana again, and I had the same soothing feeling of being near her as I had when we met.

After her ordeal, she looked okay.

Who was I kidding? She looked beautiful.

Even the small frown that creased her brow couldn't detract from that. She paused in her work and looked up as if feeling the intrusion of my senses around her. After a beat, she turned to face the window and saw me watching her. Moving toward the door, I figured I'd better go inside now she'd seen me rather than continuing to stare like a creep.

Her expression was neutral as I approached. "Hi," I said.

"Hi, can I get you anything?" Her tone was all business but not light or friendly.

I shook my head. "I just wanted to see if you were okay."

"I'm okay," she responded flatly.

Sitting at the bar, I watched her. Even this close, I couldn't feel any darkness in her or any hint of the residual power from the Tenebrian Gateway. But there was only one way I could know for sure. I'd have to touch her. Movement in the corner of my eye caught my attention, and I turned my head to find Ralph watching me. Ralph made significant eye contact with Ana, and she gave him the smallest of nods. He retreated but kept a weary eye on me.

Standing, I leaned across the bar. Ana didn't move away from me and held her ground as I captured her eye contact and ran my hand across her cheek. She stared me down for a moment and ignored my touch, either daring me to move or daring herself to stay. Her skin was warm against my palm, and there was none of the darkness I had felt from her the other night. Her eyes were clear.

Ana's eyes softened. "I don't remember the other night, but I think I saw you."

"You did," I whispered.

"I don't know what I did, but I'm sorry if I did anything..." she trailed off. She didn't need to apologize to me. She owed me nothing. But it seemed, despite the brief nature of our connection, she, too, had some lingering feelings for me. Ana's eyes betrayed her conflict, and with the smallest movement, she leaned her cheek into my touch. Guilt flared inside me, but I couldn't pull my hand away. I had the information I needed—she was clear of the influence of Tenebris.

Every moment I spent with her potentially dragged her further into danger.

But I wanted her.

I didn't want to hurt Ana, and I could see the pain in her eyes now. Pain and confusion. She didn't understand why I kept coming and going from her life. Why I said one thing, and did another. Wishing I could tell her, I clenched my jaw to stop the truth from escaping. She kept herself so closed off, avoiding people for this exact reason, I'm sure, and now I was torturing her with my presence.

But I couldn't stop myself.

My eyes flickered between her dilated pupils, and with every second that passed, I was closing the small gap between us. When our lips met, she relaxed further into my touch, and the feeling of her rushed into me through the contact of my hand on her cheek and her lips on mine. I took the opportunity to probe her complete essence and could find no trace of what had infected her.

As if I didn't already know that.

Her inner being was bright. It was pure Ana—the Ana I knew.

I shouldn't have kissed her. I didn't *need* to kiss her to know she was clear of the infection. But being this close, feeling her near me again, the warmth of her presence and her scent, I couldn't help it. Wishing I were stronger and that I hadn't allowed myself to give in to the temptation that was Ana's lips, I pulled slowly away from her. Ana kept her eyes closed for a moment after we broke contact, as if she were holding on to the feeling of me. Her lips were slightly parted, inviting me to kiss her again.

I clenched my jaw as she whispered, "Kyle." A breath of air traveled between us and beckoned me to her.

Overwhelming guilt fell heavily on my shoulders, as though gravity had increased tenfold then, and the sensation tried to crush me to the floor.

I still couldn't be with her. Nothing had changed. Once again, I had given her false hope.

I was a terrible being for what I had done.

How could I explain to her that I needed to be as close to her as possible to make sure?

Was that even the reason I kissed her?

When the vapor and influence of Tenebris completely took Ana, it permeated her skin and flashed through her eyes. But even as it dissipated, there was a chance it would lie dormant in her system. This use of a Gateway was new to me, and I needed to cover all bases. It was only when we touched that I could be sure that the darkness didn't still radiate from her and was completely gone from her system. But she was innocent, and I was drawing her deeper into this battle. It was painful to let her go, but I couldn't have her in harm's way.

You're lying to yourself.

I didn't *need* to kiss her. I kissed her only because I wanted to feel her again. Because I wanted to lie to myself for a moment longer. I lied to myself about what these feelings that stirred in my chest meant. I lied to myself about our chances of having *anything* together when I had a duty to uphold. It didn't matter that I relaxed with Ana the same way she had melted when I kissed her.

She watched me, and when I didn't speak, that small frown returned.

Beautiful.

Heartbreaking.

"Why did you kiss me?" She pulled away from my hand, and the cool air penetrated my senses the instant the warmth of her skin was gone from my palm.

"There are so many reasons." I went to take her hand that rested on the bar, and she slid it out from under mine slowly and purposefully. The pang in my chest increased.

"I don't want to play games, Kyle. Either you want to be around me, or you don't."

"I'm torn between wanting to be near you for selfish reasons and wanting to keep you safe."

She scoffed. "That's not an explanation. Safe from what? From you? Why did you come here?"

"To see if you were okay."

Her brows pulled together. "As I said, I'm okay."

"Ana—"

"I've got to get back to work."

While I couldn't blame her when she turned away, it still hurt—a sharp, twisting pain deep in my chest. I left the bar feeling worse than when I had gone in. What exactly had I been hoping for? That she'd need me to rescue her? Shaking my head, I headed down the street and away from Ana.

Kissing her had been a mistake, but my skin still tingled pleasantly from the sense of her.

I'd been on Earth too long. I'd never had emotions like this before, and I wasn't sure how to deal with them.

Or how to stop myself from hurting Ana further while I figured it out.

I held on to the sense of her and touched my fingers to my lips, because there had to be a last time, and this would have to be it.

OUTLET

Chapter Twenty-Two

Kyle

"I need blood."

"This isn't a blood bank, man."

Fidgeting, I'd been gearing myself up for this moment. I'd been forced into a corner until I had no choice, but it didn't make it any easier to face the task at hand.

"I'll pay," I said, "I won't take much. You'll barely notice it."

"What are you? Some kind of blood-drinking freak?"

Pulling a face, I eyed the man in front of me. I towered over him and tried to use my height to cover the discomfort that crept through my veins. I was average by Guardian standards, standing at slightly over six feet five, which made me perfect for blending in on Earth, and it was enough to be intimidating to some humans. Other Guardians who could stand up to seven feet tall had difficulty mixing into a crowd and, therefore, rarely set foot on Earth. We could change our skin and appearance to fit in with humans, not our height or build.

I'd gauged my targeted human and sought someone who kept to themselves. This young man dealt drugs but was otherwise quite healthy. Although his health made no difference to the effect the blood would have on the other Guardian, it was a difficult enough task without adding the weight of taking advantage of someone sick, weak, or who couldn't give consent to my conscience. I felt no negative energy around the man and no intention from him to cause harm to others. He was selling drugs on the side purely for some extra cash. I disapproved, but it wasn't my place.

Under it all, he was good.

I wasn't sure if that made this easier or harder.

Planning as much as I could, I was thoroughly unprepared for the internal battle I'd face at this moment. Technically, I was hurting a human and causing pain. But it was for the greater good. Did the end justify the means? Was this simply a consequence of my not being better at my role? Had I been able to track the Tenebrian earlier, I wouldn't be in this difficult position. The self-confidence that had pulsed through me when I first stepped through the Gateway to Earth had ebbed away and was challenged further with every second.

"Listen to me. This is for something very important." My voice was all business, as though I regularly paid people to let me take their blood. "What I do with it is none of your business."

"It is my fucking business. What if you use it to frame me for murder or some shit?"

That's a good point. I hadn't thought of that, and it didn't feel good not to be trusted. I was used to humans picking up on my energy, even if they didn't understand it, and being comfortable around me. I wanted to achieve this task with the human willing, so the harm caused would cause a lesser shift in the energies around us.

If I forced the man and made him fear me, I would undo the

work I had done so far. I needed to keep the energies positive, and therefore, he needed to be willing.

With only my voice and the energies I could project through it, I could make the man submit to me without using physical force, simply by suggesting he do it.

But that wouldn't work if he were *fully* opposed. I couldn't break free will. He needed to be hesitant but pliable in the matter.

Until this point in the conversation, I'd resisted using my powers, but I was wasting valuable time. Directing my energy inward, I projected it through my voice when I spoke, and the air shifted between us. "Let me take some of your blood."

The man shrugged. "All right, but it'll cost you."

"How much?"

"A thousand."

"Five hundred."

He shook his head. "Nah, man."

I repeated the offer and added influence to my voice.

"Okay, fine."

The act of our influence never ceased to surprise me. Humans never appeared under a trance or spell but would simply change their minds, as though that's what they were going to do anyway.

The dealer followed me around a corner, leaned against a closed shop front, and watched as I pulled out the sharpened moonstone. Holding my hand out, I waited for him to place his palm in mine. When I sliced into the fleshy part of his palm, he flinched but didn't protest. But his pain mingled within me with my guilt at having caused it, and my stomach churned. I'd never wanted to know what it felt like to hold a blade as it cut through human skin, and I never wanted to experience the emotional reaction to pain so close.

I reminded myself this was the only way, even as I realized the memory of these sensations would stay with me.

Blood drawn by moonstone on Guardian skin and lit by moonlight would force my enemy's skin to return to its natural form. It was a small window to simultaneously have all the elements in the right place. But I'd been spending more time at the hospital and was almost certain who I was looking for.

Once he was forced to change to his natural form, there could be no doubt, and I could send him back to Tenebris using the moonstone blade.

Then I could return to my home.

Ana.

Her name brushed through my mind, though she was never far from my thoughts.

Would I see her before I went? Would I even tell her I was leaving?

She was better off without me.

Blood dripped steadily from the wound on the man's hand and was enough to distract me from thoughts of Ana as I guided him to close his fist and squeeze as I held a small jar under the stream of blood. I handed him a wad of paper towels from my pocket, pressed them against the wound until it stopped bleeding, and then passed him the cash.

As I was screwing the jar lid on, my finger grazed some blood on the side. The man stared as the skin on my finger shifted to a vitreous blue and glinted as though it were made of sharp glass. It caught my attention, too, and it hit me how long it had been since I'd been in my natural form. I almost forgot about the human with me until he took a step back, and the terror radiated off him and hit me in waves.

"What *are* you?"

Shoving my hand in my pocket with the sealed jar, I straightened. "It was just a trick of the light. Now leave."

"But—"

"*Leave.*"

I straightened as he walked away, a little faster than a casual gait, released the breath I'd been holding, and allowed my shoulders to slump. Being menacing and portraying power and confidence wasn't my strong suit.

I was a protector, a guide, a *Guardian*, and I didn't enjoy dealing with blood, pain, influence, and force. But desperate times called for desperate measures.

And at this point, I was desperate.

Finally, the night had cleared. The few remaining clouds were wispy and floated past the moon quickly in the persistent breeze. Immediately after gathering the blood from the almost-willing human, I made my way to the hospital.

Striding through the hospital hallways and gently shifting past slow walkers, I moved across the off-white floor. It was stronger this time—the disturbance in the air that reeked of fear and seeped through my skin. I'd felt it the moment I'd stepped through the double doors and moved steadily toward it. I didn't want to run through the halls and attract unwanted attention, but I walked as quickly as possible and ran only when

I encountered an empty strip. It went against every fiber of my being not to race unabated. The feeling was so close now, and the end of my journey was within reach, but I still needed to keep a low profile as much as possible while in this world. Every move I made had an effect here.

The feeling started to fade.

"No, no, no, no, no," I mumbled as I turned another corner.

I could almost see the dark cloud coming from the staff room.

Pressing my back against the wall, voices came from inside the room, one agitated and fearful, the other full of anger.

"Hey, don't be such a prude. I'm just messing with you."

"I'd prefer it if you didn't even talk to me." A female voice responded.

There was a tousle, and the man said, "No talking it is, then."

When there was a squeal, followed by, "Get away from me, Ken!" I moved into the room.

Dr. Ken had a woman backed up against the far wall, and I took a moment to place her. It was Penny, Ana's roommate.

"I'm so sick of you pretending you don't want me. I can feel you do. I've seen the way you look at me," Ken said.

"*Ken.*" Penny slammed her hands against his chest and tried to push him away before he grasped both of her wrists in his free hand.

"Hey!" I shouted.

Ken turned to me, and his face twisted into something dark and ugly. "This room is for staff only."

He turned back to Penny as if I weren't there. "I've decided that from now on, I'm going to take what I want."

As I rushed toward them, Penny lifted a knee swiftly and

made contact with Ken's groin, and he buckled over.

"You *bitch.*" He reached out and grabbed her arm as she moved to run past, but I came up behind him, snatched at the back of his white coat, and yanked him backward.

"Are you the one I've been looking for?" I muttered to him as Penny fled the room.

Chapter Twenty-Three

Kyle

My suspicions grew with the senses that radiated from Ken as I grabbed his arms and marched him backward further into the break room. He yelled, "Let *go* of me." And I slapped a hand over his mouth and dragged him the final distance when he began to struggle. I didn't slow my pace, threw Ken into a nearby chair, and pointed a finger at him in warning when he went to stand. "I'm going to call security."

"Snap out of it. I know who you are."

Ken paused, his expression blank, before a deep frown creased his forehead. "You need to leave. *Now.*"

My hands shook. I wish they didn't. "No."

Withdrawing a small vial from my pocket—having split the blood I'd obtained into several smaller containers—I carefully removed the lid and looked out the nearby window. Crossing the room in three strides, I flicked off the light switch, turned, and emptied the vial's contents onto Ken as he leaped up to attack me. Ken shielded his face with his arms as the droplets of blood splattered over him. Holding his hands out, he glanced at the blood, and his expression morphed from anger into horror.

Fear and confusion clouded him and replaced the senses I'd picked up on earlier.

"What the fuck?" Ken said.

I watched him as the moonlight spilled through the window and cast a glow across his skin.

Nothing.

Spinning around, I left the break room. There was no time to waste being concerned because I'd frightened a human. I had felt *something*, something strong, and the other Guardian had to be close. Ken was only one of my suspects, and when he cried out for security, I bolted and searched for the nameless man in scrubs.

Please let this be over.

The sense came strongly again, as though I had walked into a wall. The fog of fear was so thick I felt it milling around me as I kept moving, like the air thickened before it passed over my skin. I allowed the increasing sense to pull me in the right direction. Other times in the city, it had seemed to be coming from everywhere at once, but this was strong and poignant, an arrow directing me to its source.

Stopping, I pressed my back against the wall and scrunched my nose in distaste as the young man in scrubs left a patient's room. He was still not wearing a name tag, and as he walked past, I almost dry-heaved at the cloud of darkness surrounding him. There was so much guilt, fear, and hatred in the air that I could practically see the black fog surrounding him.

There was a flicker of doubt in me.

He was letting his energies filter out and affect everyone he interacted with. He wasn't hiding.

Perhaps he felt safe doing so in the hospital, convinced that the protection this place provided would be enough.

The images came to my mind rapidly from my previous searches of the hospital. A young man had committed suicide with a pen, and I had felt the pain from elsewhere in the building before I knew what had happened. When I arrived outside the room, I noticed *this* man as he stood at the end of the hall, away from the chaos of the doctors and nurses who tried to save a life in vain. He never had any identification, and given that he was wearing scrubs, I doubted many in the hospital would look twice at him or even notice his lanyard had nothing on it.

The victim had been recently paralyzed, was young, and still had so much left to live for. But the hopelessness had filled him, and if my suspicions were correct, the negative feelings had been *forced* into him. A cloud of fear, regret, and pain was encased in the room and would've seeped through the victim until he had no choice but to take his own life to end the misery.

Had the Tenebrian handed him the pen himself? Had he watched while he stabbed it into his leg, hitting an artery he couldn't feel? Or had he waited at the end of the hall and enjoyed the chaos as it rained down after his actions? Another act of destruction, another human life lost, pushing the Balance further.

The entire area where I stood was clouded with fear, and I breathed heavily. My anger at all the pain caused came to the surface. That young man still had a life to live, and all the people who had loved him suffered now.

My stomach twisted.

Stepping away from the wall, I faced the man's retreating back. "Hey, you!" I shouted. As he turned, I fingered the small jar of blood in my pocket, and my expression darkened. "Time to leave."

He glanced at where my hand was hidden in my pocket, and I pressed my thumb to the lid, ready to use it as soon as I was close enough. I couldn't place his expression. It wasn't fear, but why would it be? The other Guardian was powerful and had no reason to fear me.

It was suspicion and resignation.

Stepping forward, I lowered my voice. "It's time you went home."

Before I had taken a second step, he turned and bolted.

"*Shit.*"

I gave chase and no longer cared about making a scene or drawing attention to myself. I was so close. After all this time, he was *right there*, and there's no way I would let him get away now.

As we rounded the corner, a nurse looked up at the man in scrubs as he skidded past. "Ryan, what's going on?" she asked and grunted when Ryan shoved her roughly to the side. I wanted to check on her, but there was no time.

I was closing in.

Following Ryan up several flights of stairs, I thanked my luck at every locked door my enemy encountered, funneling him into a trap. Finally, he broke through to a rooftop area. A second later, I burst through the door and kicked it closed behind me. The door slamming sounded like a finale.

Finally, it was over.

Ryan retreated away from me, his face twisted with rage. "Get away from me."

"You don't belong here."

"I know who you are. And I'm *not* going back."

Taking the vial of blood with one hand and displaying the carved moonstone knife with the other, I said, "I can't let you stay here. You're doing so much damage." Stepping slowly toward Ryan, I kept myself between him and the door. "Just come with me now, and I won't have to use force."

"I'm not going anywhere with you." Ryan lunged toward me and curved his body out of the way as I slashed at him with the crude blade. He backed up again and stepped onto the ledge at the boundary of the rooftop area.

Ryan's voice was dark. "Let me go."

"No." Maneuvering my fingers, I undid the small lid on the vial of blood and, with a flourish of my arm, propelled the contents toward Ryan. Ryan raised his hands defensively as he was splashed with blood, and his expression twisted and changed into something I could no longer read. As the moonlight hit Ryan's skin, I moved forward and watched with my blade outstretched, ready to strike the moment my suspicions were confirmed.

The seconds stretched out, and my breathing sounded loud in my ears.

Nothing.

"Is this blood?" Ryan inspected his hands before he cried out, "What the fuck is wrong with you?"

Dread washed over me, ice cold and freezing me to the spot. I stared at Ryan's skin, the blade still clutched in my hand, and held defensively between us.

"That is blood drawn with moonstone. Why hasn't your skin returned to its natural form?" I demanded as the panic rose like bile in my throat.

"What are you talking about?"

"You're a Tenebrian here to spread pain and fear." I struggled to keep my voice and my hand steady.

Ryan's face was a mixture of anger and confusion. "I don't know what the fuck you're talking about."

"Why were you running?" I matched his anger, and my voice rose with every syllable.

"You were *chasing* me! Isn't that enough? You had something hidden in your pocket. Wouldn't *you* run?"

"I..." I didn't know what to say.

"Aren't you one of May's boys?" He asked, his voice small.

The whole world fell around my shoulders. I stared at him.

Ryan's face dropped, and he looked as though all his life had been drained from him at that moment. Whatever it was he was fighting, he had completely given up.

The dark fog around him loomed larger.

"You're not here to take me back to answer for the death of May's daughter, are you?"

"I'm sorry, I—"

"It doesn't matter. I can't keep doing this." Running his hands through his hair, Ryan gripped it and twisted the strands around his fingers. He paced up and down on the ledge, and my eyes followed his movement, although I couldn't move myself. "I keep running and running, but they'll never believe me that it was an accident, that I *loved* her!" Ryan spun around to face me and looked at me desperately as if I might be able to offer some answers.

I only shook my head hopelessly.

Ryan turned and looked up at the sky and down at the street below. He had tears in his eyes, and the fog of darkness thickened again, beyond anything I've ever experienced around a human.

"I swear I never meant for it to happen," he said, and his voice cracked. "That paralyzed man with the pen... I didn't think he'd ever do that. I was trying to help and make him happy. When he asked for a pen and paper, I thought he was going to write a letter. I've been trying to make people happy. Trying to make up for..." My gaze was fixated on the concrete pavers at my feet when Ryan cried out and drew my gaze upward. "He wanted his mother to know that he loved her. Did you know that? I should've known then, but I didn't think... all I've tried to do is give people company and make them happy."

Still, I didn't move, but occasionally shook my head. I wanted to reach out and help this man. He needed it. He required the calming influences I could offer to ease the burden of pain and guilt that weighed so heavily on him.

But I could barely get my mind around what was happening. Everything was a gray blur.

Ryan was a man.

Merely a human.

I was wrong again.

"I try to do good things," Ryan said as he looked upward again. "I try to be helpful, but everything I touch just turns to shit." He sighed. "You're right..." His voice was hollow. "I don't belong here. I'm a curse on this world."

"Ryan, *no!*" I threw myself forward and grabbed at Ryan's shirt. But I was too slow as my pain and guilt clouded my judgment and reactions. My hands closed on empty air where Ryan was a moment before as he tipped forward and fell into gravity's embrace. He didn't make a sound as he fell before he hit the pavement below with a sickening thud.

I dropped to my knees as screams echoed from floors below.

Ryan was suicidal, holding on to guilt from his past and fear for the future. He had carried with him an entire world of pain, much more than any one person should. His personal cloud of self-hatred read the same emotional energy as a Tenebrian. I didn't know what else he had done or seen, but Ryan had said the man who killed himself with the pen was an accident. Maybe both of them were infected by the ever-present fog in this part of the city, exacerbating their fears.

Thanks to me, that energy was still here and stronger than ever before.

I was drained and empty. A shell of who I was only hours ago. I should give up now, risk opening a Gateway and alerting the Tenebrian of my location to call for the help of a more experienced Guardian. I was useless and hopeless, and had done more damage than prevented. I began to understand how Ryan's internal pain had grown and festered so much.

The more I tried to help, the more damage I caused.

It was torture.

How did humans stand feeling these emotions every day? I'd only experienced anything like this by feeling a human going through it—second-hand emotions. But to feel it myself was like having knives stabbed into my chest. The emotional pain manifested into a physical ache.

My stomach churned, my heart pounded, and my chest stung.

I hated it. I hated all of it. I hated that I could feel *at all* when I never knew I had the capacity.

I hated all the mistakes I had made, and my arrogance that led me there.

It took all my strength to stand as though my guilt weighed me down. Slowly, I walked to the door, dragging my feet. Everything that was left of me, I left on this rooftop.

It was over.

I was done.

Chapter Twenty-Four

Ana

The bricks were hot against my skin as I leaned against the wall of my apartment building, and my arm that was extended out shook slightly. With my other hand pressed on my chest, I closed my eyes until my breathing slowed. I'd been running while angry, which was never a good idea. When my chest started to burn and my legs felt like they were going to turn to jelly, I pushed harder and stopped only when I thought I would vomit with one more step.

All the angry thoughts swirled in my mind the entire run, and I was no closer to figuring out how Kyle had gotten under my skin so much. I was usually so good at brushing people off, the first to say *forget you* and move on when there was even a hint of games being played. But Kyle, there was something about him and *us* when we were together. The energy that passed between us was electric. Putting it simply, I felt good when I was around him. He soothed me like he could push away all the negativity in the world and create a bubble for us to exist and be happy in.

So why did he have to play these games with me? He told me he was no good, yet he kept coming back into my life, only to leave me again. Having my emotions messed with created a physical ache in my gut that weighed as heavy as cement, and every time he came and went, it reopened the wound.

He'd kissed me, and I wanted it to last forever, but something in his eyes said *this was the last time.*

I wish I'd screamed *Good*! *I never wanted you anyway.* But I *did* want him. I wanted to cling to his shirt and pull him closer, and I wanted the desperation of his hands on my body to reflect mine.

But instead, he'd left me. Again.

So, I'd tried to run it off. My shift wasn't until later tonight, and I figured I could run until I felt I was going to puke, then pass out on the couch for a while.

Once my head cleared and the gray that crept into my peripheral vision dissipated, I took a few deep breaths and ran my palm across my forehead, slicking my hair back with sweat. Fanning my t-shirt around my body, I stepped into the foyer of my apartment building.

"Hey."

I looked up as Nathaniel crossed the foyer after leaving Henry's apartment. "Oh, hey, Nathaniel," I replied.

He kept moving until he stood right next to me, so close my chest was almost brushing against his with every breath. I took a half-step back, hoping it wasn't too noticeable, but it felt like he'd invaded my space intentionally, trying to send me a message. Or perhaps to regain some misguided sense of dominance after our failed dates.

Nathaniel looked at me, staring until I felt uncomfortable. "I wanted to know if you'd like to get together again, maybe dinner at my place?" He stepped forward again to compensate for my half-step back and surveyed me, eyeing my chest where my t-shirt stuck to my skin.

I moved back again. "Listen, that's sweet of you, but I'm not in a great headspace at the moment and—"

"Bullshit."

My eyebrows shot up. "What?"

Nathaniel stepped forward as I stepped back, again and again, until my back hit the wall next to the elevator. Reaching behind me, I jammed the call button with my finger repetitively.

"All this *not in a good headspace* rubbish, it's such a load of bullshit. If you don't want to see me again, admit it."

This wasn't a side of him I had seen before, and I didn't like it. He stared down at me with such intensity. I wish he'd blink more often. "I don't think I want to see anyone at the moment," I said.

He scoffed. "Right, whatever."

He didn't leave but instead stretched one arm out against the wall next to my head, the first step to boxing me in. I looked at his hand and then back at him as, in one swift motion, he moved forward and pressed his lips to mine.

Struggling out from under his arm, I cried, "Nathaniel, *no.*"

"You didn't hear me complaining when you kissed me without asking. I bet you're fucking someone else."

"I need to go."

I couldn't help the reflexive flinch when his other palm slapped against the wall and kept me where I was. The elevator dinged, and I ducked under Nathaniel's arm and into the car and punched the close door button with my thumb until it hurt. Nathaniel didn't attempt to follow and watched me with his brow furrowed.

A silent threat if ever I'd seen one.

This isn't over.

As the doors closed, I backed against the far wall of the elevator. My breathing was already coming in hitches and gasps, and the thing had barely started moving. I repeated in my head that it was only a few floors, and I didn't have far to go before I could escape this death trap. I wasn't claustrophobic, but given an option, I would rather not be in an elevator, especially one that was so old and in desperate need of maintenance. In fact, the list of places I'd rather be was piling up in my head as the lights flickered above me.

The elevator jolted, and I gasped.

Don't be an idiot. Act like an adult.

It jolted again.

It's an old building. The elevator had been running for years without an incident.

Due for an accident then, right?

I closed my eyes when it jolted for a third time. I'd never been in the damn thing and had no idea if this was normal.

When an elevator falls...

I couldn't believe I was about to do it.

I started jumping, small jumps on the spot at first, which soon became higher as I pivoted my toes with each upward leap as high as I could get.

When the elevator rattled to a halt and the doors slid open, a middle-aged couple stopped mid-step as they faced me, where I was still jumping on the spot like a lunatic. I abruptly stopped and staggered slightly as I stepped out of the elevator.

"Ah..." I stuttered. My brain couldn't pull the words together fast enough after the interaction with Nathaniel, and then the terror-filled elevator ride. The couple watched me with confusion. "Cool down exercises?" I added, the inflection at the end of the sentence accidental. Turning, I bolted down the hall toward my apartment and fumbled with my keys before I slammed the door behind me and leaned against it, breathing hard.

I wasn't sure what bothered me more—being in the elevator or the look in Nathaniel's eyes when he'd pinned me against the wall.

RELA

Chapter Twenty-Five

Kyle

She'd found me, or I'd found her. I wasn't sure which.

I'd gone to the bar where Ana worked, and she wasn't there. Part of me was glad, as I didn't want to infect her with my pain and guilt, and she deserved better than that.

Better than me.

But this woman was oozing appeal, and her eyes darted around the bar as she sought someone to have only for tonight.

Sought *me*.

I approached her, drawn to her as she swayed to the music, and whispered sweet nothings in her ear, which had her pawing at my chest. Plastering on a smile that felt unnatural, I grabbed her wrists as she ran her fingers across my chest through my shirt. She was ready and waiting for someone to pick her up and free her for just one night. She wanted nothing more than a release. Purely physical.

Exactly what I needed too.

I didn't want to care anymore. I didn't want to feel these things that tore me apart. I needed something from her, something she wasn't even aware of, and I needed to get close to her. I could absorb her happiness, the carefree feeling she clung to tonight. I could use that, and maybe it would ease the pain in my chest.

The scent of it was all over her—she'd had a rough month and wanted to let loose and feel good. She already felt better within the atmosphere of the bar, with her friends, and, of course, with the assistance of a couple of cocktails.

But she wanted and needed more.

I did too.

When I left the hospital, I was in a daze.

Should I go home to Lucidis straight away? Should I find Ana? I could have used her help, given how my senses sharpened when I was with her. I could take her with me while I started my search from scratch and have her by my side. We could be a team.

That would be beyond foolish, and I'd dismissed the thought as soon as it came.

I had drawn so much attention to myself now. What if I were being followed or tracked by the Tenebrian? But I couldn't shake the feeling of Ana, and I guess that's why I came here. My feet carried me without thought. Ana had infiltrated my mind and gotten completely under my skin in a way no one else—not human nor Guardian—ever had.

I couldn't get her out of my head and needed a distraction.

Not just from Ana, but a distraction from everything—all my failures and pain.

And that distraction stood before me in a black and white mini dress.

Huffing out a breath as she rubbed me through my pants, my laugh staggered. "What's your name?" I asked.

She smiled, her entire body constantly moving as she swayed to the music and pressed herself against me, her ample breasts pushed against my chest. "Sophia."

"Sophia," I crooned and brushed her chestnut hair out of her face. "Want to get out of here?" Even as I asked, an uncomfortable pang of pain stabbed at my chest.

Sophia took my hand and kissed my palm. The gesture did nothing for me. "I have a better idea," she said. Turning away, she led me toward the back of the bar and stopped in front of the bathrooms.

"Wha—" My words were cut off as she shoved me hard in the chest, more from the shock of the motion than any strength, and I stumbled back a few steps through the bathroom door. I recovered quickly and backed away from Sophia as she approached. When she got to me, she kissed me hard and ran her hands over my head and through my hair.

I grabbed her arms, "Wait, wait, wait... maybe this isn't the best place?" I wanted a release, but not quite like this. This felt empty and dirty.

Another location, and surely it would feel better.

Surely.

I already knew I was lying to myself.

Sophia groaned loudly, grabbed the loops on my jeans, and yanked me toward her. "You're overthinking this. Just shut up and fuck me, will you?"

She started undoing my pants and rubbing me through my boxers, and I moaned in response. I took a moment to shake my head and rid myself of the memory of Ana touching me the same way. My body responded fast, but I felt a disconnect between my body and soul, almost like I was viewing this scene from the outside. Growling in frustration at the conflicting feelings, I lifted Sophia onto the counter between the sinks. She laughed and hiked her dress up over her thighs.

When the bathroom door opened, I yelled, "Get out!" without looking away from Sophia. The influence was heavy in my voice without my trying, and everything was bundled up inside me and exploding out. I was a conflicted mess.

The intruder turned and left without a pause.

Sophia squealed in delight, clutched onto my back, pulled herself closer, and wrapped her legs around my waist. I braced my palms on the mirror as she leaned into my shoulder and kissed my neck. I tried to get lost in the moment, closed my eyes, and breathed in her essence. It wasn't the physical touch I needed, that was incidental. Sophia was so relaxed, and the alcohol pulsed through her body.

She didn't have a care in the world right now, and I craved it. I wanted that feeling.

I needed it.

But how could I bring her pleasure and feed from that pleasure when all of this felt so wrong? Everywhere she touched me, I was reminded of Ana and what we shared.

I was tainted. My negativity would infect Sophia.

This didn't feel right.

This wasn't right.

She was beautiful, and she was everything I needed.

No.

At least what I *thought* I needed.

All I could think of was Ana's hands and lips on me.

I didn't need a distraction. I needed *Ana.*

I'm a fool.

I shuddered against Sophia's touch when she moved to pull my boxers down as her lips dragged across my cheek, and she hummed in contentment, responding to the influence I didn't have control over.

I pulled away. "I can't do this," I mumbled.

"What?" Sophia breathed out, her hands still fumbling numbly for my pants.

As I stepped away, her arms fell lazily to her sides. Sophia's eyes were glazed over, and I watched her carefully as I did my pants back up. She frowned at me, but she couldn't quite focus. This would have been wrong even if it weren't for Ana. Sophia was drunk. I sighed and dragged a hand down my face before gently lifting her from the bench. Sofia giggled quietly as I placed her on her unsteady feet.

"I'm sorry," I whispered.

When her eyes met mine, her smile dropped, and her expression filled with disappointment and uncertainty. "Is it me?"

"No, no, not at all." I ran my fingers through my hair. "You're beautiful." She smiled weakly at my words, but it fell again when I sighed. "There's someone else, we're not together technically..." Sophia cocked her head at me, and the innocent gesture made it all worse. "I... but I... this doesn't feel right."

"Oh." She whispered before she huffed out a humorless laugh. "The one night I'm just looking for a fuck, and I run into an actual gentleman." She leaned against my arm when she stumbled again, and her brows knotted together. "I don't feel so good."

"What?"

I felt the wave of nausea that radiated from her before she

moved. "I think I'm going to—"

Sophia burst past me and into the nearest cubicle to be sick. I hesitated between helping her and leaving. Guilt weighed heavily in my stomach, and something else I couldn't quite identify, but the feeling spiked when Ana popped back into my mind as she often did.

Leaning against the counter, I waited.

When Sophia was done, she staggered out of the cubicle, and I was there to meet and steady her. I guided her to the sink and held her while she rinsed her mouth and splashed water on her face. As I dabbed at her forehead with damp paper towels, Sophia watched me the entire time. Her eyes didn't leave my face, but I couldn't look directly back.

Everything hurt.

When I managed to drag my gaze to her face, her eyes watered, but they were clearer than before.

"Why are you being so nice to me?" she asked quietly.

"Because I feel bad for leading you on, and it didn't seem right to leave you when you're sick."

She laughed before mumbling, "It didn't feel right..." under her breath, and I tilted my head as I took a read on her imprint.

She needed a release tonight as much as I did, although for different reasons.

Many things about tonight didn't feel right, including the idea of leaving Sophia feeling rejected.

I stepped toward her until I had her backed against the wall. She instinctively ran her hands up my back as I rested my face in the crook of her neck and breathed in deeply. She relaxed into my touch as I balanced her energies. It may have been wrong, but I also used some of her happiness for myself. I had to. I felt like I was drowning in a negative cloud with no escape. Sophia was so bright, and I needed that. So, I drew on all the positive waves from the fun and relaxation of her night so far and let it fuel my powers so I could feed it back into her until she sighed with contentment.

When I moved away, she grinned at me and planted a delicate kiss I absolutely did not deserve on my cheek. She felt lighter. I could feel it in the small space of air between us.

But I only felt more weighed down than before.

Indicating the door, I said, "Shall we uh..."

Sophia nodded and stared at me with a small quirk of a smile and narrowed eyes as she tried to figure out what I had done. It was just a hug, a comforting hug for all she knew. But she felt better after I'd released her from my embrace that seemed to penetrate her being. She needn't know the details, but at least she left our interaction feeling better than she went in, instead of worse.

At least I did one thing right.

Sophia adjusted her dress, which had crumpled after kneeling on the floor, and I held the door open for her. "Aha," she said as she walked through. "Gallantry isn't dead."

I stopped in my tracks.

Was there no end to the reminders of Ana?

"Are you okay?" she asked.

"Yeah." I looked around. "I'm going to grab a drink."

"Okay," Sophia chimed as she fixed her hair with her fingers and returned to meet her friends on the dance floor.

I didn't get a drink, but instead, I left the bar, stepped out into the night, and disappeared down the street. It was easy to ignore your feelings, even as an empath, when you were so used to not experiencing emotion firsthand. But these feelings were harder to ignore, and apparently impossible to rid myself of.

Earth had changed me.

I clenched my fists as I walked.

Being with Sophia was a stupid thing to do. It didn't matter that I didn't follow through, because I shouldn't have gone to the bar in the first place.

I was glad Ana wasn't there. I didn't deserve her company.

OUTLET

Chapter Twenty-Six

Kyle

Shoving my hands into my jean pockets, every step was a chore, and my legs and body were heavy as I moved myself down the sidewalk. Leaving the bar, I was empty, guilty, and in a worse state than I'd been before entering. The positive emotions of those inside the bar meant nothing when they couldn't penetrate the haze I was encased in. Beyond that, my powers were inconsistent at best. How much longer could I go on without returning home? Not long, I'd wager.

But how could I return home?

I'd achieved nothing on Earth, less than nothing. I'd wasted time and pushed an innocent man over the edge. On top of that, I'd betrayed Ana by even *considering* fucking Sophia.

Even though we weren't together, Ana had apparently already begun moving on.

Rubbing my hands vigorously over my face as I walked, I groaned loudly in frustration.

Humans were so damn complicated.

The anger welled up inside me and replaced all other emotions. I was furious at myself for allowing things to get this out of hand. I should have been able to locate and return the other Guardian to where he belonged long ago. I'd spent weeks, all of which were wasted time—tracking, locating, and observing—only to draw out the wrong being. A *human.* The entire time, the Tenebrian was still out there, harming everyone he encountered, directly or otherwise.

All that pain was on my shoulders and was mine to bear.

It had never been this difficult before. It wasn't unusual for Earth to be infiltrated with both good and evil—the positive and negative forces that the world balanced on were *needed*. But it was highly unusual for it to turn out like this. When I came to Earth the first time with my mentor, the Tenebris Guardian we were tracking was only influencing, up to the same old tricks they usually were. It was a bit of *fun* for them at the expense of some humans, tired of their duty to protect and observe. We'd located and returned him within two days. I'd watched other Guardians return from their missions, sometimes within hours.

Cordus had warned me not to let my arrogance get in the way of the search, not to underestimate my enemies' powers, and not to assume I knew their intentions.

How much of the blame rested on my shoulders?

All of it. The voice in my head demanded I not hide from the truth.

Should I not have treated this the same as all other missions? How was I to know?

But it is *my fault.*

I spent time thinking about a human female rather than where my focus should have been. I hesitated to do what was necessary and draw human blood, ultimately taking too long to work myself up for the task.

I should've acted sooner.

A small bit of pain from one human was a small price.

I gritted my teeth and huffed out an angry breath through my nose. It was *hard* to think like that because I didn't see humans as purely tools. They were so much more.

The longer I was on Earth, the harder it became to separate my emotions from those around me and to focus and pinpoint my powers. Everything blurred, and my physical form was the only thing stopping me from getting lost entirely in the swirl of human emotions that permeated the air. The focus it took me to maintain this form was barely noticeable now, but how much of it was draining what little power I had left? There had already been moments where I slipped up, and my powers came out stronger than intended, or when I hadn't been trying at all. I couldn't afford to continue like this.

I need to try harder.

I can't give up.

Stopping so abruptly, a couple walking behind me murmured angrily as they passed. I stilled and assessed my location.

My thoughts had been clearing the further I'd gotten from the hospital.

Maybe I needed to head home to Lucidis and recharge, even briefly.

Would the others have noticed my failure? Would they let me come back or send someone else?

The dark thoughts retook hold.

Failure.

Cursing, I scuffed my shoes across the pavement. Had I become a victim of the very influence I was trying to save humans from? Had I been on Earth so long that I was completely compromised? No better at controlling myself than the humans who surrounded me?

Failure.

The stench of my self-loathing oozed from my skin, followed me as I walked, and created my own cloud of self-hatred.

Stopping in my tracks, I gazed around the city streets at a momentary loss.

Where do I go from here?

Should I return to my motel room or continue searching in vain? Forced to start afresh because of my inexperience and arrogance. Should I wander the streets until my feet bled and *hope* I found what I was looking for?

Running my fingers through my hair, I squeezed my eyes shut. This was too much.

To my left was a small bar, and I went in. Spending my time in places like this may not have been helping, but my thoughts were clearer at night when half the human population was asleep, not adding to the flood of emotions that invaded my mind and being. Being in bars and clubs made sense, as I couldn't be hanging out on the street every night, gaining unwanted attention.

Sitting, I rubbed my temples again, dropped my elbows on the sticky table, and closed my eyes.

Besides the obvious reasons I gave myself, I'd also grown fond of beer and bourbon. Even though I knew they were counterproductive, they added to my mind's cloudiness.

But right now, filled with self-loathing, some cloudiness wouldn't go astray.

The sound of a chair scraping on the floor drew my attention as someone sat beside me. I dropped my palms to the table with a loud whack and turned slowly to the intruder of my space.

"Can I help you?" I asked, surprising even myself with my scathing tone.

"Hey, relax, man." The stranger slapped my shoulder, and my back straightened in irritation. "You just look like you're having a rough night."

I knew the man was drunk and meant no harm, and I should have been more patient. But what I knew in my head and what I felt in my soul were at odds, and frustration weighed heavily on my shoulders. The air around me began to vibrate as my anger filtered out.

"Leave me alone," I said through gritted teeth.

"I'm just trying to help you," came the slurred response.

Standing abruptly, my chair slid out and tipped over behind me with a clatter that drew the attention of the handful of people in the bar. "Why don't you..." I began, my anger radiating invisibly throughout the bar, "... get the *fuck* away from me and go take this up with someone else?"

The drunk man stood and took a step back. His eyes were glazed, and he turned on the spot and found himself face-to-face with a staff member. There was a momentary pause where the energy of the room shifted, and the drunk looked at the man in front of him and, without a single word, swung a punch to the side of his head. The staff member fell, and his head hit the floor with a sickening crack. The drunk turned to the next person without pause and was ready to strike again.

Only to have a chair broken across his back.

I was shocked out of my stupor as fights spontaneously broke out around me. Looking down at my clenched fists, the air rippled around my hands as I radiated anger. Panic surged through me.

It was *me.*

"Oh no." I unclenched my fists and shook my hands to loosen the stiff joints as if that would help the damage I'd already done. I tried desperately to control my emotional state, but it was too late. My anger and frustration had infiltrated the air and infected the humans around me.

I couldn't stop it.

"No, *no, no, no.* Stop fighting!" Running toward the nearest brawling group to separate them, I grabbed two men by the backs of their collars, pried them apart, and forced them to release the hold they had on each other's throats. Tossing them in opposite directions, I turned on the spot, faced in every direction with the chaos of my creation. My being close to everyone was only making it worse. My frustration, not only with myself but also with humans for fighting for no reason, spiraled out of control, and in turn, it fueled their responses as they continued striking anyone within reach.

Horror and panic took over, and the sensations in my body shifted rapidly between feeling as though I was made of stone and feeling as if my legs were weakening and I would drop to the floor at any moment.

There's nothing I can do

My fear was only making everything worse.

I needed to leave and put distance between myself and them. Only then would their minds clear, and they would stop fighting.

Purposefully, I headed to the door and was a step away from the exit when I was punched in the jaw. I stumbled forward as my attacker gripped his hand and cried out, "Son of a *bitch.*"

After I stumbled onto the pavement, I fell to my knees. Moving through the doorway had been a physical effort as I passed through the barrier of the negative influence I had created.

Rubbing my jaw, I spit out a small line of blood.

I stared at it.

A human had made me bleed.

Was I getting weaker physically, as well as losing control of my powers?

I shrugged angrily when a hand landed on my shoulder, and I shouted, "Fuck off."

"Kyle, Christ, it's just me. Are you okay?"

"Ana?"

Ana reached toward my cheek when I stood facing her, and I flinched as she touched my face, where a light bruise was forming.

"What are you doing here?" I asked, brushing her hand with my fingers before breaking the contact.

The air was already clearing. All I could see was her.

"I got called in early. I'm on my way to work. Ed left early without notice." She barely restrained herself from rolling her eyes. "Are you okay?" I studied her face, and her eyes swam with concern. It only made me feel worse. Why should she care for me after how I treated her? Ana brushed my jaw with her thumb, and I covered her hand with mine as she said, "You're hurt. Let me take you home and clean you up."

"No."

"You're close, right? I really think you should let—"

"I said *no.*"

Ana recoiled at the harshness of my tone and dropped her hand from my face. The second I lost contact, my guilt and fear tripled and threatened to take me over again. "Don't take your shit out on me. I was only trying to help."

My shoulders drooped, and I rubbed my temples again. Now I was infecting Ana. Was there no end to how much I could mess up in one night?

"I'm sorry, I mean… just not to my place, and… I'm okay."

Ana frowned. "I gotta get to work, anyway. Seeya."

As she went to storm away, I grabbed her hand and swung her around to face me. "Wait, please."

Ana raised her eyebrows and looked at me expectantly before she glanced at my hand, where I gripped her wrist. When I said nothing, she prompted me with, "Yes?"

I hesitated.

I shouldn't be doing this. It was selfish of me to hold on to her and to want her in my life. But something about her balanced me, something I didn't *know* I needed before I'd met her. Something I had missed having without really knowing what it was. Having Ana near me helped silence the outside influences and calmed me. I could be more myself and purer with her than I had in weeks.

Perhaps ever.

So, I could tell myself that I needed her to find the other Guardian or that I needed clarity.

But the truth was, I needed her with me.

I just needed *her*.

"Can we talk for a bit?" I asked, my voice filled with the resignation that had built inside me. I was weak. I couldn't stop the Tenebrian, nor could I stop myself from wanting to be with

Ana.

Ana sighed. "No promises?"

Moving closer, I wrapped an arm around her waist, bent to lean my face near to her neck, and breathed in her essence as she tilted her head slightly to allow my body to mold in with hers. I could sense her fear, and I wondered if she was afraid of me or afraid of me hurting her again.

Either way, it sucked.

"I just need to be near you, be with you."

"That's the opposite of what you've told me before." I felt the crack in her voice more than I heard it.

"I know what I said, and I'm sorry."

Ana pulled away slightly. "Is this because you saw me kissing someone else?"

I frowned. "You remember that?"

Ana rubbed her arms. "I remember parts of that night, but I got pretty wasted." A flush crept over her cheeks.

Sighing, I shook my head and scanned her face for signs of any darkness having resurfaced. I was satisfied there were none. I would have felt it the moment she touched me if anything was left lingering in her system.

But I no longer knew what to think. Everything had changed, and everything I thought I knew was falling apart.

No matter what I told myself, the last time I kissed her was only because I wanted to, because *I* needed to, and not for any reason related to the mission or the greater good.

"I want you to be happy. I'm just dealing with a lot right now. I was only trying to do what was best for you, even if I went about it the wrong way." I traced my fingers along her cheek and used the influence from the calming effect she had on me to, in turn, soothe the anger I had caused in her.

"I guess I can understand that." Ana sighed and took out her cell. "This is against my better judgment as you haven't exactly given me a reason to give you another chance, but..." she glanced at the time, "... you've got fifteen minutes."

I took her hand and started walking.

"Where are we going?" she asked.

"Anywhere away from here."

We headed toward Ana's work, stopped down the street, and found a place to sit on a bench. I sat and pulled Ana gently down next to me.

She sat and didn't take her eyes off my face. "You look a mess."

Rubbing my jaw, I glanced sideways at her. "Thanks."

Ana smirked when she caught the whisper of a grin on my face, but then her expression became serious again. "I don't mean this..." she said as she brushed her fingertips over the mark on my jaw. "... I mean, in general. You look like you're a mess inside."

"I am. I am a mess inside." I sighed as the weight of it all fell on my shoulders. As if it had ever left. "Everything I'd set out to do has failed and at a very high cost. I honestly don't know where to go from here or why I bother staying around."

"I can't figure you out, Kyle," Ana said as she shook her head. She looked up at the stars, barely visible in the night sky as clouds rolled in. "I love the stars," she mumbled, and her sigh was wistful.

"You should see them from home. They're spectacular."

Ana nodded. "Maybe one day I will."

Frowning, the guilt rose in my chest again. It was another empty promise I could never keep.

Ana continued, "I bet there's no light pollution where you live."

"None at all. I've never understood the need for constant light," I mused. "Maybe people are afraid of the dark."

"Maybe they have every right to be," Ana whispered.

"What was that?"

Ana just hummed in response.

After a moment of silence, she whispered, more to herself than to me, I suspected. "Fuck it." Ana turned to me with determination, and I wondered what she had been thinking in those moments of silence. I'd given her no reason to trust me, and—from what she'd told me—she didn't give second chances. Yet here she was with me again, and from the shift in her essence, she was about to throw caution to the wind and open herself up to another chance of being hurt.

I didn't want her to hurt.

I didn't want to be the one hurting her.

Selfish.

"I like you." Ana blurted the words out and followed them with a quick glance at me before she looked away again and tucked her hair behind her ear, which immediately fell forward again. "I don't know why, and it goes against every fiber of my being to say this, but I like you." She threw me another suspicious glance. "Despite you being unpredictable, which isn't normally something I'm a fan of, and you popping in and out of my life. Every time I see you, I tell myself *this is the last time*, but every time I see you, I realize you just... radiate good. I'm not sure how else to put it."

I scoffed quietly. *Radiate good?* "Not always, apparently," I said.

"What do you mean?"

"The fight in the bar was my fault."

"What happened?"

"I was angry, and I made them all angry."

"I don't understand." She frowned at me.

"My anger made them angry... and then they started fighting. I started it, and just by being there, I made it worse."

"Kyle, you can't control what other people do, no matter what you said or how you felt. People are responsible for their actions. If someone picked up on your shitty mood, it's hardly your fault if they started fighting over something else."

"It *is* my fault, Ana."

I said it with such conviction and finality, she didn't argue, although I knew she didn't understand.

"I like you," she said again, and her hand twitched as if she were going to take mine. "Before all the bullshit, when we talked, it was like connecting with someone after so long of denying myself the opportunity. You seemed to get me." She scoffed out a laugh. "As if that wasn't scary enough, I actually fucking *like* you."

After a moment of silence during which I was filled with everything I either didn't know how to say or couldn't, she rested her hand on top of mine on the bench. I looked down at our fingers as they intertwined. She was so warm and so good, and I felt her essence begin to re-energize me.

But there was still something hiding inside her, something she protected as fiercely as she did herself. A single point of her being, almost hidden from me and my senses, a tiny light inside her that felt like home. Ana was lost, confused, and afraid, but underneath all that, there was a glimmer of hope. A hope that she probably didn't even admit to herself. A hope for better.

It was that which I clung to.

If Ana could have hope, then maybe I could too.

"I've got to get to work, Kyle."

I nodded but didn't respond. I rubbed her hand with my thumb as I fought the constant inner battle of selfishly wanting to have her near me, despite the dangers it presented to her.

"Can I see you again?" she asked as I squeezed her hand.

I can't fight this.

I need you.

I smiled sadly. "How about tomorrow night?"

"Dinner?" Ana's smile lit up her face. "Your place? I can cook."

"No, we can go out."

"It's no trouble, really, I—"

"Not my place, Ana. Just no. We'll go out."

"That's a little creepy, Kyle." Ana folded her arms across her chest and appeared to shrink away from me. I knew her well enough that I could practically read her thoughts.

I trusted you enough to bring you to my home, and you won't do the same.

There were so many things I couldn't even begin to explain to her, and as I opened my mouth to respond, she cut me off. "Why don't you want me at your place? At least tell me why, so it doesn't appear so weird."

Arguing with myself for a moment, I searched for the right answer. "I'm embarrassed."

Ana cocked her head. "Of what?"

"It's a temporary place, Ana, and it's not nice. I don't want you or anyone there."

"I don't care about that, Kyle."

"But *I* do."

Ana nodded slowly as I sighed. I had a good reason for not wanting her in the same place where I slept. It was in my training, but she was understandably suspicious of my secretiveness. "Look, I have a gig tomorrow. I should be done around nine-ish. Meet at mine in the foyer, and we'll go out. Okay?"

"At yours?" Again, my back-and-forth behavior confused her, and I had messed up something that should have been simple.

I smirked at her pout. "Yes, at mine. Then we'll go out."

Ana held up her hands in mock surrender. "Okay, all right. My cooking isn't that bad."

Smiling for the first time in days, I gave her the address and kissed her lightly on her perfectly pouted lips. "Wait for me in the foyer, okay?"

"Okay." Ana squeezed my hand and let her fingers tickle my palm before she let go and headed to work.

Watching her go, I looked at the sky as she entered the bar. Were the other Guardians at home watching me? Were they disappointed? Were they itching to pass through a Gateway and finish what I couldn't? I was certain the only reason I hadn't been joined by backup was the ever-present danger of the Tenebris Guardian going into hiding if he sensed too many were after him. He'd know if another Gateway was opened, and he'd be able to feel the imprint of any being that came through to Earth. Then we may never find him.

A resolve grew within me.

I would rid this place of evil, if only for Ana's sake.

Chapter Twenty-Seven

Ignis

She was beautiful, I'd give her that.

Evidently, she felt safe in the city and had become intoxicated to the point of barely being able to walk in a straight line. All wide eyes and bright smiles, innocence mixed blissfully with ignorance. I'd considered fucking her myself when I first saw her enter the bar, but then she'd disappeared out back with someone else.

Though he didn't know me, I had my suspicions about his identity.

I turned as there was a giggle, and Sophia stumbled out of the bathroom with the man, Kyle, and practically skipped over to her friends to the bar to order more drinks as he disappeared out the door.

I shifted closer to listen without getting their attention as Sophia's friends surrounded her as though she were the only one who'd ever touched a man and held mysteries they couldn't dream of. Like they were expecting his cock to be a magical secret.

"So, how was he?"

Sophia laughed, and the pitch grated against my eardrums, but I listened anyway. "He was the sweetest thing." She dropped the volume of her voice. "When he was touching me, it was like he was *inside me.*" She ran her hands down her neck and over her breasts as she sighed.

My teeth ground together. I wanted to touch her.

But not in the way she wanted to be touched.

"Sophia, he *was* inside you."

The giggling recommenced again, and if I closed my eyes, I'd swear I couldn't tell one from the other by their voices alone. They ordered more drinks, and Sophia turned serious as she closed her eyes a beat longer than a blink. "No, I mean, it's like he was *inside me,* like he could read my mind... feel what I felt."

My back straightened, and my gaze immediately shot to the door where her suitor had disappeared.

The Lucidian.

But his imprint was so weak I'd almost considered I had the wrong being. However, with the way Sophia had described the feeling of being near him, there's no doubt he was the Guardian.

With my suspicions cemented, I chuckled to myself.

He was *weak.*

This made things interesting, as he knew Ana, too, and she was intriguing in her own right. She was resistant.

My gaze traveled back to Sophia as she returned to the dance floor with her friends.

It was time to send a message to my rival.

And I had found exactly the vessel to deliver it.

Sophia and her friends stumbled out of the bar, and the two girls linked arms as they waited for the three men who followed shortly afterward. There was much chatting and laughter, all of which was unnecessary noise.

Until one of the men said, "Shall we continue this party back at my hotel room?"

The girls cheered like this was something worth cheering about.

Making their way down one of the main streets lined with popular bars and nightclubs, I kept my distance. Not that they would have noticed either way. They were a combination of too drunk and too naïve to consider they weren't safe, and the shadows might hold secrets they should be actively avoiding. Occasionally the guys would holler and make crude comments at the girls and speed up their steps to slap them on the ass. The girls would giggle and carry on as though it were the most romantic gesture they'd ever had.

I watched the way Sophia's ass and thighs were enunciated in that tight dress of hers.

She'd be in my hands soon enough.

As they approached the hotel, Sophia held up her hand, slipped a box of cigarettes out of her handbag, and pulled one out with her lips while searching for the lighter. The group moved to hang around the back of the hotel while she smoked, and they laughed and occasionally shushed each other when they realized how obnoxiously loud they were, before laughing again.

I approached silently and kept to the shadows.

"Well, this looks like a fun little party."

They all turned to look at me, squinted, and held their hands up to their eyes, as though it would help them see past the shadows that hid my face. "Who the hell are you?" one called.

"Just an observer."

"Go observe somewhere else, creep."

"Oh, no, I quite like it here." I leered at the girls, and my lip lifted into a satisfied smirk. "I think I'll stay for a while."

The guys moved to stand in front of the girls.

I spread my fingers dramatically at their masculine gesture. "Ooh..." I cooed before I dropped my arms. "I don't think that's going to do much good."

The other girl said, "Guys, let's just go inside, okay?" Her voice shook, unable to contain the fear I could feel rising through her chest. Even in the semi-darkness, I could see her eyes scanning the area, and her horror increased as she realized they would have to walk past me to leave the space. Her voice trembled as she spoke, and the last word barely escaped as a whisper, "Please."

I stepped toward her. "I can smell your fear..." I inhaled deeply, and she trembled even though I hadn't yet touched her. The rush of her fear fueled me, like a drug to my system, and ebbed through the air before being absorbed into my veins. They were *all* afraid, although some hid it better than others. Sophia's fear spiked higher than the rest of them, and her heart thumped so loudly I could almost hear it in a rhythm that pushed her essence toward me.

Stepping forward again, my face was bathed in the light of a nearby streetlight.

Sophia frowned. "Do I know you?"

I grinned. "You're about to."

They barely registered what was happening until it was too late to stop. Guardians could move at a speed that humans couldn't, and in the semi-darkness, with shadows and pockets of fear to play with, I could make myself almost invisible to them. I ducked and weaved through the light, and all they would see was their friends as they disappeared from around them.

One by one.

Gone. Gone. Gone. Gone.

All the while, I watched Sophia as her friends' screams echoed around her. Her eyes widened as each one disappeared, and she whipped around as the sounds came from all directions. Shouts and crashes, gurgling, ripping, and a scream so filled with terror it made her blood run cold and her heart thud harder against her ribcage as though desperate to wake her from a nightmare it couldn't. Every way Sophia turned, there was a blur of movement, and I savored every inch of fear she gave in to. I absorbed it all, and as hers mixed with the fear of her friends as the life left their bodies, I almost came with the ecstasy.

Sophia jerked to the side as I struck her, and the force of the blow threw her against a dumpster before she slid down and hit the ground.

There was silence.

Casually, I strolled toward one of the floodlights facing the car park and turned it so that it bathed the area behind the hotel in light.

Then I waited in the shadows.

Sophia groaned, slowly lifted herself into a sitting position, and rubbed her head before she looked around.

She screamed. A high-pitched sound that sent the fine hairs on the back of my neck on end, and I shuddered with pleasure. Her eyes watered as she shoved her knuckles against her teeth and stared at the wall opposite her. I followed her gaze, narrowed my eyes, and smiled as I took in my handy work. The bricks were covered in artistic splatters and streaks of blood that spoke of the violence she didn't witness. The splatters surrounded a large, dark patch in the center, where the blood dripped down the wall and passed over small chunks of flesh before it added to the growing puddle on the ground and oozed out slowly over the pavement.

I watched her body convulse as she kept in a dry heave, and her bottom lip trembled as she saw one of the men's bodies where it lay to the side, so covered in blood that he was almost completely caked in red. His eyes were wide and staring, but empty and devoid of life.

Lying at his feet was an arm—no body—just an arm.

Sophia's eyes whipped to the gold bracelet on the dismembered arm, and she screamed into her hand again.

She began gasping and sobbing, desperate for fresh air that wasn't coated in the stench of death. Choking on her tears and covering her mouth, she cried and screamed to herself as her entire body trembled. Sophia stood surrounded by what was left of her friends and looked around wildly, presumably trying to find me.

Standing slowly, she took a few tentative steps as she looked to her left and saw the street. All she had to do was move around the high fence, and then she'd be on the street. I bet it felt *so close* yet so impossibly far away, and the traffic sounded muted through the haze in her mind created by the fear that penetrated and controlled her. I knew fear so well. I lived and breathed it. I practically bathed in it. That street she was watching might as well be miles away, and somewhere in the shadows, I was hiding. She could feel it.

Her body tensed.

She was going to make a run for it.

Sophia almost collapsed again when she made the mistake of looking down to find another of her friends lying near her feet, completely torn in half at the waist, and a trickle of blood was all that was left of the pressure in his arteries. Her tears reflected the light from the lamps, and it was a wonder she could see at all. Still, her heart pounded hard, a soundtrack to her fear, and thudded in her ears and mine. She stepped over the remains of her friends and took one more look at the street.

She steeled herself, her shoulders rolled, and her spine straightened.

Sophia ran.

By the time she saw me, it was too late.

Opening her mouth to scream, the sound had no chance of escaping as I grabbed her throat and lifted her against the wall. Sophia clutched at my arm desperately, and her eyes bulged as she struggled to breathe. She kicked wildly, the tips of her toes scraping against the concrete below her.

The show she had given me, how she'd tried so hard to push through the fear that consumed her—the air around me practically vibrated with how good it felt. I was energized and driven for more.

"You humans, you just cannot take the initiative, can you?"

I said, and showed no signs of effort or concern about Sophia's struggling form. "You have all the potential for evil. I can feel it in all of you. It's right there in your core. All you need to do is tap into it, and you cannot imagine what you would be capable of."

Sophia whimpered and managed to force out a strangled word. "*Please.*"

I ignored her.

"But I guess sometimes you just need a little push." I lowered Sophia toward my face and breathed in her fear as it fell from her gasps as she clung to consciousness. "I can smell him all over you, my poor rival." I grinned.

Sophia tried to shake her head, attempting to beg for her life, no doubt.

Her feet touched the ground, and I loosened my grip on her throat only enough for her to regain her breath. She gasped loudly and gulped in the oxygen gratefully. She still held onto my arm as her eyes darted around wildly for any signs of help, and the hopelessness she felt when she saw no one coming to her aid was all-consuming, and I hummed as I breathed it in.

"You're going to send a message for me." I glanced at the night sky before looking back at her. "And the pain you're about to experience will haunt him."

Sophia's resulting scream never made it out of her throat.

Chapter Twenty-Eight

Kyle

Sitting in the middle of the floor in my small motel room, I'd decided.

Being away from the hospital, and after I'd spent those few moments with Ana, my head had partially cleared—enough for me to think straighter. There was no longer a question about the next step, and despite all the failed steps I'd taken, all the ill-advised decisions, and the reckless nature of my actions, this was something I was certain of.

I needed to recharge, re-energize, and return to my roots.

I needed to go home.

After a vigorous internal debate where I'd paced my room's thin carpet, I realized it was worth the risk. While I knew the Tenebrian Guardian would sense the Gateway being opened, if one Guardian went through and one Guardian of equal power came back, he'd know I hadn't called for backup.

Chances are, he'd recognize the sense of my leaving and returning imprint, and if he were as experienced as I knew him to be, he'd understand why I'd gone home. With any luck, the Tenebrian wouldn't leave the area. Although I suspected he was playing with me, I hoped he would soon tire of the game and face me so we could end it.

When that time came, I needed to have my power restored. Only Lucidis could bring back the power I'd lost being on Earth. There wasn't any other option. I'd only need a few minutes, enough time to clear my essence of this realm. That, plus my evening with Ana later, should be enough to set me back on the right path. Despite the nagging feeling in the recesses of my mind that I wasn't good enough for this task, and perhaps I should reconsider before facing a Guardian who was much older and more powerful than I, I had made up my mind.

Any more time to think would only result in more uncertainty.

Cordus wouldn't want me to give up. He believed in me, and I wouldn't let him down. I may be young, but like my mentor, I was stubborn, and I refused to let the influence of a Tenebrian dictate my decision based on fear. If I gave up now, everything that had been lost would be in vain, and I would have proven I was no stronger than the humans I was meant to be protecting.

Sitting cross-legged on the floor and focusing my energy, I was able to rip a small hole between the realms to create a Gateway home. The energy of opening a Gateway could linger in the air, so I would only ever do this where I couldn't be interrupted or discovered, and in a place that would remain empty for a period after my departure—usually alleyways, abandoned buildings, wooded areas, or, when possible, in our temporary accommodation.

The air around me rippled before it shattered in an instant with a sound beyond even my range of hearing, and the air appeared before me as though made of broken glass.

To my right, the light emitted from the Gateway was warm and bright, and a pale blue essence slipped through the cracks. The cracks were orange to my left, and the black vapor dripped through. Both energies met in the middle and canceled each other out.

This was Earth's role in the realms—the center of the Venn Diagram, the point between two influences.

Earth was the home of the Balance, and I was one of its Guardians.

I wouldn't let them down.

Another time, I might have watched the transition of these energies for a while. This was the only physical evidence of the Balance that could be viewed, and it was beautiful in its power. The light and dark smoky essences oozed through and met where I sat. They twisted and turned in the air around each other, and the moment they touched, they would disappear and become part of the Earth realm. They canceled each other out perfectly, and my breath caught as I watched the energies dance together momentarily.

But this was not the time for lingering.

Frowning at the Tenebris Gateway to my left, I closed it with a hasty clap of my hands. Despite the beauty of the energies, I'd always hated that both Gateways opened simultaneously when generated from Earth. Earth, as the center of the realms, meant moving between them used a significant amount of energy, and focusing that energy to create only one Gateway was impossible, no matter how experienced the Guardian was.

Even with my home realm right next to me, being so close to Tenebris was sickening. The lingering feeling of the realm made my skin crawl even after I had closed the Gateway, and pins and needles crept across my skin, followed by minor stomach cramps.

It wasn't physically impossible to enter Tenebris, but why would I want to?

Turning to my right, I expanded the Lucidis Gateway enough to allow me to move through. Leaning into it, there was a moment of bright white light and a chilling cold I felt to my bones before I reappeared in Lucidis.

Home, to recharge and refresh.

So I could come back to protect Earth.

And Ana.

Collapsing to the ground, the grass never felt so sweet. The scent of it filled my nostrils as I lay spread-eagled with my arms stretched out, and thankful I was able to catch the last of the sunlight before it ebbed away. The warmth was gentle, and I rolled onto my back, closed my eyes, breathed deeply, and filled myself with the positive energies that existed in and made up my home realm.

Being home never felt so good, and I wanted to stay.

But I couldn't.

The blades of grass tickled my palms as I pushed myself into a sitting position. I rubbed my arms, not bothering to return to my natural form. I wouldn't be here for long anyway.

"Is it done?"

I turned at the voice and bowed my head slightly at the Elder before me. "Cascus," I said.

"Is it done?" he repeated with more force behind his tone.

I shook my head and kept my gaze averted from his. Cascus was stern, and I was not as close to him as I was to Cordus. "Not yet. I needed a few minutes to recharge. Then I will return."

"Very well." He moved to turn away, and I was about to reach out to him. But I didn't need to touch him, nor did Cascus need to see the movement to stop mid-step and turn back to face me. He felt my hesitation through the air between us and sensed my question before it was on my lips.

"A lot has gone wrong," I said, pushing down the guilt that swelled in my chest lest Cascus sense the depths I was experiencing human emotion. "Do you feel another Guardian would be more equipped to finish the mission?"

Cascus stared at me with a deep frown etched on his severe features. His one clouded eye watched me with the same unwavering stare as his good eye. "Why do you offer something you have no intention of giving?"

I faltered. He was right. I wanted to finish this myself, and he would have felt that from me as easily as if I had told him outright. There was no hiding from an Elder.

The realization of my situation hit me. I was home, my mind clear of distractions and the imprints of humans who had no idea how to control or conceal them. I could think.

It was so obvious here.

Of course, the other Lucidians wouldn't be as concerned with the events that had transpired as I was. Guardians cared for humanity but showed little interest in local events or individual people. They were concerned about the greater good, the bigger picture, and the Balance, and so long as I kept to the task at hand and was able to apprehend the Tenebrian eventually, they wouldn't hesitate to send me back to Earth alone. As long as the Balance didn't begin to shift, and as long as I was making enough of a difference to keep it maintained, they didn't care as much as I did.

I was alone in my concern for the deaths and pain of the humans in the city where the Rogue had taken up residence.

But of the many things I had learned on Earth, a level of humility and the dangers of arrogance were high on the list, and I thought I should at least offer the Elder the opportunity to replace me with someone more experienced. The idea stirred resentment and anger in my chest, which I managed to keep under control, but I had to ask.

All Cascus's reaction did was show me how much I had changed during my extended time on Earth.

It was out of character for a Guardian to say something they didn't mean. It was no different from lying, and we simply didn't understand its purpose in communication between each other. Keeping secrets from humans they did not need to know was one thing, but with each other? Pointless. There were no feelings to protect from getting hurt by the truth.

Guardians didn't feel like that.

Or, they weren't supposed to.

When I didn't answer, Cascus watched me for a moment longer before he moved away. His disapproval of me and my question flowed thick from him as he left, and he *wanted* me to feel it. An Elder of Cascus's power could have easily cloaked his imprint from me, but he wanted me to know he disapproved of my giving in to the human weakness of emotion.

Straightening, I turned my back to him as he retreated and took several deep, steadying breaths. I could not stay much longer. The pull to my home realm was strong, and I feared I wouldn't have the will to return to Earth once I became comfortable.

Then I thought of Ana, and the image in my mind was so

powerful I could almost feel her skin under my fingertips.

Closing my eyes, I absorbed what strength I could from the sweet air of Lucidis before I swept my hands in front of me and created a Gateway back to Earth, right back in my apartment where I had left.

My appearance back on Earth was not quite instant, and my outline fluttered and blurred for a breath of a moment in smoky blue, and my skin lost its glow a fraction of a second later. I was back on the floor exactly as I had left, and I checked my hands to ensure I remained in my human form.

Satisfied, I breathed in deeply. The air on Earth was different, and it always took me a moment to get used to it. It was thicker and heavier, and it took more effort to pull it into my lungs and expel it. But I was clearer, stronger, and much more like my original self than I had been.

All the troubles from the past few weeks were cleansed from my system, and with the Gateway's healing transition and the energies from Lucidis, I was renewed.

I pulled on a jacket after taking another deep breath and letting the crisp air fill my lungs. I was lighter, having been relieved of the guilt and pain that had weighed me down. Tonight, I needed to work my Earth job to earn money, pay my rent, and buy some food, and then I'd spend some time with Ana.

Tomorrow, I will start my search anew.

I grabbed my guitar and left for the gig.

Chapter Twenty-Nine

Ana

The sun was setting on a day I had spent desperately trying not to overthink my date with Kyle.

I had made plans.

Romantic plans even.

It wasn't often that I tried to be romantic, and by *not often*, I would say it bordered on *literally never*. But I figured with the constant up-and-down nature of our relationship—if that were even the right word—it deserved some extra attention.

Plus, Kyle was worth the effort.

In my musings, I stopped long enough to ask myself *why* he was worth the effort. What exactly was it about him? Images ghosted my mind with the sensation of him touching me. But beyond the physical was the emotional connection we drew from each other. I'd begrudgingly admitted to myself that I'd resented the connection at the time, and maybe I shut myself down harder afterward for a bit to make him *work* for me, which he did. We'd spent hours talking as if I'd known him for years, and damned if I wasn't coaxed into dropping my defenses again.

Nathaniel had been cute, at least initially, but Kyle drew me in, and I didn't even want to try to escape it anymore. I *liked* him, and I wanted to give it a chance.

Leaving my apartment, I waved to Penny and stumbled over trying to find a way to say I might not be home tonight... just in case. "I may be... late," I finished lamely and cringed at my own choice of words, and even worse was the knowing look in her eye.

Penny replied with an exaggerated wink and a hearty laugh at the expense of my mild discomfort. "Don't do anything I wouldn't do," she teased.

"Fuck off, Penny," I snapped.

She laughed. "I love you, too, Ana."

"Love you too," I muttered as I closed the door, knowing from her following laugh she'd spotted the telltale smirk on my face. Damn her, she knew me too well.

Where did all these people come from who were so understanding of me? I wasn't sure I liked it.

I *did* like it. I missed it. But it was frightening.

Arriving at the grocery store twenty minutes before it was due to close, I walked around the aisles and carefully selected items that would allow me to make a decent meal for Kyle and me.

Although I did buy a premade dessert, I wasn't *Wonder Woman*.

Approaching the building Kyle was staying in, I stood in front of it momentarily.

"He wasn't kidding," I muttered to myself. But I wasn't there to judge, and I pressed my lips together as I eyed the dodgy-looking building. He was trying to start a life in the city, and I could imagine that wouldn't be easy.

Once again, Kyle had been honest with me, which had to

count for something.

I glanced around as I stepped into the foyer and probably looked as out of place as I felt. This was like one of those places from the movies—cheap motel, pay by the hour if you like, or stay as long as you want, no questions asked, no identification required.

I supposed the floor tiles had once been white, but they were now caked with dirt, streaked with the constant foot traffic of the tenants and visitors. Why would Kyle choose a place like this? If it were even a choice, perhaps he had no other option.

What brought him here?

Where did he come from?

I added those to the list of things I wanted to ask him over dinner. I was *so* curious about his story. We'd talked about my childhood, but I wanted to dive deep into his psyche. I wanted to know him as well as he seemed to know me, and I wanted to know if I made his skin tingle the same way he did mine.

If the way he looked at me was any indication, though, I was a precious jewel, not an overly sarcastic woman with more attitude than someone of my height had the right to be.

Maybe tonight, he'd open up about his past. Something I hadn't been able to get more than a few words from him. How could you know so little about someone but feel like you've known them your entire life?

Carrying my groceries inside, I had thought earlier that Kyle looked like he could use a home-cooked meal. Seeing his current home, however temporary it may be, I realized this might be truer than I originally thought.

Approaching the clerk, I smiled at him as I tried desperately not to react when he looked *exactly* like a clerk would in a movie in a place like this. "Hi," I said.

He looked up at me from under his brow and said nothing.

"Umm... I'm looking for Kyle. I'm a friend. I'm going to make us dinner." I unnecessarily patted the bag of groceries and was met with another blank stare. Hesitating, I realized I didn't know Kyle's last name. "Ah, he's about yay high, blond, kind of shaggy-looking, carries a guitar..." I trailed off when the clerk didn't respond and continued to stare at me.

After a pause, he finally responded, "Room 203," in a monotone, and returned to reading.

A bit taken aback, I said, "Isn't that information supposed to be confidential?"

He dropped his magazine on the counter with a slap and fixed me with a stern glare. "What are you? A cop?"

"No."

"You going to kill him?"

"I wasn't planning on it."

"Then, what's the problem?"

"Uh..." *How do I even respond to a twist of logic like that?* "I just thought you might want to protect your tenants better."

The clerk stood, and he was taller than I'd anticipated. Coupled with his considerable girth, he made quite an imposing figure. "Are we going to have a problem here?"

"No, no. I'm going, I'm going." Hugging my grocery bag closer to my chest as though it were a shield that could protect me, I scurried toward the stairway and glanced back at the disgruntled clerk as he watched me leave. Great, now I was on his radar.

When I reached Kyle's apartment, I knocked. I was early, but that was part of the surprise. At least, that's the reasoning I gave myself. There was no answer, but the door shifted slightly when I knocked again.

It wasn't latched properly.

My brow arched as I nudged the door with my foot, and it swung open with a creak.

Stupid.

Shaking my head, I reminded myself to tell him about this when he returned. I knew he wasn't from the city and was used to smaller country towns, but this wasn't the sort of place you'd want to be careless about leaving your door unlocked.

"Kyle?" I called and received no response.

A moment of panic washed over me as I considered that maybe I was in the wrong room. No matter how hard I tried not to judge, it was difficult not to, and something told me I wouldn't want to be caught in the wrong room by some disgruntled tenant. Glancing around, I searched for something I recognized. Spotting Kyle's red plaid shirt, I relaxed with a deep breath, confident I was in the correct place. Sliding the grocery bag onto the small kitchen counter, I started unpacking the items.

From the corner of my eye, something flashed—a bright orange flicker—gone before I could capture it when I turned around.

Staring at the center of the room, I squinted, stepped to the side, and tilted my head until I saw it again.

A shimmer.

Moving toward it, I lost it again for a moment before finding it with another angle of my head. As I approached it, something knocked at the back of my mind.

Hey.

I took another step forward.

Hey, don't go near it. Don't touch it.

I felt I'd seen it before, but couldn't place where. How could I have seen it before? It was just a shimmer, right? But what was it reflecting off?

Don't touch it!

I was drawn to it, this sliver of orange light. Approaching it cautiously and curiously, it seemed to draw me in closer. What was it? It seemed to be in the air itself. There was nothing to reflect that color and nothing to catch the light from the overhead lamp. If I walked to the side, it was still there. Once I was closer, it was no longer shifting in and out of my sight like a magician's trick, but was a small light floating in the room.

Leaning forward, I was practically on top of it, and my necklace dangled out from my chest as I bent over.

Cold. So cold.

"What the fuck?" I whispered.

Standing completely still, my eyes made rapid darting movements as I glanced around. A tremble ran up my spine.

This was wrong, all wrong, and I swallowed back the urge to be sick.

A moment ago, I was in Kyle's motel room.

I knew that at my very core. I wasn't crazy.

So, the fact that I was here made no sense. Wherever *here* was.

Keeping my back to the wall, I looked around again. I was in a hallway at a dead end, and ahead of me was a long, empty stretch. There was no light to beckon me in that direction, and I pressed myself against the wall behind me.

I don't want to be here.

The walls were a deep red, the kind of color people choose

when painting a cigarette lounge. Was it plaster or stone? I couldn't say for sure. Looking up, the ceiling was solid and in the same shade of red. Taking some deep breaths, I tried not to panic, but I could feel the bile rising in my throat, and I choked it down as it burned.

Wherever I was, there had to be an explanation.

And a way to get out.

This place felt wrong.

Reaching out tentatively, I touched one of the walls. It was warm and smooth. Taking a few steps forward, I paused again, looking straight ahead. I could hear something. Voices, but muffled as if I were listening to them through a wind tunnel.

But there was something else.

There was a constant sound in the background, somewhere between a scream and the whoosh of a fireball, warping and fading as though the sound was traveling past me behind the walls and back again. Neither of these sounds was comforting, but I couldn't stand still forever, and the idea of shouting out and drawing attention to myself from God knows who was too terrifying to consider.

My skin crawled, and I was hyper-alert.

This place feels wrong.

Sticking close to one of the walls, I made my way down the hallway, glancing back where I came in case there was a hidden door I hadn't seen before. But there was nothing, only the same dead end. I walked on, and the sound of my footsteps on the floor was flat and empty. There was no echo, no resonating sound, and the sensation was unnerving and unnatural.

When I reached a corner, the voices were clearer. People were having a conversation. They sounded calm, friendly, even.

Apart from the constant sound of screaming somewhere in the background, the voices around the corner seemed normal.

Peeking around the wall, my eyes fell upon a long row of stalls. The doors went from floor to ceiling and reminded me of dressing rooms in shopping centers. The row of doors stretched beyond my sight, and there was no movement down the hallway, and no people were visible.

So, who was talking?

Stepping out from around the corner, each stall had a mirror on the front. But none of them reflected my image. Instead, each mirror showed the image of a different person. All ages, races, and genders were present, and they were conversing with someone I couldn't see or hear. They were all talking at once, occasionally pausing as if there was another side of the conversation I wasn't privy to. Then they would smile and answer inaudible questions.

Approaching the first stall, I stared at the image of a tall, handsome man, and not quite game enough to reach out and touch the mirror, I whispered, "Hello?"

His image didn't respond and continued talking as if I weren't there. Slowly, I made my way down the row of stalls, unable to stop myself from shaking. A tremble started down my spine and continued through my body. The fear was all-encompassing, and I'd never experienced anything like it. My hands shook, and so did my legs. Walking was an effort. This entire place held a horrible feeling of unease that I couldn't explain or get rid of, and my skin continued to prickle unpleasantly.

When I saw movement, I stopped. One of the stall doors was slightly ajar. Approaching cautiously, the door pulsed and moved as if people on either side were fighting to open and close the door simultaneously. No one was on my side, only the image in the mirror.

Who was pushing the door?

The image was of a young woman who appeared to be in her mid-twenties, with shoulder-length brown hair and a bright smile reflected in the door. I didn't recognize her, but she was talking in the same cheery manner as all the other images.

The door continued to pulse.

I moved closer.

Jumping back, I managed to stifle the scream that rose in my throat when the terror I had been holding back finally took over. Fingers appeared around the edge of the door from the inside. The door slammed against the hand, but no matter how bruised they became, the fingers clung to the door, desperate to escape. Somehow, I found the strength to step closer again and screamed when the brunette's face appeared in the crack of the door. Her face was bloody, and her hand became mangled from the constant crashing of the door against it. She ignored it, her eyes fixed on me.

"*Help me.*" The pitch of terror in her voice made the hair on the back of my neck stand on end. Her image on the front of the door continued to talk, smile, and laugh. The laughing image in the mirror starkly contrasted with the terror in the girl's voice behind the door. She was trapped, and while the mirror image smiled and talked, the girl behind the door screamed and clawed at the door as it closed further and further on her. My gaze dragged desperately over the door, seeking something to grab onto to help. There was no door handle and no edge beyond where she was. I tried to push against the mirror to open the door inward so she could escape, but the heat from the mirror seared against my arm, and I jumped back with a yelp.

Before the door slammed, the woman managed to get her arm out briefly and swiped at me before she was dragged from sight, and the door closed with a hollow final thud.

The screaming stopped, and all that was left was the conversation in the mirror.

Happy. Laughing.

Was there one of these doors for me?

My shoulder throbbed in pain as I collided against the opposite wall when I'd thrown myself backward in terror. Every sensation piled on me all at once. All the terror I had kept barely in check until this moment clawed at my throat, and I could scarcely breathe.

Then, I heard it.

An unnatural screech grated against my eardrums. Nails on a chalkboard would've been music compared to this sound. I didn't want to look, but I had to, and I turned my head slowly to my right. There was a creature. Was it made of glass or lava? Diamonds or ice? It was orange with flecks of black, and its skin was so jagged it looked like it would shred me just from being too close.

At my gasp, it lifted its face toward me and smiled. There was no other word for it. As it bared its sharp teeth, its eyes glowed, a flash of orange against a sea of inky black.

I screamed.

And I ran.

I was reacting on pure instinct and kept running. I'd never been so terrified in my life, and I could hear the girl's screams reverberating in my eardrums and mind as I turned the corner and ran back the way I had come. The terror clawed at my throat, and I gasped for breath as the sensation moved down my chest and into my stomach. My entire body started to cramp, and I willed myself to keep moving forward, convinced the creature would be right behind me, and that if I tripped, I would die.

Reaching the dead end where I had first found myself, I clawed at the blank wall. "Oh God, there has to be a way out."

I broke several nails and my hands bled as I banged on the wall with the sides of my fists.

Looking around wildly, I cried for help, "Get me out of here. Let me out!" My screams were so loud and desperate that I barely recognized the voice as my own.

Who were those people?

How did they get there?

What was happening behind those doors?

What was that creature?

Where was I?

Would I become one of those people, trapped forever?

Dropping to the floor, I hugged my knees and sobbed. Rolling into the fetal position, I squeezed my eyes shut as my skin continued to prickle, and I wished to be anywhere but here.

Chapter Thirty

Ana

The first thing I noticed was the change in the air. It was smoother, cooler, and slid down my throat, filling my lungs better than the thin, warm air of wherever I had been. Snapping my eyes open, I was still curled in a defensive ball, but I was back in the middle of the floor in Kyle's place. The dirty carpet beneath my cheek was a comfort and a blessing.

A hand touched my shoulder. "Ana?"

Leaping to my feet, there was only a moment's pause and hesitation before I threw myself into Kyle's arms. I clung to his shirt, and my fingers curled around the fabric as he drew his arms around me.

My body stiffened as the weight of the past few minutes crashed around me.

He knew.

Kyle knew where I had been. I was sure of it. He knew, and he wasn't saying anything.

Pressing my hands against his chest, I shoved hard at him and pushed myself away from his embrace. The pain hit then, and I buckled over and clutched at my stomach.

"*Oh God.*" I groaned at the sensations as they tore their way through my body. The aftermath of the place I had been—it must be that. The cramps felt the same as the sickly sensation that had crawled up my throat. "I think I'm going to be sick."

"Are you okay?" Kyle stepped back and held a hand out to comfort me, but didn't make contact.

Slowly, I breathed my way through the cramps and stood as they subsided. They were replaced with anger, stronger than my fear and confusion. "What the fuck was that place?" I cried.

When Kyle didn't answer, I shoved his shoulders again with both hands. I wasn't strong enough to move him much, but he stepped back with each touch. I assumed this was more out of respect for my space than the force of my push, and somehow this only upset me more. "*Tell me.* What was that place? Where the fuck was I?"

The sadness in his eyes increased the sinking feeling in my stomach, and there was something else in his face—regret. Deep regret that cut straight through him.

Tears welled up in my eyes, and I swiped them away.

"Tell me," I said. This time, my voice was small, the whisper of a terrified child, and despite how pathetic it made me feel, I couldn't help it. The anger was impossible to maintain. I was confused and terrified and still shaking, and I needed answers.

Kyle opened his mouth and closed it again as though choosing his words carefully. Finally, he said, "It was another realm." He watched me as he continued, "A dark place full of evil things."

I sniffed. "Like Hell?"

"Not exactly."

"Then, *what* exactly?" I shouted and drew the last word out with a sarcastic drawl as I threw my arms up in frustration. "You owe me an explanation." I stepped forward into his space and pushed my fingertip against his chest.

Kyle snatched my hand, shifting with such speed I didn't see his arm move. "I told you *not to come here,*" he yelled.

Yanking my hand from his grip, I stepped back, the anger in his voice caught me off guard, and the air almost seemed to shake with his rage. "I just—"

"I don't want to *hear it,* Ana. You could've been killed. Or you could've ended up trapped..." He pointed a shaking hand to the floor. "*There.*"

"I just wanted to make you dinner!"

Whatever Kyle expected me to say, it wasn't that. He dropped his arms to his sides and glared at me. I glared back at him until, once again, the energy I couldn't seem to maintain drained from my body. Barely lifting my arm, I indicated the half-unpacked bag of groceries on the counter. "I just..." my shoulders dropped, "... wanted to be with you."

"Ana..." Kyle reached out to me.

"Don't." I swatted his hand away. "I don't know what the fuck just happened to me, but I need to leave. *Now.*" Kyle grabbed my arm as I tried to walk past. "Let me go, Kyle."

"You need an explanation."

"Let me go. I don't need anything."

"Ana—"

"Forget it. I changed my mind. You don't owe me a damn thing." I tugged at my arm before I tried to pry his fingers off me, but he wouldn't let me go.

"Ana, please." He released me from his grip, and his eyes shot to my arm as red marks appeared for a moment on my skin before fading, and guilt was heavy in his expression. “Please sit down and let me explain.”

I stared at him, my eyes darting between his. Sighing heavily, I knew I didn’t want to leave, not right now. At that moment, I was so vulnerable that if I stepped out onto the street, I’d probably collapse into a helpless heap.

Walking past Kyle, I dropped myself heavily onto the couch. Kyle kneeled on the floor before me and, shrugging his jacket off, placed it around my shoulders. I didn’t even realize I was still shaking.

“Kyle?” My voice broke, and tears welled again, but I was powerless to stop them.

“There are three realms,” Kyle spoke softly and patted his jacket's shoulders over me. “Earth is only one. There are also Lucidis and Tenebris. They are all things light and dark, good and evil, and are separated from each other by Earth between them.” He paused, but I didn’t speak. His words were... words, and they took a moment to sink in. *Realms?* I had so many questions, but they swirled in my mind until they were a tangled heap, and so when I said nothing, Kyle continued, “There’s a Balance between the realms, between light and dark. Sometimes the Balance is tipped, so Guardians are sent to Earth to right things.”

“But... that place...”

“Was Tenebris.”

Another realm. A *dark* realm. With all things dark and evil.

“This is crazy!” I slapped my palms on the couch. “You’ve got to be joking. This can’t be real. Different realms? What kind of talk is that?”

Kyle’s face remained impassive. “I’m not lying, Ana.”

I stared at him.

Different realms.

Where was Kyle from? Not from... Earth?

The idea seemed too wild to consider, and yet...

After a moment, he said, "You're still here."

"Well, I mean—"

"You're still here because you don't doubt what I say."

"Kyle." I cupped his face in my palms for a moment before I dropped my hands onto my lap and fidgeted, wringing my fingers together. "My mind is working desperately, trying to find an explanation f-for..." I faltered, then sighed. "... for what I saw, and I just can't." I looked at him, desperate for an answer that made sense, as if there was some reasonable explanation for being in his room one moment and in a different place the next. "If the only thing I can do right now is trust you..." I rolled my tongue in my mouth as I chose my words, "Then I don't have much choice. The alternative is to go home and pretend it didn't happen and that you're crazy, or let it drive *me* crazy." After a moment, when he said nothing, I stared at my hands in my lap and said, "This is going to sound incredibly stupid, but you know how in movies if someone reveals something shocking to another character, they never believe them? Then, it all comes back around to bite them in the ass later. I always thought that was ridiculous. As if you wouldn't believe your friend, no matter how strange it seemed, you'd trust your friend..." I shrugged and laughed hollowly, "... and here I am."

I met Kyle's eyes, and we looked at each other for a long moment.

"There are different realms?"

His nod was so slight, yet it pushed all the air from my lungs.

Kyle then reached for my hands and stilled my fidgeting. "You can trust me, Ana."

I know.

Silence filled the room as my mind raced.

"The girl..." My voice trailed off.

"What girl?"

"The girl with the dark hair, she was..." Twisting a strand of hair around my fingers, I dropped it from my grasp as panic overtook me. "She was trapped, Kyle. She was trapped in that stall." My voice broke, heavy with the guilt I hadn't had the chance to feel until the shock had eased. "I *left* her there. She was terrified, and I just ran away and left her there with that creature."

I stood, and Kyle's jacket dropped off my shoulders to the floor. Pacing, my fingers intertwined in my hair until I tugged at it. "Oh my God, I didn't even *try* to save her. What's wrong with me?"

Kyle stood slowly. "You can't help her, Ana."

"I have to go back." I grabbed Kyle's shirt as if it were my only lifeline. "Take me back. I need to go back and help her."

"You can't help her."

As my panic rose, my heart rate and breathing increased until the blood pounding in my eardrums was all I could hear. Kyle took my shoulders and shook me lightly, raising his voice. "Listen to me, you can't help her. You can't help any of them." I collapsed to my knees, and Kyle kneeled with me, stroked my hair, and cradled me against his chest. "I'm sorry, but you can't help them. Breathe, Ana, breathe."

Slowly, I managed to gain control over my hysteria, and my breathing slowed. I took a shaky gulp of air, nuzzled my face into

Kyle's chest, and filled myself with his comforting scent. "Why can't I save her?"

"She's not real."

I sniffed. "I don't understand."

Kyle sighed and threaded his fingers through my hair. "I'll tell you."

After a heavy silence, I pulled from his embrace, settled back onto my heels, and wiped my cheeks with the back of my hands. "Are you a Guardian? As in, you're not human?"

He pressed his lips together before finally answering, "Yes."

My chest clenched, and I breathed in deep to try and force myself to remain calm. I needed to understand. "Do you have powers?" I asked.

"In a way. I feel what others feel, and sometimes *they* feel what *I* do. Guardians can influence, search, and locate using emotions, among other things. Every being has an emotional imprint, like a personalized signature, and I can feel those too. I can sense who's feeling what and when. I can influence them to feel certain ways by shifting energy."

"Like an empath."

"I guess."

"Where are you from?"

"Lucidis."

I released a breath.

I believed him. God help me. I believed him.

I shook my head. "I still don't fully understand the realms..."

Kyle held his hands before him as if pressing against an invisible surface. "Think of it as a two-way mirror. We can see you, but you can't see us. Three planes of reality existing side by side at all times, practically on top of each other. We're real, but not in a sense most humans understand. We're not from this realm, from this plane of existence. The Balance we protect isn't influenced by our realms, only yours."

"You feel real to me."

"That's because I'm in your realm. You wouldn't see me or even know I existed if I were at home."

Reaching forward, I touched his chest as if to prove to myself that he was there and the entire conversation was happening. My fingertips spread across the warmth of his chest, which rose and fell with his steady breathing.

He had a heartbeat.

He lived.

I could get up and leave now, but I wanted to know more. I *needed* to know *everything*. Maybe then I wouldn't feel as though I were losing my mind.

Kyle sighed. "I'm sorry, it's hard to find the words to explain." Sitting upright, he continued, "You know how sometimes you can be overcome with a sudden wave of hope or happiness? Of dread or depression? That's us. Have you ever been driving and just had the thought that you could pull into oncoming traffic? Or stop on the train tracks? That's one of the Tenebris Guardian favorites..." Kyle breathed deeply and closed and reopened his eyes slowly. "It doesn't often work, but they keep trying. While Tenebrians feed off negative emotions like pain, fear, distrust, and hate, Lucidians feed off positive emotions like happiness, love, and hope. Human emotions, their spirits, souls, and us... We're all intertwined." He clasped his hands together, linked his fingers, and never took his eyes off mine.

My eyes were wide, but I didn't say anything, so he continued, "Now and then, all across the world, action is required to restore the Balance. It's a delicate point on which we are poised, affected by all emotions. Everything every human feels at all times is shifting the Balance, in constant motion, never still or calm. Sometimes Guardians cross over and influence, good or bad, to make necessary corrections. But I'm here because a Tenebrian Guardian has gone completely Rogue. He's acting violently for personal pleasure. It goes against everything we're meant to do, and he must be stopped."

"What happens if he isn't stopped?"

"The Balance will tip toward Tenebris, toward the negative influences in the world. You see, despite the horrid nature of Tenebris, we need it because good cannot exist without evil. But they must be kept under control. Earth exists on the Balance between Tenebris and Lucidis and cannot exist without either. Tip it too far one way and..."

"And?"

Kyle frowned. "The Balance must be maintained," he replied firmly.

I looked at the floor, my brow creased, as I tried to process and make sense of all the information being presented. When I looked at Kyle, I asked, "Why are you telling me this?"

"You need an explanation for what you experienced. If I leave you without one, you'll likely go mad. I can't allow that."

"Because it'll move the Balance?"

"Because I care about you."

I pressed my lips together. It was difficult enough to accept the feelings Kyle claimed to have for me, and it was nearly impossible to accept that a being from another realm cared about me. "So, the people in the stalls weren't real?"

Kyle rubbed his hands together slowly before he twisted

them around each other. "They are real. The humans you encounter in our realms are part of a whole that makes up the beings here on Earth. Representations of humanity that feed energy directly into your souls. We call them Reflections. The good and the bad in everyone."

"So, somewhere in Tenebris, an Ana is being tortured?"

"No, they are representations of humanity only... Reflections. There is a connection between them and the humans on Earth. They are physical representations of a billion souls, and their emotions all merged. They are not duplicates of people here."

I rubbed my temples. "So, that's why I couldn't save the girl?"

"You can't save her," he repeated. "Outside of Tenebris, she does not exist. She has no name, no home, no family. She's a Reflection only."

Fiddling absentmindedly with my necklace, I abruptly looked up at Kyle, eyes wide. "When we die, do we go to the other realms? Like Heaven and Hell?"

"No."

Disappointment flared in my chest, immediately quelled by anger at having allowed myself to feel hope under the misguided notion that I might see Mom again.

"When people die, they cross over and enter the light," Kyle said.

"What happens then?"

"I'm afraid even we don't know the answer to that." He smiled sadly. "I think that's enough, Ana. It's a considerable amount of information to absorb all at once. I'm sorry, but you're only human."

"And you're not?" I asked more defensively than I had

intended.

He studied my face, his head tilted slightly. "No."

Despite everything, I still trembled slightly at his response. *This was really real.*

"But, but..." I stuttered as I reached out to him again and let my hand drop before I touched him. "You're so real. You look like us."

"Because I choose to, and we take on identities here. We change."

"What do you normally look like?"

He shrugged, and his expression became guarded. "Different."

"I have another question."

Kyle merely looked at me and nodded slightly when I hesitated.

"How did I even end up there?" I asked.

Kyle sighed. "I have been trying to figure that out myself. I had opened the Gateways earlier tonight, and sometimes they can linger like that one you saw the other night."

"What?"

Kyle's jaw clenched. "The night you don't remember, you saw a Gateway. You didn't drink too much. You can't remember because of the influence of how close you were to the Tenebris Gateway, and it was designed to leak influence into humans."

I didn't know how to react. I wanted to be angry or upset, but I sat staring at Kyle. "Why didn't you tell me?"

"You didn't remember the night. Would you have believed me?"

Lowering my gaze, I shook my head. "No. No, I guess not." I put on a voice, fingers splayed, and waved my hands about, "*Hey, Ana. You saw a Gateway to another dimension. Just thought you should know.*"

Kyle smiled, and his brows furrowed simultaneously. "Was that supposed to be me?"

For a flicker of a moment, my lips lifted into a smile. "Yeah, I'm pretty good at impressions." Then, I remembered. "When I saw the light in the middle of the floor, something was in my mind, like it was familiar."

Kyle stared at me momentarily before his eyes flickered to my chest, face, and back again. The furrow deepened between his brows as he lifted his chin at my necklace. "Your necklace, what's it made of?"

Reflexively, I grabbed the stone pendant, hiding it from view. "Moonstone, I think. Why?"

Kyle nodded, still frowning. "Moonstone can be used to return Guardians to their realms forcibly. I've never heard of it before, but maybe it could also work for humans? But I imagine a Guardian would need to be close..." Shaking his head, he stared hard at where my hand encased the pendant. "I'm sorry, I don't have all the answers. And I'm sorry I gave you this address and put you in danger. You were so keen to be with me..." his eyes were pleading when he held my gaze. "I loved that you wanted to be with me as much as I want to be with you, and I gave in to the weakness of wanting you close. I hope you can forgive me. I never wanted to lie to you."

"You told me behind your mask, you had a lot of secrets." I glanced around the small room and swore I could still see the glinting light of the vanished Gateway, and I shivered. "I never imagined it like this..."

Kyle watched me sadly. "Neither did I."

Chapter Thirty-One

Kyle

Somewhere in the recesses of her mind, Ana had accepted what I'd told her as the truth.

Whether that was based on some inherent and ultimately undeserved trust in me, or whether she was simply seeking answers to a situation she could not explain, I couldn't be sure. Perhaps she was clinging to the one thing that eased her confusion.

I didn't have the luxury of time to dismantle her reasons.

But she believed me.

I pushed against the air around Ana with my senses as she sat staring at the floor, her brow pinched with confusion. There weren't tears anymore, but she was still confused and afraid, which was understandable. The sudden awareness of other realms, inhabited by creatures who could influence humans, was a lot to take in. My flinch when she used the word *creatures* had been unavoidable, but if Ana noticed, she didn't say anything.

What do you normally look like?

Different.

Because the truth was the creature she'd seen in Tenebris was a Tenebrian, and while my natural skin was a different color, I looked much like that. I controlled my reaction because I didn't want Ana to associate me with a monster.

I'd told her everything. Everything except the consequences of the Balance tipping. Ana need not be burdened with the knowledge that Earth was constantly teetering on the edge of destruction, prevented *only* by the Guardians doing their duty. There existed something beyond the physical in the world —a spiritual force that we could not see—a force without consciousness, but one controlled by human emotions.

Billions of humans. All feeling different things every second of every day, decade after decade.

And the only thing between them and certain death was us.

Of course, we lived in this world, albeit in different realms, and it was as much about self-preservation as protection. But humans were the ones who influenced the Balance. Humans were the ones who lived their lives letting their emotions spill out. Both positive and negative forces are needed to exist. There could be no Balance without both.

So, while humans influenced the Balance, we influenced them, as needed, to rectify things. Tenebrians acted to bring dark where there was too much light, and Lucidians did the opposite. Both roles were vital.

Until this Guardian had come to Earth, with motives unknown except his sick desires.

My loyalty to my duty was blurred because, really, I shouldn't have told Ana anything. But, if I hadn't told Ana the truth, would she have searched for answers until she was eventually driven crazy when she could find none? I couldn't allow it.

Beyond that, a much more selfish thought populated my mind.

Would she be afraid of me if she saw me as I truly am?

Ana glanced around the apartment, never quite settling on one object or space. Her shoulders slumped, and her movements were slow. She was drained of energy, her imprint was weak, and she needed rest. I watched her process and wished I could tell exactly what she was thinking, but I didn't want to rush her either. No matter how much she trusted me, she'd harbor a small seed of doubt that nothing I said was real.

Creatures.

I turned my hand over and stared at my human form. I could show her so easily, and it would instantly prove everything. But I was weak, and the horror at the idea of her being afraid of me held me back. Reaching my senses out to her again, I probed further. There was so much going on in her mind, and it was a wonder she could think straight. A jumble of emotions rolled around her, and my stomach churned simply experiencing them through her.

Placing a palm on her forehead, Ana raised her eyes to mine without lifting her head.

"What are you doing?" she whispered, barely the energy for any volume.

I shushed gently. "Trust me."

Watching her until her eyelids fluttered closed, I also closed my eyes. Focusing on her panic and fear, I found its energy center, and my mind's eye pictured the sickly yellow poison as it continued to spread through her veins. I forced it from her body and out of her mind and flooded her with calm and a sense of tranquility, pulling it from within my being. The fear vacated her body through her skin and fingertips, an invisible force dissipating into the air. Ana sighed loudly as I worked my powers around her and through her. My palm grew warm on her forehead as my control and peace moved from my being into her very essence.

There was a flash of brilliant white behind my eyelids, and my eyes snapped open at the same time hers did.

It can't be.

Withdrawing my hand, I watched her as she blinked slowly. There was something else inside of her, another part to her. I needed to know more. Desperately, I wanted to talk to her, to get to know her better, and to find out if she knew.

But now was not the time.

Instead, I asked, "Better?" and watched her with concern. Ana nodded, and I asked, "Are you hungry?"

She shook her head. "Thirsty, though."

Standing, I moved to the kitchenette and returned to the center of the room, where Ana knelt on the floor, and handed her a glass.

Ana accepted it. "Is there alcohol in this?"

I chuckled. "It's water. Drink it slowly."

Her small comment spoke volumes to me. It was good to see a flicker of Ana being herself. As much as possible, anyway. She may never be quite the same again, but she was stronger than she gave herself credit for, and I wouldn't let her sink under the weight of this knowledge.

She needed to know. She deserved to know it *all*.

Ana sipped the water a few times before she downed the glass.

"Maybe one day you can answer some questions for me." I

regretted speaking the moment the words left my lips. *One day* implied we would continue seeing each other in the future. But every step we took together reminded me I had already dragged her too far into this. She had her path to travel, and I did mine. But we were drawn together, Ana was entangled with me, and it was almost impossible for me to follow through with my internal reminders that I couldn't keep her by my side.

She was mine, and I hers.

Ana looked at me. "What do you mean? What questions?"

Shrugging, I tried to downplay the statement. "There are just some things about humanity I don't understand."

"Like what?"

Pausing for a moment, I reflected. There were so many things that observation alone didn't explain. Humans did things and participated in traditions that made little to no sense to me. Some things they had done for so long that they didn't even question them anymore, and it made it impossible for Guardians to understand *why*.

One example...

"Birthdays," I said.

Ana laughed, then covered her mouth with her hand. "I'm sorry, I don't mean to laugh. What about birthdays?"

Shrugging again, I was suddenly uncomfortable with having asked, but I couldn't help the curve of my lips at her reaction. "I don't know, I just don't get them. What are you celebrating? You didn't even do anything. You were just... *born*."

Ana smiled, then looked thoughtful. "You know, I've never really thought about it. I guess we like celebrating things. Birthdays represent a milestone in your life."

I nodded, although I didn't really understand. It seemed

like a lot of trouble. Or maybe it was because it was an excuse to socialize, which was also a foreign concept to me. Each Guardian community congregated at the end of each day to balance one another and replenish the energy we had used throughout the day. Influencing was easier when we could draw from each other.

That, and courting often took place at night. Sex was for physical pleasure or reproduction, nothing more.

"What else do you want to know?" Ana asked as she leaned forward, eager to be the one answering questions.

"Ana, I should take you home."

Ana looked up at me, her eyes wide and pleading. "Can't I stay?"

Accepting my outstretched hand, I helped her to her feet. "Ana..."

"Look," she straightened and faced me as much as possible with the height difference. "I don't fully understand what all this is, but I know you, and only a few hours ago, I was coming here to make you dinner and maybe spend the night with you." A surge of fear ran through her and disappeared almost as quickly. She didn't want to be without me. "So, can I?"

Gripping her hand, something squeezed at my heart in my chest. I resisted the urge to pull her closer to me, to feel her heartbeat against mine. I hated myself for what she'd seen, what she had been through, and most of all, for allowing myself to get so close to her. From the moment I first touched her, I knew this wasn't simply pleasures of the flesh, and I couldn't stop myself from coming back to her again and again. Every minute Ana spent with me put her in further danger. Another Guardian was out there seeking to do as much damage as possible, to turn light into darkness.

If he discovered who I was and that I was close to a human...

I shuddered. Ana had already been too close to complete evil, and I couldn't allow her to continue being at risk.

But there was another thought that fought within my mind. Was Ana safer with or away from me? Could I protect her if the other Guardian were to come for us? Should I keep her close, so I could know she was safe?

Ana watched my face and stared straight into my eyes as I battled these thoughts. In her eyes, that gorgeous deep brown, I saw complete sincerity, trust, and a remaining flicker of fear that even I couldn't take away.

And God help her, I saw love.

The realization startled me.

Ana cared. She knew what I was and that I wasn't human, and she still cared. Beyond that, she was falling for me, and even more terrifying, I was falling for her too. Falling in a way I had witnessed humans do so many times and never knew I was capable of.

Pulling Ana close, I wrapped my arms around her, and she melted against me.

"Ana, I'd feel better if you were home. I'll make sure you get there safely. I have work to do, and I want you to be with Penny. Will she be home?" I spoke as gently as possible, trying to do the right thing. All the while, my heart felt like it was being ripped from my chest at having to send her away.

Ana nodded against me but didn't let me go and continued to nuzzle against my chest.

Resting my chin on her head, my stomach rolled, and my chest tightened.

She was so close. *Too* close.
What had I done?

Chapter Thirty-Two

Ana

After walking me home, Kyle waited for me to be safely in my apartment before he left. Standing near the window, I watched him walk away, and a void opened in my chest. It took every fiber of my being not to press my hand against the cool glass of the window, seeking those inches closer to him even as he disappeared into the night. Before Kyle had left, I'd asked him what his real name was since he'd told me Guardians took on different identities on Earth.

The corner of his mouth had twitched as he held back a smirk, and I found myself getting defensive and crossing my arms over my chest.

His smirk then broke through his control. "I don't yet understand humans' obsession with names, but then again, you interact much differently than we do, driven by emotion."

I was beginning to feel like a lab rat being studied, and my back stiffened. His face changed, and I guess he picked up on the shift in my mood with those powers of his that I wasn't even close *to understanding.*

He extended his hand. "Cael."

Shaking his hand slowly, I said, "That's very similar to Kyle."

"Yes." He squeezed my hand briefly before he broke the contact. "But more unusual. Unusual draws attention." He looked down at himself and opened his arms. "Plus, different me, different name."

I dropped onto the couch with a heavy sigh.

Penny had woken when I'd gotten home and watched as I sat and stared out the window.

She rubbed her eyes. "So, not an all-nighter, then?"

"Guess not."

A furrow creased her forehead, and she sat next to me. "What happened? Do you want to talk about it?"

Continuing to stare out the window, the void in my chest filled with a range of emotions I couldn't quite put names to. The dark city skyline stared back at me from outside, every light flickering as though it were intentionally holding back the shadows and all the secrets the darkness held.

Was the other Guardian out there now? What was he doing? Was someone being hurt?

"Do you ever think about all the evil in the world?" I asked.

Penny stiffened next to me. "Ana... did he hurt you?"

Snapping back to reality, I turned to Penny. "What? No, no, nothing like that."

Penny settled on the couch, and the fake leather creaked as she shifted and linked her arm with mine before she patted my hand. "I guess I try not to think about the evil in the world too much. I try to focus on the good."

"There's just so much bad out there, you know? So many horrible things, people who need help, and others doing terrible things, and some don't even know they're doing anything wrong..." I could feel the tears forming when I turned to look out the window again. "We try so hard to stay in our safe bubble, our little world we created, our safe space..." Everything Kyle had told me was balling up inside me.

Influence was the word he'd used—the Guardians could *influence* humans.

Why were we so susceptible?

"How much of what we do is our own will? Are we vessels for evil or inherently good with a few bad seeds? Are we all capable of terrible things with a push in the wrong direction?"

"These are some big questions, Ana... bigger than we're supposed to know, I imagine."

Nodding, my lips pressed together in a thin line as I fought to keep myself together. The calm I had felt flood my body when I was with Kyle had dissipated now that we were apart, and a sense of selfishness had crept into its place. Kyle was surely more important than I, and he had things to do. A duty. But I was taking up his time, and my feelings towards him were... getting in the way. I turned to Penny, unable to stop my face from telling the tale of the turmoil inside me. Penny knew there were terrible things in the world. I knew her past and what she had been through, and I didn't need to tell her of the darkness.

I wished I had been there to protect her. Perhaps I could've laid my life down so she didn't have to go through it at all.

The world needed her and Kyle. It didn't need me so much.

"I'm worried about you," Penny whispered.

After I shook my head slowly, it felt as though I was seeing her for the first time, really seeing her.

And she was beautiful.

Everything felt different now.

"I'm sorry," I said, and when I closed my eyes, my eyelids felt heavy. "It's been a long night."

"Is there anything I can do to help?"

I shook my head. "No. Thank you. I'm just going to go to bed."

Standing abruptly, I paused for a moment and turned to look back at Penny. Bending down, I kissed her cheek, "I love you, you know that, right?" I whispered. I couldn't even be certain I'd said anything out loud.

"I love you too," Penny answered, equally as quietly, as though any loud noise would break us. She pressed her fingertips to her cheek, and the beginning of tears shone in her eyes as her face was bathed in the light from the city outside. I moved to my bedroom hastily before I broke down completely.

Surely, Penny already knew, but I wanted to tell her.

Because the world suddenly felt much larger than before, and there were so many dark forces in it—forces completely outside my control. Battles are going on with beings and realms humans didn't even know about, so close we could touch them, if only we could reach out to break through the barrier between our realms.

Not bothering to get undressed, I wrapped my blanket around my body as though, like a child, I hoped it would protect me from the monsters under my bed.

And the monsters everywhere else.

My cell rang obnoxiously loudly and startled me out of my

snooze. I'd stayed in our apartment all day and watched television when I'd failed to summon the concentration to read a book. I could be achieving something, even something as simple as cleaning the apartment. I could change the bed sheets or put a load of washing on. I could sort my clothes or do some grocery shopping.

But everything felt somewhat pointless.

Without lifting my head from the couch cushion, I fumbled for my cell and stabbed my thumb blindly at the screen to answer it.

Kyle's panicked voice cut in before I'd even had a chance to speak. "How did you get into my apartment last night?"

"What?"

"*Ana.*" He sounded frantic, forcing me to wake up completely from my doze and concentrate. "How did you get into my apartment last night?"

"I, ah..." Sitting up straight, I ran a palm down my face. "The door was unlocked, Kyle. I meant to mention it to you, but with everything that happened... I forgot." My brows furrowed at the silent response. "You really should lock your door."

"I *do* lock my door." He sounded as though he were speaking through gritted teeth.

"What's wrong?" I asked, but he didn't answer. In the background, there was shuffling and banging, and it sounded like he was turning his apartment upside down. "The man in the lobby told me what apartment you were in without much prompting."

That got his attention. "He *what*?" Kyle practically yelled.

I explained apologetically how I'd found his room and gained access. "I'm so sorry, Kyle. I shouldn't have done what I did, but

I wanted to surprise you with dinner."

"Ana, I don't care that you got in. But I do care that it was so easy to do so. I'll be having words with that man." The shuffling continued.

"Kyle, what are you doing?"

"To see if he left anything else."

"If who left what?"

Silence filled the other end of the line.

"Kyle?"

When he finally spoke, his tone sent chills down my spine. "Ana..." I gripped the cell tightly against my ear. "The Tenebrian Guardian, he knows who I am."

"What? How do you know?"

"He left something for me." His voice sounded tight.

"I don't understand. What did he leave? I thought you knew who each other were?"

"No. He took human form so he could be anyone. I know he's here, around here, but I couldn't pinpoint him exactly until I'm on Earth. We can use our human forms to get closer to humans and influence them. But he has used his human form to conduct violence as well as influence. It has taken me so long to find him because he could be *anyone,* and he hides his true form." He added, muttering, "He's so good at hiding his imprint... too good."

"How long have you been trying to find him?"

"Weeks. I'm not even supposed to be here this long. It messes with my being, with my powers. I'm getting desperate, and this proves that he's just toying with me. He's been doing so much damage. The negativity is over this entire area like a blanket."

After a moment, I asked again, "What did he leave in your

apartment?" When he didn't answer, I stood. "I'll be right there."

"Ana, *no—*"

I hung up on him and pulled on a pair of boots.

Running down the flights of stairs of the apartment building, now and then, I skipped a step, but stopped doing that when, after the third time, I lost my footing and collided with an emergency exit door. Rubbing my shoulder, I reached the ground floor and slowed to catch my breath. As I jogged through the small foyer, I passed Henry, who was talking to a teenager, and waved on autopilot. When my greeting was met with a shuffle of hands and a guilty look from the teenager, I stopped.

"Everything all right, Henry?"

"Fine, just fine. Thank you." Henry pocketed an envelope as I surveyed the teenager, his hands stuffed in his pockets. Henry waved cheerily. "Well, have a nice day, lad."

The boy took a hand from his pocket to shake Henry's outstretched hand and, in doing so, spilled the contents of his pocket onto the floor.

"Let me help," I said.

I bent as the boy said hurriedly, "No, thanks." Before he scooped up his belongings, shoved them hastily back into his pockets, and fled the foyer.

"Henry..." Standing slowly, I looked at Henry. "Are you... selling your prescription medication?"

"What?" Henry chuckled, but it sounded empty. "Don't be ridiculous."

I pointed to the door behind me. "I saw the packets he had, and they looked like heart medication. I've helped you fill your scripts. I know what they look like."

When Henry didn't respond, I tilted my head and stared until he was forced to look at me. "If he takes them or uses them to make something, people could get hurt. He's just a boy."

"I don't think I appreciate your tone."

I assessed him. This wasn't right. This wasn't the Henry I knew. Something was off.

Had the Tenebrian been near him?

Did he *have* to be near him? Could Henry have been affected simply by the negative energy in the area? I struggled to filter through all the information and bit my lip in indecision.

Physically, I was still poised to leave and glanced back and forth between the door and Henry.

"You look like you have somewhere to be," he said.

"Yeah..." I hesitated for a moment longer. "I'll talk to you about this later, Henry. Please be safe." Turning to leave, I glanced back to catch him watching me go, conflict written all over his face.

OUTLET

Chapter Thirty-Three

Kyle

Swinging the door open after Ana's urgent knocking, I said, "You shouldn't have come."

She pushed her way past me. "What happened? Are you okay?" Turning to face me as I closed the door, she asked again, "What did he leave?"

Without considering the gesture would speak the words I didn't, my eyes flickered to a table. Ana followed my gaze, strode over, picked up the envelope, and read the message on the front out loud, "*Are you enjoying your time on Earth?*" After a brief hesitation, Ana frowned and emptied the envelope's contents onto the table. She recoiled. "Is that *blood*?"

"Yes."

"Whose is it?"

"Sophia's."

Ana lifted the blood-stained dress using the end of a pen. Although *blood-stained* wasn't a suitable description—the dress was *soaked* in blood, so much so that it was hard to tell the original color. Though I remembered well. The vision of Sophia dancing in that dress swam in my mind, and my stomach churned.

It's my fault.

I watched Ana staring at the dress and knew she was imagining, as I had, all the horrible things that could have happened to the girl who wore it. Ana dropped the dress and shakily rubbed her already-clean hands on her jeans without taking her eyes off it.

She was jerked out of her stupor when I called her name, "Ana."

"Oh my God..." Ana muttered as her lip trembled. "What did he do to her?"

"I don't know."

"And you knew her?"

"Enough."

Ana glanced back at the envelope and tried to avoid looking at the dress again, but her eyes were drawn to it. "Where did you find the envelope?"

"It was on the floor but was partially hidden beneath my jacket. Far enough in the room that he must have come in but left it somewhere I'd see it. I must have missed it when I came back. I was in a rush to... to rescue you."

"Rescue me..." She frowned. "How did you even know I was in trouble?"

"I felt you cross over through the Gateway. They dispel an energy force."

Ana nodded, although I knew she didn't fully understand. She was trying, and it was more than I could ask when I had expected her to leave the moment I'd revealed the truth. "I still don't get these feelings you have..." Ana's hands twitched with unfinished gestures. "These senses."

"It's hard to explain."

She nodded again, and I could almost see her turning the information over in her mind. "Did you sense Sophia was in trouble?"

"No, yes, I mean... maybe I did."

"I don't—"

"I think I was too clouded. I was in a pit of self-loathing." I struggled to find the words to explain. My chest ached, and I resisted the urge to clutch a palm to it. I needed her to understand in a way that had never been important before. "My own feelings were so intense. Anything else I sensed wouldn't have registered as strongly. I was *completely* enveloped in negative emotions. It's not normal for Guardians to *feel* like that, to feel *at all*. I've tried to figure it out, but the normal way of things seems to change the longer I'm here. Maybe your signal of being in trouble was stronger?"

"Why?"

"Because yours involved a Gateway, and maybe also because..."

Ana prompted me when I didn't finish my sentence, "Because?"

"Because I care about you."

Ana's brows raised. "That just raises more questions. Why would he hurt her to get to you and not me?"

"I don't know. I assumed he must have seen me with her when we were together."

"Together?"

Guilt and discomfort tugged at my insides. "*Together*," I enunciated the word.

As understanding hit, Ana's expression shifted and became

stony. "Oh... oh, I see."

"Ana, I'm sorry. We didn't sleep together. Please believe me. I wouldn't lie to you."

"You don't need to apologize to me. You said no promises at the time. I understand." But her eyes betrayed her hurt.

I stepped closer to her. "I *do* need to apologize because it was a mistake to even be in the bar. I was only there to try and get you out of my mind..." I cringed. "Although I only went to *that* bar looking for you."

Fuck.

"Why?"

"Because you're the only one who makes me happy." Her breath stilted, and she held my gaze as I continued, "When Sophia kissed me, I couldn't stop thinking of you, and I couldn't do it. I *swear* I didn't have sex with her." I sighed as weight settled in my chest. "But now she has paid for just being seen with me."

Ana looked down and mumbled, "I believe you."

I kept talking, desperate to share my thoughts and feelings with Ana and to have her understand. "After I left the bar, I felt so empty, but the anger was building. Resentment at myself for having failed to find the Tenebrian. When I went into the bar where you found me, that's where I caused the bar fight."

"You started that fight?"

"Not intentionally. I influenced the fight accidentally."

"Kyle..." Ana took a breath and slowly lowered her hands. "Explain it to me as if I were... just a *human.*"

I bit my lip. I'd never had to explain this to anyone before. "In the same way Guardians influence emotions from our realms to yours, we can do the same when we're here on Earth, only it's stronger. But when we're here too long, the lines get blurred, and sometimes our emotions can cause a reaction in the humans around us without us even trying."

"So, the fight started..."

"Because I was angry at myself, and it spilled out of me and made them all angry. I never laid a hand on anyone to start a fight. I only tried to stop it."

Ana was silent for a long while as she contemplated the questions this raised. When I thought she would ask another question, her head snapped up. "Turn on the news."

"What?"

"The TV, *turn on the TV.*"

I found the remote and flicked through the channels, looking for an early evening broadcast.

Ana rubbed her temples. "Sophia, the name sounded so familiar. I think I heard something today on the news while I was flipping channels."

When I found a news report, we sat on the couch and watched in silence through the weather and smaller stories.

"There!" Ana grabbed the remote and turned up the volume. The reporter sat at his desk, his expression serious. A small picture box in the corner of the screen displayed *Mass Murder* in dramatic red writing.

"*An update on our top story. Police are still calling for any witnesses to the gruesome murders that took place last night. The murders occurred in the early hours of Sunday morning out the back of the Park Place Hotel. The five college students have been identified, and their photos have been released. Police are seeking to trace their steps leading up to the murders. If anyone recognizes any of these people, please contact the police on...*"

As the reporter spoke, the screen displayed five photographs of young adults—three men and two women, including Sophia. The pictures appeared to have been taken in social settings. They were smiling or laughing, so young and happy, with plans for the rest of their lives. My heart broke for them and their families, and when I looked at Ana, her expression was disturbingly blank, as though she simply couldn't absorb any more chaos. My stomach churned with a mixture of rage, sorrow, and guilt.

"*Police have been unable to identify what weapon or weapons were used, and I have been notified that further details are too upsetting to share...*"

Flicking off the television, I dropped my face into my hands with a heavy groan while Ana sat in shock. She was facing the full reality of what the Tenebrian Guardian was capable of, and it was far from pretty.

I turned toward Ana and took her hands in mine. "You need to leave."

"What? Why?"

Pointing angrily at the now blank television screen, I raised my voice. "You saw that, right?"

"Yes, but—"

"Ana!" I stood as anger flooded through me. "He has no limits! He's *killed* people. What if he comes for you? I can't..." I sighed, my shoulders dropped as thoughts of a reality I couldn't bear to face came to the forefront, "... I can't lose you."

"You don't even know me. Why do you care so much?" Ana's voice was small.

"I do know you." I sat again, faced her, and cupped her cheek in my palm. "You're funny, caring, and stronger than you give yourself credit for. You dance like an absolute idiot, yet I know you *can* dance when you want to. And despite what you've been through, you still have hope. I can feel it in you, which takes something special, and you're..." I paused, and Ana filled the silence.

"And '*In the few hours we had together, we loved a lifetime's worth.*'?"

I stared at her. "Is that another movie quote?"

Ana looked at her feet. "Yeah, from *The Terminator*."

Standing again, I dropped my hand from her face. "Ana, this is serious."

Ana threw her arms up. "I know. I'm sorry. I got nervous." She stood and faced me. "This! *All of this.* It's a lot to take in, okay?" She brushed her fingers down my cheek. "I care about you, and I feel drawn to you, too. Why is that? What is it about you that breaks through my walls?"

"Ana, *please*," I tilted my cheek into her touch. "I need you to be safe."

"Aren't I safer here with you?"

"What if he comes for me... or you?"

"Then, I'll have you, and you'll have me."

"I think you may be safer further away from me."

Ana squeezed her eyes shut for a moment. "But what if you need me?" she asked, and the break in her voice shattered something inside me.

"I *do* need you." I leaned in closer, pulled her against me, and wrapped my arms around her. "Which is why I need you safe."

Ana twisted her fingers in my shirt as she hugged me close. "I *am* safe."

Chapter Thirty-Four

Kyle

Sleep didn't come easily that night.

I stared at the ceiling and listened to the sounds of the city outside. Two floors down, the people around the streets had no idea of the dangers present right next to them, in their city and homes, and the constant conflict that threatened to tear their entire world apart. Looking over at Ana, I watched as she slept on her side. Her breathing was slow and steady, and every outward breath fluttered the hair that had fallen in front of her face. I'd never been so torn internally. This was torture.

Rolling onto my side to face her, I watched her for a while. Peace radiated from her, and I breathed it in. She slept the sleep of the calm, somehow able to push her troubles aside to allow her body the rest it needed, and I envied that. There was extra weight on my shoulders, the additional incentive to do what I came here to do, because I needed to protect Ana.

But what happened after I found the other Guardian? I'd have to go home to Lucidis.

Would Ana wait until I could come back?

Did I even expect her to?

Would I be able to come back?

"I can hear you thinking."

I startled. "You can?"

Ana laughed sleepily, her eyes still closed. "Not literally, you idiot."

Reaching out, I rolled her toward me and pressed her back to my chest. Ana sighed, relaxed against me, and molded her body next to mine. I could feel every curve of her, and every inch of skin-on-skin contact awakened me further. She had slept naked at her insistence that she was comfortable doing so. I'd resisted because I didn't want to pressure her or make her feel like she had to do anything physical simply because she was staying the night.

Breathing out slowly, I followed the movement of the air with my senses as it traced across her skin and left a trail of goosebumps in its wake. Shifting my weight on the bed, I couldn't concentrate on the world outside anymore, but I was content to leave that behind.

All I could feel was Ana.

Her heartbeat sounded like a drum in my head, and her skin's small divots and imperfections shaped the air around her. I could sense her being, essence, and everything that made her who she was.

Reaching out to her, I ran my fingertips across her shoulder. The air in the room changed, and she was fully awake, although she didn't move. She shivered under my touch, and there was something else I could sense. *Arousal.* Breathing out heavily, my cock hardened, and her response to my touch only fueled me further.

Tracing my fingers down her arm and over her hip, I hesitated only for a moment before continuing down her stomach and over the mound of her pubic hair. Ana moaned softly and shifted against me, and her arousal was escalated by mine as it drifted through my skin and settled over the two of us like mist. I almost couldn't contain the tension as it built in my body. When I dipped my hand lower and found the warmth between her legs, she moaned openly and loudly. I groaned with her as I felt her wetness around my fingers. She was ready for me, waiting for me.

"Kyle..." Ana panted. I'd barely touched her, and it felt as though her skin was on fire. I needed her, needed to be inside her, so much that it hurt. Ana rolled onto her back, grabbed my arms, and encouraged me to move on top of her. Bracing myself on my forearms above her, I studied her face. Her cheeks were flushed, and one lip indented lightly from her bite.

She was perfection.

"Ana..." I pressed my lips to hers, softly at first, before increasing the pressure and dominating her mouth.

"Please..." She breathed against my lips. "I need you."

Resting my face in the nook of her neck and shoulder, I planted kisses along her collarbone. Ana ran her hands up my shoulders and rubbed down my back while she opened her legs to invite me as I guided myself inside her waiting warmth. Growling as she enveloped me, I moved in her slowly and rocked my hips against hers as she opened her legs further and pulled a knee back toward her chest.

Groaning, I thrust into her and relished as she gasped.

I knew this was wrong, everything I wasn't meant to do.

Guardians were not supposed to be close to a human, not like this.

Not at all.

Ana moved her hands down my back and over my hips and pulled me into her as she started pushing up to meet my thrusts. Our pleasure was linked, and our emotions and sensations filled the room as we infected each other. Every breath we took was together. I got completely lost within her, unable to stop touching her and feeling her, all the while fighting an internal battle with the repercussions of the depth of my feelings for her.

I didn't want to stop. I never wanted to stop.

But I'd have to, one day soon.

Almost all Guardians partook in pleasures with humans while on Earth, but this was different. I'd taken it too far. I *cared* for her. I cared much more than I should, more than I thought possible.

Did I love her? Did I have it in me to love?

A single invasive thought popped into my head—*take her with you.*

I grew angry at myself, resentful of my feelings, and it started to infiltrate through my pleasure, cutting like a knife and spreading into the room. I thrust into her harder, and her moans of ecstasy drove me faster. When I bit into her shoulder, Ana cried out, and her fingers tensed against my back.

"Gentle," she whispered.

"*Quiet.*"

It was a statement, a demand, and the influence dripped from my voice even though I hadn't intended it. I was losing control in the worst of ways and dragging Ana down with me. Ana's eyes widened as she opened her mouth to speak, but only a small squeak escaped when she tried to utter a response.

What have I done?

I growled against her skin as my climax built with hers. Ana gasped intermittently. Her pleasure fed off mine and vice versa. We were one. My thrusts became sporadic, and Ana's mouth opened in a silent scream as she came at the exact moment I spilled inside her. I watched her face as she reached her climax, and her skin seemed to almost glow from it.

What have I done?

Collapsing on top of her, I trembled as Ana's leg twitched against me. As my heart rate slowed and my breathing returned to normal, the invisible fog in the room ebbed away and cleared.

Ana took a deep, shuddering breath of the cleared air.

"Kyle." She cleared her throat when her voice came out as a stumbling croak. "Kyle, what was that? Why couldn't I speak?"

Rolling off her, my weight shifted the bed, and I ran my hands over my face. "I'm sorry."

"Sorry? You're... Did you..." Ana clutched her throat, sat up, and pulled the sheet to cover her breasts. "Did you *control* me? Like those people at the bar fight?"

Frowning, I watched her face carefully. "Ana, can we talk?"

"What?" She laughed humorlessly. "What? You're trying to small-talk me now?" She stared hard at me.

I tried again when she didn't speak, asking, "Tell me about your parents. What do you remember of your father?"

"Are you serious right now?"

The air rippled with sparks of anger from her, and as it filled the room, I held my hands up. "I'm trying to calm the situation."

She laughed, and the sound was edged with tears. "That's so stupid. Don't you think I have a reason not to be calm? You. Controlled. Me."

I ran my hands over my face again. "It was an accident."

"An accident? That doesn't make it any better, Kyle."

"My powers leaked. I told you this can happen on Earth."

Ana snatched her top from the end of the bed and pulled it over her head as she slid out from under the sheets, then started getting dressed. "So, how do I know any of this is real?"

"Ana..."

She stood straight and watched me with a strange look. "How do I know you didn't just..." she spluttered as she tried to find the words. "... *influence* me to love you?"

I lifted myself onto an elbow. "Love? I..." But she had already pulled her boots on. "Ana, it's the middle of the night."

She turned. "What are you going to do, Kyle? *Influence* me to stay, so I have to?"

"It's not like that. There's always an element of free will. We can't completely take you over."

She glared at me.

Relenting, I sighed. "No, I won't make you stay with me."

"You know..." she started, and the anger practically dripped from her voice. "... I stayed because I felt safer with you. Suddenly, there's a whole world out there that I can't begin to understand fully, and you... *You* are the only constant. I thought..." Her shoulders dropped. "I thought I was safer with you than away from you. But tell me, Kyle..." I raised my eyes from my hands in my lap, "... am I?"

My mouth opened and closed several times, and I didn't speak for a moment. There were no words to express the ache that burned inside me. There were still so many things left to tell her, yet it felt wrong to burden her further than I already had.

Is she safer with me?

Finally, I whispered, "I don't know."

She stared at me, nodded stiffly, and then turned to leave.

"I love you, too," I muttered.

Ana paused, her head bowed as her shoulders shook, but she didn't turn around and left without looking back.

It was painful to move, as if lifting my limbs was an act I couldn't muster the strength to manage.

Until it hit me.

Sitting bolt upright in my bed, I focused my senses.

I'd barely moved since Ana left not long ago, but now I could feel it, seeping through the air and infecting the room and me.

Pain and fear—a lot of it.

"Ana," I whispered as I threw myself out of bed and pulled my clothes on. Grabbing my crossbow and quiver, I ran out of the room and down the hall.

In the street, I tried to gain my bearings. Focusing on the pain, I tried to ignore how it stabbed into me and ached, and I closed my eyes for a moment before I started walking. My gait turned into a sprint when the feeling intensified, and I tried to convince myself the direction was just a coincidence. My panic drove me faster and spurred me on when the source of the pain was apparent and could no longer be denied.

Ana's apartment building.

I tried desperately to pinpoint the emotional imprint behind the pain, but there was a fog around it, which meant the Tenebrian was near.

No.

Once I entered her building, I pounded the elevator button before turning and racing up the stairs two at a time. I heard the ding of the elevator doors opening as I was already at the top of the first flight.

If something had happened to her, if he had hurt her, I would never forgive myself.

It was my fault.

This whole thing was my fault.

Chapter Thirty-Five

Ignis

She was asleep, her breathing slow and steady, interrupted only by gentle murmurings of nightmares that plagued her. I wondered what she was dreaming about, not that it mattered.

Because once I had Ana, all her nightmares would become a reality.

Knocking on her apartment door, I waited. While it was late, I'm sure I could devise a decent reason for being here. Ana knew my face, and she'd follow me until it was too late to realize the danger she was in. There was no answer, but the sleepy mist from inside had dissipated. Perhaps they thought me an intruder, although hopefully, my gentle knocking would ease their nerves. Thieves tended not to knock politely.

"Who is it?" a voice yelled through the door.

That wasn't Ana. This must be the roommate.

Gritting my teeth, I then forced my jaw to relax. "I'm looking for Ana," I replied as I sought the apartment for a second imprint. "It's important."

The door opened a crack, and I was face-to-face with an attractive woman with dark hair whose features suggested an

Asian heritage. She was quite beautiful, though she looked at me with suspicion.

Smiling pleasantly, I held out my hand. "Hi, I'm—"

Her face contorted and twisted from suspicion into fear, then terror. She recoiled from my extended hand, and I watched her curiously. Strange, I wasn't letting my negative influence leak out to make her feel fear she couldn't explain. I was hidden perfectly in this human form, yet she reacted like she had seen the devil.

"I know you," she whispered, one hand raised to her throat as though she could stem the terror that gripped and spilled out of her before it filled the air between us.

I cleared my throat, unsure why she was reacting this way. "Well, of course, you do. I'm Ana's—"

"*No.* Don't touch me!" Lurching forward, she attempted to slam the door, but I moved my foot in the way. "Get out! Get out... *right now,"* she screamed, and her voice bordered on hysteria as she pushed the door uselessly against my foot.

Staring at her curiously for a beat longer, I shoved the door open and entered the apartment before quietly closing the door behind me. She scrambled away from me and almost tripped over her own feet, her face the perfect picture of terror.

Tilting my head, I frowned and studied her features. She seemed to know me.

Then it all came back in an instant, and a dark smile spread across my face and contorted my features. "Oh... I remember you now."

It was *her.*

All those years ago, I had kidnapped her from the street, taken her to an abandoned warehouse, and tortured her for hours. She had been so full of terror that night that she hadn't even begged for her life after the first hour, sure I was going to kill her at the end of her ordeal.

How about that? Her nightmares were probably still about me.

"I enjoyed myself that night," I crooned. She froze on the spot, and fear turned her legs useless as she trembled like the pathetic human she was. Sniffing the air, I got a read on her imprint. "After what I put you through, I expected you to go dark. Humans have the uncanny ability to turn their trauma into pain for someone else, as though attacking others would ease their pain." I chuckled and tilted my head. "But you didn't, did you? No, I can sense it about you. You went on to try to help people and ease your pain by helping others in pain. Seems I misjudged you."

As I approached her, something inside her snapped, and she started to scream. Launching myself at her, I clasped a hand over her mouth, and she immediately tried to fight me off, but she was too weak. "I thought about you often while I was back home," I muttered against her struggling form, my lips close to her skin. Sending memories and shivers down her spine as she recalled the last time I was this close to her body and what I did to her. "I did not intend on finding you once I came back here, but now we are together again..."

She wasn't why I was there, but since I was all about pleasure, perhaps I could make this trip more fun than I planned. I would find Ana because she was the one who would cause the most pain to the Lucidian.

Sophia had been a message, but Ana would be the end of him.

Maybe this woman even knew where Ana was, but one way

or another, I was going to use her for my pleasure again, and the air would be thick with her fear.

She fumbled around on the kitchenette bench, grabbed at something, and slashed at my face with a small pair of nail scissors. I recoiled at the sharp sting but didn't lift my hand from her mouth. Smirking, I touched the blood that dripped down my cheek.

"Oh, I like you." I chuckled. "I really do like a fighter." Grinning, I pressed myself down against her, dragging her to the floor while she screamed against my hand.

Looking up, my eyes narrowed, and I smiled down at the human woman as she trembled by my knees. She had curled into the fetal position and sobbed quietly the moment I moved away from her.

"He's coming," I said as I stood. With sure aim, I lashed out another kick at her stomach. She cried out and started coughing. "Too bad. We were only just getting started." I'd barely had time to have the fun I intended, and now there certainly wasn't time to get her clothes off. Maybe it didn't turn out to be quite the do-over from our night together years ago, but I achieved a high from the familiar sense of her fear. She had been one of my first victims when I had decided Tenebris no longer held the pull to keep me rooted there, and my trips to Earth became more frequent and more violent until finally, I came to be here, and messed with the Balance and all those that cared about it.

Her fear was thick through the space between us now, much

as it was the last time we met.

But it was stronger, sicker, and I breathed it in. This time, she had the terror of knowing what I was capable of, and all the memories I had left her with poisoned her essence the moment she'd seen my face. Glancing down, she moved on the floor as though her breathing was painful. Perhaps her mind was trying to shut down her body, fearing that I would do it first.

Reaching out, I grabbed her shoulders, forced her into a sitting position, and slapped her across the face. "Where is Ana?"

"I don't know," she cried, a trickle of blood trailing from the corner of her mouth. She looked at me in disgust, and she coughed again. "Even if I did know, I wouldn't tell you," she said before she spat blood onto my face.

I grinned. "Oh, you have such potential, my first. I wish we had more time."

Looking up again, I dropped her to the floor like discarded trash and moved to the window. The Lucidian was on his way to this building. I could feel his presence as it grew closer. While tonight would be the night we finally met face-to-face and acknowledged each other for who we were, I wasn't quite ready yet.

Because he had a weakness for Ana, the fool had allowed himself to care for a human, which meant leverage to me.

I would take her tonight, bring her pleasure and pain she'd never dreamed of, and take the body she'd denied me before.

Climbing onto the window ledge, I stole another glance at the woman on the floor, still curled up. "Until we meet again," I said and smirked before I jumped.

Chapter Thirty-Six

Kyle

Bursting through the door to Ana's apartment, I called out her name.

At the sight of me, Penny panicked and started screaming. She was on the floor, her clothes disheveled, her cheeks red, and she dragged herself away from where I stood.

Dropping my crossbow, I rushed to her and turned her over to face me. Penny immediately started beating her fists against my chest, and I tried to grab her hands, not wanting her to think I was trying to restrain her but needing her to calm down.

What had he done to her?

What would he have done if I hadn't come?

"No, no... shh, shh..." I shushed gently, and while holding her wrists, I rubbed her skin with my thumbs. "It's me, Kyle. I'm a friend of Ana's. We've met."

Penny started sobbing harder, heavy sobs that surged through her body and made her shake with the effort of breathing. I took a moment to survey the damage. She was cut and bruised, but she'd be okay, physically, at least. After blinking through the tears, she focused on my face, threw herself at me, and clutched onto my shirt. Hushing as I stroked her hair, I rocked her gently for a while.

The residual feel of the Tenebrian was all throughout the apartment, twisting and merging with the pain and fear that ebbed from Penny as she sobbed in my arms. His essence was one of pleasure. I closed my eyes, searching past Penny's pain and into the air for him.

My eyes snapped open.

Of course, his coming here was no coincidence. He had been looking for Ana specifically. His imprint felt *devious*, his thoughts framed around a single act, and I could guess what that was.

Pulling away from Penny, I cupped her face in my hands, and as gently as possible, I asked, "Where's Ana?"

Penny started shaking her head. "I don't know." Her eyes widened, panic taking over as she gripped my wrists and hissed out, "*But he's looking for her.*"

Glancing at the open window, dread rose in my chest. I'd need to concentrate and get my emotions back in check if I were going to track Ana. Previously, I had been trying to prove myself to the other Guardians, and my motivations were a messed-up combination of selfish and dutiful.

But now, everything was different, and I had to find Ana.

At any cost.

With that realization came a renewed sense of power and a renewed sense of terror.

Because now I knew what it was like to have something to lose.

Lifting Penny, I carried her to her bedroom and placed her lightly on the bed. She moaned and hiccupped as tears streamed down her cheeks. I couldn't leave her like this, so I sat on the edge of the mattress and placed my hand on her forehead. Easing her fear, I pushed it from her body in waves that shook her breathing, and I sighed as her breathing slowed and she fell into a deep, hopefully dreamless, sleep. It wasn't as much energy as I would like to give her, but time was of the essence.

Standing, I took care to close and lock all the windows. With another glance at Penny, I picked up my crossbow and carefully locked the front door behind me as I left.

By now, I knew Ana better than I knew myself. Her emotional imprint was branded onto my mind and soul as though we were two halves of one being, not complete without each other. If we made it through tonight, the questions raised about what we would do going forward, I pushed to the side because I would have to go home, and she would have to stay on Earth.

My heart already ached to think of it.

Once outside Ana's apartment building, I focused and sent a sweep of my senses across the city blocks closest to me. Surely, he couldn't have gotten far? Could he have already found her? How long had transpired between him leaving Penny's apartment and my arrival? I hadn't thought to ask her, and I wouldn't go back and wake her only to interrogate her.

My only hope was to find Ana first.

But as I increased the area I searched, I found nothing that resembled Ana's imprint. My senses grew weaker the further I stretched my limit until I was trying to cover too much ground, and they were practically useless.

But still, nothing. No Ana, nothing even close to the purity that emanated from her.

I held onto the idea that the Tenebrian planned to draw me to him using Ana, and then force me to bargain for her life. How could I have been so foolish as to get close to her? But she drew me in. We were drawn together, and I didn't want to fight it.

Logic had no place in the emotions I felt with her.

If that were his plan, then surely he wouldn't kill her.

That meant maybe he'd take her somewhere I couldn't sense her, to fill her with negative energy, and to increase her fear beyond anything she thought possible. She'd become a lighthouse of fear then, and not only would I be able to seek her out, I would be pulled to her.

There's only one place he could take her.

Tenebris.

Chapter Thirty-Seven

Ana

Storming away from Kyle's building, I crossed my arms over my chest against the night chill. I acted impulsively and was out on the street in the middle of the night. Usually, I'd never be afraid of the night, but I knew there was more to be afraid of—things that lurked in the darkness I hadn't previously considered could exist. Being out alone, given what I knew about who Kyle was and the Guardian that was after him, may not have been the best decision. I considered going home but decided against it.

What I needed was a drink.

Turning into the first bar I encountered, I plonked myself on a barstool and huffed loudly. The bartender looked up from cleaning and raised an eyebrow at me. "Rough night?"

"You don't have to small-talk with me."

He approached, rubbing his beard. "That answers that. What can I get you?"

"Bourbon. Please."

After I downed the drink in one go and indicated for another, the bartender hesitated before topping up my glass. Rolling my eyes, I sipped the second drink and stared hard at him from under my brow until he seemed satisfied I wasn't going to drink myself to death, and he moved along to serve someone else. Spinning on the stool, I leaned against the bar and surveyed the room. It wasn't busy, and small groups of people were dotted around. The few times someone made eye contact with me, I made a point to look away quickly, but not before giving them a dark look that hopefully told them to *fuck off.*

I was *not* in the mood to socialize.

At this point, so many thoughts rushed through my head that it was all simply a blur, a heavy fog that offered no solutions or insight.

So instead, I tried to dull the thoughts.

I drank silently for a long while, ignoring one man's attempt to chat me up and not being bothered by anyone again. I resisted the urge to check my cell and was on my fourth bourbon when someone touched my shoulder.

"Fancy seeing you here."

Spinning around, I found myself face-to-face with Ed. "Oh, it's you."

"Who were you expecting?"

Kyle.

"Nobody."

Ed frowned. "Is it that scrappy guitarist?"

"What's it to you?" I replied aggressively.

Ed sat next to me, uninvited. "Sounds like *nobody* is being a bit of a dick."

I scoffed. "You would know."

"Hey, hey..." He held up his hands in mock surrender. "We both know it's not me you're mad at."

"Sorry, it's been a weird… things are weird."

"This may sound hypocritical, but do you think drinking might not be the best answer?"

"No, but it certainly helps." I lifted the glass. "Salute!" Then downed it and gasped as I relished in the burn. One day, I'd try some expensive bourbon to see if it made a difference.

Ed watched me with a cocked eyebrow, and I tried to ignore the way he looked at me like he could pick up on every tiny physical cue, and people-reading was his magic power. Not an inclination he'd ever shown before, given his constant attempts to hit on me despite my lack of interest.

I'd had enough.

Leaping off the barstool, it took me a moment to find my footing, and I gripped the bar.

"You're right," I said, straightening my top as I tried to ignore how it smelled like Kyle. "I'm going home."

Ed slid gracefully off his seat. "I'll walk you."

"No, it's okay. You don't have to do that."

"Stop arguing, and just let me walk you home."

Staring at him, I sighed loudly. I should know better than to spend any time with Ed, but I'd had a rough night and, despite myself, I found that not only did I *not* fancy walking home alone, I couldn't bring myself to care about much at this point. Including the company I kept.

What did it matter?

"Fine." I threw my arms up and stomped my way to the door. Ed caught up in a few steps, held the door open for me, and followed me outside before we crossed the street together.

We walked in silence, and the streets were empty. Everyone was at home or in one of the few remaining clubs open at this hour. I stared ahead as we walked. While I was never interested in Ed, his company was comforting tonight. Something to break up the darkness that surrounded me, both figuratively and literally. He was a body, a presence that meant I wasn't alone and nothing more.

"Do you wanna talk about it?" he asked.

"Not really."

Ed nodded, and we continued to walk. After a beat, Ed placed his hand on my lower back.

Immediately, I shifted my body away from him. "Come on, Ed. No."

"Just helping a friend out." He slid his arm around my waist and pulled me next to him.

"I said *no.*" I pushed my forearms to his chest as he used his other hand to pull me against him. "If you're not happy to just walk with me, then fuck off."

It was a futile hope, but maybe he would leave me alone of his free will.

"Oh, please, Ana, we both know you want me."

"Ed, *no,*" I yelled.

Ed yanked me close, and my arms were trapped between us when he kissed me forcefully. I struggled against him, but he was stronger than I, so much stronger than I thought he would be. Ed grabbed my arm and began pulling me toward an alley.

I resisted but couldn't pull out of his grasp, and when he pressed me against the wall and started kissing my neck, I cried out, "No, no, no," turning my head toward the street, I screamed, "Help, somebody, help me!"

Ed clamped his hand over my mouth, muffling my cries.

He was an asshole, but I never thought he would force

himself on me. The combination of the alcohol and my anger at Kyle, of my fear and confusion with everything that had happened in the past few days, had clouded my judgment. The part of my gut that told me I shouldn't be anywhere alone with Ed, I'd ignored.

I screamed against Ed's hand, gathered my strength even as my head swam from the alcohol, and stomped on his foot. He grimaced but didn't release me and responded only by making a sound that was a cross between a growl and a groan as he pushed me harder against the wall, his body flush against mine.

"Like that, is it?" He breathed against my ear. "Maybe you like it a little rough? Maybe you want a little pain?"

I whimpered and released a strangled gasp as Ed clamped his hand around my throat and squeezed slightly. Grabbing his forearm, I tried to shake my head as he forced his other hand down the front of my pants and felt me roughly. Pressing my nails into his arm, I choked out another protest.

Lifting myself onto my toes to counteract the roughness of his touch, I gasped as the pressure eased on my throat. "Kyle." I grunted before calling out again, "Kyle, help me."

"You're calling out for that guy? After he ditched you to fuck some Latino chick?"

"How did you know—" I lost the words when Ed pressed harder against me.

"I saw them together," Ed said.

I didn't stop struggling. I was never going to give up and make this easy for him. I fought against his arm on my neck, gasping intermittently as his grip loosened and tightened.

Perhaps if I kept him talking, I could find an opportunity to break free.

As I opened my mouth to reply, Ed grunted. "Enough of this."

So much for talking.

He spun me around and pushed me against the wall. I braced my hands on the bricks to stop my head from colliding with them as Ed started undoing my jeans.

"Ed, *please.* Why are you doing this?"

Ed leaned against me, and his weight held me in place as he used one hand to begin yanking down my pants. "I don't know, Ana. I could've charmed you, but sometimes this just feels *so damn good.*" I whimpered as he continued, "Don't you ever want to push the boundaries, Ana? Push people? Maybe they'll like it."

Could it be him?

I hadn't known him that long, and he'd come into my life around the time Kyle had said...

"Oh my God..." I breathed out. "It's you. You're the Guard—"

My sentence was cut off as my head was cracked against the bricks.

I fell, Ed landed on top of me, and I clutched my head as lights exploded behind my eyes.

I felt Ed shift and, moments later, lost consciousness.

Chapter Thirty-Eight

Ana

Eyelids fluttering, I didn't open my eyes. I couldn't. My head throbbed, and when I reached up with one hand to rub it, I hissed out a gasp when my hand grazed the cut, already starting to swell into a bump and sticky with blood. Pushing myself into a sitting position, I groaned and took my time as every movement sent a swell of dizziness through me. Finally, I opened my eyes and blinked rapidly as I stared at the ground.

My brow furrowed, and I lifted a hand and studied my palm.

It was covered in a layer of fine red dust, and I rubbed my fingers together.

"What the hell?"

My ears prickled when I heard a familiar sound, and the panic started to rise in my chest.

It can't be.

"Oh no. Oh, please, no." The tears began to well in my eyes, and I didn't have the willpower to fight them away, too scared to look up or move. I stared at the ground as the echoes in the distance of the wailing screams and the hollow rushing sound continued, although there was no wind.

I'd been to this place before, this realm, but only this time I knew its name.

Tenebris.

Standing slowly, my shoulders heaved as I breathed in the thin, hot air, and I didn't take my eyes off the ground. Sucking in a deep breath, I attempted to brace myself for whatever I was about to see. Lifting my eyes from the ground, I stumbled backward and almost tripped over my feet.

There were no words.

I wanted to scream, but couldn't find my voice, and as I collapsed to my knees, a hooded figure turned around. "Ah, you're awake."

I looked back at the ground. "T-t-take me home." The words came out as a stutter.

"Oh, but you just got here."

"I don't know why I'm here, but I want to go home."

"So, you know *where* you are, then?" I could hear the grin in his voice as he delighted in my terror. Gripping my hair in both hands, I squeezed my eyes shut and wished I could will myself home.

All sound evaporated into the air for a moment, then returned louder than before, as though this entire realm was a dreamscape designed to disorient and terrorize.

The dark figure approached me. "Look at me, Ana."

I shook my head. "I don't want to look at you, Ed."

He laughed and grabbed a fistful of my hair, wrenched my head back, and fresh tears sprang into my eyes at the pain as I kept them squeezed shut. "I said... *look at me,*" he growled out.

I opened my eyes and looked into his face. "No."

Not Ed.

"Oh, yes."

"It was you, the Gateway, those *murders*..."

He laughed again. "Of course."

"Ed?" I choked out.

"That heap? Oh, don't worry, I didn't kill him," he answered my unasked question. "He's a fucking asshole. Why would I take that away from the world?"

I couldn't tear my eyes from his face.

This entire time, he was right there.

Nathaniel.

The sensation of pins and needles that dotted across my body intensified, feeling more like knife points against my skin. "It hurts," I said.

"I haven't touched you yet."

Hugging my arms around myself as he let go of my hair, I whispered, "It hurts being here. This place... it hurts."

He tilted his head. "Does it really? Where?"

I trembled despite the uncomfortable warmth. "Everywhere. My skin, it just hurts, like needles."

Nathaniel watched me. "Interesting," he said, before smiling widely. "Oh, that *is* good."

Abruptly, he stood and swept his arm behind him. "We will take your mind off it. Look, I have a show for you." He looked at me expectantly and tutted impatiently when I continued to stare at the ground, not daring to look any higher than his knees. "I would look when I tell you to, Ana. I can do so much worse to you than make you watch."

I slowly lifted my eyes from the ground, trying to draw out the inevitable.

I'd never recover, not from this. The images would be burned into my mind forevermore.

Spread out behind him was a giant cobweb structure crafted with barbed wire. All over the barbed web were people, hundreds of people, hung from the barbs by their skin alone. Flesh was torn from their bodies, some were missing limbs or had gaping wounds, and every one of them was covered in blood and screaming. Their screams were overwhelming, and it felt like the volume had been turned up the moment I'd looked at them.

They're not real. Kyle said they're not real.

The screams continued.

Not real. Only Reflections.

I clamped my hands over my ears, but it did nothing to stop the sound—it was in my head, in my very soul. Inescapable. As the people on the wire structure wailed and moaned, their suffering was made worse by the Guardian's complete indifference, and I couldn't hold back the tears that escaped. Nathaniel knew my fear and pain, and I knew he could feel it and sense it, and there was no point in trying to hide it.

"Please, make it stop," I cried.

"Why make it stop? I can make it better."

Nathaniel turned and surveyed the scene before him, one hand on his chin as he hummed thoughtfully. "Attention," he cried out as he spread his arms wide. "The first one to kill *that* man..." he pointed at a bald man hanging near the center, already missing a leg, leaving only a bloody stump, "... will be released."

The reaction was instant and horrifying, and the people started crawling across the wire, dragging their bodies over the barbs in desperation to get to the man in the center. He started screaming before anyone reached him—he had nowhere to go.

They're not real!

I repeated it to myself, my hands still clamped over my ears, and tried to remember the smooth tone of Kyle's voice as he told me what they were.

They're Reflections. They're not real.

The voice in my head wasn't loud enough, so I started speaking.

"They're not real. They're not real. *They're not real."* By the end, I was screaming the words, but it didn't stop the terrifying scene in front of my eyes.

People approached the man from every direction, with no regard for their injuries, as their flesh was torn and their blood rained down on those below them. The man's screams escalated, and all hell broke loose when the first person reached him. The true and complete terror in his voice, as they started tearing him apart, dug into my chest, and he screamed in agony as he was torn to pieces.

His screams died down and drowned to nothing with a final blood-curdling cry.

I screamed too, and pressed my hands against my ears. I kept screaming and couldn't stop. The images of what I'd witnessed were imprinted on my retinas.

When Nathaniel approached me, I started kicking out at him and shrieked, "How could you do this? *How could you*?"

"We will have plenty of time to talk. Come with me."

"No!"

"It wasn't a question."

He struck me across the head, and after I hit the ground, everything went black.

I came to for the second time that night, and my head spun double-time. My vision blurred and grayed around the edges, and it took several minutes to ease. Blinking a few times, I tried to clear it faster, but the best I could do was wait for my body to catch up.

With a groan, my head lolled down to my chest. I moved to lift a hand to rub my head.

I can't move.

Opening my eyes, I blinked a few times again. Looking down, I rotated my wrists. It was about all the movement I could get with the ropes that bound my wrists to the arms of the chair. My legs and torso were also wrapped with ropes, and there was no weakness, no give at all.

No hope.

Letting out a desperate squeal around the gag, I whimpered as I continued to writhe and struggle against the restraints, whining again when I couldn't get loose. Glancing around, I squeezed my eyes shut when the sudden movement grayed out my vision again. There wasn't much light, and I was in a warehouse of some sort. I tried screaming again, although I already knew it was useless.

"I wouldn't bother if I were you." He strolled casually into my line of sight.

I started shaking my head, rocking back and forth as much as the restraints would allow.

I couldn't believe it was him.

How could I *not* have known?

Nathaniel smiled. "Why couldn't it be me?"

I cringed as though he had struck me, and my eyes snapped toward him.

He laughed. "No, I can't read your thoughts, just the general..." He waved his hand lazily through the air. "... essence of them, of what you're feeling. I can deduce from there."

I was trembling, and I couldn't stop.

"Oh, and before you think it, yes, Kyle *will* find you. I'll make sure of that."

Kyle.

I tried to scream again, but the sound was too muffled.

"How will he know where we are, you ask? Well, we Guardians can... sense others' pain." As he approached, I tried to lean away from him, crying hard. "I'll make you into a beacon to call him, and your pain will be felt across the city. He'll find you, and this time, I won't leave before he makes it. I'll be right here to greet him. But, in the meantime, you and I can have some fun."

Nathaniel leaned beside me, took a deep breath near my hair, and hummed happily.

"So much fear radiates from you from our little vacation to my home. It's so *exciting.* Pity we couldn't stay longer. If the Elders found me, they'd want me dead for what I've done to the Balance." He ran his fingers down my cheek gently, like a lover would, and when I angrily pulled away from his touch, he slapped me hard enough to leave my ears ringing. "Wouldn't you rather play nice with me? I know you know how good it feels to feed off others' pain."

What was he talking about?

Nathaniel traced the furrow between my brows with his fingertip and smiled dangerously. "You don't remember, do you? Well, I can fix that."

He placed his palm against my forehead, as Kyle had done in his apartment. But I wasn't flooded with a calming sensation this time. It was with a sting, and my vision flooded black briefly. Nathaniel brought to the surface buried memories of the night of our date, and I remembered my encounter with Gateway and the darkness it held. Whimpering as all the details from that night came back to me, I tried to get away from his touch.

The mugger, the knife, the way I'd felt when I'd fed off the fear of the victim.

Then, the woman I'd hurt, all my anger bubbling to the surface as I took it out on an innocent.

Internally, I cried out in pain.

How could I?

When Nathaniel pulled his hand away from my forehead, my cheeks were wet with tears. "Now, you remember," he whispered.

My shoulders shook as I sobbed. I'd done such terrible things. How could I have done that? Did I have that capability inside me all along? How much was of my own free will?

"I opened that Gateway to infect you," he whispered next to my ear. "Influence alone is not enough to get humans to push their free will to the very limit. You needed to be *touched* by Tenebris. Little did I know what else it would reveal about you."

I shook my head furiously. I didn't want to believe him. It couldn't be true that I had done those things and hurt those innocent people. When I tried to scream *you're lying,* it only resulted in another pathetic muffled cry.

“I have learned so many things watching you, and you proved to be much more interesting than I could’ve hoped. You are so much more than just bait for Kyle, and I don’t think either of you even know why.”

I watched him knowing the confusion was written all across my face.

But there was no point in trying to hide from him.

“You know,” Nathaniel started, his tone thoughtful as though having a victim tied to a chair was a completely normal part of his day. Which I realized with a chill it probably was. He pointed his finger playfully at me and moved it in small circles. “You almost got me, you know? I think in that coffee shop when we touched. You almost felt the darkness before I internalized it.” Nathaniel chuckled and patted my cheek lightly before he turned the pat into a slap. “Now, are you going to play nice with me?” He licked my cheek, and I recoiled in disgust. “Kyle seems to like you. Maybe you’re a good fuck? Maybe I’ll help myself. After all, you did deny me.”

The tears came anew, and I shook my head in protest, but I was bound and helpless, and the knowledge of that only increased my fear of him. Nathaniel roughly worked his hands over my body and pawed at my breasts as I looked away, as if not seeing him do it would somehow erase the sensation from my mind. When he kneeled before me, he moved his hands to the front of my jeans, still undone from Ed’s attack.

“I could teach you some things. You rejected me before, but I could’ve brought you to the edge of agony and the peak of ecstasy. You know what that’s like. You’ve felt the thrill of fear. But maybe we don’t have time for that. After all, all I need to do is make you scared enough to draw Kyle here.”

As I continued to cry, Nathaniel smiled. My reactions merely seemed to excite him more. The more I recoiled and protested, the more he enjoyed it, and his cruel smile widened and twisted his once handsome features. Continuing to touch me, he ran his hands down my body, his breathing steady and heavy. I wanted to hold back my fear, knowing that he could sense and absorb it and that it was pleasurable and powerful for him.

But I couldn't stop the terror that bled through me.

As he ran his hands over my stomach, his fingers twitched, and he laughed as I tried in vain to block my emotions. The Guardians could do it. Why couldn't I?

"Oh!" He seemed delighted. "This too?" He looked up at me. "Does he know?"

Barely listening, I squeezed my eyes shut again, trying to force calm through myself as Kyle had done. I pictured the white light.

But it was all in my mind. Nothing worked.

When Nathaniel whispered, "Do *you* know?" I opened my eyes. I hadn't been paying attention the first time, and I had no idea what I was supposed to be knowing or not knowing. When I didn't answer, he continued, "No matter," and moved his hands down to roughly yank off my boots. He loosened the binds on one leg and rested my bare foot in his lap.

Immediately, I kicked out at him and tried to strike every part of him I could reach. I ceased my attempts when he pulled out a knife and stilled. Nathaniel took the blade and pressed it against the exposed sole of my foot.

He tilted it and cut slow and deep.

I screamed against the gag as blood splashed on the floor. A lightheaded rush had me almost passing out again, and sluggishly I tried again to pull away, but he held a vice grip on my ankle.

"You know..." he said, lifting the knife away from my foot, "... humans are just too easy."

He did a quick succession of small cuts on the side of my foot. Screaming into the gag, I was barely listening to him talk, unable to concentrate beyond the torture.

"It's so easy to get humans to do the wrong thing. Sometimes they only need the slightest push, the smallest hint of justification, and they'll take the darkest path." He waved the knife around as he spoke, and I traced its path with my eyes, trying to mentally prepare myself for the pain that would follow.

There was no preparation.

He was still talking as my foot throbbed, somehow both hot and cold while covered in blood. "I can convince a man that that woman really *does* want to be fucked, and it's okay to use drugs to loosen her up. I can tell your old man friend, Henry, he can make an extra buck by selling his medication, even though he felt it was wrong. I can blur the lines for people between black and white, give them a reason to steal, hurt, or do wrong, and most of them take it without a single hesitation."

He slipped the knife between my big and second toe and cut through the fragile skin, and the blood spilled into his cupped hand before he let it dribble to the ground between his fingers, playing with it as though it were a toy to him.

"But then I needed more." He held the knife still and looked at it thoughtfully, apparently deaf to my screams. "It wasn't enough to watch people playing these petty games with each other. Even most of my fellow Guardians didn't understand, they couldn't stop me either. Some were too worried about the Balance, but the world needs a shake-up. And sometimes, I want to really *feel* the fear and pain, and there's no one better than me to *create* it."

Nathaniel cocked his head and looked at my face. The shadows played games with his expression, and he looked dark and otherworldly. I pleaded to him with my eyes, although I knew it would do no good.

Tomorrow I would be in the news like Sophia, my clothes soaked in my blood.

Left for Kyle to find.

He smiled, and as he lifted the knife again, a glint of light from the blade passed across my face.

NO
PARKING
DO NOT
BLOCK

Chapter Thirty-Nine

Ana

Gritting my teeth into the rag, my throat was raw from screaming. Nathaniel moved the bloodied knife away from my foot and went to place it on the floor.

"Oh," he muttered with a glint in his eye. "Don't want to leave that on the dirty floor."

Adjusting his grip on the knife, he swung his arm out, brought it back in a sweeping motion, and embedded the blade in the side of my upper thigh. Throwing my head back, I howled in pain into the gag. For a moment, it felt as though the air had moved around me with a pulse, and I could only hope that was my pain calling Kyle for help.

Leaving the knife in my leg, Nathaniel wiped his hands on his pants, leaving behind streaks of my blood. He sighed, watching me. "Physical torture isn't always enough, you know."

I couldn't help how my eyes fell to him, pleading, begging him to stop.

A grin passed across his features, and I cringed. "Your roommate is quite something, isn't she?"

Penny? Oh God. What had he done?

"I visited her when trying to find you. We'd met before, you know."

When had Penny met Nathaniel? I didn't think she ever had. When Henry set us up, she didn't know who he was. Confused, I said nothing, and his grin widened.

"I can see what you're thinking, and no, we didn't meet on this trip to Earth. No, we met about a decade ago when I came here to find a human victim to have fun and test the boundaries. We found a nice little space to play..."

He was waiting for me to put it together, and when I did, I thought the sickness in my stomach couldn't get any more intense. I willed myself not to vomit, telling my body I would choke with the gag in.

It was him.

I let the man who tortured my best friend touch me.

He tortured Penny. He was her captor. They couldn't find him because he returned to Tenebris. That's why he didn't kill her. He needed only for her pain and fear to infiltrate the air.

Oh, Penny, I'm so sorry.

I brought him back into her life.

Still kneeling before me, he watched as I groaned and rocked back and forth, and his teeth grew more exposed as my agony flooded into the air around us. I wanted to stop because he would enjoy it, but I couldn't. All my thoughts were on Penny.

When he dropped my foot, too covered in blood to see clean skin anymore, and placed my other foot in his lap, I cried out against the gag.

Oh, please, no.

"Toes are quite cute, aren't they?" he said.

I couldn't take anymore, and I thought I would pass out if he kept going. The pain from my left foot was already throbbing up my leg, red-hot pokers of pain that continued even though the blade was no longer slicing into my sole. I could feel the blood pulsing around the blade in my thigh. Crying against the gag, I pulled on the binds that held me to the chair and looked hopelessly at him, trying in vain to pull my foot from his grip.

He grabbed my big toe between his thumb and forefinger and wiggled it slightly. "*This little piggy went to market...*" he said, a light tune in his voice before he kissed my toe. "*This little piggy stayed home...*" he kissed the next toe, grazing it with his teeth.

Shaking my head frantically, I whined, and the legs of the chair scraped against the concrete as I tried to get away.

"*This little piggy had roast beef...*" he licked the bottom of my foot, ending at the top of the middle toe. "*And this little piggy had none...*" Nathanial pressed his teeth into the base of my fourth toe, biting lightly before he kissed it.

I started trembling against the binds and rocked back and forth violently while I screamed into the gag, tears streaming down my cheeks.

"*And this little piggy...*" Nathaniel whispered, looking up at me with cold eyes as he wiggled my little toe, ignoring my protests, "*Went—*"

I screamed as my eyes rolled back. Maybe I blacked out. I couldn't tell.

Nathaniel stood and spat my amputated toe onto the concrete as I wailed and continued to rock in the chair, and he grinned as my blood dripped down his chin.

Then he paused.

"He's close," he said, glancing at me with a grin. "Good news. He's coming to rescue you."

Kyle.

I looked up through my hair, damp from sweat and tears. Nathaniel wrenched the knife from my leg, and my jeans became almost immediately stained with dark blood from the wound as he began severing the binds. Pulling away from him madly, he paused in cutting the binds to hold the knife next to my cheek, the tip of the blade near my eye.

"Stop struggling, or this blade is going through your pupil."

I stilled.

Kyle, please hurry.

When he finished cutting the binds, he pulled the gag from my mouth and used it to tie my wrists together behind my back. Wrapping an arm around my stomach, his other arm across my neck, he pressed my shoulders against his chest and yanked me to my feet.

"Get up," he yelled as I slipped, trying to stand on my bloody and throbbing feet. "*Now.*"

Nathaniel spun around, dragging me with him as Kyle entered the warehouse, holding a crossbow, which was pointed directly at us.

"Stop right there," Nathaniel shouted. "Not one step closer."

Chapter Forty

Kyle

On the way to the warehouse, I had almost buckled under the tidal wave of pain that radiated from Ana. I was so close. I could feel it. Swallowing, I tried to keep the bile from rising in my throat and not to think about what Ana was going through. Her screams echoed in my mind, and I pressed my hands against my ears, trying to concentrate on the feeling of her, searching beyond the pain.

It wasn't the time to lose focus.

I kept moving. The second the Gateway had opened, I knew my suspicions were true. Somehow, he had managed to cloak himself while leaving this realm. Whether he knew I would be with Penny and, therefore, her pain would partially blind my senses, or if he was simply more powerful than I had imagined. Either way, it made me feel sick and helpless.

When they stepped back into this realm, Ana's imprint was weak, as though she were unconscious. Then, with a blast that knocked me off my feet, she awoke, and her pain and fear were everywhere around me, consuming and confusing me.

They were well out of the city, and I managed to flag down a cab, but even he refused to go the full way because of the high number of carjackings in the area, and I was forced to take the final stretch on foot.

The Tenebrian wasn't going to run this time. This was a trap, a game to him.

It was time for this to end.

After bursting through the door into the warehouse, my hands shook as I held the crossbow braced against my shoulder. The familiar weight felt much heavier when I pointed it at someone I loved.

Oh, Ana.

Nathaniel held Ana tight against his chest. There wasn't a clear shot. I could go for his head, but Guardians were fast. It was too risky, and I didn't want to hit Ana. She wouldn't even be here if it weren't for me.

"Nathaniel," I pushed out through gritted teeth, his name a threat on my lips.

Of course, it was him.

Thinking back to when we met that night the Gateway was opened, it was either bravery or stupidity to take Ana there, but either way, I didn't doubt it was all part of the game he had been playing. Nathaniel would have known that the Gateway's presence would have hidden his imprint from me because he *must* have known I would come. Any darkness I'd picked up on, I'd assumed had been coming from the Gateway and not the being standing mere feet from me.

He scoffed. "Ignis, please. I loathe Earth names."

The anger bubbled underneath my fear. "Let her go. She has nothing to do with this," I shouted.

"She has *everything* to do with this."

Nathaniel pressed his arm harder against her throat. Ana's eyes bulged as she struggled against him, and her fingers scrambled against his skin as she gasped for breath.

He loosened his grip slightly and said to her, "Stop struggling, or I'll cut you in two right in front of him."

Ana stilled and eyed the knife in his hand. I wanted to tell her not to go for the weapon. He was too strong, and he'd break her neck before she could get near him with the blade, assuming she managed to grab it at all.

"You've done enough damage. It's time to go back."

Nathaniel laughed. "Do you know what happens when the Balance is tipped?"

I gritted my teeth. "Yes."

He paused as though leaving me to dwell on that hint of information before he continued, "You're a lot of things, but you're not a killer. You can't win this."

"You've gone too far. For God's sake, you've killed humans! This is beyond tipping the Balance. You're *sick.*"

"*I've* gone too far?" He laughed, drawing out the words. "Me? What about you? What about *this*?" He shook Ana for emphasis. "Why do you even care?"

"We're supposed to care."

"Yes." He smiled. "But about humanity collectively and only concerning the bigger picture, not caring about one in particular. Not one above all the rest. You've become corrupted by this realm, and it's pathetic."

"Just let her go, and you and I can end this."

Nathaniel grinned, and his teeth were stained red. My stomach churned, and I looked down to see Ana standing in a puddle of her own blood. She had lost so much, and her face was drained of color.

She needed medical help, and soon.

But would I be able to get her to a hospital in time?

There was a wound in her leg, and blood oozed to the ground in a slow, steady stream. She was fading fast, and I could feel her life force as it drained. I swallowed heavily. Ana was growing weak, so it was now or never. I had to finish this.

"It's going to be okay, Ana," I said.

The moment I said her name, her expression twisted, and she choked back a sob. "Kyle, why did I do those terrible things? I thought there was still free will. Why did I do those things that night?"

Maintaining as much calm as possible, I spoke softly to her, aware that my mood could affect hers. She needed to stay calm. I didn't need her heart pumping faster than it already was, pushing precious blood from her body.

Besides, if her emotions became unstable, there was no telling the effect it would have.

"There's a difference between being influenced and being infected, Ana," I said, "You're not a bad person."

"Technically, she's not a person at all," Nathaniel muttered.

"Shut *up,"* I snapped at Nathaniel.

"Kyle…" Ana was crying now. "Am I evil? I hurt that woman. Why did I do that?"

Steadying the crossbow, I said, "You're not evil. It's okay. Please stay calm."

"Careful with that crossbow, Kyle. You wouldn't want to hit her."

Glaring at Nathaniel, I adjusted the weapon against my shoulder, keeping Nathaniel firmly in my sights.

Nathaniel laughed. “What’s the matter? Don’t you recognize one of your own?”

“Leave her out of this.” My voice cracked with anger.

Not like this.

“She’s one of us. She’s a half-breed,” He shouted.

I almost dropped the crossbow as my gaze flickered quickly to Ana and then back to Nathaniel. There was a ringing silence, and I couldn’t hold Ana’s accusing gaze.

“I know,” I whispered.

I didn’t want it to happen this way.

Ana, please forgive me.

“Kyle, what’s going on?” Ana’s voice trembled as her shoulders shook.

Nathaniel laughed loudly, watching me. “Oh, you figured it out, too? When did you pick up on it? When you were fucking her? I must admit, it took me a while. What was so special about her? She didn’t feel the same as other humans. It piqued my interest when she was drawn to the Gateway and absorbed the essence so easily. But I only knew for sure when she described the pain of being in Tenebris. Only a Lucidian would have that reaction.”

Ana frowned, staring at the warehouse floor, before raising her eyes to meet mine.

I stared back at her, watching her process. I didn’t lower the crossbow. How was she going to react? Would there be an accidental response upon the realization of her hidden powers? I didn’t want her to panic and trigger a reaction from Nathaniel.

Of course I knew she was only half-human.

Although I didn’t initially see it, my feelings for her had

blinded me. All new feelings that I didn't know what to do with. I didn't even recognize a kindred spirit in her. But when I touched her forehead after I told her of my world, I felt it in her. She had already been through so much. How could I then tell her that she wasn't *all* human? Perhaps her parents had a reason for not telling her.

Her mother was human, and her father was a Guardian of Lucidis.

Chapter Forty-One

Ana

The pain of my injuries was momentarily forgotten as I got lost in my thoughts. My life flashed before my mind's eye like the reel of a movie, and so many things suddenly made sense. My grief when I'd lost my mother and my friends' subsequent reactions to my depression, as though *my* feelings were making them feel the pain too. They spoke of it, but we didn't understand what it meant. It was more than me just bringing them down by being sad—I was *influencing* them—an ache they said cleared the moment they weren't around me.

My ability to shut off my emotions.

I thought of my absent father. From what I recalled, he came and went frequently. Was he going back to Lucidis to recharge? And what of my ability to read people? It was as though I could tell if they were rotten or pure from the first meeting, and I rarely gave them time beyond that, so I was convinced of my gut feelings.

Penny, Ed, Henry. I'd had a read on them all.

Nathaniel? Kyle said he was powerful, and he hid his essence.

Kyle. I read him, too, and I knew I was safe with him.

I stared at Kyle. What about my connection with him? A connection beyond the physical that formed so quickly and strongly, I didn't even question it. He was good, I could feel it, I'd even told him so, and my feelings grew from lust into love faster than I'd imagined possible.

We were connected.

But above everything else, the sensation of loss fell heavily against my chest like a lead weight. The familiar feel of my pendant against my skin was warming—a moonstone pendant—a gift from my father to my mother and then to me. It was no coincidence.

Oh, Mom, why didn't you tell me?

When I finally spoke up, my voice was small and fragile. "Why didn't you tell me?" Kyle's face changed as I spoke, as though my words broke his heart. I didn't blame him. There was so much I didn't know, and he'd tried to find the balance between protecting me and informing me.

I wasn't angry, I was hurt.

"I'm sorry, Ana, I didn't know how you'd react. I couldn't predict..." he trailed off.

Looking at the floor again, my mind reeled as I tried to accept another world-shattering truth—my father had been a Guardian of Lucidis.

Why did he leave?

Was he still alive?

"Please..." Kyle's voice was filled with resignation, "... just let her go."

"I'm not going back. I am having too much fun here," Nathaniel said, jerking me against him and making me grunt. "I spent so long in Tenebris trying to feel satisfied watching these petty humans and throwing out negative clouds, but it wasn't enough. The Balance is no longer my priority. It's so incredibly easy to corrupt humans, and their pain feels so damn good. I can simply step back..." Nathaniel breathed against my neck, "... and watch them tear each other apart," he hissed out.

I choked back a sob at the memory of what he had shown me in Tenebris. The awareness formed in my mind as a solid thought, and I knew. I could feel Nathaniel's determination and darkness.

He's never going to stop.

I thought of Henry and everything he had told me about caring for people. I thought of Penny and the love I held for her. They deserved better than a world with creatures like Nathaniel in it.

Looking at Kyle, at the pain in his face, it tore my heart in two. I had people I cared about now, something I never thought I'd have again after my mother, because it had felt so natural to shut myself off from emotions. I couldn't help it. But people worked their way into my heart anyway—too wonderful for me to deny them the space. I didn't want Nathaniel to be in this world and hurt them or anyone else. I was all too aware of what he could do. He had *told* me how he'd manipulated Henry, and Penny's trauma was so strong it lived in my heart as a dark secret.

But what of all the things he had done that I didn't know about? How many people's lives had he ruined, scarred, or destroyed entirely?

What of all the things he *would* do, if given the chance to keep going?

"Kyle..." Kyle's eyes flickered to my face as I spoke, my voice raspy from crying. I held his eye contact. There was so much hurt there. So much pain radiated between us on the line that was our invisible connection.

I was growing weaker. I could feel it—an unpleasant sensation as the warmth from the blood that continued to spill down my leg cooled before joining the puddle already at my feet, as I cooled too, beyond what I should be feeling for the temperature in the warehouse.

Was I dying?

How badly was I hurt? I felt numb in some places.

I prayed Kyle was strong enough to do what had to be done.

Swallowing heavily, the muscles in my throat worked uncomfortably against Nathaniel's forearm. "Take the shot."

Kyle's arm started shaking where he held the crossbow. "What? *No.* You'll be killed."

I tried to smile, but gave up when it felt unnatural on my face. I could sense my energy draining. I'd not done much in my life to care for others, not after Mom had died. I'd spent more energy pushing people away than holding them close. But now I had something to fight for.

Something to die for.

I may not have done much protecting of others in my life, but I could do this.

More than once, I wished I could have protected Penny from her attacker with my life back then, and here was my chance.

The tears came thick and fast as I thought of Penny, her smile, the laughs we'd shared, and how she'd been nothing but kind. *Henry. Oh, Henry.* My stomach turned again when I thought about how close he had been to Nathaniel.

What if Nathaniel had killed him?

And Kyle, and the future we could never have.

"I'm not going to make it out of here, Kyle. I know you can feel it, too," I said.

"No." His voice broke.

"Finish this. You have to."

"No."

Nathaniel laughed. "Oh, yes, Kyle. *Finish this,"* he mimicked my voice. Turning his face toward me, he spoke into my ear, "He's not going to do it. If you get hurt, that's the opposite of what he's here to do, an act of absolute negativity. You can't win. It's over." Nathaniel looked at Kyle. "Enough talk. This is what's going to happen. I will drop Ana into Tenebris, and you'll get her. I'd act fast if I were you before she gets ripped to pieces. I'll have some friends waiting for her. When you get back to Earth, I'll be gone. Do not try to find me. Do not try to follow me. Just leave me be. I have so much more I can do in this world."

"I'm not letting you leave." Kyle's jaw tensed.

Trying to gain control, I needed to stop myself from shaking. "Kyle, take the shot. This is bigger than you and me."

"No, Ana. Stop saying that."

"Do it, Kyle. I already forgive you." Tears streamed down my face for the love I had and could never have. "I love you." My voice crackled with emotion, and tears sprang into Kyle's eyes as he tried to hold himself together.

Nathaniel laughed. I'm certain he could feel what we were feeling. To him, these emotions of loss, grief, and pain were pleasurable.

No more.

Nathaniel scoffed. "Earth has made you weak."

"Take the shot, Kyle."

"No," Kyle cried back, the crossbow lowered slightly. "I won't."

"Take. The. Shot."

"*No.*"

Slowly, I pulled air into my lungs and summoned all my remaining strength, finding everything I could and channeling it into my core. Nathaniel tightened his grip on me when he felt me stir, and I let him, gripping his arm with my nails and willing him to stay still.

Stay right where you are.

Closing my eyes momentarily, I pictured my internal strength as a white light, the same one I had seen when Kyle had calmed me in his apartment. That was my power. I only needed to focus on it once.

Only once.

Forgive me, Kyle.

Let me influence. Just this once.

Rallying every ounce of love and hate burning inside me into a ball of light, with all my remaining strength and willpower, I threw that energy into the scream I forced from my tired lungs.

"*Take the shot!*"

NO
PARKING
DO NOT
BLOCK
GATE

Chapter Forty-Two

Kyle

As my finger compressed the trigger, I roared. Ana's scream was punctuated as the arrow hit her chest. A white mist passed across her eyes as the moonstone arrowhead burst through her before it embedded itself just under Nathaniel's ribs.

Ana collapsed to the floor in a heap.

Nathaniel looked down and flicked the arrow protruding from his body. It wobbled as he stared at it in disbelief. He raised his eyes to me as he dropped to his knees and coughed up blood onto his shirt and into his hands.

Loading up a second arrow and fueled by anger, I was determined not to look at Ana's body. Lining up, I took another shot. The second arrow pierced Nathaniel just below his collarbone, and his body jerked with the impact.

As Nathaniel's wounds started to glow, I lowered my weapon. "Your Elders will deal with you now."

A brief flicker of fear passed across Nathaniel's face. He had given up his location when he had risked taking Ana back to Tenebris, and his Elders would not miss him again. He was as good as dead. The fear in his eyes was replaced with darkness, which changed the whites of his eyes to black as he let himself go. He looked at Ana and laughed. "You don't even know what you've done," Nathaniel said as his wounds burned a bright white, and then, with an orange glow and the sound of film burning, he vanished.

Dropping the crossbow to the floor with a clatter, I ran toward Ana, fell to my knees, and slid down beside her. "Ana, Ana, please wake up." Lifting her motionless body onto my lap, I cradled her against my chest.

My mind had accepted the truth before my heart.

Low guttural moans escaped me, sounds of pure and all-consuming grief.

The waves radiated around me and spread outward rapidly. I knew I would be influencing humans, affecting those even blocks away with my grief and pain. I would only be adding to the damage the Tenebrian had caused. But the grief overtook me and spilled into the air surrounding us both, encasing the area in my pain. I couldn't stop it.

"I'm sorry," I whispered, brushing her hair out of her face. She was already growing cold. "I'm so damn sorry."

As gently as I could, I undid the binds on her wrists and sobbed again as her arms dropped lifelessly to the floor. Holding her close to my chest, my arms wrapped tightly around her limp form. I squeezed my eyes shut and kept hoping I'd feel her arms wrap around my body and hold me back, and she'd nuzzle against my chest and sigh with contentment.

But she wouldn't.

Not ever again.

Squeezing her, I whispered her name into her hair and kept my strength restrained only enough. I didn't want to crush or hurt her.

Rocking back and forth, the deep moans fell from me. I couldn't control them as the pain cut through me sharper than any blade ever could.

Sirens.

The police were coming. Someone must have heard the screaming.

I didn't want to let Ana go.

Letting her go would mean a finality I wasn't ready for.

Please, no, anything but this. Take me instead.

The sirens grew louder, and I trembled, still whispering her name.

But she didn't move.

Lowering Ana gently to the ground, my stomach churned as I moved to stand and paused when a flicker caught my eye. Wiping my face with the ball of my palm, I kneeled again, tenderly removed Ana's necklace, and put it in my pocket.

I kissed her on the forehead, lingered, and waited for a breath, a stir.

Anything.

But there was nothing.

Standing, I turned to leave.

My respect for humans increased—they handled this pain, grief, and loss daily. How did they do it? I'd never felt anything like this. To love and then to have your heart torn in two when they are taken from you. Never again would I view humans as weak for allowing their emotions to be such a powerful influence.

It wasn't weakness, it was strength.

It took all my willpower to move one foot in front of the

other.

It took everything I had left to walk away from Ana.

Outside, I tilted my head at the sound of approaching sirens and ducked out of sight. Ana deserved better than this, to be found alone in an abandoned warehouse—a crime they would never solve, and I could never forgive myself for.

The Tenebrian Guardian Ignis was gone and back where he belonged.

I had done it.

I had accomplished what I came here for.

But I felt no pride.

It was at a terrible cost. How could I ever live with it?

I didn't have a choice.

Waiting until the police cars had parked and all the officers had moved inside, I came out from my hiding place, feeling dirty and like a criminal. Flicking my hood over my head and shoving my hands in my pockets, I walked toward the east.

The sun would soon rise, welcoming another day.

How can there be sun when all the light had died with Ana?

Chapter Forty-Three

Kyle

In the laundromat, I watched the machine spin.

It had been several months since Ana's death, and I'd committed my time to restoring the Balance. It had taken a lot, and would take a good while longer. I knew I was supported by the other Guardians back home, but there was only so much they could do from Lucidis.

This was the longest any Guardian had been on Earth without returning home to their realm, and it was draining, but I had a lot to do. Ana's death was just another tilt in the wrong direction, along with everything Ignis had done. While nothing I did could rid me of the sickness that penetrated my soul after Ana's death, this was bigger than me. I'd had to push that deep down inside to spread only positive waves throughout the community that recent events had rocked.

It occurred to me that I was denying myself a trip home to recharge as some self-inflicted punishment, but I didn't offer those thoughts much time.

I deserved the weakness and pain that came with being here so long.

I'd worked hard and kept a safe emotional distance from any humans. Every act of positivity helped because those people would go on and spread it further by helping others, creating an ever-growing ripple of kindness. Human nature, in the end, would prevail, and I'd found people were more often inclined to do good things than spread evil.

My work consumed me, I had nothing else now, and really, I should never have had more than my duty to start with.

Getting Ana involved was my fault, regardless of the reveal of her parentage, and every day, I punished myself for not trying to find another way to get rid of Nathaniel.

Deep down, I knew he'd have killed her, even if she didn't die from blood loss first. There was simply no end to the situation where Ana lived.

But having her die at my hand was something else entirely.

I shouldn't have even talked to her that first night.

My arrogance had been such a driving force in the beginning. Had I admitted I was out of my depth earlier, perhaps I could have saved Ana, Sophia, her friends, Ryan, and who knows how many others from heartache.

I knew that pain now. I was a different being than I was before I came to Earth.

I'd attended Ana's funeral, but stood in the back, not drawing attention to myself. It was a closed casket service, which surprised me. Surely, the parishioners would want to see her beautiful face.

Maybe it was for the best. I didn't want to see her that way. Foolishly, I'd reached my mind out toward the casket, feeling sick when I felt nothing within.

I wasn't sure what I was expecting.

Penny had organized a beautiful service, and while she gave a teary eulogy to the handful of people present as a striking red-headed woman patted her hand somberly, she had met my eyes. Her gaze held no blame, but I couldn't keep her eye contact long and left shortly afterward.

Once again, I marveled at the humans' ability to deal with grief.

I wasn't sure I'd be able to do the same when I finally succumbed and let the grief through.

I'd changed so much, would I be able to return to who I was?

I didn't think so.

Did I want to?

I didn't know the answer to that either.

To ensure Penny was okay, I'd followed her home, reading her essence as she walked alone. Maybe she knew I was there, but she didn't turn around or slow down. When she approached her block, she paused and ducked into a side alley, and I waited and watched from where I was. A few moments later, Penny had emerged with a ginger cat tucked securely into the front of her jacket. She scratched the cat's head and cooed, and I almost smiled. This must have been the cat Ana spoke of, and it seemed fitting that Penny would take it home.

At that point, Penny turned and saw me. She stared at me for a moment with red-rimmed eyes before slowly raising her hand and waving sadly. I nodded, and the invisible strings of shared grief passed between us. Then she turned and left.

I didn't see her again.

I'd kept moving around the city, only staying in one place for a few days or weeks at a time, but I couldn't move far, needing to focus on the area that had sustained the most damage from the Tenebrian.

A young lady walked into the laundromat and interrupted my thoughts as she stuffed her washing in the machine next to mine. I stood and put coins in the machine for her.

She looked at me and was about to protest, until I smiled sadly and shrugged. "Pay it forward?"

She returned the smile, nodded, and muttered, "Thank you." Before she pulled out a textbook and sat down to study, while the machine whirred.

With every act, I felt a shift in the atmosphere as the air changed and became lighter.

However small, it all added up.

As I returned to my motel, I closed the curtains on the twilight over the city and sighed. My room was dark, and I stood by the window, looking at my feet. Without turning, I spoke to the room, "I wondered when someone would come." I faced the woman sitting cross-legged on his bed. "Sasha."

She nodded. "Cael."

She had long silver-blonde hair that fell lazily down her back, and her blue-gray eyes held little emotion as she stood and approached me, keeping a few feet between us. She felt blocked off, as though she were hiding her imprint from me. Maybe she thought whatever I had was contagious—my having succumbed to my emotions being a weakness.

"You haven't been back, not even to recharge."

"I can't. There's too much to do," is what I said. But what I meant was I didn't *deserve* to go home. I didn't deserve to feel better until I had done everything I could.

Sasha nodded, feeling my hesitation. "I've been watching you. I saw what happened."

My head dropped. "I never meant to hurt her."

"I know."

"He got so out of hand. It's my fault for not finding him sooner. I didn't want it to end that way for Ana or any of them."

"You did what you had to do to maintain the Balance."

I cringed. A human death or two was of no real consequence to the Guardian community—only the Balance mattered. If they could contain the ripples of grief, they moved on. Once upon a time, I felt this way, too, but not anymore. Sasha was young like me and not quite as severe as the older generations, but she still put her duty above all else.

"Everything will be okay," she added. I glanced up at her, still unable to read her imprint. Sasha continued when I didn't respond, "It was your first mission to Earth alone. It wasn't an easy task, far harder than we were prepared for. We understood why you didn't call through for help, too many of us here would've sent him into hiding, and we would never have found him. You made tough decisions, far beyond your experience, and no one blames you."

"I do." Tears stung in my eyes, and I tried to blink them away. Guardians didn't present emotion outwardly like this. "I made so many mistakes."

"We were not prepared, but we will be next time."

My head snapped up to look at her. "Next time?"

She nodded without a change in her expression. "Just in case."

We watched each other for a while, sharing our essence. I think she was letting me draw from her power, even encouraging it.

"Are you here to take me back?" I asked.

"No." She approached and placed her hand gently on my arm in an unusual display of comfort. Her hand grew warm as she shared her essence with me, and a spike in the air felt like she was daring me to pull away. She knew I needed this energy, and I was denying myself it. Sasha brought some stability back to my power. "I'm here to help," she said.

Sasha helped for eight months, returning to Lucidis regularly to balance herself, sometimes staying away for days or weeks. She had more experience than I, but even she needed to step away from Earth every few days. She had not said goodbye the final time she moved through the Gateway, but I had felt her go and knew she wouldn't return. I knew she could feel how grateful I was for all she had done, and I would see her back home when the time was right.

Slowly, the feeling of sickness cleared from the air, the dark cloud lifted, and I took solace that we had managed to save lives. One such life was three months ago. I'd grabbed the back of a man's jacket as he walked to the edge of the train platform, so overcome with grief, he felt he had no other option. I'd taken him in, even living with him for a few days, counselling him through his grief, and shown him there was goodness in the world to live for. Later, I followed his progress after we parted ways. He'd studied to be a school counselor, as he wanted to help students find their path and be the person they could talk to when they felt they had no one else.

A flicker of a smile played in the corner of my mouth at the memory.

That man would do good things.

Sasha and I had reached out to the families of those lost—Sophia and her friends. We had come into those families' lives as strangers and left as friends, although we would never see them again. We helped them come to terms with their grief, and together we set up a charity to support causes Sophia had believed in. I liked Sophia's mother and sister. They had a warm glow about them and an inner strength. Her mother was a breast cancer survivor, and I feared she may not have the strength to survive this. But once again, human nature surprised and inspired me, and the families drew together in their grief and, from it, created love.

I'd learned Sophia wanted to be a journalist, and despite her initial capricious impression, she was incredibly good at it. I'd told her family I would have liked to have gotten to know Sophia better. It wasn't a lie.

Returning to the bar where Ana worked one night, Ed was working. My initial plan was to approach and talk to him, but something stopped me. The wall around Ed was so hard and thick that it might as well have been visible. Probing the air around Ed with my mind, I found a huge weight of regret and grief. Ed blamed himself for Ana's death, for being with her that night, and for how he treated her. I should tell him it wasn't his fault, but then I felt something else.

A need to do better, and a desire to right all the wrongs he had caused.

Redemption.

The pain had driven him to want to do better. So, I left him with the pain to make of it what he would and spend his life making things better for others.

Nodding to myself, I left the bar without a word. I don't know if he saw me.

These last few months, I'd used to fit in as much good as I could, but I had grown tired. My powers, which earlier had bled from me out of control and infected those around me, seemed to have drained almost entirely. I knew I'd recharge when I went home, but that must be soon.

Standing outside the bar, I looked up at the rays of sunlight that poked through the clouds and held out my palms as the rain started, picking up quickly. Turning, I walked toward my current motel, hunching my shoulders against the pouring rain.

There was a hand on my shoulder at the same time I felt the gun push into the small of my back.

I raised my hands slowly.

"Easy. No sudden moves. Give me your wallet."

I stumbled slightly as I was yanked sideways into an alley by my arm. "Okay, I don't want any trouble, just take the money."

As the thief riffled through my jacket pockets, I watched his face. This was a man with pain. It was clouding him, and he didn't know which way to turn anymore, but he was not a bad person. Holding the gun was like burning embers on his skin. He hated it, but he was desperate.

"Why do you do this?" I whispered.

"Shut up," the man responded by pushing the gun against my stomach.

"I can help you."

"I don't need your help."

"Don't do anything foolish now, please." Keeping my voice quiet, I tried to calm the air between us, but could not influence the man. I didn't have the power left to make him drop the gun. "Let me help you."

I grabbed for the gun, but I wasn't as fast as I used to be. The man cried out, "*Stay still.*"

The words were drowned out by the gunshot echoing through the alley. We both looked down as I touched my stomach, my hand coming away slick with blood. Sliding down the wall, the man caught me under my arms and kneeled with me when he couldn't hold me up.

"Oh my God, *no.* I just needed the money. I'm sorry." He fumbled around and watched in horror as blood oozed from around my fingers. "Why did you have to grab the gun?" He did not show any anger, only fear and regret. "Wh-what can I do? Tell me what to do."

Lifting my eyes to his, I said, "Look at me." The man trembled as he looked at my face, and I suppressed a cough. "Do good."

"What?"

A wheezing breath escaped me. "Leave the gun. Do good things. Help people." Coughing, blood splattered onto my chest and soaked into my jacket with the rain, changing from a deep red to a faded orange.

The man wiped away tears and rain from his face and hastily dropped the gun. "I'm so sorry, man. I'm—"

"It's okay. It was my time. Just go."

He hesitated, then stood, opened his mouth to speak, but said nothing. He watched me with complete sorrow and a look promising the world.

I smiled sadly, feeling the shift in him. "Go," I whispered.

The man hesitated, then ran and disappeared into the heavy

rain.

Coughing again, I looked at my stomach, and when I moved my hand away from the wound, the blood came faster. I was dying, I needed to pass through a Gateway to be healed.

Lifting my fingers, I focused. There was a spark, but then nothing happened.

I was drained, and I couldn't summon a Gateway.

I might die here.

Reaching into my pocket with trembling fingers, I pulled out Ana's necklace and gritted my teeth, grunting as I pushed the stone pendant into the bullet wound.

Moonstone.

I almost smiled as the world faded around me, or perhaps I was fading from the world.

Goodbye, Earth, you gave me some of the best memories I could have hoped for.

Chapter Forty-Four

Cael

The warmth on my face was exquisite, and the gentle sunlight caressed my skin.

Opening my eyes, I was home.

Lucidis.

Looking at my hands, I was still in human form. Glancing around, I squinted slightly. I'd never been away for so long. It felt incredible to be back, and the energy surged through me as I breathed in deep, powerful breaths. Passing through the Gateway had healed the bullet wound, and my body pushed Ana's necklace from inside me, and it landed on the grass.

I was whole again.

Almost.

The realm was bathed in warm light, not blindingly bright but comfortable and perfect, always perfect. Closing my eyes again, I tilted my face toward the sun. My essence was rebuilding and becoming stronger every minute I was here.

I stayed like that for a long while, feeling the soft breeze on my skin as the emerald grass moved playfully around my ankles.

Sighing, I smiled to myself, but the smile dropped a moment

later. I was still plagued with guilt, and I didn't think that would ever go away. I'd simply have to learn to live with it.

Home now. I could start afresh.

Guiding and influencing from Lucidis.

Maintaining the Balance.

Helping humans.

But never forgetting Ana, and carrying the pain and weight in my chest like a trophy, but never a burden. She deserved nothing less than that.

To stop feeling the pain of her loss would seem an insult to her memory.

Walking slowly across the grass, I trailed my hands along the trees and flowers as I passed, relishing in the feel of the realm. It was beyond a physical sensation—being surrounded by peacefulness and completely at one with this realm and everything in it. I could feel the Balance stronger from here and sense the core that held everything together.

Things were right again.

As I walked, the space around me was filled with the Reflections of humans, the representations of their souls that drew peace and inner happiness from this realm. Some lounged on the grass in the sun or helped themselves to the fruit trees. Their forms were almost transparent, moving about without noticing each other or the Guardians, each caught up in their happiness.

Lucidis offered the human spirit a simple thing—a return to simpler times, with no worries, stress, deadlines, or conflict.

No fear or pain.

Tenebris had to work much harder to break their spirits because humans were stronger than they knew, or perhaps they didn't want to accept it. The Lucidians didn't have to actively involve the Reflections, only protect them from the influences of the outside realms.

Heading toward an archway of vines that formed part of the structure at the border of our community, I slowed and allowed my appearance to change. My body shimmered and transformed into my natural Guardian form from the soft human skin. My skin became hard and jagged, shining in shades of blue and angular like diamonds.

As I walked through the archway, I stopped.

The trembling started again, and the ache opened up in my chest as though I was feeling the wound for the first time. Open and fresh and pounding. Love turned to loss.

It's not real.

Please.

I couldn't take it, a trick of the light or my memories teasing me.

Please, I begged my mind, *let me grieve in peace.*

What if what I'm seeing is real?

I turned achingly slowly, almost not daring to look in case it wasn't true.

"Welcome home, Cael."

My vision blurred and swam as tears flooded my eyes. I wasn't sure how, but I didn't care at that moment. Subconsciously, I hastily returned to my human form, my skin flicking over like a deck of cards.

Ana smiled. "It's okay, Cael. I know what Guardians look like now." She held her arms out, indicating her own body, but I couldn't draw my gaze from her eyes.

I truly smiled back, and my cheeks ached as it had been

so long. I'm surprised I hadn't forgotten how. But it was impossible not to. It was *her*. Ana's warmth filled the air between us. Her imprint was the same, although she looked different. I wanted to ask questions and had so many things to say, but all those welled up inside me in shock. My mind rushed through the moments of and after her death, and how I had searched her body for any sign of life and found none. Was I too weak already then? Memories of how I'd reached out my senses to her coffin and recoiled when I'd felt nothing.

Was it empty? Had her body disappeared, and they'd assumed it had been stolen?

The moonstone in the arrow would have opened a Gateway within her. But it would have taken time as it clung to her Guardian half, repaired the shot's damage, and healed her enough to pull her through to Lucidis.

She died on Earth, but she lives here.

I never thought it possible to be brought back from the brink of death.

Shakily, my voice broke as I managed to mumble, "You waited for me."

"*We* waited for you."

"We?"

Ana looked down, and I followed her gaze. My heart swelled, and the ache returned. But it was different. It was a *good* pain, and I'd never felt anything so sweet. It was as though I had so much love that it was trying to explode from me. As my eyes fell on an infant who stood shakily behind Ana, barely able to hold himself up and partially hidden by her legs, he clung to her for support. I had missed the first months of his life, and it already felt like I had missed too much. He had blazing, bright blue eyes, and his skin shone and reflected like the angles of a polished stone. A jagged, scar-like line of white traced down the side of his face and neck, disappearing over his shoulder and blending with the blues. But his face was rounder than the Guardians usually were, and his eyes held a recognizably human softness.

Looking back at Ana, I rushed to wipe the tears from my eyes to see her properly. Her skin had taken on a pale blue hue and shone in the sunlight. Her shoulders and back were angular like my skin, with a dappling of scales and quills—a blend of human and Guardian.

Perfection.

"Meet, Samael," Ana said as I looked from her back to the boy, tears of joy streaming down my face as I knelt to see him. He looked at me with those bright eyes, his essence recognizing mine, and his imprint already flooded with the memory of me, even though he had never met me. "Your son."

To be continued

Bonus — Q&A

Instead of my usual ramblings at the back of this book, I thought I'd do something a little different and have a Q&A segment. These questions have come from several sources, including questions I've been asked on social media and at events.

If you have any questions you'd like answered at the back of one of my books, please feel free to contact me through my Facebook page!

1. What made you rewrite the Guardians Trilogy?

For those who may not be aware, this trilogy is a rewrite of the first books I ever published, which have since been removed from publication. Given that they were the first complete novels I wrote and published, there were problems with the writing. Everyone needs to start somewhere, and I think the biggest lesson I learned from those books is *not to rush into publishing*. I still had a lot to learn about the art of writing and storytelling, and in my naïve excitement to rush into being a self-published author, I went full steam ahead, whereas the reality was that I should have waited at least another year.

However, in saying that, perhaps if I hadn't followed the exact path I did, the Unearthly Sins might not exist. Because The Demon in Me followed almost immediately, coming to me from nowhere. So I can't be too upset!

I loved, and still love, the story of the Guardians. I love Ana and Cael and their connection. I love the idea of a supernatural being unable to succeed despite their powers. I love having an antagonist who was stronger, smarter, and more vicious than the protagonist.

I love that the "good guy" was tested and failed more than once and that his motivations shifted. I was so taken with this story that I couldn't let it go.

But I realized that after a while, I was no longer happy selling the original books. As my writing experience grew, I became aware of all the flaws and rookie mistakes I'd made in my writing.

Not willing to let the story go, I decided to pull the trilogy from publication and give it new life. This meant a complete rewrite, with a shift from a third-person perspective to a first-person one, and a deeper focus on character connections. It also forced me to be creative, for there were key scenes where the protagonists weren't initially present, and I needed to find a way around that. Being in the first person also allowed me to delve deeply into Ana, Cael, and Ignis's psyches, which was fun.

The short answer is that I loved the story and wasn't willing to let it go, but I recognized it needed work. So, I did the work, and eighteen months later, here we are. I'm thrilled to be re-releasing these stories back into the world.

Not to mention the gorgeous new covers!

2. Where do you get your inspiration from?

Dreams sometimes, 'cause my dreams are wild and I love it.

Music is also a big one.

I'm a very visual person, and while listening to music, I see scenes unfold in my mind. Sometimes, random things with little to no meaning, other times, it's like a movie. It can be characters I already have waiting in the sidelines to be written, scenes that perhaps I'm struggling to complete, or entirely new concepts. However, I have to make sure I write them down or leave a voice message before they drift away and are replaced by something else when the next song plays.

If it *really* grabs my attention, I'll repeatedly play the same song until the scene solidifies.

Fun fact—I call them *Stef's Fun Facts* though I may be the only one who finds them fun—two songs that I played when building the Guardians Trilogy, all those years ago, were Darkside by Oshins, and Inside by Chris Avantgarde, and Red Rosamond.

3. How many vines are too many vines?

A question I received on Facebook, regarding Vitri in Rescuer, from my Elements of Abduction series.

See? I actually put it in here, bet you didn't think I was going to.

The answer is that there's never enough, especially if he knows what to do with them.

4. How long does it take to write a book?

A common, but ultimately difficult question to answer!

Because I tend to work on more than one project at once. I'm a mood writer, and will jump between two or three projects depending on my headspace.

Unless I have a deadline.

No, sometimes even if I have a deadline.

However, given the time it has taken me to write a first draft, which has varied from three weeks to twelve months, looking back, I'd say that for most projects, it'd take around two or three months for the first draft. I then let it sit for at least a month, longer if I have the time and no set release date, before I go back to it and read it beginning to end, editing, changing, and adding as I go.

Then, of course, there are edits. Layers, and layers of edits.

Let's say eight months, from beginning to end.

That seemed an unnecessarily long way to answer the question, but here we are.

5. What is your favorite book?

Nope. Nope. Even as I typed the question out, I immediately *noped* out of there.

It's impossible. There are too many, spanning too many genres. My personal library has over a thousand books. How can I pick *one?*

But, rather than leave you hanging entirely, I'll offer something that rings of nostalgia.

When I was younger, one of my favorite series was the Wind on Fire Trilogy by William Nicholson. I've read it more times than I can count, and probably will again.

I'll also leave a shout-out here for the first five books in the Chronicles of Amber series by Roger Zelazny, Robert

Silverberg's science fiction novels, particularly Up The Line and The World Inside, and Tanya Huff's Vicki Nelson series. More recently, practically anything by Lily White.

6. How do you handle writer's block?

Do anything else—clean, bake, crochet, paint, watch a movie, work on something else, dance like a buffoon. Anything that allows the creativity to simmer in the back of my mind. Because sooner or later, I'll be struck with inspiration, and will be back at it.

Another thing I do is discuss it with my amazing partner. He has an incredibly in-depth understanding of story structure and seems to know precisely which questions to ask to help me figure it out when I've written myself into a corner.

Or if my characters are being pains and have done it to themselves.

Sometimes, though, in the time it takes me to explain the back story enough to get to the part where I'm explaining the issue, something will click, and I'll have my answer.

7. Why paranormal/sci-fi romance?

Because it's fun!

Here's a random insight. When I started writing, I didn't even know the paranormal romance genre had a name, and I *certainly* didn't know about all the subgenres and just how deep the rabbit hole went. But once I was in there, I was *in.* There were books I had already read, and I could look back and go *Oh,* that's *paranormal romance.* Then the world of monster romance opened up, followed by aliens, and oh boy, anything you could think of—it was all there.

Like most people, I was a reader before I became a writer, although I recall favoring creative writing in school.

Timeline-wise, I was already writing demon/human romances before I even knew it had a name, and once I looked into it, I found my people and never looked back.

On a more serious note, I enjoy paranormal romance because of the *extra* it offers to the story. Aside from the usual angst and relationship issues that people can face, there's the added element of them *not being human.* And, from the creature's side—I'm looking at you, Zaqiel and Cade—there may be guilt, complications, and questions of morality that arise specifically from the paranormal element. I find it incredibly fun to write about demons and angels, in particular. There are many layers to peel back, and numerous different levels of faith, both within humanity and beyond, that can be explored through various pairings and character combinations. It has endless possibilities, and I especially love creating my own lore surrounding the paranormal creatures.

Writing with aliens offered a new level of creativity—they're on a different *planet,* where the rules may not be the same. I have ideas for an RH alien romance series of standalones, but I can't promise *when,* because even I don't know!

Because before that, I will dip into the lore of werewolves. But I'm going to take the lore as you know it, throw it out the window, take snippets from here and there, and create something different. I'm excited about this one, so watch this space.

Then there'll be more demons and angels, more aliens, more *everything.*

Wait, what was the question again? I was having too much

fun talking about all my future projects.

8. Who's your favorite character from your own stories?

This was a lot easier to answer when I had fewer books.

Can I choose one from each series?

Of course, I can, I'm making up the rules as I go along.

Unearthly Sins Novels—Frank. He was the first to stroll into my mind, saunter, if you will. I love that arrogant demon.

Elements of Abduction—Vitri, of course, that cheeky bastard. But Lanir is a close second, because the grumpy/sunshine trope gets me every time. If I think about this too hard, I will go through every character and realize I love them all. Then I'm going to second-guess my above answer too (what about Zaqiel? What about Ray? What about Cade?)

Better to move on now before I overthink it, because overthinking is my bread and butter.

Guardians Trilogy—John. John has a backstory, and yes, I plan to release his story as a prequel.

But *please keep that to yourself*, I'm looking at *you*... person reading this. I have *so many* story ideas swirling around in my head, and I can't type fast enough to get them all out as quickly as I want to release them! So when I say it'll be a thing, it will, but if you ask *when?* Cue me dropping a smoke bomb and disappearing into the night.

Demonic novellas—Azaziel... so far.

9. What advice would you give to someone starting to write?

Take. Your. Time.

Publishing and the idea of being published are exciting! But don't let the excitement of it make you rush your writing. Sit on it longer than you think you need to, revisit it, and rewrite. Learn all you can about writing and the art of storytelling. Watch videos and tutorials, ask lots of questions, learn the common mistakes, and how to avoid them. You love your story and your characters, so when it's out in the world, you want it to be the best version of itself, so take your time with it.

10. Finally, who would you like to acknowledge for this book?

Okay, no one actually asked me this question. This is my way of including an acknowledgments section because it feels wrong not to have one.

My partner, Jason, because holy hell, when I say this wouldn't be possible without him, I mean it. He has been incredibly supportive since the first time I announced that I was going to write a book and wanted to publish it. He's there at every event, helps me talk through plot holes, and listens when I'm complaining (this goes for everything outside of writing, too). His life insights are always valuable when I'm facing a dilemma, and no matter how obscure the subject matter I'm writing about, he'll listen patiently, albeit with one eyebrow arched.

To me, you are perfect, and I love you.

Got to thank my parents, right? For blessing the world with my awesomeness. Raising a future legend can't have been easy.

Mum, thanks for being so supportive and buying all my books, even though you and I both know you won't and *really shouldn't* read them.

Kate and Chris—here we are again, with me thanking you once more. Are there enough *thank yous* in the world? I don't think so, so this will have to do. If anyone gets tired of hearing about how pivotal these two have been in my author journey, and reading me mention them at the end of almost every book, and reading the phrase *author journey...*

Then, too bad, because I'll never stop telling them they're awesome and that I love them.

There are others, of course, and don't think that because you're not mentioned here, it means I've forgotten—although no doubt after this is published, I'll *gasp* and remember someone I should have included. Let's throw in a thank you to Pat, Ashleigh, and Kathy for good measure.

Thank you for reading my lovely readers! I do hope you enjoyed Rogue Heart!

As always, please leave a review. They help in so many ways, least of all making me smile like a fool and clutch my phone to my chest as I *squee*!

Love to all! x

Connect with Me Online

ANGELS AND FIRE BOOKS

Find our exciting stories at:

www.angelsandfirebooks.com.au

READER GROUP

https://www.facebook.com/groups/588038442170571

NEWSLETTER

https://www.subscribepage.com/angelsandfirebooks

GOODREADS

https://www.goodreads.com/author/show/21761217.Stefanie_Dawn

BOOKBUB

https://www.bookbub.com/authors/stefanie-dawn

WEBSITE

https://www.angelsandfirebooks.com.au/

FACEBOOK

https://www.facebook.com/stefaniedawnwriter

INSTAGRAM

https://www.instagram.com/stefaniedawnauthor

About the Author

Stefanie Dawn writes steamy paranormal and sci-fi romances, as well as dark and urban fantasy. She strives to give her readers stories they can escape into as they become absorbed in the worlds created, and fall in love with the characters.

Stefanie adores creating romances that will keep you hooked, with HEAs and paranormal fantasy, elements of instant attraction, and of course lots of steam!

When she isn't writing, Stefanie might be painting, reading, or watching movies. She loves the process of producing films as another form of storytelling. There's also a good chance she'll be baking some delicious treats—pretending she won't later regret consuming them—or simply enjoying a cocktail with friends.

Stefanie Dawn lives in South Australia with her ever-supportive partner and a lovable gang of rescue cats.

You can stay up to date with Stefanie and her books at

www.ingramcontent.com/pod-product-compliance
Lightning Source LLC
Chambersburg PA
CBHW020328030826
48979CB00021B/472

* 9 7 8 1 7 6 3 8 7 0 5 5 0 *